The Light of Shadows

Ryan Elledge

Book Cover by John G. Reinhart

Maps by Dewi Hargreaves

First edition 2024

For Morgan,
Who believed in this book, even at the times I didn't,
and who has all my love

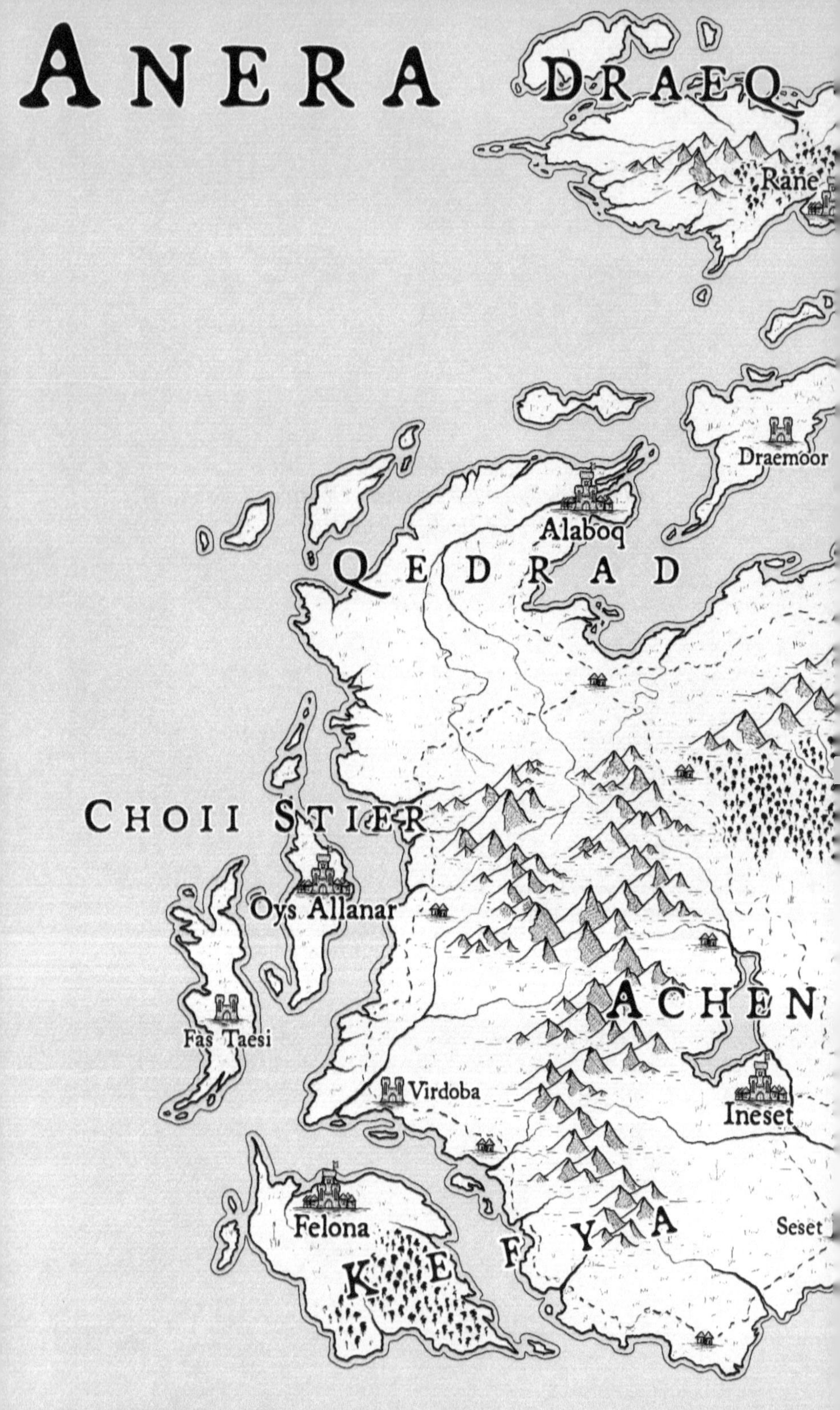
ANERA
DRAEQ
Rane
Draemoor
Alaboq
QEDRAD
CHOII STIER
Oys Allanar
Fas Taesi
ACHEN
Virdoba
Ineset
Felona
Seset
KEFYA

Qravburn
Brey
DESTUEQA
Havine
Oretol
EBKARII
Woross

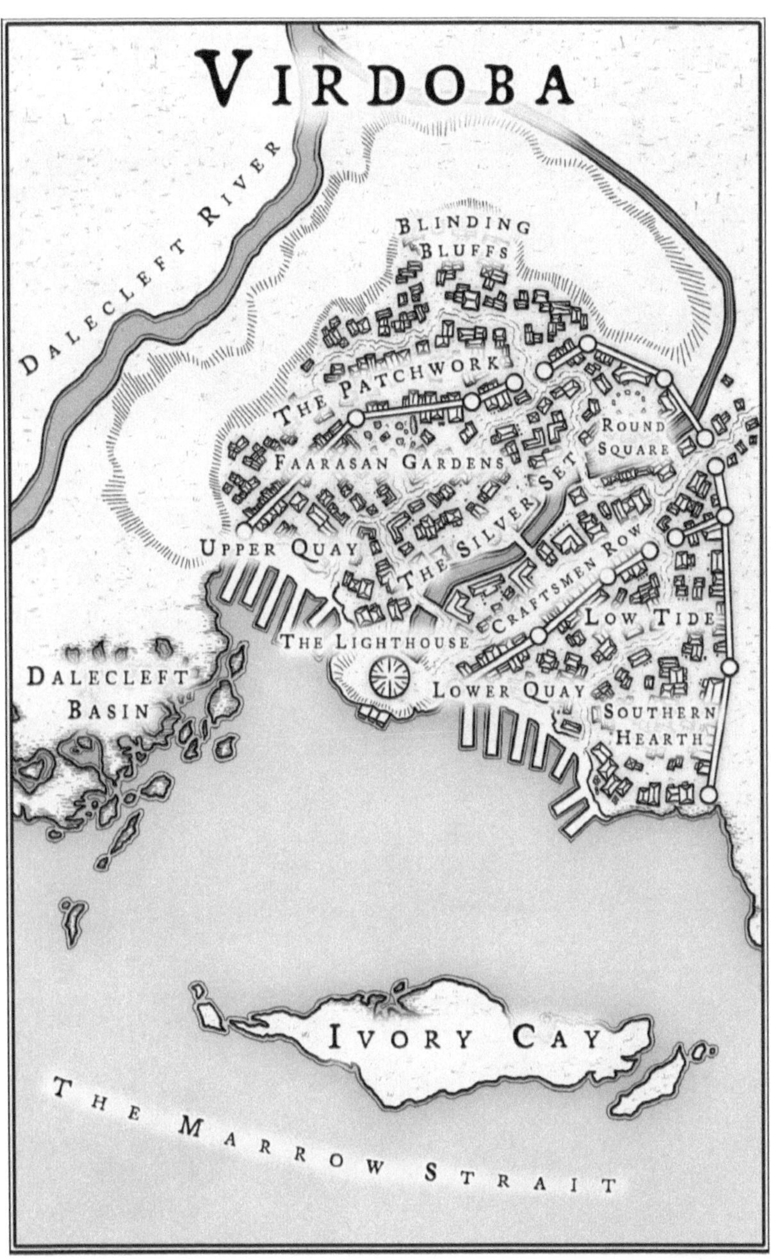
VIRDOBA
DALECLEFT RIVER
BLINDING BLUFFS
THE PATCHWORK
ROUND SQUARE
FAARASAN GARDENS
THE SILVER SET
UPPER QUAY
CRAFTSMEN ROW
LOW TIDE
THE LIGHTHOUSE
DALECLEFT BASIN
LOWER QUAY
SOUTHERN HEARTH
IVORY CAY
THE MARROW STRAIT

PART I

Chapter 1

Virdoba

Rav caught her breath in the shadows of the archway, hoping that the sound of rushing water from the aqueduct above would drown out her ragged gasps for air. The pungent slop of soil and runoff squelched beneath her boots, and she groaned as she looked down to see that the leather was irreparably stained. *Looks like they'll have to bury me barefoot,* she thought. *There's no way this stench wouldn't seep into the mausoleum. Mother would be mortified.*

Placing her left hand against the cool gray bricks for support, she pulled her right hand away from the puncture wound in her abdomen and watched the slow pulse of blood stream out of her leather cuirass. Her vision was beginning to darken around the edges, like a creeping dusk settling over her ever-narrowing field of view. Blinking rapidly, Rav ripped a strip of cloth from the shirt below her chestpiece and pressed the wad of fabric against the bleeding gash in her side, letting the leather hold it tight to the wound.

"Damn useless plagueman," she grunted. Swearing to herself that this would be the last time she trusted a tonic over a good stitch, she made her way into the bustling crowds of the Lower Quay as angry shouts and thundering footfalls echoed down the street behind her.

The sun had yet to rise over Virdoba's eastern wall, and the long shadows were welcome. Though she counted three young lamplighters in the immediate vicinity, children who struggled with poles at least twice their height, there was far less public illumination here in the docks than in the residential streets she had left behind. And with the small army of brawny men and women who were already well into their shifts loading and unloading the vessels in the port, Rav believed she could lose her pursuers among the throngs and shadows. Some of the city's undesirables were hunting her, but they were less the sneaky sort and more the bloody-knuckled variety.

Keeping the hood of her cloak pulled over her head, she crept along the edges of the warehouses that made up the border of the district. Each building rose three to four stories and softened some of the clangs, grunts, and thuds that otherwise would have drifted unhindered into the quiet homes of the Low Tide neighborhood beyond, but Rav was keener on the tightly packed network of alleys between them.

Upon hearing the thumps of her pursuers' boots growing louder and louder, Rav ducked into the nearest shadowed passage and hustled as fast as her quickly draining body would allow. Her shoulder ached from maintaining pressure against the wound in her side, and her vision continued to cloud. *I have to get to Wymund. It's his fault this is happening to me anyway, so the least he can do is patch me up.*

"Don't let the girl get away!" she heard Cater Waldwen call from around the corner. Judging by the volume, he and his lackeys had gained some ground on her. Only a few short hours ago, she had not thought much of the man beyond the loyalty he inspired in his crew, but she had to credit him for running a group capable of discovering her. Not many people caught Ravael Trisarin when she didn't want to be caught.

As she darted down the branching alleyways, Rav did her best to leave no trail, but the effort was wasted. This close to the bay and the aqueducts that lined the city's outer walls, there was always a thin film of moisture that soaked into the unpaved paths of the district. Muddy footprints would be unavoidable. Still, she doubted Waldwen and his men spent much time honing their urban tracking skills, so with some effort and a little luck, she could disguise her route behind a veneer of randomness. Rav doubled back a few times and made loops, all while moving in a northerly direction. The looming silhouette of the Lighthouse stood out in the distance against the predawn light. If only she could walk in a straight path with no interruptions, help would be less than ten minutes away. The warm, damp rag in her hand reminded her she might not have ten minutes left.

Shouts rang down passages ahead and behind her as she felt herself being boxed in. No matter how slippery she thought she was, Waldwen had numbers on his side. He could comb the Lower Quay all night if he wanted, but he wouldn't need to—Rav wouldn't last that long. The salvation of the Inner City gate beckoned to her, no more than four blocks away. She could see the cobblestone archway and the disinterested sentries posted there. They would not be much help to her; Wymund had kept her work a secret from most of the Virdoban guards. But if she could just get inside the gate, maybe the relative safety of the Inner City wards would prevent Waldwen from sending his entire force through after her. The monied nobility simply would not stand for his ilk charging down their nicely paved streets, and he wouldn't want that attention on his organization.

Cater's hunters began closing their vice around her, and Rav made a quick decision. If she couldn't outrun them in her current state, she would have to hide, gambling with the precious few minutes of consciousness she had left. However, the alternative would be certain death at their hands. Rav sank down beside a workbench outside the nearest storage building, draping her cloak over herself and a few nearby piles of kindling to appear more of a misshapen lump than a crouched body. She shuddered as a chill ran through her, and she told herself it was from fear rather than blood loss.

The first pair of thugs to appear came from behind her, moving out of the alley she had just passed. One was a giant of a man with a thick mane of graying dark hair and an eyepatch barely covering a long scar from the center of his forehead to the middle of his right cheek. He strode into the intersection with all the confidence of a man who had never lost a fight and had likely instigated many. He glowered and scanned the passageways around him as another man stepped out next to him, much smaller by comparison but with a more discerning gaze. His head was shaved on the sides while the rest of his hair was pulled back into a tight tail, a streamlined look that accentuated the hawklike features of his face.

"I don't see her," the larger man said with a huff.

"Patience, Reg," said the other, smirking beneath his beak of a nose. "Give someone with both their eyes a chance."

Reg threw his elbow back into the smaller man's bony chest, knocking him backward into a wooden wall. "Asshole. Keep it up and I'll take one of yours to complete my set."

The man rolled his shoulders and stood as tall as he could manage to, just reaching Reg's shoulder. "C'mon, big guy," he muttered before continuing down the path away from Rav.

Before she could spring up and continue her dash to the Lighthouse, another duo materialized from the shadowed alley to the north of her, one pressing a hand to his side with a pained expression. He folded over, causing his tunic to stretch tight across the bulk of his belly, and placed his hands on his knees as he gasped for breath. The other, a draqesh woman with sandy hair pulled back into a tight braid and arms bulging out of her sleeveless shirt, stopped a few paces ahead of him and turned back with a grimace. "Edis's eye, Carn!" she said, staring daggers up at him. "How many people did you cheat at the boards last night to deserve this?"

Though bent over, Carn was still at least a head taller than the draqesh woman, but he swallowed hard and did what he could to calm his breathing. Despite the natural height advantage, even the most fit human would be hesitant to confront an angry draqeshi, and he certainly didn't fit into that category. But something about her no-nonsense stare made Rav hope the man said something smart. Maybe the woman would take care of this particular obstacle for her.

Instead, Carn said, "Just give me a minute, Lariq! Not all of us are born with bodies like an ox."

Lariq scoffed and patted the side of his face. "You weren't born with *that* body either. That came from a lifetime of poor decisions."

Carn regained his full height, now half again as tall the woman before him, but kept his hand pressed against the stitch in his side. His imposing frame was still dwarfed in comparison to Lariq's mere presence, glowering up at him as she was from his navel. "Well, right now, I'm decidin' to have a rest and a leak. So if a lady such as yourself ain't looking for a show, I suggest you go on ahead. I'll catch up."

"Sure, I'll see you next week then." She laughed, turning to continue her journey east down the alley. "If Cater asks, I'll just tell him you decided a quick nap was more important than catching the rat."

Rav swore under her breath as Carn opened the front of his trousers and began to relieve himself in the alleyway. At any other time, this buffoon wouldn't have troubled her. If deception failed, she could always rely on swift feet or a well-timed jab to get out of a situation, with the twin daggers at her sides as a contingency plan. But, bleeding out and exhausted, no option sounded promising. The lanes to the east were occupied by the hunters she had just watched pass by, and to the west, back toward the docks, she could hear more men entering the maze of warehouse backstreets. How many men was Cater willing to throw at finding her? How many seconds did she have left before it no longer mattered?

The entrance to the Inner City seemed to sway in the distance. The two guards posted there doubled to four, then snapped back to two again. Rav blinked and pressed harder on the puncture wound, hoping both to slow the bleeding and use the pain to regain focus. This was it. There was a straight shot to the archway and then on to Wymund, with only an oafish and winded man standing in her way. Time would have allowed for stealth or guile, but it was ticking away far too quickly now. There was only time for a final charge. At least, she hoped there was time.

Flinging her cloak off herself and the wood piles around her, she harnessed every bit of energy she had to burst forward into a sprint. Rav closed the distance to Carn in seconds, just enough time for him look up from his task and see her lithe figure dart behind him. She kicked at the back of his left knee as she passed, causing it to buckle as she caught the back of his head in her bloody hand. His startled cry was stifled as she slammed his face into the wooden boards before him, and an arcing trail of blood marked his path downward as his head dragged against the building's façade. It would be some time before he could continue his hunt for her.

Lights flared at the sides of her vision, appearing to streak past in her mad dash for the gate. The early-morning stockers would be arriving to their storage buildings with the first intakes of the day, and Rav could already feel Waldwen's hounds nipping at her heels. The hairs on the back of her neck stood on end, and gooseflesh tickled down her arms as if their fingers already brushed against her skin in their desperate attempts to grasp her. Her lungs burned, her arms ached, and the pain from her wound radiated across her entire flank. Despite the humid sea air and her exertion, a chill settled over her body. The only thing that mattered was continuing to place one foot in front of the other.

The gate loomed large before her as she exited the final block of the alley maze. Her sudden appearance in the more open street startled the city guards from their relaxed stances, each man bolting to attention. The first, a man just out of boyhood with less hair on his face than she had, brought his hand to the hilt of his blade. The traditional teal wool coat worn by the Virdoban City Guard swallowed his frame whole, and his eyes were wide as he looked across the archway to his partner for guidance. The other, an elven man judging by his delicate face and the shimmering ring of gold around his irises, was more collected. Rather than reaching for his own longsword, he crouched into a readied stance.

She had nothing left in reserve to fight her way through. As much fun as it would be to tussle with the lawmen under better circumstances, she could only hope to slip by them. Taking in her surroundings, she could see multiple paths she would have preferred to take to bypass the sentries, most of which involved vaulting the wall without being seen in the first place. Instead, she would have to rely on raw agility, her supply of which was draining drop by bloody drop. However, she surprised herself as her legs and arms pumped faster and faster. More lights flickered to life down the street and beyond the wall into the Inner City, some oddly extinguishing as quickly as they appeared. Maybe those inside the buildings could see what Rav could swear she felt: dozens of Waldwen's men on the edge of grabbing her by the neck.

As she reached the guardsmen, the elven man sprung forward out of his crouch to tackle her to the ground, but Rav caught his tell. She watched his legs flex into a tighter bend before he launched, giving her just enough time to throw her left shoulder into a backward spin away from him. The man grunted as he landed face-first on the slick cobblestone street, skidding several feet in the mud before coming to a stop. Using the momentum of her twirl, she slammed her palm into the younger man's chest, sending him stumbling back into the bricks of the archway, winded and gasping for air. Not stopping to relish in her small victory, Rav raced toward the tower rising high into the sky over the Upper Quay. Of course, she knew she wouldn't get far if the elf could draw from the World Shroud, but there was little chance of that. He would have leaned on those tricks immediately if he could, but that was beside the point. She didn't believe Virdoba would employ someone like that to protect the populace. It was surprising enough that they had hired an elf.

The roads beyond the gate into the Inner City were well-maintained, without an ounce of the muck that permeated the paths behind her. Money was no object within those walls, so it was not uncommon to find street cleaners making their rounds throughout the day to ensure the fine leather boots and silk slippers walking the roads remained unsullied. Rav assumed today would be the first time they encountered a trail of blood, though, and a part of her brightened at the idea of her wound creating a stain on some unsuspecting lady's shoe.

To her left the waters of the Marrow Strait glistened under the dawn light with a near-blinding intensity. She had never been in the Upper Quay at this hour, and she wondered why the same body of water appeared to sparkle here, as if it knew it were surrounded by gold and gemstones. She squinted against the glare and gritted her teeth as the base of her skull began to throb. The muscles in her legs and arms twitched, but rather than causing her to stumble, the fasciculations made her limbs vibrate with a thrumming energy. The Lighthouse was close now. Wymund was close. *Just keep moving.*

Merchant carts and stalls lined the right side of the road, each one bare in anticipation of the soon-to-be unloaded wares from the docked boats. Unlike the more rugged and practical vessels found in the Lower Quay, the ornate ships bobbing in the harbor had been constructed from the finest Achen lumber, complete with beautiful figureheads styled after everything from Qedradan royalty to mythical sea serpents. She even saw one sculpted to depict Teachers Leros and Melan plotting a course as they hung from the bow of the ship, and she wondered about the confusing message the captain was presenting to the world. Maybe it was her dwindling blood supply, but she couldn't work out if the Siblings featured together was meant to be an aspirational declaration or an insult to both congregations.

The workday did not start quite as early here in the genteel districts of the city, so Rav's path forward was unobstructed by hustling dockhands or early morning customers. That was both a blessing and a curse—the more visibility she had, the more visible she was herself. Lanterns hanging from poles peppered either side of the street, and she could now see the calm waters of the Silver Set reflecting their light just down the road. Rav was annoyed every time she saw the man-made canal that ran through the center of the Inner City. It reminded her that enough gold could make people think it was their right to divert the course of nature for their own gain—in this case, the creation of waterfront villas and a scenic backdrop for lazy afternoons spent gazing at the teal-fringed ducks residing there. But at that moment, the sight of it was the sweetest thing she could imagine.

Just across a wooden bridge stood the Lighthouse, Virdoba's guard tower and barracks, rising out of the waters of the canal before it ended and drained through a sluice gate into the sea. Constructed from the gleaming limestone that lined the cliff faces along much of Kefya's coast, the Lighthouse was often the first landmark sailors could see as they approached the city's harbor, and true to its name, the tower served as a beacon of safety to all who viewed it. Once she was over that bridge and inside the building, she would be protected, and Wymund could rally the guards against Cater Waldwen and his goons.

However, the beautiful vision of security was marred as Cater Waldwen himself emerged on horseback and stopped in front of the bridge, flanked by two of his pawns. The bald man was just into his middle years, though a lifetime of physical labor had made those years land harder on his skin than they might have otherwise. But that same work had also ensured he maintained the physique of a much younger man, and his light cotton shirt and vest did little to hide the damage he could inflict. He stared down the road toward her as she ran, crossing his arms in satisfaction. From this distance, Rav could make out a smirk plastered across his broad face.

Bypassing city guards had been one thing, but these men would strike her down and leave her to be swept aside on the streetcleaners' first pass of the morning. She had to lose them, so she slipped between the stalls to her right. The intensity of the strange spasms in her arms and legs continued to build, the fatigue that had been settling in now seeming to melt away. Faster and faster she ran.

"You can't scurry away forever, little rat," Waldwen shouted over the sound of approaching hoofbeats.

How did he even get inside the gate? Cater isn't the type to be granted free passage throughout the city, especially with those thugs at his side. Rav assumed the man must be better connected than she and Wymund had thought, and that meant she had been nowhere close to bringing down the root of his organization. But why would a noble be interested in helping Waldwen run his little protection racket in the city's outer wards?

The pins and needles danced more vigorously across her skin now, appearing to match her pace as she darted between the storefronts and homes of the affluent. The sensation had gone from unpleasant to painful, but it paled in comparison to the knot of muscle wrenching the back of her neck. Still, despite the pain, Rav had never felt so alive. Instead of hampering her circuitous progress back to the Lighthouse bridge, the pulsing waves radiating from the base of her skull fueled her. Each step was bolstered by their energy. She held her hand in front of her eyes as she ran. *Why is it so bright this early?*

No matter how fast her legs could carry her though, she couldn't outpace a horse at full gallop. One of Waldwen's companions, a short man with a mouse-like face and short-cropped hair, came careening around the corner before her. His eyes bulged and he smiled. "She's here, boss! I've got her!"

Rav dashed down an alley to the right, moving farther from safety. But that didn't matter anymore. She felt as if she could run all morning if she needed, and some of the day as well. More calls rang out behind her. Then again to her right and left. The rider spotting her had been enough to make her lose her edge against Waldwen's numbers. She was being corralled, and there was nowhere left to hide.

Skidding to a stop in the alley, she tried the only door available to find it was locked. A simple mechanism, she was sure, and one that could be picked with ease. If only riders had not just arrived at both ends of the corridor.

With a sneer displaying teeth almost too large for his face, the short man who had found her hopped off his mount, landing with surprising grace. "Come now, little rat," he said as he flipped his riding cloak back to place a hand on the wooden truncheon hanging at his waist. "That's enough running for the day. Cater just wants to have a word with ya. We just need to get this all sorted."

Rav heard the rider behind her dismount as well and chanced a glimpse back. Standing at the other end of the alleyway was a woman who looked to be the same age as Waldwen, her reddish-blond hair pulled out of her face and loosely bound in a tail that draped over her shoulder. It was starting to gray around the temples, but that only spoke to a greater threat rather than a sign of frailty. A woman of her years who had made it this long with this crowd had to have earned her experience. Rav knew firsthand the danger she posed. The dagger that had punctured her side was hanging beneath the woman's cloak.

The rat moniker stung with irony. A rat would be able to squeeze its way out of her predicament, but Rav could see no escape. Here within the Inner City, the added space between structures was an affordable luxury to most, so reaching the rooftops by leaping from wall to wall was out of the question. Likewise, she had allowed herself to be caught in one of the barest alleys she had ever seen. No crates, barrels, or furniture were present to use as a launching pad. She widened her stance and dropped low, using one hand to unfasten the cloak from around her collar and letting it drop to the ground. If she was going to have to fight her way out, she didn't want any loose fabric that could make her easier to restrain. She also wanted it out of the way of her daggers if Waldwen's men insisted it come to that.

As if the thought summoned him, Waldwen and his horse trotted into view behind the sneering man, followed closely by Reg and his sharp-featured partner. Each man looked winded, as Rav would expect of anyone keeping pace with her movements through a city, but they were far from out of commission. "Hello again," Cater said from atop his mount. The man made no move to join his men on the ground, and instead settled into a more relaxed position, laying his hands loosely across the saddle. "You've caused us some trouble this morning. Forcing us to chase you all around the damned city. It's enough to make a man wonder who you were off to see."

Rav stayed quiet. Wymund might have been a pain in her side from time to time, but he was loyal and he kept his word. That was more than could be said for most of the men living here in Virdoba. She wasn't about to say anything that could give away her connection to him. If this encounter didn't go well for her, maybe he would have another chance to bring Waldwen down.

"Not in the mood for talking? That's strange." He leaned back in the saddle, cocking his eyebrow in mock surprise. If Rav was the rat, Waldwen had assumed the cat's role. "Something tells me you were getting ready to spread some nasty rumors about us. But as you must've picked up while you were snooping around, we're in a tricky position right now. I can't have some criminal running their mouth about me to the wrong set of ears. There's too much at stake for the people of Virdoba."

Heaving gasps for air announced a new arrival behind her, and Rav spun to find Carn leaning his bulk against the wall at the end of the corridor. His once bulbous nose was now smashed flat against his face, and blood streamed down either side of his mouth. Despite the exhaustion, she could see pure hatred in his eyes. Standing beside him was Lariq, the only one of Waldwen's thugs who had arrived on foot and seemed no worse for wear. Draqesh strides were shorter, but their endurance more than compensated.

Every muscle in her body was vibrating now, as if the energy within was screaming to be unleashed. The tingling sensation felt like liquid fire scorching each inch of skin, the heat seeming to worsen the gooseflesh that was normally reserved for the cold. Lights sparked brighter and brighter, streaming from around the corners of the alley but also flaring at random from the walls to either side. *There are no windows*, she thought before Waldwen grabbed her attention once again.

"Obviously, we can't let you live," he said, though Rav now saw little more than his silhouette against the glare. "Torran, make sure you lot take care of our rodent problem. I have to go explain why I had our benefactor dragged out of bed at this hour."

The man beside Reg nodded and drew a shortsword from the scabbard across his back. Waldwen tapped his heels against his mount and spun the animal around. "Don't be sad, little rat," he called behind him. "Your death will serve Virdoba's future."

All was silent in the alley for a moment, with only the sound of Waldwen's horse clopping farther into the Silver Set neighborhood breaking the silence. Rav was surrounded. No one would mistake these six for highly trained combatants, but at a certain point, numbers became more important than skill. Still, her muscles ached with anticipation, quivering like a taut rope about to snap. She knew the odds. She had lost. But some of them would too.

"You heard him," said Torran as he stepped out in front of Reg and the short rider. "Let's show her how we treat rats that get caught sneaking around our house."

The man rushed forward with his fist already cocked, no more than a dark outline against the bright lights flaring all around her. He was either winded from the chase or generally out of shape, though, because Rav had ample time to sidestep the obvious strike and grab his wrist from the air. She jerked his arm out straight with the aid of his forward momentum, then drove her right fist up under his extended elbow. The joint bowed in the wrong direction with a loud wet pop, which was followed by Torran's anguished scream. He hunched over and cradled his arm gingerly with the opposite hand as Lariq and the older woman came charging from behind him.

Rav could hear Reg's heavy footfalls landing closer and closer from the opposite direction and knew she could not allow the two sides to crowd around her. Launching herself at the wall to her left, she kicked off the surface and managed to flip over the oncoming women, driving her knee into Torran's exposed back before rolling into a three-point stance. She had heard stories of cornered beasts lashing out with incredible ferocity but experiencing it herself was almost beyond comprehension. Minutes ago, Rav had felt as if one foot was already in the grave, but the cool dampness of her blood-soaked shirt was the only reminder of her wound now. Its pain had been eclipsed by the waves of heat coursing over her skin and the blunt pressure building at the base of her skull, and her sense of power only seemed to grow in concert.

With one threat prone and unmoving on the ground, she prepared for the next attack. The human woman had already doubled back, reacting to Rav's leap faster than she anticipated. As the woman closed the distance between them, Rav could just make out her face despite the blinding lights obscuring most of her form. Present was the same stony calm that was there when she had plunged her dagger into Rav's side earlier. Unlike the other bruisers Cater had ordered to stay behind, this was a seasoned fighter who moved with a confidence and grace that could strike fear into anyone's heart. But Rav only felt anticipation to release the quaking tension stored within, and so she pounced.

Slamming into the woman's abdomen with her shoulder, she locked her arms around her waist and drove her target into the opposite wall. Rav held tight and blocked the woman's access to the dagger at her belt, but that did not stop the woman from crashing her elbow down onto Rav's spine. Blows that once would have sent shockwaves around her body only melded into the pain she was already experiencing, leaving her with the focus to reach down and grasp the woman behind her left knee.

Rav pulled up and away from the wall with everything she had, throwing the woman off balance and shoving her onto her back. The pair fell to the ground hard, Rav landing with all her weight against the woman's leg, held in a flexed position against her body. There was a sudden laxity to the limb as something tore in the woman's hip on impact, but before she could capitalize on the injury, Rav was knocked away by a heavy blow to her ribs.

She rolled with the punch, stopping on her side, and looked up to see Lariq, stout arm still extended in her follow through. Rav hated fighting draqeshis. Their bodies could have been chiseled from stone, as dense as they were, and they were always quicker than expected. But if that were not enough, Reg had moved himself into a flanking position with her, and he looked as if he had spent his life trying to emulate the draqesh form, only with added human height. Unlike Torran and the older woman, Rav wouldn't last long exchanging blows with these two. She had one recourse available to her now, no matter how much she disliked it. Rav pushed her torso off the ground and swung her legs around in an arc, swiping Reg's legs out from under him, and finished her spin in a crouch before slipping the twin daggers out from her belt.

Both he and Lariq appeared to be moving sluggishly, and Rav was thankful that her chase through the city had taken more out of them than it had from her. Feeling a surge of confidence, Rav struck out with her blade at the mountain of a man lying on his back. He brought up his arm to deflect, but she had already buried the blade up to its hilt in his stomach. Without pausing, she spun with her other dagger in hand and found purchase in Lariq's side. The draqesh woman winced, but whereas Rav had expected to stop Lariq in her tracks, she carried through with her haymaker unbothered. Rav heard more than felt her cheekbone crack against Lariq's fist. Not only was there no pain from the blow, but the maelstrom of fiery pins and needles had vanished as well. Now Rav was left with an alien numbness, everywhere except the knot of muscle that seemed like it would break through her skull at any moment.

She sank low into her stance once again, readying herself for the next punch. But before it could come, her arms were yanked back behind her as she was lifted off the ground. A heavy nasal wheeze near her ear told her that Carn had finally joined the fight. She struggled against the hold, but she could find no leverage. Her feet dangled half a foot from the ground and her back had been pulled into an arch over his gut.

"You broke my nose." His voice was stuffy, but there was no mistaking its malice. "Now we break you."

Rav was helpless as Lariq slammed fist after fist into her stomach. She was sure she would be seeing stars if the light had not been so blinding already, but the fight had not left her yet. The draqeshi unleashed another blow, and Rav crossed her lower legs around the woman's neck, locking her boots together behind the draqeshi's skull. If physically damaging Lariq's hardened body wasn't possible, she could still cut off her air. Mallet-like fists rained down on Rav's shins, but she felt nothing, and the vise grip remained locked in place. Panicky gasps for air turned to silence as she tightened her hold, and Lariq opted for flight instead of fight. Just as Rav had hoped.

Lariq's heels dug into the ground as she began to pull away like an ox hitched to a cart. However, Carn was not fitted with wheels, and as she exerted her force, he toppled forward, landing on both women in a heap. He released his hold on Rav's arms to catch himself, freeing her hands to plunge her daggers into both sides of the draqeshi below her. Her kind might have been tougher than most, but they certainly were not immortal.

"Oh no," Carn started before Rav flung her head back into his busted nose. The man collapsed on top of her, no longer conscious.

Rav wriggled her way out to the side just as a loud crack landed across her back and she was forced to the ground. She threw up an elbow in anticipation of the next blow, rolling over to see the mouse-like rider bringing down his truncheon again. Her arm took the brunt of the strike, and she dropped her dagger to latch onto his forearm. Before he even seemed to realize he was caught, Rav pulled him off balance and sunk her other blade up under his chin.

After shoving the little man's body off her, she stumbled to her feet. The explosive pain behind her neck was her entire world now, no longer accompanied by the intoxicating power that had been humming throughout her body. Her muscles continued to quake, but the spasms had become violent and irregular. She was spent, and all at once the fatigue from the blood loss and exertion washed over her.

Rav placed a hand on the wall to steady herself, but she only managed to guide her fall back to the ground. She heard a scraping sound and looked up to see the silhouette of the older woman hobbling her way toward her, favoring her injured leg. Barely managing to keep her eyes open against the storm of light sparking all around her, Rav tried to throw the dagger at her chest. But her arm refused to move, remaining locked in place at her side while her hand was stuck, contracted around the hilt.

Five out of six is admirable, she thought. *Sorry to prove you right, Mother, but it seems I will be dying in an alley somewhere after all.*

The woman hesitated, looking down at Rav but keeping her distance. "What's wrong with you?" she asked just as the locked door at the side of the alley flew open and another silhouette darted out, slamming into Rav's attacker. The woman's head cracked against the wall and her form slumped to the ground next to her.

"Damn fool girl," said a new matronly voice, somehow tinged with equal parts annoyance and concern. She grabbed Rav by the shoulders and dragged her inside the building from where she had come. "I guess we'll be fools together," she muttered. "But I won't watch this happen again."

She placed Rav on the ground inside the threshold. Rav's body was now shaking uncontrollably and her vision was nothing more than pure white light. The woman ran back outside and down the alley, and Rav could hear her shouting. “Guards! Guards! There’s been an attack!”

That’s an understatement. The pure white light was suddenly snuffed out, and there was only blackness.

Chapter 2

Virdoba

No one was supposed to be in the house. A simple in-and-out job, and everyone would go their own way with their share of the spoils. But the simplicity of the score vanished with the rising flames that licked up the walls, embers now reaching the rafters above. She couldn't imagine why anyone she was with would have started the blaze; attention was sure to follow such a spectacle. But the eyes that the fire would attract were a secondary concern, eclipsed by the whimpering she could hear through the next doorway. The huddled form of a child rocking back and forth on the floor, arms wrapped tightly around their knees, was backlit by the flames filling the room.

Rav rushed forward. Windows were smashed open behind her and the sounds of her partners escaping made her seethe. There was no honor among thieves, but did that apathy extend to the life of an innocent child? As she reached the threshold, a flaming rafter snapped and fell across the doorway with a deafening crash. She placed her hands underneath to lift the beam, only to jerk them back quickly when the heat scalded her skin. Panic began to rise within her. She wouldn't allow her actions to contribute to this child's death, no matter how much risk she had to take upon herself. Wrapping her hands in her cloak, she tried to lift the beam once more with everything she had, but it wouldn't budge. She screamed with the effort, her heels digging into the floor below. The child stopped rocking.

"Take that sash from around your head, girl. You're not hiding anything from me."

Rav stirred out of unconsciousness, her eyelids flickering to adjust to the flame in the hearth. She must have heard the fire crackling in her sleep. Why else would she have dreamed about that night? The cot she was lying on groaned as she tested her stiff muscles. Upon realizing another person was in the room, she turned to see a woman stooped over a heavy iron pot that was hanging over the heat. Thick waves of gray-black hair were pulled back into a loose bun behind her head, and her bronze skin marked her as a native Kefyan. If it weren't for Rav's straight hair, this woman could have passed for a long-lost relative. And although the coat she wore was simple in its design, Rav noted the garment was woven of a fine black silk. The stranger lifted the lid and sniffed before nodding her head at whatever meal she was brewing within.

Rav gasped and slapped a hand over the wound in her abdomen, her mind finally catching up to her current circumstances. However, she only discovered a fresh bandage and mild tenderness. She tested her jaw, gratefully finding no clicking or laxity. The sparking lights and throbbing neck pain were gone, replaced by a fatigue that seemed to be nestled deep into her bones.

The older woman glanced across the room, and Rav sat up to meet her scrutinizing gaze. "I told you to take that sash off," she said. "But it seems as if you can't hear a thing with those ears hidden like that."

Rav carefully slipped the sash down so it dangled around her neck, the rounded points of her ears breaking through her hair for the first time since she had left Felona. "How did you know?" she asked, casing the room for any exits or concealed threats the woman could be hiding.

The longer she stayed in this city, the more she focused on humanity's dark side, a fact that had only been bolstered by the company she kept. Her mother's gentle eyes and soft smile came to mind, and she felt a brief pang of regret for thinking in such broad strokes. But she shoved the guilty thoughts aside, deciding she wouldn't offer the benefit of the doubt to people who wouldn't extend as much to her.

The old woman chuckled. "If you spend all your time with the dregs down at the docks, you may get away with it. Most of them are lucky if they've seen a book in their lives, much less read one. But you're in the presence of an educated woman now, girl." She hurried forward with a grace that belied her age and hunched over, leaning toward Rav's face.

"I've read *many* books, so there's no use trying to hide what you were doing out in that alley from me." Smiling, she added, "Plus, those bright rings of blue around your irises are a dead giveaway."

"So what? You're holding me here until the guards arrive so you can pin the deaths of all those *upstanding Virdobans* outside on me? There's another side to that story."

The woman laughed and pulled a stool up beside the cot. "The guards have already come and gone in the few hours you spent napping, child. I told them it was some territorial spat, and I'm sure they'll take my word over the protests of the survivors. But I doubt they'll mention you to the authorities anyway. It doesn't help their image to share that they were thoroughly handled by a slight thing like you."

Rav winced as she repositioned herself to face her captor and rescuer. Although her body seemed to have been healed to a degree that defied explanation, every shift of her weight caused an ache in her side. "Well, if you saw what I could do to those thugs, you've decided to put yourself at great risk holding me here. What does that say about your vast education?"

"I just saved your life, and at great personal cost. More than you could comprehend." Her eyes flicked over to a small cherrywood box sitting open on the floor. The exterior was etched with beautiful intricate wave patterns and the trumpet-shaped bulbs of what looked like the seafoam bindweed, a flower popular with the Kefyan nobility living out on the island. Inside, the container held nothing but a red velvet lining. Rav caught a hint of mistiness when she looked back, but the woman blinked it away. "I won't have my loss be for naught."

Rav rolled her eyes as she stood from the cot, her legs feeling surprisingly steady. Once she recognized the design on the wooden box, everything had clicked. Her heart wasn't going to ache for the tears of the wealthy. "*Of course.* You're from the capital. Only a Felonian would be this arrogant."

"Watch what stones you throw, girl. You may not be from Felona itself, but you're definitely from the island." She smirked at Rav's obvious jolt of surprise. "You're too trusting."

"I *don't* trust you, old woman."

The self-assured grin dropped from the woman's face, her smile softening as her eyes ran up and down Rav in appraisal. "Maybe not," she said. "But there's a stillness to your eyes that can only come from being raised in a safe home. You at least have the *capacity* for trust in you, and with those ears of yours that can only mean you aren't from here in Virdoba."

Uncomfortable being read like an open book, Rav decided it was time to leave. The condescending lectures had been enough to drive her away from home, and she wouldn't stand for them here, regardless of whether the woman had saved her life. Rav's cloak was neatly folded at the end of the cot, and as she snatched it up to make her escape, she could feel the familiar heft of her twin daggers tucked within. She unfurled the garment and inspected each blade, both of which had been cleaned and cared for while she was sleeping. Tracing a finger along the engraved name on the cross guard, she took a breath and tried to center herself.

"You picked up my stuff?"

"When covering up a murder, one doesn't typically leave the evidence lying around."

Rav smiled despite herself. The woman was opaque and seemed to enjoy being difficult, but how many times had those same traits been attributed to her? Maybe that was why she found her so grating.

"How do you know Ilphas Trisarin?"

Her father's name cut through the quiet moment, sharp as the blade upon which it had been engraved. The memory of his beaming face as he knelt to pick her up flashed to mind. Besides his daggers, it was the only thing she had left of him. Her earliest memory, the warm feelings it summoned untainted by his later absence. But that was what she had always heard about her father: No matter how he disappointed you, he always left you with a smile on your face and love in your heart.

"My father. These belonged to him."

"Ah, I'm sorry for your loss then, girl," the woman said, genuine empathy in her voice. It made Rav's heart ache. "When those Clipped Gull bastards stole him from us, Felona suffered a great blow. But I'm sure it was nothing compared to the crater his assassination left in your home. I must admit, though, I was unaware he was a stormforger in addition to a civil servant. I'm surprised that he would bother with a layman's weapon, but I suppose someone must've taught you to fight like that."

"Stormforger?" Rav laughed. "I've heard my father was a lot of things. Charming, curious, restless. But he couldn't draw from the World Shroud. Trisarins aren't special stock."

The woman cocked an eyebrow, and Rav thought she could see her mind at work behind those sharp eyes. "Well, all right then. I was mistaken." Stepping forward, she extended her hand. "Let's start again. My name is Annika Iatorii. Who are you and why were you stabbing people in my alley?"

Rav blinked at the surname. She would have had to marry into that name, as the woman obviously did not have a drop of elven blood in her veins. *First the condescending tone and now this. It's like Mother has found a way to be in two places at once.*

Grasping the outstretched hand in return, she said, "Rav. And let's just say they didn't leave me much of a choice." She donned her cloak and slipped the blades back into her belt. "I suppose I should thank you for saving me. I'm . . . not sure what happened out there, but I'm certain I would be dead right now if it weren't for you." Her fingers brushed against the closed wound, still tender but somehow whole. "How did you do that exactly?"

"You should really be thanking my sister," Annika replied as she turned to pick up the empty wooden container on the floor. She clicked the lid closed and sat the box on a shelf over the fireplace, taking the time to adjust its position until it was centered perfectly on the mantel. "It was her talents that saved you. Her last knitting serum for that hole in your side, and then her own special concoction to bring you back from the brink." Still facing the hearth, Annika whispered, "She would be glad to know it worked."

Rav knew healing potions like knitting serums were exceedingly rare and powerful. The witches who brewed them would spend days, or in some cases weeks, draining enough life energy from the World Shroud to imbue the tonics with their restorative qualities. The more time that was spent infusing the power into the liquid, the greater the effect could be on the recipient. If she *had* been on the verge of dying, then Annika's sister must have spent a great deal of time and energy crafting those potions.

"Your sister is an elf?"

"She was," Annika answered with the barest hint of a smile. There was a distant look in her eyes for a moment, startling in contrast to their usual intensity. Then the gaze was gone. "And since she gave you a second chance, she wouldn't want you wasting it on some half-cocked vendetta against those thugs. But I can also see you aren't the type to be satisfied sitting on your hands. Why don't I give you a better way to put your skills to use? You need to slow down for a bit anyway, after what I just witnessed."

I don't think Wymund is going to alter the terms of my deal for you, old woman. But if Annika had used everything she had left of her sister to save the life of a stranger, how could she just shut her out now? Rav hated being in someone's debt. Sighing, she said, "I still have responsibilities to people that I can't just run out on, but what do you have in mind?"

"Have you heard of the Allies of Edis?"

Teacher Edis wasn't a figure that members of polite society would rally around, so any group that called themselves allies of *the* Ally would have to be composed of unsavory folk. The Dawn One of the wretched and maimed didn't inspire any sanctioned congregations; the acts of vengeance he espoused for the wronged could never really be justified under the laws of most communities. If a chapter of his followers had gathered within Virdoba's walls, they might be able to tip the scales of the city's uneasy peace. It all depended on who they targeted for retribution. Feelings of persecution were often a matter of perspective.

"I can't say that I have, but they sound like a fun bunch."

"Yes, I'm sure they're a riot," Annika said with a sardonic grin. "Although they may not be your crowd. Some Kefyans still haven't adjusted to the nation's changing demographics after the War of Arrival."

Rav slipped her sash back around her ears. "Believe me, I got the message. Are they planning something more than shouting slurs across the street?"

Annika's brow furrowed. "I don't know for sure. I've only begun to hear whispers of them organizing within the city, but the sentiment is growing stronger. Choii Stier is forming deeper trade ties with Qedrad, and Virdoba's merchant class feels threatened. Impotent as they are in the realm of international economics, they may want to lash out at the closest surrogates."

"In this case, being their elven neighbors. Most of whom have never set foot on the shores of Choii Stier."

"Rationality is not a trait they possess in abundance," Annika replied.

"How do you know all this? I would think secret revenge mobs would hold their ideas closer to their vests."

"People can sometimes feel more comfortable than they should expressing their more colorful opinions to a person who looks like them."

A horn sounded in the distance, breaking through the somber mood that had settled over the room. Wymund's shift was ending, and Rav knew he would be preparing for an ill-conceived rescue attempt since she had failed to return the previous night. After gathering her cloak to hide her bloodstained clothes, she turned to head for the door. "I'll look into it. I owe you that much. But right now, I have to go stop a friend from getting himself killed in my name. Give me a few days and I'll fill you in on what I find."

Annika followed her to the door, holding it open as Rav entered the alley. "Do be more discreet about it than whatever you were doing earlier this morning." Her features were softer than they had been inside; concern for a woman she barely knew etched across her face. "I don't have the means to save your life for a second time, so try not to get into anymore brawls or chases."

"Espionage is an unpredictable trade, old woman," Rav joked, hoping to ease Annika's mind with a laugh, though her frown only deepened. *Great job, Rav. You've replaced one fretting maternal presence with another.*

She made it halfway out of the alley before she stopped, turning to find the woman still watching her go. "I never asked. Why did you save me?"

Annika's gentle smile returned. "Because I had the chance to."

Chapter 3

Alaboq

"Now I know all of you are lying to me," Mareq said as he plucked a fiery red cinder plum from the top of the crate. He squeezed it between his first two fingers and his thumb, testing the firmness before sniffing the fruit. "A great fish the size of *The Fortune's Rose?* You just want everyone in the kitchen to have a laugh at my expense when I go repeat your wild tale."

Captain Tomau clutched his hand to his chest and staggered backward a few steps, a mock pained expression barely visible through the matted tangle he called a beard. The two sailors standing at his side chuckled at his antics before hefting the last crate and carrying it down the ramp to the sandstone dock below. "You insult my honor, son. How many days and nights did you share the sea with us? Months, at least. And you think we would deceive you just so someone else could have a laugh?" A familiar twinkle returned to his dark eyes as he looked down at Mareq from the railing. "We would much rather have that laugh ourselves, Greenboots!"

The two sailors laughed so hard at the nickname that one almost dropped his side of the crate. Mareq shifted his feet. He had, of course, bought fresh shoes once they had docked in Alaboq, but the reminder of his sick-stained boots caused his face to flush. All his boasting about seeing the world had only made it that much funnier to his shipmates when he couldn't find his sea legs. That had been months ago, and he refused to be the butt of the joke each time Tomau and his band of buffoonish traders made their way to this port. Mareq had no choice but to continue working with them, though; no one else could deliver the exotic produce he peddled in a timelier fashion.

Joining in the laughter as he accepted the crate from the two men, he said, "I understand, Captain. The inability to laugh at oneself is a sign of a weak-minded man. I bet you all still joke about the time we found you passed out from drink, draped over the boom with your bare ass to the stars."

Mareq heard a choked laugh from the man to his right, who had done his best to disguise it as a coughing fit. The other just stared at his own feet with wide eyes. Tomau glared down at him, and for a moment he wondered if he had overstepped. They were reputable merchants who liked to play pirate for the mystique; Tomau probably thought it brought him business. Mareq was sure the captain and his men wouldn't hurt him. Mostly sure, anyway.

After an uncomfortable pause, Tomau gave in to a fit of uproarious laughter, slapping the side of his ship for good measure. His men took the cue that it was safe to join in, and each patted a hand on Mareq's broad shoulders before making their way back onboard. Wiping a tear from his eye, Tomau said, "That was a good night, boy. And here I thought you draqeshis didn't have a sense of humor."

"Of course we do. It's just a bit more subdued." Mareq removed several gold crests from his pouch to settle with his supplier, leaving it far emptier than he liked. He had been living and working out of Alaboq for nearly six months now but hadn't managed to save many more crests than were needed to refill his wares each week. The itch to leave was always with him, but he had been patiently waiting for most of his life, enduring taunts from his siblings that he was not cut out for a life of adventure. What were a few more months of scrounging up coin if it meant a lifetime of exploration and knowledge?

Captain Tomau and his men went back to work unloading the rest of their cargo as Mareq hefted his crates into the wagon hitched to his coal-black mule. Although he could manage the weight of the containers on his own, their bulk would be awkward for his shorter arms. The animal's long ears twitched as the weight of the packages settled into place, and she clipped her front hoof a few times on the sandstone below.

"Oh, don't be like that," Mareq said. "You know the shop's only a short walk from here."

Leading her by the reins, Mareq began to walk up the winding path that led from the docks to his storeroom in the Lyri Blossom Market. The street was crowded with men, women, and children hustling this way and that, transporting goods to their merchant stalls, searching for the perfect place to grab a morning meal, or just enjoying the sunshine and clear skies. Despite the teeming masses, everyone had a smile on their face, politely stepping aside whenever Mareq and his cart approached and greeting him warmly. Growing up in Brey, he had always been told that the people living in massive cities like Alaboq were inconsiderate or even outright callous, but since arriving here, he often found himself wondering if those who told him had ever left their hometown. Here he was in a city nearly eightfold the size of Brey, and with few exceptions, everyone he met seemed to go out of their way to be kind.

Mareq was still not used to the beauty of the city itself. The architects who had designed the buildings of the capital must have had an eye for art as well as function, as each shop and home seemed to rise naturally out of the sandstone below. The appearance was so striking that a less educated person could be forgiven for believing the city had been sculpted from the stone itself rather than constructed on top of it. Color popped all around, from the rust-colored tiled roofs to the cerulean and snow-white petals of the lyri blossom trees that served as a median, separating opposing lanes of foot traffic. He smiled as he reflected on how far he had come. His home was not small by the standards of most people, but relative to Alaboq, he might as well have come from a rustic fishing village. And there was so much more left in the world to see. *Just preferably not by boat.*

He reached the circle that marked the midpoint of the market, where a towering bronze statue of the Accountant watched over the business transactions that took place below him, one hand outstretched as if to receive payment, the other raised in greeting. Teacher Leros's delicate facial features had been captured expertly by the craftsman who had created the likeness, but they had smartly kept the Dawn One's shoulder-length hair draped in such a way as to obscure the ears. His high cheek bones and narrow nose told one story, but humans had always liked to claim Teacher Leros as one of their own as well, and in the spirit of fairness that he taught, most artisans left a little ambiguity in their work. Every time Mareq looked at the statue from the window of his storeroom, he could hear his father muttering in his mind. *Hmph. Even the Westlanders' gods are soft.*

After unloading the produce from his cart and stabling his mule down the street, Mareq sat at the small wooden table that served as both his desk and dining table. The building he had rented here in the center of Alaboq's market district was little more than a large closet, but it was all he could afford. In this room, he slept, ate, and organized his deliveries into the individual orders he received from his wealthy clients. Other than the table and a set of chairs, the only objects occupying the space were his stack of crates and a bedroll tucked into the back corner.

Operating a storefront from this glorified alcove wasn't feasible; most in the city simply could not afford the imported fruits at the rates he charged to make the business worthwhile. But Mareq had found a niche for himself in the months he had lived in the city, including regular deliveries to Vinsart Hold, the king's blockish citadel that overlooked Alaboq from the peak of the north hill. Propping his feet up on the table, he closed his eyes and told himself he had time for a short rest before he had to start dividing up his wares.

A sharp series of knocks rapped against the door, followed by a feminine voice shouting, "Mareq Iq'Urlset! I've traveled a long way to see you and I insist you get me out of this scorching sun immediately."

A broad grin broke across his face as he recognized the voice, and he leaped up to get the door. Mareq swung it open to reveal a young woman with golden-red hair that had been pulled back into a loose knot, her emerald-ringed eyes staring at him intently as she muscled her way into the room. She was holding her cloak above her head so that it formed a canopy to shade her from the early morning sun. Being from Draemoor, her skin was fairer than other Qedradans, closer to Mareq's own hue, in fact, but Tiialya had always fared especially poorly in the heat. She took a seat at his desk and hung her head so she could fan the back of her neck.

"It's good to see you too, Tiialya. With a little warning, I could have suggested that you plan your visit in the evening. I know how sensitive your constitution can be."

Without lifting her head, she glanced up at him with a flash of annoyance. Mareq knew she was not to be trifled with; he had seen Captain Tomau and his men on the receiving end of her scolding, often defending him from their taunts. But she just sighed and stood to hug her friend.

"Honestly, how you can live in this tinderbox remains a mystery to me. The one place in the north with buildings that seem to function as a brick oven." She pulled back and her smile lit up the cramped room. "I've missed you, my friend."

"How are Ormuq and the young ones?"

Tiialya groaned. "Oh, they are absolute terrors. I wish one of them could've taken after me, but they're both troublemakers like their father."

"That's right." Mareq laughed. "How could I forget that steadfast and cautious Ormuq was always hiding a wild streak? They couldn't possibly have picked up their mother's restlessness."

"I'm not restless. I'm simply good at what I do, and it would be a shame to waste my talents." Her smile softened, though it lost none of its intensity. "But as the boys have gotten older, I've decided my international excursions are becoming less important than my time with them. I'm here for my last job, at least for a while."

"I never thought I would see the day that you would succumb to the draw of domesticity."

Tiialya rolled her eyes. "I won't have Ormuq being the only one educating the boys. Someone needs to be there to teach them the intricacies of societal dynamics. Otherwise, they'll stumble their way through life naïve and trusting, and I can't have that on my conscience." Scanning the room, she walked over and plucked a cinder plum from the open crate. "I trust you're putting my connections to good use?"

Mareq nodded. "I've been making weekly deliveries to Vinsart Hold. I still don't understand how you know so many people in such lofty positions."

"A lifetime of fortuitous introductions and information gathering can result in a favor or two." She paused, her forehead knitting together with concern. "But that *particular* connection is actually one of the reasons I wanted to see you. Have you noticed anyone out of the ordinary on the citadel's grounds lately?"

"I think you're overestimating my familiarity with who should and shouldn't be there. Plus, I'm not allowed anywhere inside beyond the kitchen and storeroom."

Tiialya nodded her head, lost in thought. "Just . . . be careful, Mareq. The job that brought me to Alaboq involved *discreetly* delivering a message to one of the king's advisors from a member of the Kefyan Council. It referred to some 'plot in Virdoba' that would 'break down trust before new relationships could flourish.' When communications between heads of state are covert instead of matters of official record, there's always cause for concern."

Of course, secret messages signaled a need for suspicion, but Mareq didn't believe that equated to danger. For all he knew, that letter could refer to an uncovered romantic tryst and some scheme to undermine it. *Motherhood is making her anxious.*

"I will be cautious, Tiialya. Thank you for the warning." He walked the short distance across the room to place a hand on his shipments. "But speaking of the citadel, I'm due for a delivery this morning. It's been so long since we've had a chance to catch up, and I don't want to rush you out. How about you stick around and help sort the orders, and I could fill you in on my winning repartee with Captain Tomau this morning."

At the mention of manual labor, her worries disappeared behind her typical playfulness. "I'm afraid I would rather take my chances with that monstrous sun than heft those crates around. You're much more suited to that kind of work." She embraced her friend once again. "And I really should make my way back to my wooded paradise. I fear for what my children have gotten Ormuq into in my absence. If you ever find yourself south of the city, please stop by for a longer visit."

"You know me," he said as she departed. "I can't stay in one place for long."

CHAPTER 4

VIRDOBA

Rav could feel the disappointment emanating from Wymund as he buried his face in his palm and sighed, the worried creases on his bronze skin still apparent despite the shadows in the lamplit office. After leaving Annika's home, she had hurried over to meet him at the Lighthouse, still marveling at how replenished her body felt considering she had nearly died. Growing up, she had been given knitting serums a handful of times to mend broken bones or close a gash, as Rav had not always been the graceful cutpurse she now was, but she had never experienced this type of rejuvenation from a potion. However, Wymund's palpable frustration was beginning to have a draining effect.

She had filled him in on the events of the night before, starting with her being discovered as she was trailing Cater's men. He jumped out of his seat to inspect her when she mentioned being stabbed, but she shooed him back down and carried on, relaying to him the tale of her chase through the city and confrontation in the alleyway. She left out the parts about flaring lights and burning pain; Rav had heard that a dying mind was prone to playing tricks on itself and she didn't want him to think she was going mad. He might just throw her back into a cell.

After a long moment of silently massaging his forehead, Wymund looked up at her. There was more concern in his eyes than exasperation as he said, "Well, at least your injuries don't appear to be too serious. Otherwise, I doubt you would've been able to make it back here."

He rose from his seat and clasped his hands on her shoulders, standing half a head taller than her. With her partial elven blood Rav could stand eye to eye with most human men, but Wymund's lean towering frame seemed built for this line of work.

"Though I think you may have oversold your clandestine abilities if those oafs managed to pick you out," he said. "And your staging of an internecine gang war won't hold up under scrutiny. I'll have to talk to whoever will be leading that inquiry." He closed his eyes and shook his head; subterfuge was never his natural inclination.

As she watched him stand before her in his teal coat, somehow still neatly pressed at the end of his shift, Rav felt guilt at the element of chaos she had brought into his life. *This arrangement was his choice*, she thought as she tried to quash the feeling. *But I did know what I was doing when I talked him into it.*

"That interpretation of events wasn't my idea. The old woman that patched me up talked to the city guards."

"Right, I'll have to meet this plaguewoman," Wymund said. "Though I don't know yet whether to thank her or have her arrested."

Rav broke away from his grasp and sat on the corner of the desk. The room she had met him in was not his office, as corporals were not afforded such luxuries without the burden of command, but Wymund possessed an air of seniority that the privates on his shift didn't question. She was sure they believed the room would be his before long. Leather-bound books discussing military tactics and city management lined the many shelves along the walls, and hanging behind the desk was a framed map of Virdoba. To the artist's credit, they had taken the time to differentiate the neighborhoods of the outer wards. Most maps she had seen since arriving in this city depicted a detailed Inner City surrounded by a grayed-out mass labeled "Outer Virdoba."

"She isn't a plaguewoman. She's human, and she definitely wasn't peddling some quack cure-all." Rav patted a hand over her closed wound. "Whatever she had was the real thing."

"Interesting. Someone with such means is definitely a person the Virdoban Guard needs to know." He crossed his arms and looked at her expectantly. "Well, I didn't let you out of your cell to pick fights and befriend strange women. Were you at least able to learn anything before you were discovered?"

"As I recall, I let myself out. You just approved of my continued freedom." Rav caught the slightest hint of a smile on his otherwise stoic face. Rare as it was, his grin had a mischievous quality to it that was not unlike her own.

"And as I recall, that freedom was conditional on information. I don't make a habit of releasing thieves and arsonists without cause."

"You damn well know I didn't start that fire," she snapped. The man's smile flickered from view as he realized he had crossed a line.

Wymund unfolded his arms and his mouth opened slightly. Finally, he said, "Apologies, Ravael. I misspoke. But please, tell me we gained something from your excursion."

She took a breath, the memory of the child's screams echoing in her head. "Not as much as we hoped. I caught a few phrases while I was following them that seemed like they were looking to expand their scheme into the Inner City, but they didn't mention any specific targets. I'll go back out tonight and see if I can learn more."

"Did you enjoy being stabbed?" he asked. "No, you'll stick with me from now on. Out in the open and holding to the letter of the law. Maybe you can learn how to be a proper investigator." Rav started to protest but stopped as Wymund held up his hand. "But what you did learn is certainly curious. I wonder how successful this group thinks they can be by extorting more affluent people for protection. There's less criminal activity here within the inner walls to need protection from."

Rav laughed. *That you know of. What's defined as "criminal" is determined by those rich pricks.*

"All you'll do is slow me down, Wymund. I work best on my own. Last night was just an unfortunate fluke."

He frowned and ran his hand along the top of his closely shorn dark hair. It was a habit of his when he was concentrating, as if he needed the friction to get his thoughts moving. "Cater's men could be actively hunting you now that you put a dent in their ranks. You no longer have your anonymity, and without that, I'm not comfortable sending you out there alone. While you're not my prisoner anymore, you're still my responsibility."

"Well, *I'm* not comfortable being on a leash."

"Think of it less like a leash and more like a partnership. You may not think you need someone to watch your back, but I'm not as useless as you seem to believe." He fastened his sword belt around his waist and rested his hand on the pommel of his longsword. "Now if you don't mind, your antics have kept me here long past my normal waking hours, and I would like to get some rest. I suggest you do the same."

Despite her restorative nap, Rav knew he was right; she could use some actual sleep in an actual bed. This slap on the wrist stung, but she didn't want to push the matter any further. Wymund wasn't as incompetent as she had suggested, and, if she were honest with herself, the thought of another blade at her side made sense. Plus, she hadn't considered that maybe the recent reversal from predator to prey would be a permanent arrangement now that Cater knew her face. However, there was one other matter that needed to be discussed before either of them could rest.

"I will," she said as Wymund finished collecting his things. "But first, there may be another cause for concern that I wanted to bring to your attention. When the old woman learned I had elven blood, she thought that I had been attacked by a group calling themselves the Allies of Edis." She didn't need to ask if the Virdoban Guard was already monitoring such a group; his blank expression revealed his ignorance. "They are supposedly a faction of people who feel slighted by Choii Stier making economic inroads with the mainland. Rather than outcompeting their trade rivals, they may be looking to scapegoat the elves living here for their misfortune."

Wymund's brow furrowed; his fist clenched tightly and pressed into his desk. "If this is true, I will personally see to it that an end is brought to their schemes. The Guard will open up an inquiry into the matter and see what can be learned."

He dropped his head, the anger on his face softening into grief for his city. Rav knew Wymund well enough to know that people like the Allies did more than just conflict with his ethical duties, although that certainly played a role. Elves had every right to live free within Virdoba's walls, as did humans and draqeshis. But ultimately, it offended his sense of honor that one person would plot to harm another, whatever the motive. She found the quality both endearing and naïve.

"It is truly a shame that a group would adopt Teacher Edis's name as their public moniker," he said. "We are meant to learn from the Ally's quest for vengeance as a cautionary tale, not celebrate his aims and champion his cause."

"There have always been, and always will be, hateful people in the world," Rav said. "The only difference now is that they are labeling themselves as such, which if you ask me, might prove helpful in rooting them out."

The hint of a smile returned as he looked back at her. "Careful now, Rav. I may start to believe you have the heart of a leader hidden beneath all that cynicism. That sounded dangerously close to hope."

She flicked her hand in a dismissive wave as she turned to leave, hiding her puckish grin from view. "Nonsense. I've simply built up a lifetime of emotional callouses like every other elf in Kefya. It will take much more than the idle threats of disgruntled tradesmen to break our spirits. We're not as delicate as we look.

"Now, I plan to return home and sleep until someone wakes me," Rav added from the doorway. "If you want to prevent another debacle, I suggest you rest up and find me before Cater and his thugs do. Otherwise, you will only have your tardiness to blame for what happens to them." His protests were cut short as she closed the door and hurried down the corridor.

CHAPTER 5

VIRDOBA

The scent of charred wood surrounded Tetamii as he strode onto the production floor, leaving behind the wafting aromas of spiced hen and citrus-soaked peas that were cooking over the many hearths of the Low Tide District. But the scorched smell was a familiar sensation, one that had been with him nearly all his life, so while the men and women tending to the kilns kept their faces wrapped in damp cloth for protection and comfort, his confident, dour expression was on full display. The workers scrambled to stay out of his way, pressing their backs against the brilliant limestone furnaces, worried less about potential burns than his wrath. He smirked at the irony. They knew so little of his capabilities.

Tetamii stopped short as a pair of children rushed across his path, a mound of empty bottles clinking in their arms. Rage flared inside him. He would have to have a word with that fool Waldwen for dragging the innocence of youth into their work. His scruples had been beaten or bought out of him when he was little more than a child himself, and he hated to see the cycle continuing with a new generation. Not that bottling distillation runoff compared to his initiation into the criminal underworld, but they had time yet before the harsh realities of life broke them down. Wispy tendrils seemed to rise from the ground and distort his vision as his connection to the World Shroud strengthened with his fury. Clenching his fists tight, he managed to tamp down the burning anger within. Cater Waldwen would have to answer to him, but Tetamii answered to someone as well, and that someone had paid for his professionalism.

Rows of bottles filled with a clear liquid were sitting on tables and work benches that occupied the center of the distillery. He stopped to inspect a few, reluctantly admitting that their process had improved. The fluid appeared no different from water, while just a few weeks before, swirling black particles could be found in each container.

It appears these hicks can follow directions when properly motivated, he thought, smiling at the memory of their fearful faces during his last visit. *But the real test will be if their product does more than just look the part.*

Cater Waldwen stood at the other end of the production floor, his bald head reflecting the flames atop the nearby limestone kilns. He was barking orders at an elderly draqesh man on a step stool who was struggling to pack more dry moss into the base of the fire. It was the most important step in the process. Moss had to be packed tightly enough into the body of the furnace so the pine wood inside wouldn't ignite. The goal was to heat the wood until it broke down, not burn it. Otherwise, the distillate would include smoke rather than the fumes that would become pure wood alcohol as it cooled. Cater had learned from his last encounter with Tetamii, it seemed, but it wouldn't save him from further scorn today.

Beside Waldwen was a woman he had seen around him before, just into her fifth decade, with red-blonde hair that was starting to gray with age at the sides. She reminded Tetamii of the large island cats that hunted the shallow channels of the Choii Stier archipelago, confident and deadly whether on land or in the water. He sensed in her an admirable grace and precision, thinking that of all the members of Cater's group, she was the only one he would describe as capable. However, someone had gotten the better of her in the weeks since his last inspection. She sported a bulbous red knot on the right side of her forehead and was clearly favoring one leg. Unless he had been wrong in his appraisal of her skill, an eventuality he very much doubted, then the person who had inflicted this damage was someone he needed to meet. Fortunately, learning about this person was why he had come.

"Seal it up tight," Cater shouted at the draqeshi, whose hands were now dangerously close to the flames as he fought to maintain balance on the wobbling stool. "The product needs to be crystal clear when it comes out of the chute for the damn thing to work. If I have to hear about cloudy swill from Mr. Swithred's enforcer again, I promise I'll share the experience around with the lot of you."

Tetamii cleared his throat. Cater's head snapped around, his face that of a child caught sneaking a pastry before supper. The woman beside him turned more calmly, arching an impressed eyebrow at him despite her swollen forehead.

"Refer to me as Swithred's enforcer again and the only experience you will be offering is a funeral service, Cater. Your benefactor and I share an employer, but one of us was hired based on mere proximity to the problem while the other was shipped here for oversight. Care to wager which of us is more important?"

Waldwen's arms tensed beneath his shirt, but he could not hide the quiver in his voice or the sweat beading on his scalp. "My apologies, Mr. Fiadar. We weren't expecting you here so soon."

Fiadar was a surname as good as any other to Tetamii's mind, as he hadn't used his own in decades. Identity was a fluid concept to him at this point in his life, his job demanding that he be able to fit into any setting as needed while maintaining an air of anonymity. He was who he needed to be for the task at hand. Unfortunately for him, that meant he was currently responsible for this insipid bunch.

"It's surprising to me that after what transpired this morning, you wouldn't expect a little more supervision. You allowed a common footpad to tail you and your men, possibly overhearing secrets relevant to our employer's interests, and then you failed to slit her throat." Tetamii gestured behind him with a broad sweep of his arm. "And now I arrive to find you have expanded our operation to include children, who can easily be bought off by inquisitive authorities with nothing more than warm sweetbread." He shrugged and adjusted the polished black leather strap holding the bastard sword to his back. "Out of professional courtesy, more than you deserve, I will remind you that while your role in this is integral, you as an *individual* are not. So choose your next words well; they will be the most pivotal ones of your life. What happened?"

To the man's credit, whether from sheer bravado or stupidity, he managed to regain some composure. "You're right, Mr. Fiadar. We did have a rat among us in the early hours, but Ninev here spotted her and stuck her between the ribs." Cater placed a hand on the red-haired woman's shoulders, who wisely remained stone-faced. Pride in a failed kill would be misplaced at best. "She's the most skilled fighter we have, and on my word, she doesn't miss her mark. The fact that the slippery bitch made off into the city bleeding like she was . . . well, that tells me that she wasn't a simple thief."

Tetamii glanced over to Ninev, who still betrayed no defiance or fear at the interrogation. If it weren't for the loyalty Cater commanded over his crew, Tetamii would have disposed of him and put her in charge then and there. "Is this true? Do you have no doubt in the placement of your blade?"

Ninev nodded. "It was a killing blow. I had no interest in finding out who she was, only in getting rid of her."

"But that's not the strangest part," Cater continued. "We pinned her down in an alley just inside the Inner City, and I left six of my best there to finish her off. But she took out all of them single-handedly, then disappeared before those teal ducklings arrived and rounded up the survivors as if they started a turf war."

"I just managed to get away before the guardsmen made it down the street," Ninev added.

"As for the kids," Cater stammered as he looked down at his feet, "I just thought that their small hands would be better suited to squeezing past my crew working the furnaces. It's crowded in here and sometimes it's hard to reach the chute and bottle the alcohol. But don't worry, we'll give them a preview of how we punish disloyalty in this organization."

"If you lay a hand on them, I'll personally lop off a few of your fingers. Then you will have tiny hands to replace theirs." Cater's eyes widened, but he remained silent. "Just let them scurry back to their mothers' skirts and do a better job yourself. Beating them will only make them more eager to turn on you."

Turning back to Ninev, Tetamii said, "Since your boss left you behind to clean up his mess for him, please fill me in on what I'm missing. As it stands right now, I fail to see how a lone girl could hold her own against six of you."

"She moved faster than most of us could react, sir. After seeing how she fought in the alley, how she was able to dance around us like she knew where we were going to be, I have to believe my blade only found purchase initially out of blind luck." Ninev winced as she gingerly touched her hip, shifting her weight. "It has been some time since someone has been able to knock me on my ass like that."

"She must be a highly skilled fighter," Tetamii said. "How was her form? Could she be an Achen blade serpent, or is she more likely a professional assassin?"

"No, Mr. Fiadar. I could tell she knows her way around a fight, but that's just it. She fights like a brawler, unrefined and undisciplined. Definitely not Achen military or anyone a noble would want to hire for a hit. When I say she knew where we would be, I don't mean she has had practice predicting the forms of her opponents. She just seemed to *know* and reacted accordingly." She smiled wryly. "That is, before she collapsed into a shaking heap. I've never seen anything like it."

Tetamii clenched his jaw to mask his surprise. "Her eyes. Tell me about her eyes."

Ninev looked to Cater, who gave a slight nod. "Well, I was *told* that the pain was playing tricks on my mind, but I would swear that her eyes were glowing. Flickering with a blue so bright that it was almost pure white."

"A lightblood," Tetamii muttered, keeping his gaze downcast, lost in thought.

"An elf, then," Cater stammered, managing to find his voice once again. "What have you and Mr. Swithred gotten us into? We were assured that nothing would blow back on us!" He began to nervously tap his foot, his arms crossed and tensed, while Ninev's expression finally betrayed the slightest hint of concern.

Idiot. This is truly the best help Cyrilke could find to enact his plans?

Of course, Cater hated and feared elves, so why would he have taken the time to learn the differences between an elf and one with partial elven blood? They were all the same to him. Tetamii wondered how that revulsion would grow if Cater knew he was currently being cowed by one. Apparently, his auricular tribute to the Clipped Gulls and focus on hiding his own lithe frame behind a wall of muscle was disguise enough for these simpletons.

"There was an elf with us that night we set that house on fire," said the draqeshi on the stool. "She was probably just some local talent they hired to help get inside. I don't think she was a full-fledged member of the Ghosts, but then again neither were Groven and me, so what do I know?"

"And your unsanctioned trial run almost started a war with those spooks. There was a damn child inside," Cater said with a glance that caused the draqesh man to turn back to loading the kiln. "Bloody dagger-heads," he fumed. "Is it not enough to boot us out of trade deals and infiltrate our cities like vermin? Now they have to spy on us as well?"

As the man's tirade continued, Tetamii turned his attention to the wispy contortions of the World Shroud all around him. He could feel the warmth of it, distinct from the heat one might sense on their skin. This was the *essence* of heat, sensed within his mind. It rippled at his direction as he mentally reached out to it, an action as natural as flickering the eyes to focus or tilting the head to hear. Drawing from the World Shroud was sensory and instinctual, with training allowing for deeper connections and greater control. Tetamii flattened a section of it across the top of a nearby kiln, thinning the membrane as it was pulled taut at the base of the flames rising from the furnace. Then he tore it.

A spout of flames erupted from the limestone kiln, licking all the way up to the wooden beams crisscrossing the top of distillery. Ninev covered her face with her arm, stumbling away from the intense wave of heat that bathed the area. Cater cut off his diatribe and transitioned seamlessly to panicked shouting, shoving the draqeshi who had been tending the flames toward the furnace and demanding that he control the conflagration. Terrified cries rang out through the room as many of the workers made for the exits, some looking for buckets of water while others aimed to escape. Several of the children stood still, tears filling their eyes as they stared at the geyser of fire consuming that end of the room.

Just as the draqeshi's hand reached toward the towering inferno, his head turned away from the intense radiating heat, Tetamii folded the tear in the World Shroud on itself. The flames returned to their original state, leaving only a blackened wall and charred beams as evidence that it was once anything more. A few startled faces peered back in through the open doorways, and the billows of smoke that collected under the vaulted ceiling emphasized the stunned silence below. The only sound was that of the crackling furnaces that ringed the room, until a resounding smack rang out.

Cater's backhanded slap completed its wide arc as the draqesh man fell to the ground. It took a great deal of strength for a human to fell a draqeshi, and Tetamii was almost impressed.

"How many times have I instructed you to control the flames?" Cater yelled. "The bottles in this room could roast us alive with a single spark!"

Before he could bring his hand down for a follow up, Tetamii grabbed Cater by the wrist and spun him around. The man's rage-filled face lingered for only a moment before dropping in deference.

"Always so quick to blame others, Mr. Waldwen. First Mr. Swithred and me for 'getting you into trouble' with the elves, and now this poor man. He can only be expected to meet the level of competence that is demonstrated for him." He released Cater from his grasp with a slight shove, causing the man to stumble backward. "No, what I see here is a consistent failure of leadership that I will bring to Cyrilke's attention. You're his man, after all. But if this pattern of behavior continues"—he paused, drumming his fingers along the leather strap holding his blade—"more immediate measures will need to be taken."

Cater tugged at the bottom of his vest and straightened to his full height, not quite measuring up to Tetamii's towering form. "That won't be necessary, Mr. Fiadar. I will strive to do better." Giving a slight bow of his head, he added, "How would you advise that we proceed?"

The presence of a lightblood in the city complicated his mission, although Ninev's report indicated this person lacked the formal training that would make her truly dangerous. However raw she was, though, he couldn't entrust this group of thugs to take care of her; their efforts would be more effective as a smokescreen. But keeping them off her trail was as much a selfish decision as it was a tactical one. It had been too long since his work had offered up a real challenge.

"You will have to accelerate the timetable of your demonstrations. With a rogue lightblood on the loose who is interested in our actions, we may not have the time to gently sway the public's opinion as instructed.

I need you to stop being discreet, and hopefully keep the Virdoban authorities occupied."

Ninev simply nodded, having regained her stony disposition while Cater couldn't hide the deepening worry lines across his forehead. Tetamii could see the man trying to plan how he could accomplish this safely and coming up short. However, Cater didn't allow his concern to dig himself into a deeper hole.

"We won't let you or Mr. Swithred down," Cater said. "But if this woman is as troublesome as you believe, what should we do if she returns?"

Tetamii's mouth ticked upward slightly at one side, despite himself. "Hold the eyes of the law. I'll handle the elf."

Chapter 6

Virdoba

Two small children darted to either side of Annika's legs, using the folds of her dress as obstacles in their game of tag. They stretched their arms around and toward each other, pulling fabric to block attempted grasps and squealing in delight. Annika balanced herself on the counter in front of her, careful not to scald her hand on the iron cooking surface just inches away, and looked down at them with a frown, her lips twitching to hold back the smile that threatened to appear. "All right, that's enough out of you two. You'll have me cooking my hand right here in the market if you aren't careful."

The pair stopped and looked at her with blank expressions, seemingly unaware that their cover had been a person all along.

"And if my hand gets cooked, Mr. Brennad will need some little fingers to sell as sides." She smirked at the heavily bearded man on the other side of the counter, who chuckled as he brought his knife down into the breast meat of the bird cooking before him. The children's eyes grew wide as their mother scampered over and grabbed each around the shoulders.

"How many times have I told you not to wander off in the Round Square," the mother scolded, holding them tight to her sides. "You will end up starting a fire one of these days."

The young woman had a darker complexion than the typical bronze skin of a Kefyan and spoke with a thick Achen accent that landed harder on the consonants than the vowels. Flowing linen pants hung loosely around her legs but cinched tight at her waist, where they met a sleeveless, dull yellow blouse made of silk. Annika recognized the typical Achen attire from the visiting dignitaries who had frequented her family's dining table in Felona as a child, inferring that the young mother must be married to a traveling merchant, or was one herself, to be able to afford such quality material. She had done her part to fit in, though, as she wore the narrow cotton caps of the Choii Stier elves that had become fashionable for Kefyan ladies of late. Hers was a sandy brown and covered only the crown of her head, and a small white feather fitted into the short brim on both sides.

"I am so sorry for their behavior. I swear, they never behave like this at home." The woman stood, taking one hand from each child in hers so they remained locked in place. "Please, let me pay for your meal as compensation. I saw that they almost knocked you over."

Just as Annika held up a hand to dismiss the gesture as unnecessary, Brennad cleared his throat and began tugging at his beard, his go-to move when he wanted to put on a show of making monetary calculations.

"Let's see, Ms. Iatorii here wanted a little taste of home, so she asked me to grill up the Felonian trail fowl I just had imported." Brennad paused to flip the breast meat of the common chicken he had butchered this morning, furrowing his brow. "Now normally the lads at the docks give me a good rate per bird, but they said the Marrow Strait has been choppier than usual lately, causing damages and such to their vessel. I told them I didn't see how that was my problem, but they saddled me with a property damage tax anyway." Releasing his beard, he smiled warmly at the kids and then beamed at their mother, revealing a missing front tooth behind his ruddy brown tangle of facial hair.

"But since you're doing my friend a kindness," he continued, "I'll return the favor and just charge you for the cost of the bird. I wouldn't want to profit off such a beauty with a magnanimous spirit. It'll be one silver liber."

It was an outrageous sum for the meal, even if the chicken actually had been imported from Felona. Brennad had also picked up on the young woman's wealth and was hoping to take advantage of her foreign naivety—a disgusting practice for a merchant to employ on their customers. But she would be damned if there was another street vendor in

Virdoba that could cook a chicken without drying it out. Annika also saw the opportunity that had fallen into her lap.

She shot Brennad a look that snapped the smile off his face, then turned back to the young woman and said, "That won't be necessary. Children will be children, and it's nice to be reminded of that carefree energy every once in a while. But if you feel so indebted, perhaps you could repay me in another way?"

"Certainly, Ms. Iatorii. I am Majaila of the Rehmanik Guild, by the way." Placing a hand on the heads of her children, she added, "And these terrors are Hibaya and Nazmi." The pair looked sheepishly at Annika. "Tell me what you had in mind, and my guild will honor the request."

Annika had heard of the Rehmaniks, an up-and-coming textiles family based out of Ineset, and was elated at her good fortune. The rumblings of animosity toward elves that had been building in Virdoba seemed to be strongest in the outer wards; specifically, from the men and women working in the Lower Quay. She understood their perspective, in a way. A threat to one's livelihood was a personal affront that also threatened the lives and health of one's family. But their anger had been misdirected, guided away from the actual source of their troubles. After all, it was not their elven neighbors that were decreasing mercantile traffic into the docks. It was further up the chain, where money was exchanged for a signature here and a handshake there, the decision-makers often caring little for lives that were being altered in the process so long as their purses stayed full.

An Achen guild-family like the Rehmaniks were perfectly positioned to have the type of information she needed, not so established that they could be beholden to those pulling the strings, but not so new as to have no powerful connections at all.

"Oh, it is nothing so formal, Trademaster Rehmanik. I just find myself in need of information, and I pray that the Arbiter may allow a place at your table so that we may talk." Familial dining was revered in Achen, with time set aside for each member, no matter the age, to share their opinions openly and to be heard with respect. Inviting herself, even metaphorically, was bold and bordering on uncouth, but it was the only way she could be sure that anything she learned would be the whole truth. Invoking the nation's patron deity would hopefully soften the request.

Majaila's eyes flickered over to Brennad, who had begun muttering under his breath as he fussed with the cooking bird. "Teacher Aton says that anyone who treats a family with honor may dine as one with them." She smiled as her gaze returned to Annika. "You respected my cultural ignorance today, and likely saved me a fair bit of coin, so your place at my table has been earned. Perhaps you will join us for an afternoon break?"

Returning the smile with a slight bow of the head, Annika said, "I am honored, Trademaster Rehmanik. Please, find a comfortable setting for us to share this meal and I will join you shortly. Mr. Brennad and I just have some business to settle." Majaila nodded and led her children away into the Round Square, allowing herself one last disdainful side-eye at the street vendor before departing.

"What did you have to do something like that for?" growled Brennad as he lifted the cooked chicken from the iron surface and dropped it on a clean parchment wrap. "It was disrespectful to the spirit of free commerce, is what it was. The push and pull between merchant and customer is a game of skill, and a third party tipping the scales is cheating."

She pulled three copper libers and one silver liber from her coin purse, then placed them on the counter with enough force to make the cook flinch. "That's not how the game is played, Mr. Brennad. If you're going to extort someone, make it someone like me, who wants something from you." She removed her hand so the man could see the amount of coin she offered, and his gap-tooth grin reappeared as if it had never left.

"Three coppers for the bird, half again what it's worth, but I don't mind paying a premium for quality. And a full silver liber for your greed." Brennad chuckled at that, and Annika smiled despite herself. "In return, I expect an answer to my question."

Brennad picked up the coins, giving them a quick toss in the air before slipping them into the pocket of his apron. "All right, well played. I haven't heard much, and I've seen even less. Folks have been saying that the dagger-heads have been torching businesses and homes in the outer wards. Just burning them to the ground for no reason at all. Even after we welcomed their kind into our city . . . " He trailed off as he focused on folding the parchment around Annika's meal.

"You and I have differing opinions on what it means to be 'welcoming,' then."

He flicked his eyes up to her from his work before blinking and shaking his head. "Uh, right. Sorry, Ms. Iatorii. I meant no offense by what I said, just repeating what I heard. I don't personally have a problem with them; elves have to eat just as much as we do, and their coin works just as well. I am surprised they stop by my cart though, what with all that fancy elven *cuisine* they like to tout so much."

Taking her wrapped bird from the man, Annika said, "Fine cuisine is like fine art, Brennad. The preparation and composition are to be appreciated, but when it comes to the sensory experience, sometimes the best examples are found on a street corner." She nodded her head in farewell and turned in search of her dining companion.

The Round Square formed the eastern section of the Inner City, where Virdoba's large Market Gate admitted venerated guests from civil officials to High Scholars of the Dawn Ones. Less prestigious visitors were diverted to either the Patchwork Gate to the north or the Hearth Gate to the south, and were therefore deprived of the mesmerizing sights, sounds, and smells that bombarded the senses upon entering the market. Mouth- and eye-watering spices drifted through the air from those offering traditional Achen meals, while the sounds of Virdobans learning to play music on an Ebkarish shifting staff mingled joyfully with the laughter of onlookers watching them fail. Brightly dyed silks were draped across Qedradan vendor carts, often with multiple colors on each sheet of fabric. It was a luxury material that many Kefyans hated admitting to needing in the scorching summer months, even if tensions had cooled between the two nations since Kefya won its independence over two centuries ago. An international rivalry remained, though, and so the more subdued silks from Achen frequently sold better.

The district's name was taken from the layout of merchant stalls and carts that had taken shape over time, somehow organizing themselves into a chaotic circle rather than into neat rows. But that was part of the market's charm. If one knew exactly what they were searching for, they could travel to one of the established shops in Craftsmen Row or even in the Patchwork. Spending time in the Round Square was more about discovery than planned purchasing. While there were a handful of regulars like Brennad, most of the carts and stalls were rented out on specific terms by the city to local farmers and traveling vendors from across Anera. This multicultural shopping center was one of only a few places in Kefya where people could purchase more exotic goods than their typical options, and despite the national pride that ran particularly deep within Virdoba's walls, this district was considered a bright spot for its residents.

As she squeezed past a man trying to peddle his recent mudroot crop, a legume more useful for its aid in digestive regularity than its flavor potential, Annika spotted Majaila sitting on a stone bench against the northern wall of the square. Her two children had taken to playing a frenetic game with some loose pebbles that they hopped around the cobblestones, seemingly at random to any outside observer, but she was sure the logic of the rules made sense to them.

After carrying her warm parcel through the crowd of shoppers, Annika took a seat beside Majaila and began to unwrap their lunch.

"It may not ignite the tongue like the traditional Achen technique, but I promise you will find it difficult to obtain a better prepared bird in all of Kefya."

Majaila smiled and plucked some meat from the thigh as it was offered to her. It left the bone without resistance. "You are familiar with the Three Heats, then? I have found that most foreigners are not so fond of our dining experience."

"Familiar, yes." Annika laughed. "Though I would not go as far as saying fond. I obviously appreciate the importance of the cooking flame for feasting, but I've always failed to grasp the need for the body flame and the sky flame. I prefer my meals in the shade and my tongue in working order when I'm finished."

"Well, I suppose there is no accounting for taste." Majaila ate the chunk of grilled chicken, her smile widening in recognition of the meal's quality. She turned to face Annika, wiping her fingers on a handkerchief she kept folded over the waistline over her pants. "Now, with the blessing of Teacher Aton, let our dialogue be open and honest."

Annika maintained her polite smile, not wanting to hint at the severity of her concerns. She didn't believe the Rehmaniks would be involved in the growing tension within the city, and she certainly didn't see Majaila as the conniving type, but there was always the chance that an enterprising outside agent could twist the situation to their advantage with enough information. This conversation called for a modicum of discretion; luckily for her, there was no more important training in her aristocratic childhood than the art of subtlety.

"Has news reached Achen of any discontent brewing here in Virdoba?"

Majaila thought for a moment, chewing slowly, her expression changing briefly to one of contentment before returning to seriousness. Finally, she said, "No more than usual. I am sure you are aware that the . . . *strain* between the humans and elves in Kefya is no secret to the rest of the continent, but I have heard nothing new that would indicate that relationship souring further."

Nodding thoughtfully, Annika said, "There have been rumors here in the city that elven insurgents are destroying property in the outer wards." Majaila gasped at the suggestion, but Annika continued to ensure there was no misunderstanding. "I don't believe a word of it, mind you. I think there are forces at work manipulating the existing friction for their own ends."

Annika watched the woman carefully, having shown just enough of her hand to elicit a hidden motive if one existed. However, Majaila demonstrated nothing beyond genuine concern, placing one hand over her heart and the other over Annika's. She had forgotten Achen's laxer views on personal boundaries. "The conflict among your people saddens me. But no, these rumors have not reached Achen, to the best of my knowledge. Is there a reason you believe my people would be involved?"

A pebble bounced off Annika's leg and Nazmi leaped up to retrieve it, her arm and fingers outstretched. But before she reached the stone, her head turned as if her chin had been caught by a hook. Annika followed the child's line of sight to the vibrant flowering trees and immaculately manicured shrubberies of the Faarasan Gardens, a district beside the Round Square that was home to Virdoba's most prominent artists. She glanced back to Nazmi, whose profile was lit with delight. It was unlikely, given the arid climate of Achen, that the child had ever seen anything like the Gardens. Annika and Majaila smiled at each other as Hibaya followed his sister over to stare at the vista, vicariously holding on to the wonderment of youth before it could be chipped away by the ways of the world.

The warm glow of nostalgia was transient, though, as the city's brewing turmoil reasserted itself. "Not directly. Much of the animosity seems to stem from the belief that Choii Stier is attempting to cut Kefya out of their trade agreements, so in fairness to their concerns, I was hoping to learn if the elves had approached Achen with such an arrangement. Seset would make for a plausible southern port city, after all."

"I wish I could be of more help to you," Majaila said, furrowing her brow. "But I have not heard anything to that effect. The little business my guild-family does with Choii Stier is always facilitated by Kefyan vessels."

"You have been a great help, Trademaster Rehmanik. Lack of evidence is a form of evidence itse—"

A shattering crash followed by panicked screams burst from their right, and Annika snapped her head around to see the silhouette of Majaila's two children backlit by a blaze engulfing a building on the outskirts of the Faarasan Gardens. She knew the place well—a prominent Virdoban floristry shop called The Glorious Forest, the contents of which were now going up in smoke. A handful of bystanders rushed off in the direction of the Silver Set, buckets in hand and aiming to help. The scant amount of water they would be able to carry back wouldn't do much, but Annika respected them more than the other onlookers who had formed a semicircular crowd around the building and seemed content to watch it burn.

"Gather your little ones," Annika said as she stood from the bench and began to move toward the inferno. Billows of smoke poured forth from the shattered window at the side of the shop, filling the air with a sickly sweet charred odor. Covering her mouth and nose with her sleeve, she shouldered her way through the bystanders, admonishing them for their uselessness along the way. "If you all see fit to watch your neighbors burn to a crisp, I would hate to be one of your enemies!" Annika received little more than scoffs of indignation in return.

As she got clear of the crowd and made it into the small space that had been created just outside the front door, a few men and women returned from their trip to the canal, each desperately trying to keep most of the contents of their buckets from sloshing out onto the cobblestones. "Go around the side," Annika shouted to them. "There's an open window. Try and aim for the center of the flames." The group nodded and hustled around the corner, accepting her command without question. With her upbringing, issuing orders came naturally to her.

Satisfied that the impromptu fire brigade would do what it could to mitigate the damage, Annika turned back to the crowd. "Has the owner come out of the building?" A few murmurs and shrugs greeted her in response. "Useless, the lot of you," she muttered before saying more loudly, "Go home! You'll be more comfortable as idle lumps near your chamber pots!"

The gasps and sneers of the crowd went unnoticed, though, as she hurried toward the front door, reaching for the handle as it swung wide. Annika fell back on to the ground as four hooded figures flew out of the burning building, each crouching low, appearing ready to defend themselves or dart away as needed.

Looking up at them, Annika recognized the oval wooden masks covering their faces, each painted white with red lines drawn down from the forehead and across each eye before meeting at the chin. These were elven war masks. When she was young, her father had hung several of these masks in his study, regarding them not with reverence but with historical interest. Masks of this type had not been worn in earnest for centuries, though, not since the War of Arrival. Judging by the reactions of this well-to-do Virdoban crowd, time had dulled the memory that the masks had last been donned in *defense* of this Kefya's independence.

The onlookers scattered, clutching the arms of their loved ones and screaming as they sought the safety of their homes. One of the masked figures stepped forward, standing feet from Annika as he shouted, "The time has come for Kefya's debt to be paid! Elven lives were lost in defense of your homes, with nothing but scorn for our kind given in return! We will have what is owed; whether it is taken or given matters little to us."

Annika struggled to her feet, the wear of age fighting against her joints more than fear. But before she could stand to face the attackers, a blunt force cracked against her jaw, forcing her back to the ground. For a moment her vision swam, the large, hooded figure towering over her seeming to split into four. Every sound was muffled, as if she were submerged under water, but she could just make out his voice as he said, "Stay down, crone. Or the next one will melt your skin."

A soot-covered man stumbled out of the floristry shop, coughing and grasping at the threshold to remain upright. "Guards," he choked out. "Guards, they're still here!"

Annika's hearing returned to normal and the sound of hoofbeats racing from the Lighthouse and along the Silver Set rang out over the shouts of neighbors hurrying back for another bucketful of water. The four masked assailants turned to one another before nodding and running off to the north, presumably hoping to lose the Virdoban guardsmen in the maze of the Patchwork neighborhood.

Regaining her footing, Annika helped the coughing florist to a safe distance, glancing over to see Majaila crouched beside Nazmi and Hibaya, one arm clutched around each of their chests. The children appeared terrified but unharmed, and Annika breathed a sigh of relief tinged with a lingering concern. This attack was over, but more were sure to follow.

Chapter 7

Virdoba

"They were dressed for war, Corporal Sylnorin. All four of them. Just like they say they used to in the War." Timmer Bynik, the florist, mopped his brow with his sleeve, wiping away the mixture of sweat and ash that had settled there. "As sure as the Artist's stroke, I've never feared more for my life, sir."

Wymund nodded, taking in the man's account while keeping an eye on Rav several yards away. Despite her insistence that she would lay low after the debacle with Cater's men, Wymund found her waiting for him outside the Lighthouse as he and his regiment came charging out in response to news of the attack. Her covert abilities were still in question, but she was certainly tapped into what was happening in Virdoba, a trait that was both promising and concerning. He had told her working together was for her own safety, but that was only a half-truth. Now, he didn't mind that Rav wanted to tag along—she needed to be watched. A charming one she might be, but she was still a criminal.

The bronze-skinned thief was talking to an older woman who had witnessed the attack, but their body language suggested a familiarity that he hadn't expected. The witness was obviously well off, a member of the Virdoban upper crust, something Wymund could infer by how she carried herself. She was a person who knew how to take charge of a situation and get results. He wouldn't be surprised if she had connections to the Kefyan Council in Felona.

But to see his partner at such ease with the woman was perplexing. Rav hadn't told him much about her background, which was consistent in his experience with footpads. Keeping personal details vague and close to the chest were tools of the trade. However, he was familiar with the behavioral patterns of the criminal element, and when they mixed and mingled with aristocracy, one of two personalities was adopted. The first was the fawning beggar, grateful for their moment to bask in the glow of greatness, while the second was the silver-tongued conman who spoke fast and above their target's heads. Each was a survival mechanism in its own way, a method of appearing unworthy of attention or above reproach. But Rav hadn't taken on either persona. She stood with a relaxed posture, leaning casually against a lantern post with her hands resting on her hips. To Wymund, the two women seemed to be peers.

"We'll find the people responsible for the attack, Mr. Bynik," Wymund said, pulling his eyes back to the shop owner. "Please, have a seat and try to settle yourself while I speak with the other witness. If you are feeling up to it, I would like you to join us in the shop shortly so we can move through the incident step by step."

Timmer nodded, eyes still wide from his recent dance with death, and shuffled over to sit on a bench at the edge of the Faarasan Gardens. As Wymund headed toward Rav and her new friend, he surveyed the damage to the structure. Blackened wood panels at the side of the shop creaked and groaned as they cooled, damp from continual dousing with buckets of water. The amateur firefighters had performed admirably, but extensive repairs would still be required to the building's façade if the florist hoped to remain in business. Not many people in the Inner City would want to purchase bouquets from such an eyesore.

The scent of charred vegetation hung in the air, wafting out of the window that had been blown apart by the eruption of flames. It was a stark contrast to the sweet floral aromas Wymund would catch as a child, when the wind gusted in off the Marrow Strait, over the inner wall, and into his bedroom window in the Patchwork. He remembered staring at the tops of the trees in the Gardens, at the pinks and blues and yellows that couldn't be found anywhere in his own cramped and dull neighborhood, and thinking that one day he would make a home for himself there.

His father was a struggling painter who eventually traded canvas for walls to make ends meet, but Wymund had been determined to succeed with his inherited talents where his father had failed. He had spent the better part of his youth studying the murals decorating the art district, learning what techniques he could from the public works that were on offer to a working-class child. Upward mobility was a steep incline though, and practical concerns came for him as well. Walking through the district now, in his long teal guard's coat speckled with ash, he realized that he had finally added some more color to the Gardens. Just not the kind he had hoped.

"—haven't heard anything about them yet, but I'm keeping my ears open," Rav said, before turning to him with the smile of a person hoping to change the subject. "Ears open" meant she was still out working on her own. *Stubborn woman*, he thought, too unsurprised to be annoyed. "Wymund! The old woman here has kindly decided to save you some time by witnessing two crimes in as many days. You said you wanted to meet the woman who saved my life, so allow me to introduce you to Annika Iatorii."

"It's a pleasure to meet you, Ms. Iatorii," Wymund said, extending his hand to shake hers. The grip was firm and confident, a fact he filed away into his assessment of her as a potential diplomat. "It seems you're making a habit of being in places of interest to my investigations."

Annika returned a polite smile. "Over the years, I've found that many places are interesting if a person cares to look. Virdoba should be grateful that it has one such as yourself looking after it."

Wymund couldn't help but be impressed. The woman was unbothered by his implication of her involvement. She knew this world and her place in it, and there was nothing a lowly corporal would be able to do about that. Still, her smile was genuine enough, and Wymund didn't think it was likely she knew more than she let on. Experience had taught him it was safer to err on the side of coincidence rather than conspiracy.

"I must thank you for saving Ravael's life. She does have a tendency to leap before she looks, but also a streak of uncanny luck that I'm sure brought her to you." Rav shot a look in his direction that would give a stranger pause. "I hear you are quite gifted with potions."

"Not me, I'm afraid. They were gifts from my late sister, and Rav had the honor of receiving her last vial." Annika glanced at Rav as a parent might when reinforcing a lesson to their child. "So, I have advised her that it would be best to avoid similar predicaments in the future. I won't be able to do that again." Then, more to herself than to the others, she added, "Though I suspect with proper instruction, those services may not be needed."

Rav pushed herself off the lantern post with her shoulder, straightening her cuirass with a scowl. "If you two insist on speaking about me as if I'm not here, allow me to oblige. Meet me inside when you're done and maybe we can get around to doing some actual work." Turning on her heel, she marched around the corner and into the still smoking shop. Annika chuckled and followed, with Wymund bringing up the rear, pausing only to beckon the florist over.

Inside, the damage to the building looked far more extensive than the outside suggested. While most of the scorch marks were concentrated around the window behind the counter at the back of the shop, the flames must have licked up the vines that decorated the sides of the store and carried the burn farther forward. Black streaks coursed up and across the walls toward the charred remains of his potted flowers, which must have filled the space with every color imaginable. Now, there were only gray stalks sticking up like gravestones from their clay pots, with whatever was left of the petals floating through the air as ash.

Rav stood with her back to them as they followed her in, locked in place and taking in the scene. Annika brushed past her to survey the damage behind the counter, but she didn't even seem to notice. Sidling up next to her, Wymund saw only a blank, distant expression on her face as she stared at the scorched room, her gaze never seeming to land on anything in particular. He had known fellow guardsmen who would drift into these modes, often after witnessing a murder or some other heinous crime, and he guessed what she had gone through might not have been too different for her. He nudged her shoulder with his and she blinked several times before looking over at him. Without saying anything, he gave her a quick nod. She returned one in kind, adding only a simple, sad smile before joining Annika.

"They've ruined me," Timmer muttered as he followed the group into the room, shuffling aside a clay pot that had fallen near the doorway with his foot. "What am I going to do now? It took me decades to purchase a storefront in the Gardens. I don't have enough years left to earn my way back here." He rubbed his hand along his balding scalp as he scanned the remains of his shop. "Elves just don't understand the level of sacrifice it takes to build a business like this from the ground up. They're born into their lofty positions and expect the same treatment when they come her—"

"It'll be all right, flower man!" Rav called from the back of the shop, carelessly snapping a shelf from the wall as she poked around. "You found your way into this rarified air once before. I'm sure such a *brilliant* businessman can do it again."

Wymund stepped between them as Timmer's gaze flared in her direction, placing a firm hand on his chest. He was aware of the effect his frame could have on mounting tensions. It took a lot for a person to remain agitated when their eye level only reached his sternum.

"What the lady meant to say is that the Virdoban Guard will advocate on your behalf to the council in Felona. I'm sure some aid could be set aside as recompense for the losses of a loyal citizen with such standing in the community." The florist cleared his throat as the indignation drained from his face. Sometimes a little ego stroking was worth the effort. *Although that's one lesson I'm sure Rav will never be willing to learn from me.*

"Now that we're all in here," Wymund continued, gesturing around the shop, "please walk us through exactly what you saw."

Timmer stepped forward and moved into the center of the room. "Well, the four of them burst through the door there and ran to this spot. They started shouting about how they were *owed* a life within the Inner City, and how they would take it by force if needed." The man's voice trembled now, the bravado that came with his anger at Rav all but subsided. "I tried to tell them that I had no control over how they were treated in Virdoba, and that if they just worked hard like I did they could make it out of the slums. But they just laughed at me. Laughed and said that I would serve as an example of what would come if those in power didn't start offering aid to their kind."

He raised his hands in the air, pointing them palms forward at Annika, who was standing near the destroyed window. "Then they started using their magic to summon the fire, like this," and he traced a path through the air with his fingers, following no discernible pattern, before clenching his fists. "That's when the fireball erupted behind me at the counter. They stayed for a few more seconds and were saying something about 'telling everyone they would be coming back,' but I wasn't really listening." Timmer hung his head. "I'm sorry, Corporal Sylnorin, but I was panicking. Listening to their threats wasn't my top priority at the time."

"It's all right, Mr. Bynik. That was an informative account."

"Did they really move their hands around like that?" Annika asked from the back of the shop. Wymund looked over at her as she shifted some glass shards around the counter, her eyebrow cocked in disbelief.

"Yes, I can't recall the exact patterns they made with their fingers, but they waved them around and then, well, *boom*." Timmer punctuated his statement with his hands spreading apart in a mock explosion.

Annika scoffed. "You weren't attacked by scorchers, then. Superstitious rumors aside, people with the ability to draw from the World Shroud don't need to utter magic words or draw arcane symbols in the air to release the power. True scorchers could stand motionless in your shop and achieve similar results. Their abilities are instinctual and natural. Whoever these people were, for some reason they wanted to put on a show."

"You think this was just a silly performance?" Timmer exclaimed, color filling his face as he flung his arms wide to indicate the devastation of his life's work. "Those elves could've killed me!"

"Oh, calm yourself, Mr. Bynik." Annika replied, doing little to hide her exasperation at his theatrics. "I merely meant that their movements were an attempt to draw your attention."

"Was something stolen?" Rav asked. "Misdirection can be a useful tool for obtaining things that aren't explicitly yours." She winked at Wymund, self-confidence once again oozing from her pores now that the mystery had washed the fire from her mind. "Or so I've heard."

"No, they never left the front of the shop, so they had no access to my personal funds. The only thing they could've taken was a potted plant, and I feel like that would've been easy to spot as they ran off."

"I'm not suggesting the distraction was for a theft," Annika said, holding a shard of glass from the window up to the light. For the first time Wymund noticed how extensive the spray of glass bits across the counter and floor had been. Most of the pieces were hidden by a layer of soot, but a few glints of sunlight reflected off those that remained uncovered. The connection she had made clicked in his mind as well, but that somehow only made the incident more confusing.

"They didn't want you to notice where the fire came from," he said as he hurried over to Annika's side. "The glass is scattered inside the building, so whatever caused the fire came in from outside. If they had created an explosion in here, this glass would be out in the street."

"So what?" Timmer asked, looking over the damage himself. "They created an explosion out there instead of right behind me. What difference does that make? What are you going to do about this scourge they're threatening to unleash on our city?"

"I don't think there is going to be a scourge," Annika said coolly, casting a sidelong glance at Rav, who nodded her understanding. "I think they just wanted *you* to think one is coming."

Wymund caught the women's shared look. *The Allies of Edis.* An act like this, within the Inner City no less, would certainly foment Virdobans' distrust of their elven neighbors. But to what end? Closed borders, incarceration, or something worse? He shuddered at the thought of what his people could be manipulated into doing. But something else Rav had mentioned at the Lighthouse came to mind, and he wondered if he and Annika might be more aligned in purpose than either of them knew.

"What?" Timmer asked, eyes wide and slamming a hand onto the countertop. "What are you even talking about, woman? These dirty dagger-heads incinerate my shop, almost killing me in the process, and you're saying they just wanted to play mind games?" The man stared around at the three of them, incredulous and infuriated. Either he had not seen the brilliant blue rings around Rav's irises, or worse, he didn't care. However, Rav seemed unmoved by the slur.

Striding over to the florist, Wymund slapped a gloved hand down on the man's shoulder, just hard enough to make him question if the gesture was meant as comfort or to suggest restraint. "Ms. Iatorii is saying you weren't attacked by elves at all." The red drained from Timmer's face under the weight of Wymund's palm as he swallowed hard. Wymund looked up at Rav and Annika, both of whom were failing to hide their smirks at the man being cowed. "If someone wants to offer *protection* within the Inner City, it would certainly be convenient for an enemy force to spring up as an incentive."

Chapter 8

Virdoba

More information. That was what Rav had promised Wymund after they left Timmer Bynik's ruined shop. His connection between Cater's extortion scheme and the "scorcher" attack made a certain sense, though she didn't want to admit that would-be crime boss could think so many steps ahead. She hadn't been sure at the time exactly *how* she was going to find out more, but she did know where to start looking. Her partner, as expected, wanted to join her in the Patchwork that evening, but she was able to convince him his efforts would be better served elsewhere. Wymund might have been born in the district, but there was no one she had ever met who embodied the essence of a guardsman more than he. With him hanging around, lips were sure to be tighter.

She walked through the cramped streets, hood up, hugging the exterior walls of the hodgepodge buildings. Their lack of unifying architectural design had given the neighborhood its name, and often more than one style comprised one structure. Upper floors had been stacked on to existing homes and shops as the city's population grew, with each new tenant adding their own flair to the streets. On this road alone, Rav could spot the old Qedradan designs closest to ground level, appearing to be sculpted from the limestone that served as the bedrock of Virdoba. No cobblestones had ever been placed in this district, so the sight of homes forming right out of the ground was always striking. They were reminiscent of the draqesh homes built into the side of the Blinding

Bluffs forming the city's northern border, which Rav could glimpse looming over the rooftops.

As her eyeline drew upward, only awnings of rust-colored tile jutting out from the buildings served as a reminder of the Qedradan roofing style. In their place, second and third floors built of bricks in the Achen style or the staggered wooden planks used by the Ebkarii filed down the path. There were even some newer floors in the Choii Stieren mold, though the elves living in Virdoba had to settle for clay bricks instead of the marble that was traditionally used in their homeland. That was the only concession they had made though, as the owners of these apartments had commissioned the fluted spires that dotted the skylines of most elven cities, each roof sporting three to five swirling decorative peaks.

One such tiered structure caught her eye. It bore a sign hanging from the awning that depicted a ladle fractured into multiple pieces, complete with bold lettering beneath that read THE PUZZLED SPOON. The tavern itself looked very much like the few she had already visited that evening, with the exception that the structure had only two levels instead of three. Rav took this as a positive sign for her quest. More floors meant more rooms for rent, which in turn meant more patrons. The secretive sort she was after were more likely to frequent a quiet dive than a bustling bar.

A handful of distressed wooden tables filled most of the tavern's main room, each with matching benches or chairs that held no customers. In fact, Rav counted only three people inside, two men at the bar and a draqesh woman toward the back of the room. The draqeshi had short blond hair that fell just past her ears and wore a white apron tied tight around the middle to emphasize her waistline; clearly a barmaid hoping to increase her wages for the evening. She had taken a spot on a makeshift stage composed of two tables near the back wall where she seemed to be practicing a slow and sultry dance despite the lack of music. Rav noted the young woman still had a long way to go before she could capture the attention of a crowd, though, as she could never get too far into the routine before having to start again.

Her boss, a barrel-chested man with a sharp widow's peak at the top of his tall forehead, eyed her from behind the bar as he cleaned a tankard with a ratty towel. He appeared to be waiting for an excuse to snap at her if she so much as scuffed his already shoddy tables but was holding his tongue at the prospect of increased business.

However, The Puzzled Spoon's only patron didn't seem interested in much beyond the flagon of ale in his fist. He was a scrawny man with short-cropped wavy hair and a prominent Adam's apple who didn't flinch as Rav let the door shut behind her. In her experience, she had found that entering a near-vacant space often came with unwelcome stares from the few occupants inside, but here, she was just another lonely customer out for an evening drink. The man behind the bar nodded to her and tilted his head toward one of the many empty stools.

"I'll be right with ya, lass," he grumbled.

Rav took the seat to the right of the indicated stool, leaving her only a foot away from the other patron at the bar. If the man had any normal notion of personal space, then the alcohol must have expanded his radius of comfort, because he didn't care enough to acknowledge her presence. The bartender finished cleaning the cup and looked her up and down.

"Sorry miss, but I don't keep shandy around," he said. "Best I can do is water down the house ale for ya."

She smirked at his assessment of her. Rav's thin frame didn't just lend itself to quick escapes and acrobatic feats; it was also a constant source of underestimation and another tool in her arsenal. "I'll have a Pregnant Pirate," she said, savoring the man's look of astonishment. He could probably count on one hand the number of times he had served a drink that stout to a woman her size.

The cocktail was a traditional Felonian concoction, calling for equal parts of a spirit triple distilled from molasses and a sweetened Felonian wine that had been fortified with brandy, before finishing with a floating dollop of molasses suspended in the drink. The spoonful of black syrup was meant to signify the undistilled, or "unborn," base liquor, or so Rav had always heard it told. Maybe the sailors who invented the drink just used whatever they had on hand to sweeten the potent combination.

Looking at the bottles behind him, the bartender said, "I've got the rum here and I think the missus may have some treacle upstairs in the kitchen . . . " He paused and rubbed his chin, then ducked below the counter and returned holding two dusty bottles of wine, one red and one white. "But there ain't much call for that fancy islander wine from my clientele. Best I can do is pour a little of each of these and give it a quick stir."

Rav could envision her mother's grimace as if she were seated next to her. The drink would be horrid. "Sounds perfect," she said.

The bartender grunted, nodding and turning toward the stairs at the back of the common room. Just as he reached the banister, he stuck a finger out at the man sitting next to Rav and said, "Jorna, I know how much drink I have left in each of those bottles. I find any missing when I come back, I'll get an equal amount back in blood."

"Yeah, yeah," Jorna answered, waving his tankard toward the stairs. "Just go get the syrup for the lady. You can't live off my purse alone."

Heavy footfalls resounded up the stairs until they were muffled by a closing door. As soon as it clicked shut, Jorna stood on the crossbar of his stool and leaned over the bar, head hanging upside down as he unstoppered a small keg on the other side. He dangled his cup below, allowing the dark ale to fill to the brim before plugging the keg once again. The man flicked a copper liber at the barmaid in the back of the room, who caught it in the air and quickly tucked it into her apron while shooting a furtive glance up the stairs. Reseating himself, he flashed a yellow-toothed smile at Rav and tapped a finger to his temple.

"A man can't see how much drink is left inside a wooden cask."

"Until he runs out of it before he knows he should," Rav replied.

Jorna frowned, a look of bewilderment flashing across his face before the smile returned. "Bah, what're the odds I'll be here when that happens. Plus I'd rather fill the pockets of the fairer sex for their discretion than pay for this swill. The name's Jorna, by the way, Miss . . . ?"

"Armela," she replied, keeping her hood drawn low to cast a slight shadow over her eyes. For this to work, she was counting on that shade and the dimly lit room to hide the blue rings around her irises, though judging by his eyeline, he was more interested in other parts of her anatomy. Another tool she had at her disposal, and one she could work to her advantage. "And your secret is safe with me. I'm not one to get in the way of a man and what he wants."

He twisted in his seat to face her, almost slipping off the side in the process but playing it off by resting an elbow on the bar. "So, what brings you all the way to this side of the Marrow, Miss Armela? The way you have Ol' Bratock running around for your posh drink tells me you're used to the high life on the island. I can't say I've seen anyone order something more complicated than a splash of whiskey in their ale for years now."

"My hope was to find a nice man in a nice town to start a family. Felona is certainly beautiful, but the community has become too *prickly* for my taste." She hoped the coded bigotry was not so subtle that this man wouldn't pick it up. Referring to elven immigrants with a word that captured both the appearance of their ears and their supposed haughty nature was common within certain narrow-minded yet polite societies, but Rav wasn't sure if in his current state he could catch anything short of a slur.

Jorna's smile widened, red filling his cheeks. "Oh, yes. I've heard about how crowded Felona has become lately. Coming to Virdoba was a smart choice then. We've got a little bit of a pest problem ourselves." He paused, leaning forward and resting a hand on her knee. The stench of malt and rot drifted out of his mouth as he closed the distance between them, and Rav bit down on the side of her tongue to suppress a gag. "But there are good people here who are working to keep our streets safe for pretty ladies like yourself."

Rav swallowed hard, the slight coppery taste of her blood a distraction from the man's breath. "That is so good to hear. When it was suggested to me that I make a home for myself in Virdoba, I was told that I could find *allies* here that would protect me."

He let out a soft chuckle, squeezing her leg as his hand drifted higher. "You've found an *ally* in me, Miss Armela. In fact, you're fortunate you've happened upon me here tonight. I have a function to attend with some like-minded folks, and with a woman like you on my arm, we would be certain to make a statement. After that, perhaps I could help arrange some bedding for you in the city. I have a warm spot in mind." His hand crept farther up her thigh, now dangerously close to touching the dagger hidden behind her cloak. Whether his encounter with the blade would be an accident or not, Rav hadn't yet decided.

"It's a date," Rav said, placing her hand on his to stop its advancement. There was only so much of this man she could stomach, but she felt confident he was on the hook now. *Best to leave him wanting more. The fool will be even more loose-lipped if he thinks it will lead to a bedroom conquest.* "Tell me the time and location of this meeting and I would be delighted to attend it at your side."

"Oh, it's not long now," Jorna said before tipping his tankard back to drain the rest of the ale. "Just spend some time with me at the bar, have a drink or two, and then we can be on our way."

"I'm afraid I must make arrangements at the inn where I have rented a room first." The man's face sunk, so she was quick to add, "You know, so that I can have my things ready to be transported to my new living quarters." With that, Jorna's rotten yellow teeth reappeared just as Bratock's boots began to thud down the steps.

"I found yer molasses, lass. It may not be the quality yer used to, but its sweet enough if you ask me."

Rav thanked the bartender and Jorna straightened in his stool. She guessed the man was either intimidated by Bratock being nearly twice his size or that the barkeep wouldn't tolerate his lecherous behavior. Whichever was true, the effect was the same and she was grateful for the relatively odor-free air inside the rest of the tavern. Bratock emptied a heavy pour of the triple distilled rum into a mixing glass, followed by an equal amount of his cheap wines. As promised, he swirled the wines together, hoping to create a poor imitation of the Felonian beverage, and then slipped a scoop of the molasses into the churning concoction. Without the sweetened element of the traditional wine to provide buoyancy, the treacle sunk quickly, where it landed like silt at the bottom of the cloudy drink.

Bratock passed the glass to Rav, who took a sip and fought the urge to wince at the taste. It was far drier than the cocktail she enjoyed back home, and somehow sour in a way she couldn't understand given the ingredients he used. Still, she would sip her drink slowly as if she were enjoying both it and the company until Jorna let slip the information she needed. She just hoped she could keep the contents of her stomach down long enough to draw it out of him.

Chapter 9

Alaboq

The kitchens of Vinsart Hold bustled with their typical midday duties as chefs and apprentices dashed about to prepare the evening's meal. A dozen fires crackled in clay stoves lining the expansive room, each manned by a unit of two or three cooks such that the large space was always a roiling mass of activity. There was no special occasion or diplomatic dinner, but King Berenqar was a formal man who enjoyed a formal meal, and his kitchen staff knew what was expected of them. Qedrad's ruler was also known to be kind and fair, often seen laughing and walking with his daughter Cailynne in the streets of Alaboq and speaking directly with his subjects, so the daily dinner production wasn't viewed as a chore. They were all compensated justly, and most counted themselves fortunate to live in a land ruled by the People's King.

Mareq finished stacking his boxes of produce in the storeroom off to the side of the central kitchen, already filled with more varieties of food than he could have imagined growing up in Brey. The citadel was supplied with fresh grains from the Achen plains that could be baked into light and flaky flatbreads, as well as the more common Destueqan strain that resulted in a hearty loaf with a thick crust. Cheeses from across the continent were delivered frequently, some hard and some soft, but each with their own distinct aroma that always set his stomach rumbling. Fresh game hung from hooks, birds and small mammals mostly, all hunted daily from the surrounding woodlands. But there was so much more every day, and Mareq doubted the royal family could ever complain of boredom regarding the meals that were prepared for them. In fact, he doubted if a meal was ever repeated within the same year, given this wide selection of ingredients.

As he stepped out of the storeroom, he was caught off guard by a minty fragrance so strong that his eyes watered. Blinking away the tears, he saw Mrs. Luviire sitting on a wooden stool with her back against the wall, eyes closed, with a serene smile on her face. Despite her age, the woman only had the faintest of lines at the corners of her eyes and no wrinkles to speak of, one of the few remaining indications of her elven blood. After decades working in a royal kitchen, though, even her kind could develop a softness at the waistline. Her palms were held together like an open bowl in front of her, containing a bushel of red-speckled herbs. Mareq was no expert, but these were decidedly not mint leaves.

She cracked open one eye. "Did you have a request, Mr. Iq'Urlset? I've only enough ruby sage for Lady Cailynne's unsettled stomach, but if you grant me enough time perhaps, I could gather some spices that would sharpen your manners." One corner of her grin crept up mischievously. "Or does the weather back home freeze you in place so often that staring is commonplace?"

Mareq laughed. "My apologies, Mrs. Luviire. I'm just not accustomed to smelling something this delightful from your corner of the kitchen." The comment elicited a full laugh in response. Both knew it was ludicrous. She was one of Vinsart Hold's greatest culinary talents. But while offense hadn't been taken, he did manage to break her concentration as her hands crumpled slightly around the herbs.

"Damn," she said as the smell of mint dissipated. She looked down at the leaves in her grasp with a tilt of her head. "Oh well, I'm sure what I managed to accomplish will be sufficient for the young lady's nausea. I've been infusing this batch since dawn, anyway."

Since dawn? Mareq thought. Princess Cailynne's stomach must have been doing somersaults if Berenqar had called for his herb nurse to spend that much time on a remedy. In his travels, Mareq had learned that infusions worked differently than drawing straight from the World Shroud. The process often took longer, and the results were not as flashy, but that also meant there was less strain on the practitioner. Still, there was always a chance when using these abilities of going too far, pushing past one's limits and causing lasting damage. But he supposed Mrs. Luviire was more familiar with her capabilities than he was, and Cailynne was the royal daughter, after all. What father would not use everything at his disposal to ensure her life of comfort?

"Good," said Waemish, a jovial rotund man who stood at his washing station several feet away, his thinning hair flat against his scalp from sweat. Like Mareq, Waemish was from northern Destueqa, fair-skinned and unaccustomed to Alaboq's heat, something that was only intensified in a working kitchen. "Maybe now you can take over the meal preparations for tonight. I'm not in the mood for any of Ptolon's creations."

The young man to his left, Chaevin, handed him a freshly dirtied pot before adding, "Yeah, the last time he was in charge of dinner, it took a full week for my bowels to be regular again. Must've been some kind of jungle weed that tied up my insides." The pair laughed and glanced behind them across the room at the tall Ebkarish man standing with his back to them, furiously stirring whatever was in his saucepan. The rigidity of his posture told everyone that their barbs had landed as intended.

"Contrary to what you fools are led to believe, my people had the foresight to never set foot within those wildlands. The only things that live among those trees are creatures that want to keep civilization *out*, so we settled in the borderlands and not a yard farther." The man turned to face the dishwashers, face stern and ebony skin unblemished by perspiration. Vinsart Hold's kitchen was no match for a humid summer in Ebkarii. "It's you fair-folk that are so determined to venture into the heart of that jungle, never satisfied with the lands you have. Well, be my guest, I say. At least I won't have to hear your uncultured tongues insult my food any longer."

"Oh, calm yourself, Ptolon," Mrs. Luviire said as she rose from her stool, her motherly tone carrying an edge of authority with it. Waemish and Chaevin continued their snickering while Ptolon straightened his shirt with a huff. "They can't help if they were born with a constitution unsuited for the varieties of cuisine life has to offer. It's a character flaw, really. But we shouldn't hold that against them." The chef cracked the slightest hint of a smile before returning to his sauce, while the pair resumed their cleaning duties with grinning faces, able to take a ribbing as good as they gave.

The herb nurse started to join Ptolon at the clay stove but was brushed aside by an individual walking briskly from the stairwell leading up into Vinsart Hold's administrative wing. It wasn't enough to knock her from her feet but rather a gentle redirection, and Mrs. Luviire looked more surprised than offended. The man was of average height and build and wore a simple brown linen tunic and trousers, with a black, broad-brimmed sun hat pulled low over his face. What little Mareq could make of his face as he passed was unremarkable—no facial hair, no scars, no hooked nose or large ears. He moved with purpose toward the service entrance, not rushing but also clearly not open to engaging in pleasantries with the staff. It was as if everything about the man was *designed* to be forgettable, from his appearance to his behavior.

"The Ghost is back," Chaevin muttered, pausing with a soapy knife in hand to glance toward the exit as the man disappeared into the daylight. "And gone just like that. When my gran told us stories of hauntings growing up, there was always a lot of chains rattling and doors slamming. I never thought being part of one of those tales would be so dull."

Mareq was never one for superstitious folklore. That man had been as much flesh and blood as anyone else in the kitchen. But despite the man's clear attempts at anonymity, he had at the very least made an impression on the workers here, and what Mareq lacked in superstition he more than made up for in curiosity. "Ghosts, Chaevin? I'll grant you he glided out of here with impressive silence, but I think you took a few too many of those stories to heart."

"The child is not speaking of literal phantoms," Ptolon shouted back over the din of meal preparation. "Though I wouldn't be surprised if his proclivity toward hearsay confused him on the subject." Chaevin made a show of sniffing the air and feigning a gag at the Ebkarii's cooking.

Mrs. Luviire returned to her spot near Mareq and had to lean down so that she could speak softly near his ear. "He means Teacher Ias's Ghosts, Mareq. We've been seeing them come and go through the kitchens for some time now, always moving through like they own the place but never breathing a word to any of us."

By her hushed tone, he guessed the situation was more serious than visitors with poor social etiquette. The Apparition embodied the ideas of thievery and deception, and as such, wasn't worshipped by an organized church. At least, not formally. But if there was a group that operated by her teachings, he could see how it might lead to trouble.

"I wasn't aware Teacher Ias had followers that pursued any kind of coordinated effort," Mareq said. "What happened to no honor among thieves?"

She smiled warmly, as an instructor might at an inquisitive pupil. "With as worldly as you present yourself, I sometimes forget that Brey is not a large place to grow up. The Ghosts supposedly have chapters in all Anera's major cities. More people means more guards, which means tougher jobs for a lone thief to accomplish on their own. The chapters form a network of sorts, somehow able to communicate over vast distances, and while I wouldn't characterize them as honorable, they do have a reputation to uphold." Mrs. Luviire rubbed the tips of her first two fingers against her thumb. "Providing a reliable service can be just as lucrative as thievery, with the right clientele."

"Nonsense," Waemish barked. "Don't let that old fool fill your head with rumors. She may have been blessed with that elven skin, but we can all become senile after a few too many seasons, and she's seen more than her fair share." The man draped his washrag over the lip of the basin as he turned, drying his hands on his apron. "Teacher Ias is the goddess of *deception*. It's all right there, plain as day. Her followers just want you to *think* there's more of them around so they can slink about with their own schemes."

Chaevin slung the clean knife into the water with a splash. "I've heard them myself, you bald bastard! Talking in their weird whispers. How many times are you gonna call me a liar?"

As the pair faced off, all puffed chests and red faces, Mrs. Luviire simply raised a hand and cleared her throat. They each glanced her way sheepishly before returning to their work in silence. "Whoever is correct, it does us no good to cause a scene. We don't want to get involved."

"Involved in what, exactly?" Mareq asked, keeping his voice low. Tiialya had mentioned surreptitious communications going on at the citadel. In fact, that was why she had journeyed to Alaboq in the first place. She had always had a talent for completing jobs discreetly. Perhaps he had been too quick to dismiss her concerns about under-the-table negotiations, but where she had seen risk, he thought he saw an opportunity.

Mrs. Luviire took a moment to glance around for listening ears before answering. "Exactness is not something I can provide. However, the Ghosts only seem to be meeting with one person when they come to Vinsart Hold, which we only know because the woman is so impatient that she sometimes stalks the kitchen waiting for them to arrive." She tilted her head toward the stairwell, pausing one more time to listen for any descending diplomats. Satisfied that no one was coming, she said, "Sylicera Hadac, the king's chief trade minister."

The possibility of corrupted trade deals could certainly be dangerous; where someone stood to profit, they would often defend it at a bloody cost. But if these agreements were being made in secret, King Berenqar might be grateful to learn of their existence. As much as Mareq had enjoyed his time in Alaboq, the only matter keeping him there was a lack of finances to fund his further exploration of the globe. If he were to gather a little bit of evidence, he was sure the royal stables would be happy to provide him a strong mare and a sturdy cart.

Already feeling the call of the open road, Mareq joined Chaevin at the wash basin. "So, how often are these Ghosts haunting the place?"

Chapter 10

Virdoba

Wymund tugged at the sleeves of his shirt, uncomfortable in this gathering of people without his teal guardsman's coat. But with the absence of his longsword's familiar weight at his side, he thought he might as well have been naked. However, Rav had been right. With this crowd, the city guard uniform wouldn't have commanded respect. It would just label him as a "duckling," a derogatory term lumping the guardsmen together with their teal-feathered neighbors flapping about the Silver Set. They were often seen as following on the heels of the superior officers, much like the actual ducklings trailed behind their mothers on the man-made canal. The color of their coats was an unfortunate coincidence.

While on their way to the warehouse in the Lower Quay, Wymund spotted a skeletal man dressed in a linen tunic and breeches with a purple velvet vest that was two sizes too big. It had dark splotches along the sides and over the stomach, though whether they were stains or simply from mishandling the fabric, Wymund wasn't certain. What he did know was that the relative expense of the material, the untrimmed fistful of wildflowers, and the hopeful yellow grin complete with searching eyes all spoke of a man who had fallen prey to his partner's charms. He supposed he couldn't blame him; Rav had her moments. But due to the meeting the man was here to support, Wymund felt no pity as she ducked past him and blended into the people lining the walls.

Inside, a strong fishy odor that permeated the air. Looking around, Wymund saw clusters of fishing gear—rods, tackle boxes, and leather boots still damp from that morning's excursion into the Marrow Strait. Large hemp nets were draped over stacks of wooden crates, presumably laid out to dry, as puddle rings had formed around each. It was obvious a local fishing crew used the space for storage between trips, but he hoped the meeting location was just a coincidence. The last thing Virdoba needed was a bigoted group with power over the city's food supply.

Rav maintained her position against the wall as Wymund moved through the crowd. It wasn't a tactic they had discussed beforehand, as most of his instructions to her often resulted in the opposite occurring, but it was one he agreed with nonetheless. If he was right and the Allies of Edis were connected with Cater Waldwen and his extortion racket, then there would be people on-site that would recognize her. *Best that the close observation is left to me tonight*, he thought, making his way toward the center of the room. *She did such an outstanding job remaining hidden last time, after all.*

Wymund scanned the faces around him, recognizing more than a few from his early days in the city guard. At that time, he'd spent most of his shifts near the top of the Lighthouse, posted as a sentry in the Iron Spiral, the name for the ramp of prison cells twisting up the tower. Most of his frequent visitors were petty criminals, staying for just a night or two after drunkenly assaulting a neighbor or failing to pay for a meal at a tavern. They were people prone to poor decisions and who could be rash in the heat of the moment, but he knew they could be reasoned with. He had done it himself many times. Making that reasoning stick, however, often proved to be difficult when they were preyed upon by those who knew how to pull their strings, like Cater Waldwen.

A semicircle had formed near the back of the room, the base of which was a wood-paneled wall with a single door that opened into a foreman's office. Anxious excitement filled the air as the people in the crowd chattered away, laughing and slapping backs, obviously anticipating whatever was about to occur. Wymund suspected most were here for the chance at some coin, but the could have been misplaced optimism for the people of his city. His stomach twisted into knots when he considered the alternative.

Standing to either side of the entrance were two men he only recognized from Rav's descriptions. One stood taller and wider than the doorframe itself and surveyed the crowd through two black eyes the color and shape of ripe cinder plums overhanging a mangled nose. The other was avian-featured and leaned against the wall, right arm cradled in a cloth sling wrapped around his neck. Carn and Torran, which likely meant Cater was waiting behind that door to greet his followers.

Wymund and Cater had crossed paths a few times over the years, and while the dockhand was tough and commanded a certain loyalty from his crew, he never seemed to possess the charisma necessary for this type of scheme. He also couldn't bankroll an operation at this scale without financial assistance of some kind. There was a missing piece to the puzzle, but Wymund suspected he wouldn't have to wait long to figure out what it was.

As if on cue, the wooden door swung open to reveal Cater Waldwen striding forth, hands clasped behind his back as he surveyed the crowd. Wymund kept his head down, hoping the dockhand wouldn't recognize his face, a feat easier said than done with the several inches of height he had over most in the room. Given his size, Wymund wasn't intimidated by many, but he had to admit that Cater's broad-shouldered frame gave even him pause, not to mention the air of confidence exuding from the man. But he wasn't there to make an arrest. This was a fact-finding operation; direct confrontation would come later with the backing of a solid plan and more men.

"All right, all right," Cater said, holding his hands up. The murmurs that had intensified with his entrance softened at the sound of his voice. "All of you have this place sounding like a schoolhouse with all that gossiping. Showing up tonight was a good first step, but we need strong men and women to protect Virdoba and the Kefyan way of life. Not a pack of bratty school children."

"We're all here for our country, Cater!" The shout came from behind Wymund, followed shortly by another off to his left. "We won't let them take away our homes!" Calls of assent echoed around him, along with claps, whoops, and cheers. His faith in his neighbors was dwindling by the second.

A thin-lipped smile broke across Waldwen's face. He nodded in satisfaction and held up a hand to once again quiet his audience. "I hear you, my friends. I hear you and I'm with you. We've broken our backs in the humid air our whole lives, all to make sure the people of the city we love can keep food on the table and clothes on their backs. Fishing, sailing, unloading cargo. All the jobs those in the Inner City couldn't stomach but needed done just the same. All the jobs that let them live their comfortable lives, like the council members in Felona and their *sharp-eared* friends."

Shouts and curses surrounded Wymund at the mention of the Council. Kefya's ruling body had certainly become less popular over the years, even more so after Relus Vunii was offered a seat as first secretary of culture. He was the son of a wealthy playwright and her Choii Stieren dalliance, and now the first councilmember to possess even an ounce of elven blood, but Wymund had never heard the discontent amount to much more than a grumble. These flames had been fanned, and he worried the blaze was only beginning.

"But what they don't know is that one among them is a true Kefyan at heart. A man who cares so deeply for this soil that he empties libers from his own pockets to strike back at those who have stolen our way of life. But the cost of justice is high, even for a man with his connections, and now we have to help him with his plan to maintain our independence. Please welcome our patron, our *Ally*, Harbormaster Cyrilke Swithred!"

Wymund watched as a short and squat figure exited the foreman's office, his graying, oily hair slicked across his scalp a match for the greasy goatee trimmed close to his skin. Even if he had not been introduced as Virdoba's harbormaster, he would have been recognizable as a man of importance based on his clothing alone. Intricate gold designs were embroidered across his black vest as it stretched across a paunch that could only come from a steady diet and living off the manual labor of others. Below it was a white silk shirt that bunched around his comparatively narrow shoulders; the man did not carry his weight evenly.

Cyrilke scanned the room with black eyes set deep in his round face, complete with the stately smile of a practiced politician. Next to Cater, Swithred looked to be the less imposing figure as his head just managed to reach the dockhand's shoulders, but Wymund knew where the power rested. What difference would size make if one man could afford a small army for protection?

"Thank you all for joining us tonight. Mr. Waldwen and his associates have done an outstanding job thus far in the early stages of our operation, but as you may expect, time is not on our side. It seems like every day, more and more pile into our city from their island beachhead, bringing all their problems along with them.

"Some in the Gardens celebrate their *cultural contributions*, but where does that lead us? What happens when our children no longer learn about the great Kefyan architects and sculptors that were born and raised here in Virdoba because their teachers are so enamored by the pretentiousness being passed off as superior talent? At what point will we no longer see our home through all the horrendous twisting spires they have filling our skies?"

Where Waldwen had been whipping the crowd into a fervor, Swithred had them hanging from his every word. It was nothing Wymund hadn't heard before. Many of his fellow guardsmen often expressed similar views when the few elven recruits weren't around. He had always found the argument lacking, though. Cultures and societies had exchanged ideas and values for as long as they had existed. It was how civilization advanced. For all their desire to protect the "true Kefya," they seemed to forget that their homeland wouldn't exist without democratic ideals seeding their way across the Drae Divide from Achen. Not to mention the elves who had fought side by side with those Kefyans seeking their independence from Qedradan rule centuries ago.

Swithred grew quieter, furrowing his brows in concern and displaying a faux sincerity that would make the most seasoned politician jealous. Wymund couldn't be sure if this man was a true believer in this cause, but he did know one thing: Cyrilke Swithred was a talented orator, and with the backing of a large purse, he would likely be able to get damn near anything he wanted.

"Thankfully, there is plan in motion that will prevent this scourge from taking further root in our community. But I need your help. I'm sure by now most of you have heard of the terrorist scorcher attack on the florist shop within the Inner City. As friends, I will confess to you now that the assailants were actually disguised members of Mr. Waldwen's crew, who have been tirelessly working on distilling a chemical firebomb to demonstrate the threat these Shroud-tearing insurgents pose."

Back against the wall, Carn and Torran beamed with pride, while Cater gave the crowd a slight tilted bow of his head. "We don't seek to sow carnage on our own soil without purpose, though," Swithred continued. "Only to open our neighbors' eyes to the truth about what *will come* when we Virdobans are overrun by their kind."

To their credit, Wymund caught a few concerned murmurs and shared glances when the harbormaster admitted to destroying someone's property. But ultimately, not one member of the crowd voiced dissent. Instead, they all listened as Swithred paced closer to them.

"But our operation needs to expand if we hope to achieve our goals, and that unfortunately requires more funding than I am able to provide. This is where you come in." He reached the front row of the crowd and held a hand out, palm up, his expression changing to one of softness and entreaty. He locked eyes with a crowd member, who stretched out a hand.

Swithred clasped it and gave it a firm shake. "Join us. Work with Mr. Waldwen as we demonstrate the horrors coming to our lands, or join our new militia, which will offer protection to Virdoba's citizens from this threat." Swithred moved on to the next person in the front row, shaking their hand, and then the next, and the next. "Each storeowner or head of household will gladly pay for the strength that those featherless ducklings could never hope to possess. The payments we receive for the security provided by our militia will fund this project, safeguarding the future of Kefya and our very identity."

He shook the last hand at the front of the semicircle and returned to the center, standing outside the door to the office. "Your family needs you. Your country needs you. This is your time to honor the sacrifices of your forefathers, who spilled their blood to live a life free of tyranny. By the Ally's example, we will set right what has been wronged. Speak with Mr. Waldwen and join our fight." Now finished with his speech, the short man spun on his heels and vanished into the room behind him. Carn reached in and pulled the door shut just as the crowd closed in around the three of them, their excitement palpable.

This confirmed it. He and Annika had been correct to assume that the extortion scheme and staged elven attack were connected. To what end, Wymund still didn't know, but now that he had learned who was heading the operation, he suspected Annika might have an idea. Aristocracy tended to be a small club, with few secrets between members.

Passersby jostled his shoulders as they moved forward, each adding their names to a growing list of illegal vigilantes. Once he was clear of the masses, Wymund retreated to the exit, closely shadowed by Rav. Their nascent band of private investigators had much to discuss, but time was now a factor. As was the existence of firebombs.

Chapter 11

Virdoba

"So Cyrilke was the missing financier?" Annika asked, looking across the table at Wymund and Rav. The pair had arrived at her home late into the evening, long after the sun had dipped below the horizon across the Marrow Strait. She viewed the sunset most nights from her patio near the western end of the Silver Set, the brilliant reds and oranges glancing off the stone façade of the Lighthouse and creating a mesmerizing pattern on the still waters of the canal below. The result was painterly and beautiful, but she watched each evening only to catch that brief moment when the silhouette of her former island home eclipsed the setting star. It was there Rav and Wymund had found her, leaning against the railing and staring westward, awestruck at the patterns of history and determined that this time, she would do more to prevent its repetition.

"Seems like it," Rav answered, leaning back in her chair with her boots propped on the table. Annika couldn't help but be amused at how the woman's rebellious streak had lasted so long beyond adolescence and so far away from the demands of an overbearing mother, but she knew that also came with an inherent danger. The illusion of youthful invulnerability was often protected by an elder's watchful eye. "It shouldn't be too much of a surprise to discover that a city like Virdoba has officials who share its more unsavory values."

"No, there's a deeper motive here," Annika said, resting her chin on her fist. "At least for Cyrilke. The Swithreds have long been a part of Kefyan high society. They have mixed and mingled with the wealthy elven families in Felona, and I'm sure they've even hosted a dignitary or two from Choii Stier itself. I agree that the man is lacking moral fortitude, but I don't believe it's because he shares this group's opinions on demography. He just has no qualms about mobilizing and directing their discontent toward some end that is beneficial to him."

Wymund's eyes narrowed for a moment as he stared at her. The guard was a perfect picture of discipline juxtaposed with Rav, sitting straight-spined with hands crossed in his lap below the table. "And you've spent time in those circles as well, haven't you Ms. Iatorii?"

Rav glanced at her from behind her boots and shifted in her chair to sit a bit higher. Wymund's reminder of Annika's upbringing was seemingly enough to summon the specter of her mother. *Damn you, guardsman. All this work gaining her trust and you make old suspicions resurface.*

Sighing, she said, "Yes, Mr. Sylnorin. My family was quite prominent in Felona during my childhood. As you might have guessed by the surprising drabness of my eyes, I was not born into their line, but I did have the great fortune of being raised as one of their own." Annika smiled sardonically. "The lone perk of being the orphan of Iatorii housekeepers, I suppose."

"So it wouldn't be unreasonable to suspect you have *mixed and mingled* with the Swithreds yourself, then?"

"It wouldn't be unreasonable, but it would be incorrect," Annika replied, digging her fingers into her knee to avoid biting her tongue. His appetite for investigation was admirable, but he would need to learn to temper his accusatory tone if he intended to excel in his field. Honeyed wine could elicit more secrets than sour grapes. "The Swithreds have always been a shipping family, dipping their hands in as many trade deals as they could manage. But my family operated a vineyard outside Felona, so by the time our wines made it to the water's edge for travel, our business had already concluded."

The guardsman glanced at Rav, who was still trying her best to force nonchalance over years of what Annika assumed was thorough etiquette training. Finally, he nodded. "Very well. Perhaps this knowledge could aid us in our investigation. If he is in fact not a true zealot, then the appropriate *political pressure* may put a halt to this plot before it escalates into a city-wide war."

Rav scoffed. "*Political pressure?* Dress it up however you like, but blackmail is blackmail. Not that I object, mind you. This is my kind of scheme. I'm just surprised an idea like that could bubble up past your pressed and cinched guard's coat to reach your tongue."

"It's not my preferred method of problem solving, Ravael. But as you may remember from your brief stint in the Iron Spiral, I can be willing to bend the law if I see a greater good as the result."

"That's enough bickering," Annika said as Rav swung her legs off the table to face Wymund, her stubborn need for the last word spelled across her face as plainly as if it were written on parchment. "I didn't forgo having children just to end up wrangling adults who insist on acting like them. The idea is sound, but we'll need proof that the man is involved if any accusation is to carry weight. People with his connections tend to weasel out of allegations if it is just one person's word against another."

"Can't you just arrest him?" Rav asked. "Then once he's in the Lighthouse, we get him to talk. We wouldn't even have to touch him. A man like that is bound to spill what he knows out of fear alone."

"I said I was willing to bend the law, not dash it against the rocks. The Virdoban Guard will not be arresting anyone in this city without cause under my direction. But if I can lead a patrol somewhere we know Cyrilke will be exposed while demonstrating criminal intent, then it won't be hearsay any longer."

"I doubt Cyrilke will be joining the intimidation crews or personally collecting the protection money," Annika said. "If they *are* moving into the Inner City, he wouldn't want to reveal his involvement to his own neighbors. Plus, I'm sure he wouldn't want to dirty his hands with work that is below his station."

"True," Wymund said, dark eyes widening with inspiration, "but now that he has made his face known to his recruits, do you believe he is the type of person who would want to strut around in a managerial capacity?"

A slight smile dawned across Annika's face. "That is an unfortunate trait bestowed upon many of us during our upbringing. If we aren't being told how brilliant we are by our parents and instructors anymore, we like to make sure others know the heights of our status." She turned her gaze toward Rav. "Or we try so hard to appear average that we circle back around to insufferable just the same." The young woman rolled her eyes and looked away.

"Then I think there's a chance we could find him overseeing the distillation of those firebombs. There are only a handful of buildings in the Outer City large enough to hide an operation like that; it wouldn't take long to discover the correct location." Wymund stood from the table as he spoke, rubbing his hand back and forth across his closely cropped hair, and began to pace. "After that, a well-timed raid could not only place more eyes on Cyrilke Swithred engaging in criminal activity, but also put a stop to the production of these horrible explosives."

Annika was reminded of the devastation a single one of the firebombs could unleash, with images of cindered floral arrangements and ash-filled air surfacing in her mind. It had been good fortune that no one was seriously injured during that attack, but if those explosives were being produced on a larger scale, that luck was sure to expire sooner rather than later. She had lived through the horrors of rebellion once before and was not eager to relive the experience.

"I have contacts in the Lower Quay who stay apprised of what is going on behind closed doors. We can find out which warehouse they have set up in before you and your brothers-at-arms start kicking in doors." Annika softened her tone as Wymund stopped pacing and glanced at her. "But the plan is sound. I can have the information for you in a matter of hours." *And if I can manage the information gathering, maybe Rav can stay clear of the whole affair.*

"And don't think about keeping me out of it, Wymund," Rav said, causing Annika to wince. "You'll need someone to confirm that rich weasel is inside before you and your patrol come clomping down the street and wake up the whole neighborhood."

Damn fool girl. My sister didn't leave another potion to save you from your own recklessness again.

Wymund opened his mouth to reply but closed it and simply nodded before returning to his pacing. "I'll gather my men. Tomorrow night we will douse this flame before it burns the city down to the limestone."

Chapter 12

Virdoba

Cyrilke Swithred entered through the front door of his home at the eastern end of the Silver Set, pausing for a moment in the foyer to remove his vest and carefully drape it across a wooden rack. From his vantage point in the sitting room, Tetamii watched the older man smooth the wrinkles from the garment. He hated that he was being forced to work with a man prone to such preening, but the job was the job. Nothing else came before it. That was a lesson he had learned through physical reinforcement long ago.

Satisfied with his vest's resting position, Cyrilke stepped to the left to check his reflection in the mirror hanging on the wall. He smoothed down his goatee with one hand, smiling with a sense of self-satisfaction that Tetamii only saw on others when it was unearned. However, the man's smirk dropped as his eyes met the intruder sitting on his wood-backed sofa, a man who now bore a more sincere version of the grin across his own face.

"Mr. Fiadar," Cyrilke said, straightening his sleeves at the cuffs in a poor attempt at indifference, "I don't recall allowing you free passage into my home."

Tetamii watched a bead of sweat form at his temple as the man struggled to maintain a casual stroll into the room. He took a seat across from the couch in a chair made from solid cherry wood, with armrest ends whittled into ship bows cresting over gilded waves. Tetamii had spent the last hour growing more and more annoyed at the ostentatious details that decorated the sitting room. There was so much gold plastered throughout the building, even woven into the twinkling curtains, that if the sun had been up, he was certain they would be blinded by the glare. He had spent time in the chambers of some of the wealthiest people in Anera and had come to appreciate a sense of elegance and understated beauty. By contrast, he thought this house was a rube's idea of how wealth should appear.

"It's important you keep in mind that you have no bearing on what I am allowed to do, Mr. Swithred. Forgetfulness in this regard may lead to lapses in my own memory." Tetamii tapped a finger on the hilt of his bastard sword, still resting in its black leather scabbard and propped against the side of the couch. "I may forget where I am meant to sheathe my blade."

The sweat droplet began to roll down Cyrilke's cheek, and Tetamii had to admire the man's restraint in not dabbing it away. "We have been made partners in this operation," Cyrilke stammered. "There's no need for such open hostility." The man managed a halfhearted smile. "Particularly when I am on the cusp of organizing a campaign throughout this city that will tip the trade balance back in Kefya's favor."

"You and I are partners in the same way a farmer is in a partnership with the ox that pulls his plow. My role is to ensure the work is done; yours is to do as you're told." Cyrilke tried to disguise a choke as a cough. "And from where I sit, the fields have been plowed and the seeds planted. What use does Elikar have for a beast of burden that thinks he has earned himself a seat at the table?"

The harbormaster's eyes widened. Using the councilman's given name had the desired effect. A man like Cyrilke would never dare drop his employer's title. "My apologies if I spoke out of turn. Please inform Councilman Thymes when next you speak that I continue to be grateful for this opportunity to repay my debt to his family."

"I'll pass along your humility when I can. Elikar views it as an honor to return some grace to the failed scion of one of Kefya's great family lines. We're all quite impressed with how you have managed not to gamble all your new wealth away since being gifted your position." Cyrilke swallowed hard but remained silent.

"Just remember that you were only placed in this official role because the fuse is shorter here in Virdoba than it is across the Marrow Strait. If we could have managed this insurrection in Felona, we would have done so. You owe your livelihood to your geographic utility, nothing more."

"Again," Cyrilke said. "I will forever be indebted to the councilman for this chance to prove my worth. Our production of the wood alcohol explosives has ramped up and tonight, I have gathered more men to the cause. Soon, pockets of Virdoba will burn, and the mainland will resort to old ties for safety. Choii Stier won't be making many economic connections with the mainland when they're viewed as enemy combatants."

Tetamii felt the World Shroud ripple within the room, as if beckoning him to reach out for it. As if the membrane could feel his desire to put a fine point on this discussion. He could melt all the gilded finery this pompous buffoon took so much pride in with no more than a moment's concentration. Or more directly, he could simply char the man's flesh for daring to assume he was anything more than a puppet on a string. But he knew it was an illusion; the World Shroud was not calling him to strike any more than a blade would before a duel. He was simply gripping the hilt.

He had more control over his baser instincts than that, though, and he released his hold on the membrane, the near-transparent wisps clearing from his vision. Cyrilke didn't know Tetamii was an elf, thanks in large part to blindness derived from intimidation. The natural amber rings around his irises were more subtle than most of his kind, and his service to the Clipped Gulls had taken care of the rest of the signs. Years of layering hardened muscles over his frame and severing the tips from his ears during his initiation completed the disguise. It would be best to keep Cyrilke ignorant of that fact. The man's prejudice was not as real as his subordinates, but he could use that information to gain more power over Cater and his dogs.

After allowing the man to stew in uncertainty for several moments of agonizing silence, Tetamii nodded. "Be sure that you speak true. I will be leaving for Alaboq in a few days' time, where I will be granted a personal meeting with King Berenqar through your Qedradan counterpart. I expect news of an elven uprising on the Kefyan coast to have reached his ears before I do. This should make him more sympathetic to Elikar's wishes."

Tetamii uncrossed his legs and leaned forward, holding Cyrilke's gaze like a vise. "But if I arrive without the support of this news behind my words, my task becomes much more difficult, and I spend a great deal of effort preparing for jobs to ensure difficulties are dealt with ahead of time. Do not make my efforts be in vain, Mr. Swithred."

"Yes, of course," Cyrilke said as he stood, smoothing his silk shirt anxiously with both hands. "Will you be needing any means of conveyance? I have many friends at my beck and call in Virdoba. I could have a cart and driver ready for you as early as the morning."

"No cart," Tetamii said, standing to tower over the chubby little man. "And I can procure my own horse. But I have promised your ragtag militia that I will take care of a potential thorn in their side before I leave. Once I find the lightblood and remove her from the equation, I will depart." The distortions in his vision returned as the World Shroud reacted in concert with his quickening pulse. Soon it would dance at his direction, as would she.

Chapter 13

Virdoba

The rooftops were uneven, both in height and construction. Some of the warehouses in the Lower Quay that were owned and operated by the city's more affluent citizens stood a story or two higher than those built by the men and women who actually used them every day. The tops of the taller structures were lined with slick clay tiles, sturdier and more fashionable than the thatched roofs around them but much less accommodating for traversal. That was what Rav had been warned of anyway, but as she skulked her way across the skyline of the district, she found herself at home no matter what material was under her boots.

Gaps between the buildings averaged around ten feet, slightly wider than the distances she was used to in the cramped metropolis of Felona, but the leaps from rooftop to rooftop proved little challenge for her. While the jumps might have been a bit farther here, she had spent too many nights scampering from pillar to balcony to spire at dizzying heights in her home city to be bothered by these spaces. Still, her heart raced. She had missed this.

Rav had feared that her new life along Wymund's narrow path of righteousness would steal this thrill from her. There was nothing else like it. The time she climbed through that crone Lady Helenorin's window to snatch her beloved brooch from the dresser, or the early morning she was nearly trampled "liberating" Mr. Jinris's abused stable of show horses. She counted those nights, and many others of the kind, among the greatest of her life. But as she grew closer to her destination, she realized her concerns had been unfounded. Partnering with Wymund might have removed criminality from the equation, but the excitement had been in the execution all along. The end goal was irrelevant.

She paused on a slanted tile roof, one arm wrapped around a flue for support, and glanced back along her path. The streets below her were largely empty at this time of night, with only the occasional scuffle of hurried feet audible over the sounds of waves lapping against the docks ahead of her. Several blocks away, Rav had passed Wymund and half of his patrol who were waiting in silence for her to confirm Cyrilke Swithred's presence in the Allies' warehouse. Somewhere on the opposite side of the building waited the other half of his patrol, meant to seal off the only other exit while Wymund and his team entered and started making arrests. It was a simple plan, and to Rav it sounded too neat and clean. Wymund wanted the Allies of Edis to surrender and for this plot to be tied up with a nice little bow before the morning, but her intuition told her there would more to it than that.

She had tried to advise a subtler approach, picking up the people they knew to be involved from their homes or workplaces and leaning on them until they turned on their co-conspirators. Going after these terrorists one at a time seemed like better odds to her, but Rav's logic had proved no match for Wymund's scruples. His adherence to the law intrigued her. It was admirable and frustrating in equal measure, but she couldn't blame him. He wasn't born into the world of lawmakers and monied interests as she had been, so he didn't see the justice system in the same light. Where he saw himself as a member of a team working to protect his neighbors and uphold order, she only saw a framework designed by those in power to keep themselves there. But despite her cynicism, she had to admit there was something endearing about believing in a purpose so strongly that he could only see the good in it. *Who knows. Maybe he can shape things into the mold he sees.*

Leaping across the next gap, she landed on another sloped roof, the thatch giving slightly underfoot. She scampered up the side, fingers finding hold with expert precision until she reached the top and peered over the peak. Her target was the next building in the row, another thatched roof warehouse with at least a dozen limestone flues jutting out across its surface. Annika had learned that the process of creating these firebombs generated a great deal of heat, and thus this vented warehouse had been selected by the group for their production. More important to Rav's purposes, though, were the large windows at either end of the long structure. Each was set into the slope of the roof and was likely meant as another source of ventilation; the one she could see was currently hanging open. But that also meant for anyone daring enough to scale the rooftops, everything going on inside would be on clear display. One last jump, and then she could signal the others.

"You're a difficult woman to find."

Her head snapped to the side at the sound of another's voice. She couldn't recall the last time someone had been able to catch her by surprise. But now, standing not more than thirty feet from her was a man she hadn't heard approach, at ease on the brown clay tiled roof to her left.

He was dressed in a white tailcoat that flapped gently behind him with the breeze coming in from the strait, moving in concert with raven-black hair that fell past his shoulders. The man was easily a head taller than even Wymund's towering frame, so despite his attempts to hide his ears and build an intimidating physique, she knew an elf when she saw one. His facial features were too fine, too *pretty*, to be anything else. A dark leather scabbard was strapped across his back, and Rav could see the long hilt of a blade rising above his left shoulder. Given its length, what little weapons training she possessed told her that it would be unwieldy for the man to draw it quickly from behind. That meant he thought he wouldn't need it.

She pulled herself up onto the flat narrow strip at the apex of the roof to face the intruder. Rav wasn't sure why the man was trying to find her, but the fact that he was another elf didn't set her mind at ease. In her experience, the few people she had run into while darting across rooftops could rarely be described as innocent. From the opposing rooftop, the man's smile was somehow both disarming and predatory.

"I think we're overdue for a chat," he said. "Perhaps we can find a place a little less precarious to work out our differences."

"I'm afraid I'm busy at the moment," Rav replied, spacing her feet apart on the thin surface, ready to defend herself or flee, depending on his next move. "And you really should be careful traipsing about up here. That nice white coat may end up with a stain or two."

The man chuckled but made no move from his position. "Oh, I wouldn't concern yourself on my account. In fact, the only reason I have to remain in this filthy city is standing right in front of me. As soon as our business is concluded, I'll be on my way."

"Sorry, never been one for business. I don't have the head for it." Rav was suddenly aware of her twin daggers' weight as they hung from her belt. Her fingers twitched before she could ball them into a fist. She couldn't allow him to see that she felt threatened.

"But if you wait until morning," she said, "I'm sure you can find whatever you're looking to buy or sell over in the Round Square. With the way you're dressed, those people will probably strike a fine bargain just to get in your good graces. You could be their ticket out of here to bigger and better things."

He shook his head, the smirk of superiority never leaving his face. Finally, he turned and began to walk away from her, up the gentle sloping roof. "Fine. You may come to me on your own terms. I know you and your friends have been busy establishing an amateur fire brigade of sorts, and I would hate to pull you away from such an important task." At the opposite edge of the building, he faced her once again, his expression now level and unreadable. "I even heard a home went up in flames with a child trapped inside recently, and I could not bear to think of anything like that happening again."

Rav saw the child's silhouette in her mind, rocking back and forth on the ground before becoming still. Always out of reach. Her blood began to boil and she could no longer stop her fists from shaking at her sides. She was sure this man had not been on the job with her. The presence of another elf wouldn't have escaped her notice. *No one in this city can keep their mouth shut. Anyone could know about what happened that night.*

Rolling tears down her cheeks brought her back to the present moment and the realization that she had been squeezing her eyes closed. Across the other rooftop, the man's grin had returned. He knew he had struck a nerve.

"Next time, I'll make sure no one can make it out of there alive."

A bright flash sparked in the distance, over the waters beyond the docks, but Rav hardly registered it. The world was already a blur around her as she charged along the narrow beam under her and leaped toward the elf. Any thoughts of reconnaissance or Wymund's plan were now lost to the buzzing in her mind.

***

Minutes had passed since Rav had separated from Wymund's patrol as they filed down the winding streets of the Lower Quay. As they had discussed, Wymund and his unit were now stationed in the shadows of an aqueduct archway several blocks east of the Allies' warehouse. Waiting for her signal call was becoming distressing, however, and he wondered if this location had been the best choice. The sound of rushing water above wasn't deafening, but it was constant, and Wymund grew worried that it would drown out the sign he was waiting to hear.

Rav was quick. Wymund had seen her dart up and around buildings before. The distance between their location and Rav's vantage point wasn't far, and she should have been there by now with ample time to report back. Wymund glanced around at the half dozen guardsmen that accompanied him, some of whom were shifting their weight back and forth or checking and re-checking that their blades were securely fastened by their sides. Private Abalk, a serious young man who had quickly become a trusted member of the patrol, met his gaze. Wymund wasn't alone in his worry.

Farther into the district, on the opposite side of the Allies' base of operations, Wymund had stationed Private Sunia with the other half of his patrol. He had faith in her ability to lead the other side of the raid; she had joined the Virdoban Guard around the same time and would likely follow in his footsteps to become a corporal soon. Still, anxious energy could wreak havoc on even the most disciplined mind, and Rav's tardiness might lead her to breach the building before she was given leave to do so.

Minutes dragged on, and Wymund checked the fastening of his own scabbarded longsword, choosing a monotonous learned behavior as a focus for his roaming mind. Ideally, the blade wouldn't need to leave its sheath during this raid. A dozen guards surrounding a chemical production house should be more than sufficient to prompt a calm surrender. But he had learned that the lot who fell into the criminal lifestyle often thought they could outmaneuver or outthink the law, so it was better to ensure proper weapon storage than to trust his targets to behave rationally.

A series of loud *thuds*, like wood on wood, echoed down the narrow passageways ahead of him, originating beyond the Allies' warehouse. "It's a raid," cried a voice in the distance. "The ducklings are here!" Confused shouts and clomping boots came in response, as Wymund guessed that Sunia had chosen the only option available to her now that they had been discovered. If the plan was to be salvaged, he would have to do the same.

"Edis's eye," he cursed, before waving his hand forward. "On me. Private Sunia is moving in and they will need us on the other exit." Without hesitation, all seven advanced down the path just as the ringing of steel on steel reached their ears. Sunia and her patrol should have no trouble securing whatever scouting party had discovered their position, but he hoped they were given the option to do so without bloodshed.

The blocks separating their position from the warehouse passed by in a flash, and soon the wide double doors on the eastern edge of the structure appeared before them. Wymund glanced toward the open window a few stories above, out of which sounds of glass clanking and wood scraping broke out into the night. However, Rav was notably absent from the perch outside the opening. *If you went inside on your own, I swear you will never see the outside of the Iron Spiral again.*

Abalk positioned his shoulder against one door as Wymund took the other. Sharing a quick nod, they rammed their full weight against the wood, causing the doors to swing wide as the other five guardsmen rushed in behind them. Inside, nearly two dozen men and women darted about, some dousing massive limestone kilns that lined the entire room while others packed glass jugs of clear liquid into crates. Standing near the center of the room, shouting orders as the veins bulged in his neck, was Cater Waldwen, doing all he could to direct the chaos. Next to him, Wymund recognized Carn and Torran, as well as a mature woman that matched Rav's description of the woman who stabbed her.

In his cursory assessment of the scene, Wymund saw no sign of Rav in the rafters above. If she had entered from the window, she must have remained well hidden. A whimper drew his gaze back to the ground, where for the first time he noticed Cyrilke Swithred was scrambling away on his back, panic etched across his round face, blood trickling from split skin on his forehead. With Rav's disappearance, their raid was going to be messier than anticipated, but Swithred's presence meant success was still in reach.

***

Rav's heart pounded louder than the stomps of her boots across the thatch and tile as she chased after the elven man, the pair of them leaping from rooftop to rooftop with no hesitation. He had responded to her charge by darting toward the docks, an unexpected move from someone Rav had read as holding the power in their standoff. Underneath her haze of vengeful fury, she understood he was leading her away from her mission. She didn't care.

He was taking a circuitous route along the skyline, at times jumping across alleys to the left or right. She guessed he had no intention of losing her—with his bulk, he wouldn't have been able to outpace her forever—but he must have had a finish line in mind, if he could just elude her until they reached it.

The familiar tingling sensation began to creep up her legs as she landed hard on a wooden beam jutting out of the side of a large square warehouse. Her quarry was already rolling into a crouch on the next rooftop ahead, brilliant sparks flaring to life across the night sky around him. If her recent encounter with Cater's crew was any indication, he would not be able to avoid her for long.

Unlike that fight, she knew what to expect. Whatever was causing the flashes of light and the jolts racing across her skin, they were accompanied by a potent benefit. She could already feel herself gaining on the elven man, and her muscles seemed to replenish with each step before fatigue could set in. With one notable exception, as the muscles at the base of her skull began to throb once again. Rav remembered the wrenching knot that formed there several nights before and tempered her excitement. She didn't know her new physical limits, but she did still have them.

The sodden planks at the western edge of the Lower Quay grew closer as the temperature dropped from the breeze off the strait. The two of them shared each rooftop now, the delay between their landings lessening. Rav could hear the man's tailcoat flapping violently ahead of her, his sword jostling in its scabbard. Only seconds were left before she caught him, before she tackled him from the rooftop onto the docks below.

Her skin grew warm, but the heat was different this time. When she ran from Cater and his men, she had felt as if arcing flames licked along her skin. Now, though, she could have been slipping into a warm bath. However, she knew the pain would intensify soon. But not before she brought down the man who set fire to a child's home.

The elf jumped off the edge in front of them with nothing to land on but the docks at least three stories down. They had reached the end of the line and she had him pinned between herself and the ocean. Rav raced forward as the air around her began to feel less like a bath and more like a pot set to boil. The heat was in front of her, not dancing around her body as it had before, but as she reached the lip of the thatched roof and planted her feet to jump, she passed through a scorching pocket of air.

Suddenly, the cool breeze was on her face once more as the source of the heat was now at her back. Glancing down, she saw the man had landed on his feet and was removing the long blade from his back, tossing his black leather scabbard to the side. She propelled herself off the roof, reaching under her cloak for her father's daggers, when an explosive fireball tore through the space behind her. Rav was sent tumbling through the sky over her target before crashing into the pier beyond him. She rolled end over end before skidding to a stop, her face scraping against the boards.

The man smiled as he looked down at her, silhouetted by the conflagration he had started in the building behind him. "Thank you for choosing to make this entertaining, lightblood."

***

The double doors on the far side of the warehouse flung open as a young draqesh man stumbled inside. He was holding his arm, his hand resting over what must have been a deep wound given the heavy stream of blood running down to the floor. Through clenched teeth he shouted, "They're right behind me! Make for the other—" The man's voice caught in his throat as he noticed Wymund and his contingent across the room, standing over Swithred. "They have us surrounded!"

For the first time, Cater broke from screaming orders at his crew to look at his presumed exit. His mouth thinned into a tight line and he locked eyes with Wymund, turning to square his shoulders with him. The thug's steely demeanor was the picture of a man who wouldn't go down without a fight. He was a zealot, a man with a cause who felt his livelihood was being taken from him, and he didn't seem prepared to let the law prevent him from reaching his goals.

"We've been found out," Cater announced to the room. "No use trying to cover our tracks now." He reached out to grab an iron mallet that was resting on one of the central tables and tested its balance. "Only way out is to clear a path."

What had once been hurried but stationary activities of dousing flames and stowing bottles was now a frenzy of movement. The Allies darted about the room picking up whatever impromptu weapons they could find: more iron mallets, broomsticks, and even broken glass jugs. Sunia and her patrol rushed in on the opposite side of the warehouse floor, weapons already drawn and taking in the scene. A stream of blood flowed down her face and across her left eye. The wounded scout who discovered her must have put up a good fight to land that blow before escaping back here.

"Weapons ready," Wymund ordered as he drew his own longsword. "Spread out. Aim to subdue if they will allow it."

Swithred mustered enough initiative at last to flip over and scramble to his feet. "Set up the ladder, you imbeciles," he shouted as he scampered back toward the safety of his comrades. "I can get out though the loft window!"

Carn and Torran jumped at his orders, looking briefly at Cater for his approval, but found their boss's attention was elsewhere. The two men lifted either end of a twenty-foot wooden ladder and began to position it against the edge of the rectangular loft running around the perimeter of the warehouse.

By the time the harbormaster reached the center of the room, grunts and ringing steel filled the space. Guardsmen were engaged with Allies all around, outnumbered two to one even with the arrival of Sunia and her band, but the thugs were untrained, their bodies jostling and tripping over each other in the chaos of the moment. His unit's swords were drawn but only being used to cleave tools in half and knock hammers aside before shoving the criminals back.

Wymund was grateful his call for restraint had been heeded, but he wasn't sure how long that would last. He didn't expect the Allies to fight fair, and his unit would be forced to end their skirmishes with bloody precision if it meant self-preservation. Cater and Ninev stood alone in the center of the work floor now. If Wymund could remove the head from the serpent, maybe the Allies would stand down.

"Throw down your weapon and tell your crew to do the same!" Wymund shouted over the din, holding his blade at his side as he walked toward them. "There doesn't need to be a cost in blood for your crimes. Your time in the Iron Spiral will be payment enough."

"I will never understand why people like you side with *them*," Cater said, his face still a calm pond obscuring the roiling fury beneath. "They give you a nice shiny tower from which you're expected to watch over their safety, but you'll never be one of them. The stain of *mediocrity*, of having the misfortune to be born outside their walls, is a mark of otherness that sets you apart."

Cater looked down at the mallet, palming its iron head in his other hand. "You're nothing more than a tool to them, useful only to hammer people back into line if they dare to upset the balance. All the while ingratiating themselves with the very foreigners making the lives you and I had growing up impossible."

The man was too far gone to listen to reason. Cater had been gaslit for the financial gain of others, and no amount of contrary evidence would sway him. Searching for better luck elsewhere, Wymund said, "It's Ninev, right? You are not bound by his decisions. There is still time to surrender." The woman remained silent, choosing only to draw her dagger in response.

Cyrilke Swithred was starting up the ladder now, struggling to maintain his grip as two members of Wymund's patrol had engaged Carn and Torran, tearing them away from supporting his ascent. In the split second Wymund spent assessing his true target's escape, Ninev dashed forward. She was favoring her left leg after her fight with Rav, but her speed hadn't been exaggerated. He had just enough time to position his blade between her and his right flank, causing her to peel away at the last moment.

But her feint had been enough, as Cater was now suddenly at his side, landing a crushing blow across Wymund's left shoulder blade. Roaring in pain, he swung his right fist wide, still gripping the hilt of his longsword as it cracked across Cater's jaw.

Wymund took two steps back in a guarded retreat, blade held at the ready before him. He rolled his shoulder forward and back. The chainmail he wore under his guard's coat had absorbed much of the impact, preventing any broken bones, but he would feel the sting of that mallet for weeks. His attackers were now standing apart, Cater to the left and Ninev to the right. He could position himself so that she remained in his periphery, but with her speed, that wouldn't provide enough warning. If she got inside the reach of his blade, he would be at her mercy.

She dashed toward him again, but this time he was ready. Wymund shifted to face her, maintaining a stance to turn and deflect another body blow from Cater, but to his surprise, Ninev was not attempting another feint. She slashed at him again and again with swift precision as he struggled to parry her attacks; it was a challenge given her speed, but not an insurmountable one. Cater's heavy footfalls plodded from behind and Wymund ducked, avoiding a swooping mallet swung wide enough to force Ninev back a few steps.

From his crouched position Wymund twisted on his heel, bringing his longsword around in a narrow arc that sliced into the man's thigh. As Cater screamed, Wymund sprang up and slammed his shoulder into the man's chest, shoving him back onto one of the central tables. Glass jugs toppled off the side and shattered, releasing their clear contents onto the production floor. Wymund's head swam briefly as the potent aroma expanded to fill the space, as if an entire tavern's worth of liquor had been spilled.

Wymund felt Ninev's body slam into his back, the woman apparently unfazed by the fumes as her legs wrapped around his waist from behind and one arm closed across his throat. He fought the urge to pull at her grip; her blade would end him before she could choke the life out of him. His hand shot up to grasp her wrist on the downswing, the point of her dagger a hair's width from his clavicle.

He twisted her arm into a painful rotation, forcing her to drop her weapon before the bones in her wrist would snap. Ninev let out a short scream and slid off his back, turning with Wymund's hold to release the strain, but he moved with her, pulling her arm up and behind her until her shoulder bulged nearly out of its socket. She froze.

Wymund glanced back to find Cater. The dockhand had regained his footing, though his broad frame was less imposing as he leaned his weight onto his unwounded leg. "Those who have wronged you shall be wronged in turn," he said through gritted teeth. "By your hand or mine." Wymund recognized the quote. It was known as Edis's Promise and was often depicted in the reliefs left behind by the Dawn Ones to denote the Ally's drive for vengeance. "He will guide my hand this day, duckling."

Wymund lifted Ninev and threw her forward, realizing that creating some distance would have to be enough without the time to restrain her. He turned to face Cater, now lumbering at him with his mallet cocked. The ladder slid off its feet at Ninev's impact and Swithred's yelp was cut short by a solid *thud* just as Cater brought down his first blow.

Side-stepping each wild downswing, Wymund looked for an opening to incapacitate his attacker. No matter Cater's murderous intent, he still preferred ending this in a way that would force the man to face justice. Wymund felt sympathy for him. If he hadn't joined the ranks of the Virdoban Guard, he couldn't be sure what a struggling existence would have led him to believe about the world. Scapegoats were tempting when the alternative was critical introspection.

But during Wymund's hesitation, Cater suddenly changed tacks and landed a heavy left hook across Wymund's jaw, followed by a side-armed mallet blow to his ribcage. Doubled over and breathless, Wymund tilted his head up in time to see his foe looming over him, mallet held in both hands over his head and ready to be brought down on his skull. Seeing no other option left, Wymund stepped inside the man's reach and brought his longsword up, running Cater through. The mallet clattered to the floor and Cater spat up a frothy red mixture as he looked down at the hilt sticking out of his chest.

"You chose this death," Wymund said, pained from more than his bruised ribs.

"What use is a dockhand if our ports are always empty?" Cater sputtered. "I had . . . no choice at all."

***

Splinters of wood and bits of thatch rained down over the pier, some blackened while others glowed a bright red-orange as they continued to burn. Sparks of light flickered throughout Rav's vision, disappearing almost as soon as they appeared and contributing to the chaos around her. She struggled to her feet, aware she was bleeding from the scratches on her face only by the blood spattering to the planks below. The rapid twitches firing to life around her body and gooseflesh bursting over her skin drowned out that pain. The top of her neck throbbed. She knew where this was heading.

The elven man, now revealed to be a scorcher, was still standing in the same position no more than twenty feet away. He was relaxed, his abnormally long blade held at his side, and wore a curious smirk.

"Honestly, I'm impressed," he said. "That you were able to get so close to catching me up there truly speaks to your potential, untrained though it may be. It's been so long since I've faced one of your kind that I forgot how powerful you can be, despite the dilution."

"Did you hit your head on the way down here? You're making as much sense as a day-drunk." *Keep him talking. Another one of those explosions and I'm done.* Her mind drifted back to the night Annika saved her, and the woman's warnings to avoid situations like this. *Maybe I'm done anyway. But I won't be alone.*

He laughed. "Outstanding. You don't even know what you are and still managed to draw enough from the World Shroud to match my pace. Operating on nothing more than pure instinct," he said, shaking his head with incredulity. "You could have done great things with that connection."

Now a second person was insinuating she was a lightblood, the child of a stormforger and another parent with no sense of the World Shroud. But that was impossible. She was no expert, but she had never seen "the cloak of all" that was described by people who could tap into its power. More importantly, her mother couldn't summon lightning, at least not more than metaphorically. And how could a detail like that about her father never come up over the years?

"Could have? I may not have the benefit of two elven parents, but I still plan on having many decades left to achieve greatness."

"A part of me is truly sorry about this. With the right guiding hand, you could become a formidable force in this world. But I'm being paid too much to allow a prying lightblood to interfere. Choii Stier will be crippled. Whether it's by bank note or blood matters little."

As the man spoke, Rav could see the blade's color begin to shift first to a dull red and then progress into a blinding yellow. Waves of heat danced around the steel, just visible amidst the chaos of light flares bursting across her vision.

"Either way," he said, "you won't be around to bear witness."

He stalked toward her along the pier, moving with a calm sense of purpose. He knew he was in control. There would be no need for a frenzied assault. Rav readied her daggers and crouched low, feeling her muscles hum with a crackling anticipation she didn't share. Scorchers carried a reputation for lethality that was well earned.

She parried his first swing, then the next, the heat emanating from his bastard sword licking against her skin. Her smaller weapons weren't meant to defend against his swooping strikes, but despite her speed, she couldn't find an opening to get inside his reach. She could track his swings as they bore down on her, knew where he would aim thanks to this strange new energy coursing through her body, but his sheer size advantage couldn't be overcome. Each successful parry came with enough force that she was forced backward toward the ocean.

His slash came in low and wide, but her dagger was there to deflect the cutting edge. Still, the power of the attack forced her to take another step back, leaving her heel hanging off the end of the pier. Based on what her opponent could do to his blade, she feared ending up in the waters behind her. There was no way to parry being boiled alive.

She crouched even lower as he drove his blade forward in a thrust meant to impale her, springing up and over him at the last moment. The pain at the base of her skull spiked with the effort, but she knew this was her only chance. As she twisted to plant a kick in the center of the man's back, she saw a jagged orange line tear across the air between them, then a geyser of flames erupting toward her.

Rav dropped to the planks below and rolled away from the scorcher and the conflagration he had created. The smell of scorched hair and flesh tickled her nose, but she couldn't tell where she had been burned. Her whole body was once again thrumming with the liquid fire that both fueled and threatened to consume her. She stood and readied herself, her vision more filled with sparks of light than not. The elf at the end of the pier stood still, his sword returned to his side.

"Your eyes are already going white," he said. "I don't think you have many more escapes like that in you. Let's find out, shall we?"

Another tear ripped open in the space to her left and released a spout of fire. Rav managed to spring backward with only the tail of her cloak getting scorched but was forced to continue her desperate retreat as more and more fiery lances shot out of the air around her. Each time her feet found purchase on the pier, another tear opened, pushing her farther and farther back, the knot crunching down on her spine harder with each landing. Her knees buckled as she reached the main dock, the muscles in her legs no longer vibrating but violently spasming. The energy had turned on her, just as it had before. She squinted along the length of the pier, the lights blinding her to all but the silhouette of the elven man standing at the end. He hadn't moved an inch during his onslaught.

"I found your limit," he shouted to her. There was no malice in his voice; he was just stating a fact. "Well, this has been entertaining. But as I said earlier, I really do have to be on my way. Monarchs do not look kindly on tardiness, even ones they call the People's King."

He strolled toward her at an easy pace, but Rav couldn't stand from where she had collapsed. Her body was once again locked in place. All she could do was wait for him, stuck kneeling on the pier, the stench of the sea and cinders and tar wrapped around her.

At least he's leaving. She pictured the warehouse going up in flames, her friend trapped inside as the child had been not long ago. *Maybe I spared Wymund by chasing this guy away.*

The man crouched down to meet her gaze. She could not see much more than his shadowed form, but as the breeze off the strait shifted his hair, Rav recognized the abrupt blunting of his ear, and her heart skipped a beat. It was a characteristic Felonians knew all too well—one her *family* knew all too well.

When he spoke, though, a semblance of empathy found its way into his words. "Look at you; you've killed yourself. Though I suppose it'll be better this way," he said as he pushed her onto her side. "People like us are eventually betrayed by those we trust. Compelled into this life of violent servitude, as if this path was predestined from birth. I envy you in this." He rose and placed the sole of his boot against her back. "You get to go out on your own terms," he said as he shoved her off the docks and into the waters below.

For a moment, Rav couldn't distinguish the burning in her lungs from the searing heat that arced across her body. But the lights filling her vision began to flicker, blinking out of existence as a creeping darkness moved in from the edges. The surface of the ocean drifted farther away until her tunneled vision filled completely with black, her sight finally disappearing with the pain.

Chapter 14

Virdoba

The beam refused to budge. Rav could no longer see the shape of the child through the flames painting everything in the room with an orange haze. Smoke stung her eyes, and the cloth protecting her palms from the burning wood had long since turned to ash, but she wouldn't leave the child.

A shadowed form began to take shape within the dancing blaze, gliding toward her. It was tall, broad-shouldered, and seemed to be cradling something in its arms. Rav blinked the tears away, squinting to block out what little smoke she could, and heaved with her legs. Her grip slipped from the stubborn beam, only managing to scrape skin from her already burned hands. Bringing her fist down on the wood with a frustrated cry, she looked back toward the advancing figure. Despite her surroundings, a chill washed over her as the elven man stepped out of the fires, his white tailcoat unscorched and a limp young boy held in the crook of his left arm.

This isn't right, *she thought.* He wasn't there. *Not long after she had slipped from the beam, Wymund had arrived and helped her lift it, allowing her to dart in and rescue the child. It was where they had met, where he had mistaken her for an arsonist rather than just a thief. But her friend was nowhere to be found now, and her murderer stood a few yards away, his hand ablaze with a fire that seemed to form around his skin. The man held his palm closer to the boy's face, portions of which were already blistered and burned. He pulled away from the heat, but Rav knew it was an unconscious reaction. The boy was barely clinging to life.*

"Have it your way, lightblood," the elf said, caressing his captive's cheek as it bubbled at his touch. "I gave you the option of a warrior's death, but you seem to have chosen a life destined for betrayal or pain. For your sake, I hope it's not both."

Rav gulped in air as she snapped her eyes open. Stooped over her was a pale, lanky man with loose blond curls that fell around the sides of his face, eyebrows knitted together above a set of brilliant green eyes. He didn't have distinct iris rings that would mark him as elven, but the color was striking just the same. More like sparkling emeralds than the typical dark greens found among the northern populations. Rather than concern over her state, the man radiated curiosity. In her clouded mind, she took that as a sign that her condition wasn't as severe as it felt.

"Hmm, there *is* elven blood in you," he muttered. "Fascinating." He stood and turned away from her, hands clasped behind his back as he crossed the room toward a leather satchel sitting on a set of drawers. There was something almost otherworldly about the way he moved, as if each step was made with perfect precision and grace but without need for a second thought.

She sat up on the bed, her hand on her forehead as she tried to focus. They were in what appeared to be a one-room home, furnished with nothing more than a single bed, a dresser, and a small dining table. Morning light poured in from a partially drawn window, and the sound of water lapping against the pier outside meant she was likely still close to the Marrow Strait.

"Where am I?" she croaked before succumbing to a coughing fit.

"Careful," the man replied without turning back around. "You inhaled a substantial amount of water before I pulled you out. It may be difficult to talk for some time." He slung the satchel over his shoulder and began to gather some loose parchment and a quill into a tidy bundle. "Rest here for a while. I do not believe the owners will return until the evening."

"Wh—" She coughed. "Why did you save me?"

Packing his bundle into the satchel, he faced her once again. "You were making quite the splash," he said matter-of-factly, followed by a slight smile. "In the World Shroud, that is. Your language is imprecise and lends itself to unintentional word play, so I apologize if my word choice reminded you of your time under the waves."

"Nobody likes puns, but it's not because of hurt feelings."

The man's smile broadened. "Then the apology remains just the same. As to why, the answer is simple mistaken identity. The distortions you created in the World Shroud were significant enough that I believed you to be someone I have been searching for. When I discovered that was not the case, I acted as I thought was best."

"Yeah?" Rav asked, rubbing her temples. "Best for who?"

The question seemed to give the man pause as he cocked his head in thought. Finally, he said, "I am not sure yet. The world, perhaps? I think you could be important."

"I left a life of importance for a life all my own," she rasped. "I don't have any intention of giving that up."

He walked back across the room, stopping in front of her. "Ironically, one may be bound to certain actions for the sake of freedom's preservation. If my assessment of you is correct, our paths will cross again." Before she could reply, he reached a finger forward and tapped her forehead. Sleep found her before her head hit the pillow.

PART II

Chapter 15

Virdoba

Annika watched the trio of Virdoban guards file out of her home, Wymund holding the door open for them in the vestibule and thanking each one as they passed. Good soldier that he was, she noted he betrayed little of the worry that had gripped him for most of the morning following the raid. Command was in his future, and he knew the importance of keeping his emotions in check. But Annika had lived too many years for a man's concern to escape her notice. They were all the same. A mask of stoicism barely hiding a shortening temper.

She heard the door click closed as Wymund returned to her side, each staring in silence at Rav resting on the sitting room couch. Despite whatever had happened by the piers in the Lower Quay, the girl did not have a scratch on her.

Wymund exhaled and the tension finally melted from his face. "She'll have a lot to answer for when she wakes."

"She certainly will," Annika replied, though she knew her questions for the girl would be of a different nature. Wymund wanted to know why Rav had deviated from the plan. Two of his patrol had been wounded inside that warehouse, and he shouldered some of that responsibility. But Annika was curious about a more fundamental point. Namely, Rav's continuing ability to draw breath.

No one was sure what had transpired by the docks. The hour had been too early for any witnesses to be out and about, but Annika had heard enough description of the property damage to form a picture of the events. The explosion that had sent burning thatch through the air could be explained away as an errant firebomb that had already been secreted out of the warehouse prior to Wymund's arrival, but the presence of smaller singed blemishes along one of the piers told her a different story. She would need Rav's corroboration, but perhaps they had been wrong at the florist's shop.

It was true that Cater Waldwen and his thugs had used their concoction to implicate a crew of elven scorchers as violent extremists, but now it appeared that a scorcher had been present in Virdoba all along. Were they connected? And if so, why go through the trouble of feigning the ability to draw flames from the World Shroud when they had access to a person who could level a city block before any opposition arrived? Perhaps the Allies of Edis didn't know they counted an elf among their ranks.

Annika watched Rav's chest rise and fall with the slow rhythm that could only come from a peaceful rest, an outcome she knew shouldn't be possible if the girl had come face-to-face with this threat. Either she would have ended up a charred corpse still smoking on the sodden planks of the Lower Quay, or she would have instinctively drawn from the World Shroud herself, much as she had the day they had met. The end result would have been the same. If battling those brutes in the alley had pushed her past her limits and toward the threshold of the Illuminated Death, then a fight for survival against a seasoned scorcher certainly would.

Wymund eased himself into a chair across from the couch, sighing as he leaned his head back and rubbed his eyes. "Part of me wants to wake her now just so this business can be concluded," he said. "I feel . . . unsettled somehow. Normally I prefer these matters to wrap up in a clean fashion, but this time there are so many gaps in our knowledge. And in our current circumstances, I don't have much hope we will ever see them filled."

"You don't think the woman will talk?"

"Ninev is made of tough stock, from what I can tell. The guard has interrogators working on her now, but I don't believe she'll ever reveal more than we already know." He leaned forward and rubbed the top of his head. "She may not even know more herself. The woman is clearly a skilled fighter, but I didn't get the sense that she was in a leadership role."

Taking the other empty seat in the den, Annika poured herself another cup of tea from the kettle she had steeped earlier that morning. Neither she nor Wymund had slept since the raid, but that would have been the case regardless of the beverage. Annika felt as incomplete as he did, like they were missing some element of closure. But with Cater and Swithred each lying dead in the care of Virdoba's undertaker, they might be forced to live with not knowing the full scope of the Allies' plan.

"Agh," Wymund growled, slamming his fist down on the arm of the chair. "If I hadn't been so careless tossing that damn woman away from me, then Swithred would still be alive to question. But I threw her *right into* that ladder, like it was pre-destined to slip and drop the man on his head."

"Based on the chaos you described, they didn't leave you much of a choice," Annika said. "You had the options of life or death presented to you. In either outcome, you still wouldn't possess the information we lack, but at least alive," she gestured toward Rav, "you can continue to pester that one with your strait-laced moral code."

Wymund looked over as Rav seemed to stir in response to being referenced. "It's not pestering," he said with the first hint of a smile. "It's a proper education."

"Yeah," Rav muttered, peeking one eye open and beginning to stretch. "The problem is I was never one for tutors. They always wanted me to sit still, and I always wanted them to feel like their salary wasn't worth the effort."

She sat up on the couch and blinked the sleep from her eyes. "Well, it's a nice change of pace to regain consciousness in a more hospitable room. The cot you had me on in your kitchen was little more than a thin board."

Annika's relief at hearing Rav's typical snark in full effect was tinged with annoyance. "I decided that if you wouldn't heed my warnings about keeping out of lethal situations, perhaps I could measure you for your coffin based on the length of my couch."

She scoffed and glanced over to Wymund, who met her gaze with a softness that seemed to temper her edge. "Ravael, you almost died. Again."

Rav opened her mouth for a retort but held her tongue. After a beat, she said, "You're right, I shouldn't be so flippant. How was the raid on the Allies? I heard you say Cater and Swithred were dead, but were any of ours hurt? Did we at least shut down their produc—"

Wymund waved his hand. "Yes, yes. The city is safe for now. A few of the guards were wounded, but we need to know what happened to you. Why did you abandon the mission?"

Hanging her head, Rav said, "There was a man tailing me up there. An elf. He . . . baited me into chasing him away from the warehouse." She glanced up at him, her eyes misty for a moment before she blinked the tears away. "He was a scorcher, Wymund. He said he was there that night . . . "

He reached across and placed a hand on Rav's shoulder. "We got that boy out of there, Ravael. He's alive today because you refused to give up on him."

Annika had heard of the house in the Low Tide neighborhood that had burned to the ground recently, almost killing a child in the process. It had been deemed a burglary gone wrong per her sources and felt too petty for the involvement of such a powerful individual.

"I think he was playing you like a fiddle, girl," Annika said. "A scorcher wouldn't concern himself with robbing a working-class home, nor would he have started a burn that allowed you and Corporal Sylnorin the time to save anyone inside. This man likely discovered your involvement and used your trauma to goad you into following him."

She poured tea into a third cup and pushed the saucer across the table to Rav. "Still, the moment you realized you were facing someone like him, you should've darted away. But you continue to insist on dancing with fate." Annika sighed. "It's my fault, really. I should've pushed more when you denied being a lightblood." Wymund's head snapped back to her at that, puzzlement scrawled across his face.

"I couldn't determine if you were keeping your secrets from a stranger or if you truly didn't know," Annika continued, "but obviously there are aspects of yourself of which you are ignorant. That needs to change, because I don't believe there will be any altering your rash tendencies."

"That's the second time you've insinuated that I have this connection to the World Shroud," Rav said. "The scorcher said the same thing. But as I said before, neither of my parents are a stormforger." She waved her hands through the air, eyes wandering as she added, "And I've never seen any 'cloak' drifting around my vision for me to yank on."

Annika smiled, glad that the woman's fire had returned. "But you *have* been blinded by spontaneous flares, yes?" That caused Rav to settle back into the couch, her expression confirming what Annika had already seen.

"I know what I saw in the alley. You were convulsing, eyes wide and shining with a blue-white light. That only happens when a lightblood draws more lightning from the World Shroud than their body can handle. It's a state called the Illuminated Death, an apt name considering that once that threshold is passed it is always fatal." Annika crossed her legs and took a sip from her cup. "Unless an *old woman* appears with a lifesaving serum, that is."

"Drawing lightning?" Wymund asked, his shocked stare transitioning from Annika to Rav.

"I don't know what you're talking about," she replied, shaking her head. "In the alley and facing this scorcher, I *did* feel a rush. Like I was able to outmaneuver and outthink my opponents, even if it was barely the case on the pier. But drawing from the World Shroud . . . I wouldn't even know how to do something like that. Even *if* one of my parents is a stormforger, which I'm not convinced is the case."

It had been decades since Annika had studied World Shroud theory alongside her sister, but the information was as fresh in her mind as if their last tutoring session had just ended. Ironically, she had always understood the mechanics of accessing these forces better than Alauvar, witch-in-training she might have been. Her sister had always been more preoccupied with the frivolities of life as a noble. At least, before she became enamored with playing hero for the revolution that cost her life. As noble as their intentions had been, the rebellion had leaned on her too much to mend bones and knit flesh with her infusions, and Alauvar couldn't say no.

"Only those with two gifted parents have the potential to directly draw from the World Shroud," Annika said. "Having just one parent with the ability produces a child with a lesser connection and no real control over their own talents. Your body was acting on instinct, tearing small holes in the membrane to funnel the energy through you as you needed it. But that is precisely what makes life with a passive connection so dangerous. Lacking control means you can't stop as easily before burning yourself out."

Rav stood unsteadily, reaching down to balance herself on the arm of the couch. "You seem to know a lot about this stuff for someone who has no connection herself."

"I've often found knowledge to be a suitable substitute for one not fortunate enough to be born with innate special talents," Annika said. "With your temperament, you'll need both if you hope to stay alive. Speaking of which, you haven't yet told us how you continue to draw breath after your encounter this morning."

"Honestly, I don't have much of an explanation myself," Rav said, crossing her arms and furrowing her brow. "I should be dead. That state you mentioned, where all I can see is light and my body locks up? That's how I was when the scorcher kicked me into the Strait." Her body shuddered.

"I remember my vision going dark, the lights dying down just enough for me to see the surface of the water moving farther and farther away. Then the next thing I know I'm waking up in a shack near the pier with a bizarre man standing over me like I was nothing more than a curiosity to him."

"You didn't recognize this man?" Wymund asked.

"No, and I've never seen anyone like him. His eyes were . . . impossible? I don't know how else to describe them. They were a radiant green that you might find among elves, but he appeared human and the color filled the entire iris. And the way he moved was almost unnatural. His movements were too . . . perfect?" She shook her head again. "Sorry, I know that sounds like nonsense."

"So, not an elf?" Annika asked, thoughts churning in her mind. Odd characteristics aside, Rav would have recognized one of her own kind. The strange, colored eyes and surreal movements were likely the result of a brain that had spent too much time under the waves to have fully recovered. "That rules out a knitter or a witch. He must have had access to powerful potions then, like the ones my sister created."

"Maybe," Rav said. "He did have a bag with him. He could've had them in there."

"As intriguing as this merciful stranger may be, there's an important element of your story you have yet to share," Wymund said, holding his hand up as if to recapture the veering conversation. "Why was this elf leading you away from the Allies? Moreover, why would an elf be helping these bigots at all? It doesn't fit with what we know about the group's motivations."

"Doesn't it, though?" Annika asked. "Cater's crew must not have known they were working with an elf, otherwise they wouldn't have bothered with the firebombs, and we've already surmised Swithred was only interested in the potential for financial gain. If this scorcher is connected to the Allies, it would just mean he is positioned in a leadership role, above the need for motives beyond more coin lining his purse."

Wymund grunted in agreement as Rav's eyes narrowed. "I do remember him saying something about crippling Choii Stier," she muttered, adding, "and about visiting the 'People's King' once he was done with me here. That's what the Qedradans call their ruler, right?"

Annika nodded. "Yes, King Berenqar has a reputation for being relatively accessible, as far as monarchs go. And by all accounts a decent and fair man. I don't believe he would be aiming to sow any discontent between Choii Stier and Kefya after years trying to build stronger ties between his neighboring nations." She paused, a larger picture beginning to form in her mind.

"But perhaps this plot is looking to manipulate him as well. Swithred was Virdoba's harbormaster, and therefore financially interested in ensuring that trade from Choii Stier passes through our port before traveling over land to the rest of Anera. We've heard rumors that the elves want to expand trade agreements with other port cities, but if Berenqar could be tricked into believing that elven terrorists were assaulting his southern neighbors, he may be less inclined to open his own borders to a potential threat."

"Your logic is sound," Wymund said, "but Swithred is dead. Is there any reason for continued concern? Without the harbormaster's purse backing that elven mercenary, what incentive would he have to follow through with this journey to Alaboq?"

"Swithred was ambitious but lacked the imagination or audacity to attempt something like this on his own." Annika shook her head. "No, I fear there was another person guiding his hand, and could just as easily be funding the scorcher's mission north."

Rav looked to Wymund. "So when are we leaving?"

"What?" he asked, his mouth agape briefly before he sighed. "You aren't going anywhere, Ravael. You've nearly died twice in a matter of days."

"The old woman comes with us, then," she replied, flashing a smirk at Annika. "She seems pretty invested in the idea that I need an education in World Shroud theory, so she can be my traveling tutor. You *know* this isn't finished." She paced over and crouched down in front of his seat, locking her eyes on Wymund's. "And I know you won't be able to rest until Virdoba's safety is secured."

"We could send a warning by courier—"

"And chance interception by another rich society-type who's bribed the messenger's guild?" Rav asked. "Annika just said more of these pricks are involved. Who knows how connected they are or how high this goes?"

Studying Rav's face, Annika asked, "Why are you so personally invested? I understand that he insinuated he caused that fire you were involved in, but as I explained, it is more likely he was using that knowledge to provoke you."

The girl's cocky eagerness dropped for a moment as she looked to Annika. "I noticed something else about the scorcher. He was missing the tips of his ears."

The Clipped Gulls. Of course Rav would want to chase this man across all Anera; he represented the moment she believed her life spun off course.

Wymund looked down and away from them. "Felonian mercenaries working out of country or no, I *am* worried that if Berenqar believes the attacks could travel up the coast, he may not just end things with a canceled trade deal. This could spark a war."

Annika placed her saucer on the table before them and stood with a groan. "As loath as I am to get these stiff joints up on a horse day in and day out, Rav is right. I've lived through armed conflict once in my life and I don't wish to see it again." She swatted the back of Rav's head lightly. "And if this one insists on joining the hunt, my hands may as well be tied to hers."

Meeting each of their eyes for a moment, Wymund said, "Even outside the Lighthouse, I continue to find myself outranked. Very well, I will request to be granted leave from my duties in order to track an external threat to Virdoba. Time is a factor, so I believe they will see the sense in sending me without waiting for word to reach the council in Felona first. Though we will have to travel light and move swiftly. The goal cannot be to catch the scorcher and confront him; I don't see that ending well. We will have to try and bypass him, reach the Qedradan capital first, and spoil his plans. Do the two of you think you can manage that kind of journey?"

Rav laughed as she stood. "Try and keep up."

Chapter 16

Alaboq

Despite days of loitering in the kitchens of Vinsart Hold after making his deliveries, Mareq had been unable to pick out a pattern in the comings and goings of the Ghosts. He made a note each day one of the plainly clad figures appeared and met with Trade Minister Hadac, but the intervals were irregular and random. Even the time of day seemed to fluctuate, a fact he only learned when he arrived one morning and heard that the night shift had mentioned a visitor. Perhaps most frustrating, though, was that there was no continuity of the individuals themselves. Each messenger was as indistinct as the last, but heights and weights fluctuated enough that Mareq was sure most of the Ghost sightings were of unique individuals. If Mrs. Luviire was right about Teacher Ias's followers forming a network of chapters across the continent, the division hosted in Alaboq must be substantial.

"One day the wrong guard is gonna notice you lagging about, and then you're gonna be sorry you've been listening to Chaevin and that old bat," Waemish whispered from his post at the sinks. Mareq finished his fourth stock count of the afternoon and turned to face the man, who had taken to resting a towel across his shelf of a belly so he wouldn't need to reach down as far for it. "Someone might get the idea that you're planning a route through the citadel for thieving or some such nonsense."

"And where might they get an idea like that?" Mareq asked.

The portly dishwasher grunted his disapproval. "Not from me. I don't tell tales out of turn. I'm just warning you, is all." As he wiped the suds off a ladle with the towel draped across him, he added, "You're wasting your time, anyway. There's no such thing as a chain of Ias's Ghosts carrying messages between fancy lords and ladies."

"They're meeting here for some reason," Mareq muttered to himself, turning back to the shelves for another round of tallying.

He had considered the possibility that these clandestine visitors were simply delivering adulterous notes or instructions for the next romantic rendezvous, but Tiialya's urge for caution around these individuals spoke to something deeper. She had been freelancing in Alaboq to deliver a message from the Kefyan Council to Qedrad's chief trade minister. However, Mareq found the temptation of resuming his travels too strong to ignore.

If I can just find a little proof of impropriety, he thought as he ran his eyes over the crate of icy blue frostdew berries for the fifth time that day, *then Berenqar will* have *to set me up for the next leg of my journey.*

A loud *clang* snapped him out of his trance, and he peeked around the edge of the storeroom threshold to see Ptolon staring down at the trade minister herself, who was still clutching the handle of the copper pot she'd slammed against the counter. Even without her official rank, Sylicera Hadac possessed an intimidating aura that was all her own. Mareq had never spoken to the woman, and in fairness she had likely never noticed his presence, but each time he had seen her hanging around the kitchens, she was wearing the same stern expression. As if she were using every ounce of willpower she could muster to restrain a fierce outburst. Whatever Ptolon had done must have put the final crack in her resolve.

"You request these *repellent* spices to be shipped all the way from your backwater village, at great expense to the Crown, and then proceed to smother all your preparations with them," she shouted up at him, her long auburn braid flicking from side to side as she drove her points home with emphatic finger jabs to his chest. "I'm beginning to suspect you're using your position in the kitchens to finance some cousin's farm back home, then burning through your supply so another order has to be rushed through."

To the Ebkarish man's credit, he met her gaze with a straight back and hands clasped behind him; respectful, but not rolling over to be tread upon. "The aromatic quality added to my sauces by this spice blend is a particular source of joy to Lady Cailynne, Minister Hadac," Ptolon said, no trace of emotion crossing his face. "However, I am sure if you explain to her that her tastes are placing an inordinate strain on the kingdom's budget, she would be willing to forgo this simple pleasure for the good of the nation."

Hadac sniffed, releasing her grip on the pot and holding his gaze in a vice. "That will not be necessary, Ptolon. The lady is due her sources of happiness." She scanned the kitchen, her eyes lingering on members of the staff. "We may just be required to trim the fat in other areas at our next meeting with the minister of the purse."

"King Berenqar trusts your judgement on these matters," Ptolon replied. "Your decision will be the right one for Vinsart Hold and the Qedradan people, I am sure."

She opened her mouth to reply, but something appeared to catch her notice just beyond the chef's shoulder. Her eyes widened for a brief moment before returning to normal, and she turned to head back toward the stairs leading up to the citadel's administrative offices.

"Keep your line workers on task," she said. "Hiring replacements is a torturous process, but their lower rates may be what is needed to justify the lady's palate." Then she disappeared from view, taking the steps two at a time.

As Mareq glanced back for Ptolon's reaction, another brown-clothed individual brushed past him and followed Hadac into Vinsart Hold's main halls. Mareq had grown accustomed to the uniform over the days he had been waiting to spot one. Some variety of unremarkable clothing and something to obscure the head; in this case, a headscarf that rested low enough to cast a shadow over the eyes, as well as nondescript facial features or body mass. This Ghost appeared to be female, which wasn't shocking considering he'd noted several females in the role during his observations. He added the day and time to his mental list of their appearances, but still couldn't make sense of any discernible pattern in their movements.

"Waemish is right, you know," Mrs. Luviire said, walking over from her station, where she had spent the morning overseeing preparations for the afternoon meal. "At least in part. Hadac has been more on edge than usual lately, more prone to lash out at her underlings. If she catches you lurking around, you may not be locked away, but she could stop buying from you. Those purchasing decisions are ultimately under her purview."

"It seems that everyone is warning me about getting caught up with these people and their schemes," Mareq said. He stepped out of the storeroom, hefting his empty delivery crates with him. "Are the Ghosts really that dangerous?"

"The Ghosts? No, Teacher Ias doesn't promote violence. Her followers will smile to your face while dipping a hand in your purse, but I wouldn't expect them to cause any physical harm." Mrs. Luviire glanced around the room before adding with a whisper, "Standing between a noble and their money, though, can at times be a lethal mistake."

Mareq finished collecting his handful of crates, stacking them inside each other until the pile was as high as his chest. "Perhaps you're right." He sighed. "It's not like I've had any luck deciphering anything about them so far, so my time could be better spent elsew—"

The words froze in his mouth as the drab figure slipped down the stairs and headed for the exit. He felt his heart flutter in his chest, and before he could think better of it, he followed. "Watch these for me," he shot back at Mrs. Luviire as he moved toward the door.

"Mareq!" Mrs. Luviire whispered, but he had already given in to the whim. If he couldn't learn anything more by studying their activity within Vinsart Hold, maybe he could glean more by following a Ghost to the source.

Mareq had never been an impulsive individual. Restless, perhaps, and eager to grow and see the variety the world had to offer, but he wasn't the type to act on a spur-of-the-moment decision. When he had left his home in Brey, it had been after months of saving up funds and planning his route, along with convincing his family that the life he wanted was worthwhile. But in that moment, tailing the woman out of the kitchens and into the cramped streets of the Thistle Hare Warren, he discovered a thrill that he hadn't felt since he first set foot on Captain Tomau's ship.

Built in Alaboq's earliest days, the Thistle Hare Warren popped up organically just beyond the walls of Vinsart Hold as an impromptu housing district. There had been no design or forethought to the neighborhood layout, as wooden shacks were constructed ad hoc for the families of the individuals working on the citadel's creation. Consequently, the area of the city closest to the towering majesty of Vinsart Hold was also its largest eyesore. Relative to the vibrant beauty of the Lyri Blossom Market, this district was a restrictive labyrinth teeming with laborers and tradespeople of every kind who constantly bumped elbows. The people there were hardy, though, and like their neighborhood's namesake, found ways to subsist despite the prickles of life.

Over the centuries, the wooden shacks had been built into multistory homes and shops that loomed above Mareq's head. Because of their height and the narrow alleys weaving between them, he found that this district was always cooler than the rest of the city. The sun couldn't heat the sandstone underfoot like a clay oven without a direct angle to focus its rays. However, this also meant the shadows were longer, and coupled with the sheer number of people crowding the thin paths, the Ghost would be difficult to track. Being a little over waist high to most of the others in the Warren and dense enough to force his way through the crowd, Mareq suspected he may be able to remain hidden from her while also keeping pace, though. Managing that feat without creating a scene would be the trick.

Mareq followed the flick of her cloak through the sea of legs before him, marking new landmarks in his mind as she turned corner after corner. He didn't know if he would need to follow this path again, but her journey through the Warren appeared to be a deliberate attempt to disguise her destination, so he thought it best that he commit it to memory. The woman frequently doubled back, often block by block, which in this neighborhood was no longer than the length of one home before another alley split off to separate it from the next one. Whether or not these Ghosts were as secretive as he had been told, they were certainly proving themselves adept at obfuscating their movements through the city.

Still, he managed to keep her in his sights as he muscled his way through the throngs. Mareq was grateful for the bustle of activity that permeated the district, allowing his jostling to blend in with other invasions of personal space. Young children chased small dogs between the legs of strangers, their laughter met with equal amounts of annoyed grunts and calls for caution. Stray cats hunted mice and other vermin along the edges of the alleys, occasionally skittering across a sandaled foot and eliciting a startled yelp. And above it all, neighbors shouted across the passageways from their windows as they navigated who would have the first use of the laundry lines that day. Next to that commotion, a gentle shove on Mareq's part warranted little more than an afterthought.

Although he couldn't see the sun via the narrow strips of sky above, judging by the shadows being cast, Mareq guessed they were generally heading east. That meant she was moving in the direction of the Alaboqan coast, though not the city's docks, which were located on its southern face. To the best of Mareq's knowledge, the Thistle Hare Warren extended all the way to the city's eastern wall, with nothing of any significance along the way and only a rocky beach beyond.

He watched her disappear around another corner, his mind wrapping around the puzzle of what nondescript building in the district could serve as a haven for Teacher Ias's followers, when he felt a hand clasp around his bicep. His head snapped back to see a woman leaning with her other hand on the lip of a small garden filled with succulents, her face lined after a long life of laughter. She smiled warmly at him, the hunch in her back reducing her to his eye level as she released her grip and patted his arm.

"Young man," she said, her voice raspy but brimming with vitality. "Everyone around here is in such a rush that I haven't been able to catch anyone's attention." She gestured back to the oak door behind her, which appeared to be warped with age and was now jutting against the threshold below. "This door gets caught on the ground all the time, and I just don't have the strength anymore to force it open. Would you mind giving it a yank for me?"

His heart rate spiked as he glanced back in the direction of the woman, who had disappeared down another path by this point and would be impossible to find again. Sighing, he said, "It would be my pleasure." He gripped the handle and jerked it back, the door swinging open once the swollen portion had been dislodged. The woman caught the door's edge as it swung and stepped between it and Mareq, gliding inside with a surprising amount of dexterity.

She closed the door partially, leaving only her upper half sticking out into the street. "Thank you so much, young man. May the sea breeze speed your story." And with a wink, she shut the door behind her, leaving Mareq flustered in the street.

Though he knew there was no hope of catching up to the Ghost now, he at least wanted to see what was around the last turn he had watched her make, so he pushed his way up the street and rounded the corner. His brow furrowed as he found himself in a dead-end alley, the purpose of which appeared to be a repository for discarded furniture pieces, broken crates and barrels, as well as other general refuse. The alley's three sides were each three stories tall, the external walls of separate apartment structures that had somehow been built even closer together than the other buildings in the Warren. Mareq glanced to his left and right, deciding he must have misjudged which path she had chosen, but he noticed the swinging sign above him that read THE HOBBLED COBBLER above a painted boot missing its heel. It was the landmark he had memorized when he watched her disappear. Scratching his head, he took a hesitant step into the alley.

He hefted chair legs and barrel hoops with broken oak staves still attached, finding nothing of note below the piles of garbage. No footprints in the dusty street, no crevices large enough to squeeze through, not even any discarded climbing rope. Mareq knew the "Ghost" moniker was a reference to their discreet reputation, but he began to wonder if perhaps the name was more apt than he thought. The World Shroud allowed certain people to do incredible things. Maybe this group could pass through walls, as their namesake would suggest.

I'll have to see if Mrs. Luviire knows more about the World Shroud than her own infusions, he thought, as his eye caught a semicircle that appeared to be scratched into the wooden paneling on one of the alley's walls, the bottom of the image obscured by the broken back of a bench resting against it.

A human would have missed it, but whatever this carving was, it was right in Mareq's eyeline. He strode over and flipped the bench back down, revealing a completed circle scraped into the building's façade, no bigger than a dinner plate. Within the circle was an etching of the Alaboqan coastline, instantly recognizable from Captain Tomau's survey maps, along with a raised wooden bird pointing west. Judging by the sculpt, with its narrow, pointed wings and short stubby bill, Mareq guessed it was meant to depict a coastal swallow, making its orientation on the image confusing. The birds stuck to the coast without fail, feeding off the crustaceans and fish in the shallows, but this representation had the bird flying inland. He reached out to touch it and the figure wobbled beneath his fingers. The etching wasn't one solid piece.

His curiosity sparked, Mareq attempted to twist the wooden bird figure in the wall, but it only shifted a few degrees before catching. Digging his fingernails behind the piece, he pulled it away from the wall, easily slipping the sculpt away with him. The underside of the figure consisted of a square peg, and behind it were two square slots in the wall. Holding the figure back in front of the image, he could see that when it was slotted into its original spot, the other hole would be obscured by the figure's wing.

Fascinating. Mareq thought back to the bedtime stories he had heard as a child. Fantastical Destueqan heroes who had plumbed the depths of the Dawn Ones's ruins, solving mechanical puzzles and disarming traps in the name of riches and fame. Those had all been fairytales, though. He never thought he would get a chance at something similar in an Alaboqan back alley.

Mareq placed the square peg into the previously hidden slot, orienting the bird so that it flew north along the coast rather than away from it. He heard a soft click as the figure slid into place and watched as the circular image popped away from the wall on a concealed hinge. Flipping the round panel up revealed four lines of strange script etched into another wooden panel behind it.

Mareq did not recognize any of the symbols or characters, nor could he tell if they were meant to be individual words or separate letters. Even the flow of the characters, running parallel up and down the panel rather than side to side, was foreign to him. However, he recalled that Chaevin had said the Ghosts spoke to one another in "weird whispers." If this was the language they spoke, it had to have an internal logic to it.

He picked up a ratty cloth from the ground and plucked a piece of charcoal from The Hobbled Cobbler's extinguished sconce, then rubbed a copy of the etching onto the fabric. Dreams of the open road were now secondary as he began to turn this new puzzle over in his mind.

Chapter 17

Central Kefya

For all her bluster, a part of Rav was coming to regret joining Wymund on this journey, if only to spare her aching tailbone. She had ridden horses in her childhood, riding being one of the few acceptable leisure activities for well-to-do young ladies in Felona. But after several days in the saddle, with the only reprieve a bedroll set up off the trail or, in the best case so far, inside a farmer's barn, she was beginning to wonder how much more of this she could stand. The only thing that had kept her complaints locked behind closed lips was the fact that Annika seemed to be holding up with no issues, and she would be damned if she would let the old woman outlast her own stores of endurance.

Wymund had procured three solid trail horses, one gray, one black, and one a white-speckled fawn. Rav had gravitated toward the latter, naming her Doe. The mare was well trained but if left to her own devices, wouldn't stand still, her hooves in ceaseless motion even while grazing. When her companions noted that Rav and her mount were a fitting pair, she chose to take it as a compliment.

The Tesigan Peaks to the east spared their skin from the sun's wrath for much of the morning as they traveled north, and each day, as the main road leading into Qedrad took them closer to the mountain range, the time spent in the shade grew longer as they traced the lazy current of the Dalecleft River in reverse. Still, nothing could be done as midday approached. The verdant, rolling hills of the Kefyan countryside offered little more than a beautiful view as they were slowly baked from above. Living close to the ocean kept the weather temperate for much of the year, but as Rav pulled her cloak down lower over her face to hide from the rays bearing down on them, she thought she might as well be traveling through the Dune Sea in Ebkarii.

"Hwen will be just over the next rise," Wymund said from the back of his gray horse. The animal was as deliberate and sure-footed as the man riding him, yet no one saw fit to point out *that* similarity. "They should have an inn there, and traders to resupply. We've made good time so far," he said, patting his mount on the side of his neck. "And pushed our friends here for their best efforts. It will cost us some time, but stabling them for the night and giving them proper care should reap rewards later. There's a long road yet to Alaboq."

"Not to mention stabling *us* with proper care," Rav grumbled. When Wymund shot her a quizzical look, she added, "Annika began this journey as a frail old woman. Let's not allow the road to grind her to dust in the saddle so soon."

A few paces to the left, Annika leaned forward in her saddle. "I'm more concerned with how you keep squirming and shifting your weight, girl. You're going to wear a hole in that animal's hide."

Rav sniffed. "We'll get there faster if we don't slow down to chat. Let's go," she said, digging her heels into Doe's side and setting off at a trot. As she reached the top of the hill, she discovered that Wymund had been correct. Just a few miles farther, across a mossy stone bridge spanning an offshoot of the Dalecleft River, was an assortment of single-story wooden buildings and a handful of taller structures organized into a central concourse that marked the city of Hwen. It didn't look like much to her eyes, nestled between two calm mountain streams and with no semblance of a wall or watchtower in sight, but she supposed spending her entire life in Kefya's two largest cities had skewed her perception. For many in Anera, Hwen would be an overwhelming experience.

It was what lay beyond the town that caught Rav's attention. Extending in neat rows over the foothills and as far back as her vision permitted were acres and acres of grains, olive shrubs, and sugar chestnut trees, recognizable by their distinctive red-brown bark. Dark, fenced-in patches interrupted the sea of crops, each patch containing livestock shuffling lazily around their enclosures.

From this distance, Rav couldn't see how far this cultivated land stretched, but it appeared as if the people of Hwen had ploughed the entire expanse between the tributaries and the beginnings of the Tesigan Peaks. In Felona, she had become accustomed to plots of land dedicated to orchards or vineyards, but those had always been more vanity projects of bored aristocrats than actual production farms. Even if a family sold what fruits or wines they produced, the goal would have been prestige rather than financial gain. But production at this scale, for the sole purposes of sustenance and livelihood, was a fact of life she was ashamed to acknowledge she had never considered before. The immensity of it was breathtaking.

"They don't call it Kefya's Bounty for nothing," Annika said, trotting her black mare up beside Doe, each horse attempting to hold its head a little higher than the other. The old woman was smiling at Rav's slack-jawed amazement. "There is more to life than back alleys and rooftops, you know?"

The trio rode on in silence, the activity of the city coming more into focus as they approached. Men and women hefted bushels of oat grain and sacks of ground oats onto long river boats, along with ale kegs, bottles of oil, and salted slabs of pork and beef. At the stern of each flat-bottomed vessel stood a muscular individual, some of which were draqeshi, gripping a long pole that extended into the waters of the Dalecleft below them. The river's current would be sufficient to carry the boats downstream toward Virdoba and on to the Marrow Straight, but these men and women would be handy for steering and dislodging if the need arose. Some of the workers stopped loading to stare at Rav and her group as they neared the stone bridge arching over the piers. Incoming traffic must have been an unusual sight. Virdobans had little to offer these people besides an open purse once their goods arrived.

"While we're here, you should thank the good people who run these farms," Annika said, nodding to the two guards on either side of the bridge as they rode past them. Unlike the Virdoban Guard, these men didn't appear to have an official uniform, wearing instead simple brown leather doublets, and were only recognizable as guards by the shortswords at their waists. They nodded in return, not bothering to stand up from their relaxed postures leaning against the bridge's walls.

"They're the only reason you have ever eaten fresh meat that didn't come from the sea or enjoyed a loaf of bread that wasn't covered in mold," Annika continued. Rav's stomach growled. Their trail rations of flat-bread and dried meat had grown old already, so if the people of Hwen were able to supply her with *anything* more flavorful, she would be grateful indeed.

The dirt road leading from the bridge directed them straight toward the central strip of buildings in the city, each no more than two stories high, while smaller shops and homes spread out behind them on either side of the thoroughfare. The structures were quaint relative to the business districts Rav was used to in Felona and Virdoba, even compared to shops in neighborhoods like the Low Tide and the Patchwork. Those shop owners might have had a lower quality of life than their counterparts here in Hwen, but there were some luxuries, like panes of glass for windows, which were exceedingly rare outside of major cities. Instead, the stores here all had open, shutterless windows proudly displaying their wares, be they fresh baked foods, leather goods, or, most surprisingly, silver jewelry. The crime rate in this town must not have justified the expense of importing glass to protect items from nimble fingers.

However, there was one element of the main street that stood out from its surroundings. Nestled between a bookbinder and a barber shop sat a raised square platform of gold-veined marble, along with a matching set of steps leading up to it. In the center was a square relief of polished black stone that depicted Teacher Leros, fine-featured and confident as always, overseeing a trade auction with hundreds of spectators in attendance. At three corners of the dais stood cone-tipped columns about a meter high, each with a fluted spiral rising to the top. But at the front left corner, the column appeared to have been snapped on a diagonal, leaving only a snubbed remnant in its place. Some damage was to be expected. The Dawn One's ruin had been in this spot long before Hwen was founded, after all.

"It really is as bizarre as they say," Wymund said, eyeing the stage that seemed so alien and timeless among the rustic surroundings. "How could they have shaped this stone without a leaving a single seam, or even brought the material to this spot? I've never seen anything like it."

"This is nothing," Rav replied, stopping Doe next to his mount while Wymund paused to take in the sight. "The Hall of Merchants in Felona was built from another of Teacher Leros's ruins, at least five times this size. The spires climb as high as trees, and there's a raised central dais made of that black rock where the person holding the floor speaks." His eyebrow cocked as she spoke, but his eyes never left the smooth marble. "Sure, some of the seating was already crumbled when it was discovered, but I have to say the sight of that hall took my breath away each time I passed it."

The transfixing hold the platform had on him finally broke, and Wymund grabbed the reins and began to turn back onto the path. "It's good the traders there still have a place to voice their opinions. I know the Dawn Ones were powerful enough fight off dragons, but I'm surprised what remains of their ruin wasn't brought to dust by the Council during the rebellion."

"It wasn't for lack of trying," Annika said as she trotted past, face blank. "Look, there's an inn just up ahead."

Following Annika's finger with her eyes, Rav spotted a painted gold sign that read DAMARA'S BOUNTY, complete with a bushel of oats drawn underneath the name. Two young stable hands, neither one much into their teenage years, waited near the door, mindlessly kicking a rock back and forth until the three riders stopped in front of them. Plastering on beaming smiles, the pair rushed up to help Annika and Rav down from the saddles, a gesture Rav batted away the second it was extended, then offered to bring the animals around to the stables behind the inn for food and water.

"That would be lovely," Annika said. "I assume the cost for stabling our friends is included with our room and board?"

The two shared a quick glance before nodding, their eyes suddenly downcast. "Yes, miss. Ms. Damara is the only innkeeper in Hwen that lets her boarders keep their animals in the stables for nothin' extra."

Smiling, Annika replied, "Good lads. Honesty is usually more lucrative in the long run than flashy salesmanship." She tipped the boys two copper libers apiece, the action lighting their eyes up once more, and walked into the open doorway, Rav and Wymund following close behind.

Inside, a lingering, toasty sweetness filled the air, wafting out of the open kitchen doorway to the right. A handful of voices shouted orders back and forth, everything from a need to whisk faster to taking a pot away from the flame. Directly ahead was a staircase that made a sharp left turn at the first landing before disappearing up into the boarding rooms above, while another open doorway to the left led into a large common room that was impressively full for the middle of the afternoon. There were a couple of elven guards eating a lunch of lamb and potatoes at a table in the corner, also wearing the same leather doublets she had seen on the guards on the bridge, as well as a handful of men sitting at the bar and chatting over mugs of ale. Toward the back, behind a wooden partition that rose to half the height of the room, was a larger table around which sat eight people immersed in a card game, some of who appeared to be in the process of losing a small fortune, judging by their expressions. Two women in low-cut shirts, the drawstrings across their chests loosened to the point of being strictly decorative, sat on a bench against the back wall with their legs crossed as they watched the game of chance.

"Hello there," came a cheery voice from their rear. Rav turned from the threshold of the common room to see a middle-aged woman stepping out of the kitchen with a welcome smile as she wiped the flour from her hands onto her apron. She was soft around the middle and had her dark hair pulled back into a bun, though many strands had come loose and now hung frazzled around her face. "I'm Romi Damara. Are you looking to stay with us tonight?"

"We are," Wymund answered. "And whatever is being prepared in there smells much better than the dry provisions we've had on the road the past few days. We would appreciate a couple of rooms and a warm meal."

"Good, good. We would love to have you." The innkeeper hurried past them and gestured toward an open table in the middle of the common room. "Just rest here for now and we'll get to work making up some rooms for you and fixing your plates. You can settle up with Tarrem whenever you get a moment," she said, motioning to a rotund draqeshi standing behind the bar, little more than his plump face visible over the counter at this distance. The bartender simply nodded at them as Ms.

Damara rushed off, stopping a moment to fuss at him for being a grump to their customers before disappearing back into the hall.

As they settled into their seats, Wymund unbuckling his scabbard belt and Rav removing the sash that covered her ears, a fist slammed down on the table in the back. It was followed by the jostling of coins.

"I'm telling all of you that this pretty-boy bastard is cheating," a man growled, his jaw clenched so tight that Rav thought his bushy mustache was quaking. He was glaring at an elven man sitting across from him, who looked comically out of place among the rest of the workmen at the table. In contrast to their drab and utilitarian attire, this man wore a stylish, slim-cut jacket that had been dyed a deep violet, along with a matching pair of tapered pants running down to black leather boots that likely cost more than his playmates made in a month. But rather than flinch at the man's accusation, the elf didn't budge from his relaxed posture, leaning his chair on its back legs and draping one arm across the top of it.

"And as I've said now countless times, I have never cheated at anything a day in my life. Wouldn't dream of it," he said, the cool smile on his lips doing more to flare tensions than ease them. Most of his blond hair was tied behind his head, but a few wavy strands hung down in front of his peaked ears. "Now if you don't mind, I believe it's your turn to start the betting. Each time I win more of your money, your face turns a new shade of red, and I want to see how many hues are left. I'm using them to decide what color cape I'll buy with my winnings."

The man threw his cards on the table with a roar. "How about I show you what red looks like on your face," he said, leaping up from the table and reaching for a dagger at his side. But the hilt caught the lip of the table, dragging the husky man's belt down with it and leaving him standing bare as the day he was born with his pants around his ankles.

The elf chuckled. "It's going to take much more than that to color my cheeks."

In a mad scramble, the man bent over to grab his pants but slammed his forehead on the table in the process. He slumped to his knees, unconscious, with his head resting where it hit.

"Wilman!" another man at the table shouted, while another threw his own cards down and pointed at the elf. "You goaded him into that, dagger-head!"

Not far enough out of Virdoba to escape the slurs, then, Rav thought, though she left her ears uncovered. If the elven guards in the corner, who were looking on with more amusement than concern, felt comfortable here, then so would she.

"Gentlemen," the elf said, unfazed as he spun out of the chair to stand behind it, somehow maintaining its tilt throughout the flourish. "There's no need for name-calling. I thought we were having a friendly game."

The two men who had spoken each stood from the table, the first rushing to check on Wilman. On his way to care for his unconscious friend, he tripped on the table leg and landed hard on his knee with a thud that made Rav wince. The other stalked toward the elf, still standing casually behind his chair as the man approached.

"Friends don't cheat at cards, little man."

Being an elf, he maintained a slight height advantage over the hulking craftsman walking toward him, but he was a wisp of a thing compared to the muscular form of a day laborer. Still, he remained unperturbed even as a calloused fist was launched at his delicate face. At the last second the elf took a step back, making the punch come up short and causing the man to stumble and slide his hand along the table for support.

Cloth napkins and playing cards fluttered to the floor as he regained his composure and went for another swing. However, the elf sidestepped again while keeping one hand on the balanced chair. In a rage, the larger man planted his feet to leap forward in a tackle but found himself falling flat on the floor as the cards slid under his weight. His nose crunched against the boards just as the elf lifted his hand from the chair, allowing it to topple onto the man bleeding on the ground.

"All right, that's enough of all that," said one of the guards, standing and wiping sauce from his mouth onto his sleeve. "Get out of here before we have to lock you up for the night."

Grumbling, the rest of the men at the table stood to leave, scraping their chairs against the floorboards in a huff. Two of them grabbed

Wilman's unconscious form and hefted him out of the room while the others served as crutches for the two injured men, allowing them to hobble out with what shreds of their dignity remained. But the elf remained where he was, dragging his arms across the table to collect the small fortune that had accumulated there. Pulling a white handkerchief from his pocket, he began to neatly bundle up the pile of coins, all the while humming a cheerful melody.

"Oy," shouted the other guard. "That means you too, blondie."

"Oh, Mr. Adii is all right to stay," Ms. Damara said as she hustled into the room, carrying three platters of food. "He means well. Some people just can't lose a bet with any grace." She smiled at him, the elf flashing a dazzling one in return.

Rav could see his eyes for the first time now, the rings around his irises the same brilliant violet as his attire, and found that she was immediately annoyed at his poshness.

The guards looked at each other and shrugged. "It's your place, miss. We're not eager to make more work for ourselves if you don't want it." They each took one last bite of their meals, then marched out of the room, tipping their heads to the innkeeper on the way out.

Ms. Damara finished her walk over with their food, setting down a cut of lamb with steamed potatoes in front of each of them. The meal was topped with a yellow cream sauce that smelled faintly of citrus, along with a dusting of crushed sugar chestnuts. Rav's mouth began to water as soon as the plates hit the table.

"I promise we don't have outbursts like that too often around here," Ms. Damara said. "Please, enjoy the food, and I'll get Tarrem to wipe up that blood before it turns your stomachs."

Annika waved away her concern. "Don't worry about us. I can assure you our sensibilities are not so delicate that a little fighting will ruin this delicious meal."

The innkeeper smiled broadly and bowed her thanks, rushing back over to the barman and pointing back at the mess. The round-faced draqeshi grunted a response but flung a cloth over his shoulder before trudging toward his task.

As Rav glanced back, she could see that the elf was handing the makeshift pouch of coins to the two women at the back of the room, one boot propped up on their bench as he leaned forward to whisper to them. Whatever he was saying had them giggling like little girls, and Rav rolled her eyes. But before she could turn her full attention to the food in front of her, the elven man caught her gaze. She forced a grin that she knew would not be passably authentic and dug her fork into her potatoes.

Her nose had been right; there was a lemony element to the sauce that reminded her of the cuisine back home in Felona. For all her mother's faults, Rav had to credit the woman for her skills in the kitchen. They had always employed a few people as kitchen staff to live in their home and keep them fed, but Rav and her mother had spent some evenings together preparing meals just for the shared experience. Before she could be lost to nostalgia, though, her eyes opened to see the elf striding toward them, beaming like a man who had every confidence that he could sell water to a drowning man.

"Well, I do hope that little display didn't spoil your appetites," he said, arms spread wide as if he were welcoming them into his home. "It would be a shame for you to miss out on sweet Romi's cooking." He paused, eyes sparkling as he took them in. "Though you all look like a worldly bunch, so I don't expect that to be an issue. The name's Kymil Adii, storyteller, philosopher, and gentleman wanderer."

"Where does tavern brawler rank among your occupations?" Wymund asked, sharing a look of exasperation across the table with Rav. It was good to know she wasn't the only one irritated by this pretense.

Kymil clutched his hand to his chest in mock dismay. "You have me all wrong. I wasn't involved in that scuffle." Taking an uninvited seat next to Wymund, he winked and added, "I simply avoided it until they gave up."

"Yeah, and I've never lifted valuables off anyone," Rav said. "I just happen to find what they lose *before* they lose it." Kymil laughed despite her tone, and she clenched her jaw. "If you don't mind, we have an early morning and a long road ahead of us. Why don't you go enjoy what you paid for before someone else demands their attention?" she said, gesturing toward the women on the bench.

The elf half turned and pointed back at them. "You mean those fine ladies? No, no. I don't pay in coin for what I can earn through charm and wit. My esteemed tablemates had run up quite a tab with them though, so I made sure they paid their debts."

"Be that as it may," Annika said, amused curiosity painted across her face, which only served to heighten Rav's annoyance. "My companion is correct. While I don't mind the conversation, we really do need to get some rest this evening."

"I bet you do," Kymil said, leaning his his elbows on the table and resting his chin on interlocked fingers. "In my travels, I don't often see an eclectic grouping like this unless there's an interesting tale driving them." His eyes passed over each of them once again, and he grinned like a fool as he appraised them. "A strapping, stoic soldier type, a wise woman finally making the adventurous choices she never took, and a half-blood scion playing at mischief. What could have brought this crew together?"

"Your intuition could use some work," Rav said. "We're just a family making one last trip to see our dear ill cousin in Qedrad. It's a personal tragedy for us, but not a tale that your audiences would find captivating, I'm afraid."

"Oh my," Kymil said, smile widening from ear to ear. "You three really are up to something. That settles it." He rapped his knuckles on the table twice and stood. "Rest up tonight and I'll meet you down here in the morning. I have a feeling that wherever your road leads, I'll end up with quite the story to add to my repertoire." With another wink, he turned and strode from the room, resuming his joyful hum.

Rav huffed and made to follow him from the room, but Wymund caught her arm. "It's not worth making a scene, Ravael. We'll just wake before sunup and leave before he has a chance to follow." Sighing, she settled back into her seat and returned to her meal.

The three ate until their stomachs protested another bite, having been unable to turn away Ms. Damara's offer of another helping. They settled their tab with Tarrem, who despite his aloofness managed to persuade Rav and Wymund to try his own house-brewed Hwen ale, which turned out to be the source of the sweet, toasty aroma filling the inn. It seemed that fermenting the drink from fresh oats made for a significant improvement over the swill they served in Virdoba.

Finally, as the sun began to set and the sounds of the town outside began to quiet, they retreated upstairs to their rooms for the night. Rav hated how much she had missed the simple comforts of a mattress and pillow over the last few days, but not so much that it kept her awake.

What did trouble her mind as she slept were dreams of the scorcher setting homes ablaze as he cut his path north to Alaboq. He may not be the man responsible for carving her father out of her life so soon—he was far too young for that—but he was a member of that murderous crew just the same. The law in Felona had failed to quash the Clipped Gulls after all these years, but she wouldn't fail where they had. She was used to finding ways around the law's shortcomings.

When Wymund's soft knocks came to wake her, she was already dressed and ready for the road, eager to depart without adding a parasitic bard to their party. As they gathered at the top of the stairs, Rav held up her hand and motioned that she would creep down to check the common room before her less surreptitious allies hazarded the steps. She gingerly lowered herself down step by step, shifting her weight with precision and repositioning her foot at the first hint of give in the wood. But at the last step, as soon as the tip of her boot tapped the surface, a sudden creak ruptured the tense silence of the early morning.

"Oh good," Kymil said, suddenly appearing at the doorway to the common room, smug grin in place as if it had never left. "You're already up and ready to set out. I do appreciate a trot through the crisp morning air." He made for the front door, adding, "I'll have the lads bring the horses around front. This is going to be fun!"

Rav hung her head, speechless at the bottom of the stairs, mind swirling with embarrassment and anger. A hand on her shoulder revealed that Annika and Wymund had descended behind her without a sound, only adding to her disappointment. "I'll go have a word with him," Wymund said. "We'll see if he understands the word 'no' more easily in the morning than he does in the afternoon."

"Let him come," Annika said with a small smile. "If nothing else, he'll be a distraction from the monotony of the road." She gave each of them a small push toward the door. "But entertainers have their uses. It may be easier to gain an audience with King Berenqar in his company than on the request of a Virdoban guard far outside his jurisdiction."

Wymund tilted his head in thought for a moment before finally shrugging and walking toward the door. Rav, still fuming at her own failure, looked to Annika and said, "Fine. But if he starts singing road songs, I can't guarantee his safety."

Chapter 18

Alaboq

Shadowmaw. That was what Chaevin called the strange symbols in the charcoal rubbing. He guessed it was the language used by followers of Teacher Ias, a fact that Mareq knew would be trouble. As the Dawn One who embodied the notion of deception, her script would likely have a hidden meaning or a concealed code beyond the basic translation. But Mareq liked puzzles; he normally would be content to pluck away at deciphering the writing at his own pace. Now, though, he didn't have the luxury of time. He needed proof to bring to King Berenqar of whatever plot was occurring under his nose *before* the scheme was complete if Mareq expected any type of reward. And he held little hope that one of Ias's secretive Ghosts would be willing to provide a cipher.

Mareq placed his head in his hands and rubbed his eyes. He could still see the four parallel lines swimming behind his eyelids, as if they had imprinted themselves in his vision during the hours he had spent studying the charcoal rubbing. Mrs. Luviire had graciously offered the use of her desk, which was built for one of elven height and required Mareq to sit on an iron pot to use, but it still provided some seclusion, as it was tucked away in a back corner. He sat in the kitchens of Vinsart Hold for hours each day, desperate to pick out a pattern in the Ghosts' appearances while he worked on uncovering the secrets in their writings.

Though the visitors continued to be difficult to predict, he believed Sylicera Hadac's anxiety was beginning to tip their hand. Mareq had noticed that on the days the Ghosts showed up to the citadel, the trade minister would take to pacing around the kitchens, scowling more than was usual. *Now I can guess when I have an opening to return to that alley*, Mareq thought as he looked back down at the obscure writing. *If only I could just figure out what this says, maybe I would know what to do when I get there.*

"There are easier ways to get funds for travel," Mrs. Luviire said as she walked up behind him and placed a hand on his shoulder. "I'm sure you can find other buyers for your produce if we spread the word that Mareq Iq'Urlset is King Berenqar's royal supplier of fruit."

Mareq laughed. "The amount of cinder plums and frostdew Berries I would need to sell just to make it to the next town over would keep me here for at least the rest of the year. And I mean no offense, Alaboq is an amazing city with enjoyable company, but I didn't set out from Brey just to get stuck in the first place I landed."

"I can understand that," she replied. "Just remember that wanderlust only culminates in endless stretches of boring roads if you don't pause to enjoy the destinations along the way." Leaning down over his shoulder, she squinted at the charcoal rubbing on the desk. "Have you been able to make any sense of these scribbles yet?"

"I'm afraid I would have better luck understanding drunken mumblings in another language," he said. "I've just never seen any form of writing structured vertically, and these characters have no similarities to the ones we use." Mareq sighed. "You may as well put me to use here in the kitchens for all the good I've accomplished trying to decipher this."

Pushing the rag away from him on the table, he reached over to a utensil rack affixed to the wall and grasped one of the ladles hanging from it. "Someone else needs to organize these, for example. There's no sense of order to the tools hanging from these pegs. Ladles are next to knives, then there are just open gaps and suddenly a handful of wooden spoons. It's as chaotic as the writing, but it's a chaos I can control."

Mrs. Luviire chuckled and grabbed his forearm. "You take your life into your hands if you fool around with Ptolon's utensils. There's a pattern to them, inscrutable as it may be, but it's something to do with Ebkarish tradition of using the same tool for certain dishes and not others. I've seen him hurl a fork at Waemish for 'daring to bring a cream sauce spoon to stir a fish sauce.'"

As he stared at the rack once more, he agreed the organization was impenetrable to a person not well versed in Ebkarish meal preparation. However, it must have had something to do with the number of empty pegs between utensils, possibly a mnemonic device to remember which tool was for which dish. At another time, he would likely enjoy picking Ptolon's brain about how the structure worked, but now it was just another puzzle with a solution that eluded him.

"I should definitely rearrange these then," he said dryly. "Perhaps if he hits me in the head with an iron pan, I'll be struck with the inspiration to make sense of this flowing script . . . "

As his gaze returned to the cloth, he noticed for the first time a detail that would have been obvious if the text were written in a language he knew. Like the gaps in the utensil rack, segments of characters were missing in the three shorter lines of script, as if the tool used to etch the words onto the alley wall had been deliberately lifted away before starting a new line. However, Mareq could now see those three lines appeared to be the same sequence of characters with arbitrary gaps in the lines forming them, to a degree that the missing chunks gave the impression of different letters entirely. But what if the line breaks were not random? And if these were in fact the same sequence of characters, then another quirk became appreciable in the script. The base stem of the initial character in each line was unique: the first extended straight down, the second curved right, and the third curved left.

"What is it?" Mrs. Luviire asked.

"I believed these to be unique characters, but these last three lines of text appear to be repetitions of the same sequence of letters. There are small portions missing here and there to make the characters appear different, but look," he said, pointing out the similarities. "It's the same word or sentence repeated three times. What would be the point in that?"

"That would be wasted effort," Mrs. Luviire said. "Unless the point *was* the small differences between them."

"Of course," Mareq said, standing as the epiphany overwhelmed him. "They made the lines of text look different enough to lead wandering eyes down the wrong path, when really it's the slight differences that matter!" He looked up at the matronly elf, her face as bright as his felt as they found themselves wrapped up in the excitement of discovery. "We may have found the hidden code within the message. Any ideas on how to crack it?"

"I'm afraid not, Mareq." She laughed. "The closest things to puzzles I've worked on over the last few decades are directions for centuries-old recipes that use different measurements than we use today. I don't think that will be of much use to you here."

But he hadn't heard another word beyond "directions" as his mind began connecting the dots, thoughts coming to him faster than he could speak aloud. "It's a map," he said breathlessly. Growing up near the Draeq Sea with all its fabled seafaring adventurers, he had listened to many tales of piracy and buried treasures in his childhood. Finding himself in the middle of one of these stories now was exactly the thrill he had been searching for when he left home. He just hoped it would be an adventure with a happy ending.

"A classic treasure map," he continued. "The way the stem of the first character curves indicates a direction to walk, and the number of missing gaps in each character could indicate the number of steps to take with that heading."

"Maybe," she said, a note of caution in her voice. "But it could just as easily be the number of miles in a certain direction, or even minutes. You're leaping to more than a few conclusions."

Mareq took a breath, but his smile never left his face. "You're right, of course. But there's only one way to find out. The next time a Ghost shows up, I'm going to try and race back to that alley and see what I can dig up."

Mrs. Luviire frowned. "Just be careful. I know Teacher Ias doesn't promote violence like Edis or even Dynnir, but I have to imagine these Ghosts would not like their secrets being exposed."

"Oh, don't worry about me," he said, patting his arm. "My people are made of sterner stuff than most. But thank you, your wisdom has been indispensable." Mareq began to gather his things from the desk, his mind still churning over the potential secrets he might uncover in the alley. "May the sea breeze speed your story, Mrs. Luviire," he added, remembering the offering of thanks that the old woman in the Warren had extended to him.

When only silence followed, he looked back up to find the woman staring at him with a furrowed brow. "What did you say?"

"Is that not Alaboqan saying for expressing gratitude? A woman said it to me recently after I helped her with her door."

"No," she said, pointing back to the stairwell leading up into the citadel proper. "The only time I've heard that phrase is from the top of those stairs, when Hadac finishes a meeting with one of her hooded friends."

Mareq could feel the color drain from his face as his heart skipped a beat. He remembered the grinning wink he had mistaken as a friendly gesture, but now he could only see as a taunt. *The old woman was in on it*, he thought as he shoved the charcoal rubbing back into his pouch and began to head for the exit. "I'll be back tomorrow, Mrs. Luviire," he said. "Hopefully with more answers than questions."

The haphazard paths of the Thistle Hare Warren were as busy as usual, but without the need to keep pace with a figure accustomed to losing themselves in a crowd, Mareq had an easier time picking his way through the throngs of people. That didn't prevent this journey from feeling any less harried, though, as he spent the walk punishing himself for his failure to see what was right in front of him. *How could I be so naïve? That old woman was spryer than I am after I dislodged her door, and I didn't think that was odd?*

The twists and turns through the maze of a neighborhood were marked in his mental map from his last race through the streets, and before long, he found himself standing in front of the door he had forced open only a few days ago. It looked the same as it had before, the oak swollen and warped near the bottom, but somehow it seemed more artificial now; even staged. There was not much wearing at the edges, or even signs of exposure to the elements over the years. Whether it was from something as simple as the weather or from thousands of pedestrians squeezing and scraping by, a door that was supposed to be a longtime inconvenience for that old woman would surely be showing signs of age by this point. But now as he stood before it, less distracted by losing sight of his quarry, Mareq thought the door looked relatively new.

He reached out to grab the handle and pulled back hard, expecting to meet some resistance when the door caught on the threshold. But instead, the door swung open fast, nearly catching him in the face. Surprised, he looked down to see that just inside the lip of the threshold was another thin strip of wood folded back on a hinge. He flipped it forward with his boot and groaned as it laid flat on the door's actual threshold, adding less than half an inch of height, which was enough to impede its process as it swung open. If that hadn't been enough to validate his fears, though, the rest of the room sufficed. The single-room apartment was completely empty. No seating, no bedding, not one morsel of food. The woman had been a sentry, and this was her post.

Dread wound up from his stomach as he closed the door and moved back into the bustling street. The warnings from Mrs. Luviire and even the suggestion of caution from Tiialya swam through his mind. If his friend had been freelancing for them during her time in Alaboq, the Ghosts could not be too dangerous. Tiialya was a good person. Fiery for sure, but she would never want to take a job that would harm someone else. But there was a nagging itch at the back of his mind, a feeling of disquiet he couldn't shake. Now they certainly knew he was watching them.

Chapter 19

Northern Kefya

As the main road along the western coast of Anera wound ever closer to the Tesigan Peaks, the party left behind the gentle rolling hills that made up much of Kefya's landscape and progressed into the hardened and rocky paths nearer to the Qedradan border, the Dalecleft River and its nourishment now a distant memory. The gradual slopes of waving, verdant grasses gave way to a sparser shrubland, with smaller bushes and clusters of wildflowers dotting the gray-brown ridges to either side of the trails. Cliff faces grew higher to their left and right as they moved farther north, looming over them and casting an impending shadow over their journey.

Wymund felt as if he were being funneled, and in a sense he was. Following the War of Arrival, when the dividing lines were drawn to allow Kefyans their own independent nation, the Qedradan king had insisted on the border crossing through this narrow valley, such that unchecked international travel would be hindered by the mountains to the east and the treacherous limestone bluffs to the west. While tensions between the neighboring lands had cooled over the last two and a half centuries, the decision was a stroke of genius at the time. An alliance between rebellious former subjects and strange new beings with pointed ears from across the ocean, some of who possessed the ability to summon powerful forces into existence, must have been a terrifying prospect for the people of Qedrad.

A gray stone archway grew steadily in the distance as they were led down the path, a man-made structure spanning the gap a quarter mile ahead of them. Even from this distance, Wymund could see that a cart was stopped at the checkpoint, its driver unfurling a tarp from across the back to reveal bolts of multicolored cloth. Given the more muted hues on display, he assumed the driver was likely an Achen trademaster looking to peddle their wares up north. Qedrad was known for its bright, eye-catching fabrics, so while there would be fewer clients interested in more subdued silks, they would certainly be willing to pay a higher price for the rarity.

Two Qedradan King's Guards poked and prodded the merchant's wares, their telltale padded crimson tunics visible under gleaming breastplates, while another spoke with the driver off to the side of the path. The Kefyan Council had never felt it necessary to man the border crossing, as there had never been any acts of aggression from the north since the treaty was signed. More importantly, though, staffing this post would require dipping further into the Council's coffers, and most were reluctant to do that for a job that felt more than a little symbolic. But from what Wymund understood, that symbolism had remained important over the years to the King's Guard, with the few soldiers stationed there seeing it as a badge of honor. However, he failed to see how it could be anything more than a tedious vanity position.

"Why are they stopping people?" Rav asked from the back of her fawn-colored mare. She had become better adjusted to riding over long stretches of road since their stay in Hwen, though a part of him thought Rav might have been putting on a stiff upper lip in front of their new travel companion. As much as Wymund had been put off by Kymil's presence, Rav had been more caustic than usual for days. If it wasn't for Annika's insistence that the bard could be useful, he didn't know if Rav would have made it this far without snapping his head off, figuratively or otherwise. Though he had to wonder if Annika only wanted Kymil along for the company. The pair had been chatty since the morning they had set out from the inn.

"Not much of a traveler, I'm guessing?" Kymil asked, sitting astride his flaxen chestnut mount, the animal's mane impressively matching that of its rider's. "The King's Guard like to stick their noses in the business of anyone looking to enter or leave their domain. It's rather arrogant, if you ask me."

Rav snorted, but the man continued unabated. "The border is supposed to be open, after all. But with the nearest town still half a day's ride to the north, and a city with a guard captain even farther still, who's going to argue with them?" Putting on a dramatic affectation, he added, "In this valley, these three are the absolute law!"

Wymund reached into the saddlebag hanging from Resin's side. He had told the others that his horse's name was a reference to the support he offered them, bolstering their endurance as they traveled, which was mostly true. He didn't feel the need to add that it was his father who had always stressed the substance's importance in preserving their oil paintings; his lost dream was a heartache he would rather keep to himself. After a few seconds of fishing around, he finally retrieved his teal coat and donned it.

"We tend to recognize our own kind," Wymund said. "Hopefully they will let us pass without much delay."

Kymil began tuning his lute, a task that Wymund had to admit still managed to produce a melodic lilt, as if the man could turn even the most monotonous chore into a performance. "Ah yes. The noble fraternity of guardsmen. Known throughout the lands as paragons of virtue and moral judgment, with the dark taint of corruption or the sultry temptress named 'Authority' never once deigning to fall upon their ilk."

Annika tittered from behind them and Wymund felt his face flush. "Your point is taken, Mr. Adii. I know all too well the types of men who can be attracted to this occupation, hoping to use it as a shield for themselves rather than others. But most of the men and women who stand by my side I'm proud to call my brothers and sisters, and I have to believe this would be true of those who answer the call to serve elsewhere."

The elf played a series of chords that called to mind tales of triumph, then took a bow. "And that is why I am leaning toward you, Corporal Sylnorin, as the hero of this journey. That certitude and strength of character are what the masses yearn for to give meaning to their repetitive daily lives!"

Wymund sighed. "This is not an epic tale for the ages, bard. Though I suppose when you carry an instrument like that, every trek looks like a grand adventure."

"Yes! A reluctant hero. All the more irresistible." Kymil sidled between Wymund and Rav, forcing her to shift left to accommodate him. He placed a hand to the side of his mouth and leaned toward Wymund, then spoke in a stage whisper. "We certainly can't have her as a protagonist. She's far too unlikable."

"You've only met my pleasant side so far, songman," Rav said. "And you're wrong besides. The people love a roguish scoundrel to root for."

Up ahead, the silk merchant's cart was beginning to trundle away over the rough earth. One of the King's Guard, a sandy-haired woman and the only one of the three wearing pauldrons, draped a length of taupe cloth around her neck and tied it off like a kerchief. She beamed like a child at their first festival as she held the material between her fingers, only breaking her attention when she was nudged by her comrade to take note of the approaching travelers.

The last guard moved into the center of the path and held one hand up, leaving the other resting on the pommel of the shortsword at his side. Wymund felt the weight of their stares as the four slowed their horses to a stop several yards away from the stone arch. Each of the guards bore a welcoming grin that was just shy of neighborly hospitality. Wymund slid down from Resin's saddle and straightened the cuffs on his coat, hoping to appeal to their sense of professional courtesy. He didn't know if he could handle it if the border guards were taking advantage of travelers. The bard's head might swell until it popped from sheer arrogance.

"Wait right there," the nearest guard said, lowering his hand and striding toward them. "By order of King Berenqar, the People's King and just ruler of Vinsart Hold, all visitors from Kefya must have on their person an official travel grant signed by a member of the Kefyan Council in Felona stating their business in the great nation of Qedrad." The man finished his practiced spiel and crossed his broad arms over his breastplate. His two companions watched smugly from behind without a word. "If such a document cannot be provided, *collateral* may be offered as a measure of good faith for our consideration."

The man's speech was all bluster. Kymil had been correct. The three of them were using their distance from higher authorities to take advantage of travelers who didn't know the migratory laws as dictated by the treaty between the nations. *I won't let him have this*, he thought, though a part of him wondered whether, if he managed to talk the guards down, it would only grow his own legend for the bard's tales. His jaw clenched, the sounds of Kymil's songs already echoing around his mind, but he shook his head and cleared all that away. There would be time later to convince the elf that he wasn't a new folkloric hero.

"Good afternoon, guardsman. My name is Corporal Wymund Sylnorin of the Virdoban City Guard, and these are my companions," he said while gesturing behind him. "Our mission is one of great urgency, and unfortunately we were not able to obtain this pass from the Council prior to our departure. However, I'm sure you understand the need for such measures to be taken when countless lives may hang in the balance." Wymund placed a fist over his chest and added, "Our oaths may be to different authorities, but they are not to different ideals. The protection of those we serve must come before all else."

The man turned his head slightly to look at the two behind him, taking no pains to hide his amusement. His ranking officer strode forward to join them, the harsh angles of her pauldrons jutting up under her silk scarf.

"We're familiar with the call to serve, Corporal," she said. "Regrettably, our hands are bound by those same ideals. We are responsible for the safety of King Berenqar's subjects, and it is his wisdom that entreats us to watch this post for any who may threaten his land or his people. I'm afraid without a writ from your Council or the king, you and your comrades are a little outside of your jurisdiction."

She reached up and brushed some road dust from Wymund's shoulder. "But we aren't inflexible. As you said, at times the demands of the mission must come before the requirements of the law. If you could leave us with something of yours, something of *value* that you'll need to come back for, we could be willing to grant temporary passage."

Wymund adjusted his coat after the unwelcome ruffling, taking a deep breath. The tension in his body grew with each second they were delayed, knowing that the scorcher was growing closer and closer to

Alaboq. "I assure you that King Berenqar will be happy to provide us with such a document upon our arrival to Vinsart Hold, and you may inspect it upon our return."

The three guards laughed, the one in the back doubling over and holding his sides. "And I'm having tea with the Dual Monarchs in Qravburn next month," the officer said between bouts of laughter. "We'll be discussing how sweaty my ass gets under this steel shell. The ruling class does so love to meet with foreign soldiers and hear about our struggles."

Grinding his teeth, Wymund searched his head for a solution but came up empty. If he explained who they were chasing and what they hoped to prevent, he would sound like nothing more than a lunatic shouting nonsense from the gutter. But the only alternative they allowed was bribery, a thought that made his stomach turn and his belt tighten. His reluctant hand dipped down to the coin purse inside his coat, which was already feeling lighter than he liked. He didn't want to rely on Annika's funds for room and board on this journey, but after this shakedown, they would have little choice. At least if he was the one who offered to pay, their extorters wouldn't be able to see the heft of the woman's purse compared to his own.

Flipping the front of his coat aside, he hung his head as he began to pull his pouch free. But he paused as he heard the crunch of boots settling onto the dirt path behind him. "What is causing this delay, Corporal? Haven't you told them about the order?" Wymund turned to see Kymil striding toward them, chin high and flashing that disarming grin. "We really must be on our way if we expect to catch up to this ruffian."

"What's this about an order?" the officer asked, recovering from her fit of laughter. She combed her hair neatly to the side with a gloved hand as she took in the bard, and Wymund thought he saw some color rush to her cheeks. Her voice suddenly increased in pitch as she spoke to him. "Your hired muscle here said you all had to leave in such a hurry that there was no documentation."

Kymil winked at the guard. "You know how it is, dear. When you're in a position of leadership like us, sometimes it's necessary to keep the information need-to-know." The elf reached up and rapped Wymund lightly on the side of his head. "Too much going on can addle their brains, as I'm sure you're aware."

Wymund shot a sideways look at him but held his tongue.

"I'm afraid this has all been my fault, though," Kymil said, reaching into his violet jacket and pulling out a folded parchment. "I should've made a note to repeat myself when I informed the good corporal about our documents. At times he gets lost, worrying over our security concerns."

All three of the guards chuckled at that, each hanging on Kymil's every word. "But here is our Order of Bounty, signed by Felonian Guard Captain Prandon himself. I do apologize if the script is a little difficult to read. You know how these council members are; one of them gets a scribe from Choii Stier and then they all have to have one."

The officer took the parchment from Kymil and studied it, squinting her eyes as her compatriots did the same over her shoulders. Finally, she folded it again and handed it back to him. "Everything seems to be in order. Next time remember to have your representatives carry the required documentation and we won't have to hold you up."

"Of course," Kymil said, allowing his hand to linger on hers before accepting the document. "But at least this unfortunate happenstance allowed us to have the most delightful introduction."

Her face turned a sharper shade of red. "Perhaps I can escort the four of you into town? If this criminal is as dangerous as you imply, I would be honored to provide added protection." Her eyes flickered down to her feet for a moment before adding, "And I do know of a wonderful inn there that should have rooms for the night."

"Oh, I couldn't possibly pull you from your duty like that," he replied. "But you know where to find me tonight if you have someone coming to relieve you."

The woman smiled wide and nodded, ushering the other two guards out of the path as Kymil and Wymund mounted their horses once again. They rode through the archway in silence, and several miles passed before the ridges lining the road began to shrink and reveal the scrubland of the Qedradan plains. In the distance, the small city of Neumane Ridge was just coming into view, no more than a dark speck on the horizon that Wymund hoped they would reach before nightfall.

"What did you show them?" Annika asked, nearly bouncing in her saddle. Wymund guessed the need for her curiosity to be sated had been close to boiling over until they were sufficiently out of earshot. "Or was that just an exercise in pure charisma?"

Kymil laughed. "Charm is never an exercise, dear. It comes as natural to me as the breath in my lungs."

"Or the vomit in my throat," Rav muttered to Wymund.

The elf pulled the parchment from his coat once again and passed it back to Annika, who took one glance at it and let out a deep belly laugh. "You could talk an Acolyte out of her skirts, couldn't you?"

"The real challenge would be a High Scholar," he said with a smirk. "Acolytes are still curious about the experiences the world has to offer, and I've been known to oblige their interests from time to time."

"Let me see that," Wymund said. Annika passed the document over to him and as he looked at it, he was only filled with more questions. "This is in Liiashan. There's no way any of those guards could read this."

"Not only that, but it's also just a performance contract for a stage show I put on at a small theater in Oys Allenar. Most people in Anera think that everyone in Felona speaks my native tongue, though. All the settlers in Choii Stier who decided to move south to the warmer island *must* have taught them the language of their homeland, right?" Kymil shrugged. "Playing into a person's misconceptions with a dazzling smile usually gets you where you need to go. But it was a nice try appealing to their sense of honor, Corporal."

For the first time, the bard managed to make Wymund grin. He had to admit there were certain advantages to having such a smooth talker around. At least, once one got past the intensity of the man's ego.

Rav glanced over at him and scoffed. "Ugh, not you too."

Chapter 20

Southern Qedrad

"Your words sound like the ramblings of a diseased mind, old woman," Rav said, cinching her saddlebag tightly at Doe's side.

Wymund was still inside the Dancing Lily, settling their tab from the night before while the rest had stepped out front to ready their horses. Kymil's priority was brushing the knots from his mount's golden mane before making any practical preparations, but Annika was more frustrated with the stubborn girl who she felt compelled to protect.

Maybe I'm becoming senile if I still feel such responsibility for a brat like you, Annika thought, taking a deep breath before replying. In all their days together, she had learned her inclination toward acerbic wit only fueled Rav's fire for obstinance. Patience and a light touch would be warranted if she expected the girl to learn anything.

"I understand that discussing World Shroud theory can bend the mind beyond its typical bounds, and it's difficult to grasp," Annika said. "I'm not even sure the ones who consider themselves experts on the topic truly comprehend how it all works, but that doesn't mean that what little they do know is incorrect. Please have some caution before you toss aside generations of study."

Wymund finally joined them on the street, his teal coat having been returned to his satchel after garnering too many stares when they arrived in town. Neumane Ridge had turned out to be a modest village, smaller even than Hwen and without the impressive expanse of farmland to pad its size, and consequently it had no standing outfit of guardsmen. Annika guessed the city had a reeve and a cadre of volunteer deputies to handle local disputes, but they had seen no law enforcement presence to speak of since their arrival.

In fact, they hadn't seen many people at all, with most of the population seemingly content with spending quiet nights in their small homes rather than carousing at an inn. Although Annika shared in proclivity, she couldn't shake a feeling of unease with the city's stillness. Felona was a dense city with tens of thousands living and working in close proximity, and Virdoba, at half the size, was still a metropolis by most standards. Even Hwen had a bustling river trade that gave the place a sense of vitality. But after a lifetime spent around the sights and sounds of so many people going about their daily lives, she found this sleepy town unnerving. As much as she dreaded getting closer to their target, the call of a capital city like Alaboq urged her onward.

"So you're saying these pockets of energy—"

"Wellsprings," Annika corrected.

"Sure, Wellsprings," Rav said as she hoisted herself onto Doe's saddle. "These Wellsprings are behind the World Shroud, and that's where people who have a connection draw their power from? How does anyone know the energy doesn't just come from the veil itself?"

"What purpose would a cloak serve if it wasn't separating one thing from another?" Kymil interjected. "While it's not my favorite of their qualities, as I much prefer the way they look crumpled on the floor, *separation* is more or less the fundamental property of a shroud."

Rav frowned, turning over Kymil's common-sensical logic in her mind. "I suppose that is a solid point. But then where does the energy come from? And is there anything beyond the Wellsprings? What abou—"

Annika waved her hand and laughed. "Take a breath. It's easy to lose yourself in questioning the nature of the World Shroud. If you're really interested in the answers to those questions, I suggest you find work at a university after we settle our business. You can spend your remaining years delving into dusty tomes rather than diving across rooftops."

"I think I'll leave those questions to people better suited to sitting still," Rav said, shaking her head. "We can pick the lessons up another time. I will need to hear more about this Illuminated Death you mentioned before." She dug her heels into Doe's sides, spurring the animal forward to join Wymund as he mounted Resin. "However, Wymund believes his investigative skills translate to tracking. If I leave him to lead the way, I'm certain we'll end up back in Kefya by nightfall."

Annika watched as the pair began to bicker about the route and duration of that day's journey before she and Kymil fell in behind them. The four rode back in the direction from which they had entered the city, as it was the only path in or out of Neumane Ridge, situated as it was at the top of a gray butte overlooking the expansive grasslands of Qedrad to the north. Now morning, Annika noted that more people were out and about, though no one appeared to be moving faster than a casual stroll. Bakers were opening their shops for the day, but unlike the bakeries back home, there were no lines ready to snatch up the first batches of bread. Nor did she see any messengers darting through the streets, carrying orders or payments to and from the handful of clothiers or smiths who were also opening their doors. This was certainly a different pace of life than Annika was accustomed to, and she was ready to be on her way.

"So the girl is a lightblood?" Kymil asked, snapping Annika out of her musings. She looked over at him to discover a sly smirk had crept onto the elf's face.

"How do you mean?" she asked.

"Well, I see no reason why you would've brought the Illuminated Death to her attention, other than as a word of caution." For the first time in the days since they had met, Kymil was keeping his voice low. "The real question I have is why a human has taken such an interest in the World Shroud." He leaned closer to her, making his voice lower still. "Is this the beginning of a new family drama unfolding before me? You, Rav's long-lost mother returning to make up for a stormforger father who failed to pass on the training necessary to protect her from self-harm?"

Annika suppressed a laugh, not wanting to draw Rav's attention. She could only take so much of her grumbling at the bard in one day, and the sun was only just rising. "I assure you, I'm not the girl's mother. Though I suspect I remind Rav of her, which unfortunately has resulted in more bullheadedness between us than there would be otherwise." Considering for a moment how much to reveal to this relative stranger, she decided a little trust could lead to some answers on theories she had held since that evening in Hwen.

"As for your question, my sister Alauvar was a witch. Our parents insisted we study together, so I picked up a thing or two. I believe they hoped my natural aptitude would make her want to compete with me." She smiled wistfully. "They always underestimated her uncanny ability to avoid hard work, though."

"A woman after my own heart," Kymil replied.

"Yes, I believe you and Alauvar would've greatly enjoyed each other's company," Annika said. "You're both impulsive and prone to the dramatic."

"It's called being interesting, dear."

"But if I'm not mistaken," Annika said, studying the bard for his reaction. "You also would've had much to discuss, given you view *the world* in a similar way."

Kymil's smile widened. "What gave me away?"

"Unless you were incalculably stupid, which I believe you've proven is not the case, only a fatestitcher would have the audacity to cheat at cards with a table full of men who could grind you into a thin paste."

He feigned an exasperated sigh. "Cheating is such a dirty word, Ms. Iatorii. And inaccurate. I simply plan ahead better than others."

Satisfied that her hunch had been correct and that the elf was comfortable revealing his abilities to her, Annika relaxed a bit more into her saddle. Her suspicion that Kymil was a fatestitcher was the central reason she had talked Rav and Wymund into allowing the man to join them in their quest. While Kymil did not yet know what they were chasing, it certainly wouldn't hurt to have a man with his talents beside them if they ran into the scorcher before they reached King Berenqar's chambers.

"So it's true what they say?" Annika asked. "That witches and fatestitchers draw from the same Wellspring during their infusions."

Kymil shrugged. "I'm no scholar. This talk of theoretical sources of energy is all beyond me, but I will say that of the few artistically minded witches I've met in my travels, their poems and songs all seem to describe the World Shroud in a way that sounds familiar to me."

He paused as he looked off into the distance, his eyes not appearing to focus on anything that Annika could see. "There are differences, of course. They seem to view the Shroud as more substantial, more tangible than it appears to my eyes. But they describe it with the same beautiful luminescence that I have come to know well over the years."

Upon reaching the bottom of the trail, Rav and Wymund settled on a path heading north that continued to run closer to the Tesigan Peaks. The road appeared more trodden than the others, with shrubs flattened along the sides of a hard-packed dirt trail; they reasoned that merchants heading to Alaboq would likely have chosen the most direct path over the scenic routes. They also hoped the scorcher would have avoided the more frequently traveled trail, but Annika knew in her gut that the elven mercenary wouldn't be bothered by the presence of others. Subtlety had not been a priority for his plans in Virdoba, so why should it be any different now?

As the party continued their trek, streaks of oranges and yellows stretching across the sky as the sun began to peek over the mountains to the east, Annika's mind turned back to the elf they pursued and the unknowns that still plagued her. Someone was pulling the scorcher's strings; she could feel it in her bones. Which meant that even if they succeeded in preventing his lies from reaching Berenqar's ears, there would just be another attempt to break down relations between Qedrad and Choii Stier. Whatever journey she had originally thought she signed up for, Annika was coming to realize the road ahead of her would be longer and more fraught than she once expected. The comforts offered by her life in sprawling cities would have to wait.

Chapter 21

Central Qedrad

Grass crunched underneath the bedroll as Rav turned over for what seemed like the hundredth time. Since leaving her home in Felona, she had learned to find comfort without the amenities that had been afforded to her growing up. A four-post bed with a down mattress was undeniably pleasant, but she had spent nights in alleys and gutters when hiding from a search party of guardsmen demanded it. But there was something unnerving about bedding down in a wide-open steppe that kept her mind from rest. She felt exposed, uncovered by the welcoming shadows in which she had always slumbered. Without the canopy draped across her childhood bedframe or the towering walls of Virdoba's alleyways casting their shade across her, she felt as if the light of every star in the sky were shining on her for anyone around to see.

Despite this discomfort, though, many days of travel had left her physically drained, and she found herself dipping in and out of unconsciousness each night. Those brief moments of rest that existed between the stirring of her restless mind were all she was running on at this point, but as each day broke, she noticed that she was never as exhausted as she expected. As much as Rav had resisted Annika's assertion that she was a lightblood, she couldn't help but see the woman's logic. She was making it through day after day of travel on little sleep; that reserve of energy must be coming from somewhere.

Finding a new divot in the earth that allowed her hip to settle in place, Rav slipped her hand back underneath the bundled cloak she used as a pillow, resting it across the hilt of her dagger. Having her blades within reach at night was a habit independent of where she laid her head. Nestling down into the fabric, she exhaled slowly before snapping her eyes open. Her hand had come to rest on *a* dagger under her head. Singular.

Rav bolted upright, staring out into the darkness that surrounded them. A low flame in the center of their camp lit the immediate vicinity, ironically making it harder to see beyond the perimeter as her eyes adjusted to the light. However, she didn't have to scan far to find what she was looking for: Kymil, sitting near the fire with his knees bent in front of him and balancing the point of her dagger on the tip of one finger. The bard was also squinting into the dark grassland beyond the illuminated area while Annika and Wymund slept soundly across from them.

"If you needed a weapon for your watch," Rav said, fighting her urge to grab her blade back with a little more downward pressure than would be necessary, "there were smarter options than taking one of mine without asking."

Kymil blinked twice, still staring off into the distance as if he had not heard her. But just before she moved to make a more forceful statement, he turned to her with his typical self-satisfied grin. "Would asking permission really have made any difference?"

"Other than arming you with the knowledge that you would be better protected by not stealing from me?"

The bard laughed quietly, flipping the dagger up and catching the end of the hilt on the pad of his outstretched finger. "I was just admiring the weapon's craftsmanship, nothing more sinister than that." He tossed it into the air once more, this time catching the blade between his thumb and forefinger before extending the hilt toward Rav. "Besides, I barely know which end to stick someone with."

Rav exhaled as she took her dagger back, the tension draining out of her shoulders. Tucking it back away under her cloak, she asked, "How did you get it anyway?"

"You didn't think it was just this smile that was disarming, did you?" he replied with a wink.

"Irasil be damned," Rav cursed, burying her face in her palm with a groan. "Why do I keep waking up next to men who insist on making puns?"

"Wordplay is my calling," he said. "And there is no form I consider higher than another. There is an art to quips that is as beautiful as an exquisitely constructed sonnet. Verses course through my veins as naturally as lightning arcs through yours."

Rav surprised herself with how little resistance she felt at the insinuation now. After her discussions with Annika, being a lightblood seemed to be the only logical explanation for how she had survived as long as she had against Cater's crew and a trained scorcher. But it did mean that her mother had kept secrets from her about her father, and that there would be a reckoning the next time she returned to Felona. That thought *did* surprise her though, as returning to her home had never been on the horizon before. Now, the call to confront her mother over this lapse in her judgment was an alluring beacon. *I just have to survive this mission first, then I get to finally be the one who plays guilt like a classical instrument.*

"The old woman told you?"

Kymil shrugged. "Not in so many words. I pride myself on reading people and picking up on conversational cues."

"You mean eavesdropping," Rav said with a laugh.

"Being open to what is going on around me," Kymil replied with grand sweep of his arm. After a moment of stillness, only disrupted by the soft crackling fire before them, his face softened, his smile becoming more sincere. "It must be disorienting to learn something so fundamental about who you are at this point in your life. Especially learning about it second hand."

Staring into the low flames, Rav said, "Well, when you have a mother who largely refuses to talk about a murdered father, it can be hard to learn things about him. The little fact that he was a stormforger must have slipped her mind." She sighed. "Maybe if he had been more interested in staying home with us than parading about the city . . . "

"Fathers aren't always as great as they're made out to be," Kymil said softly, tearing his eyes away from her to join in gazing at the fire. "But anyhow, you have Ms. Iatorii to dispense her wisdom now," he said, rebounding to his usual tenor. "I encourage you to listen to her words of caution. Life with a passive connection to the World Shroud can be quite short when one doesn't know their limits yet insists on butting into danger at every turn."

"Oh?" Rav asked. "Do we have another esteemed World Shroud philosopher in our midst?"

"I did mention I was a philosopher when we first met," he said. "Though I spend my time pondering the depths of love and passion more than the inner workings of the cosmos."

Rav found herself laughing, a part of her hating every second of it. Though she supposed he wouldn't have made much of a traveling bard without his magnetic personality. Kymil looked up at the night sky, adding, "No, I just grew up immersed in this world of Wellsprings and fancy talents. That's all."

"Right, you had that performance contract for the show in Oys Allenar. I'm sure there are many more people like me around in Choii Stier."

Kymil pulled his eyes away from the stars, looking at her with a raised brow. "Ah," he said as his momentary confusion cleared. "No, my family and I didn't immigrate to the colony until my adolescence. I was born in Liiashae. However many people with a connection to the World Shroud you had in mind, I assure you there were much more back across the ocean."

Rav had heard stories of the elven continent from the Choii Stieren transplants living in Felona, its gleaming marble cities and natural splendor making Anera seem rather dull in comparison. The colonists had tried their best to replicate some of that beauty in their new home, but they always spoke of the land they had left behind with a reverence that indicated nothing would ever come close to its grandeur. In fact, if it weren't for Teacher Irasil's call for charity and outreach, she believed many of the elves never would have left their shores. It was odd to consider that her birth would likely not have occurred if not for the ancient musings of a Dawn One.

"You don't have an accent," Rav noted, a bit discouraged at her inability to read him as well as she read others.

"I do when I want to, and I don't when I don't," Kymil replied, dipping into a musical way of speaking, his words flowing together like a song. "The performance never stops."

Stretching his legs out and lying back with his hands behind his head, he shut his eyes and nestled into his bedroll. "Since you're already up, you may as well start your watch for the night. Some of us require more beauty rest than others." He cracked an eye open to look at her as one edge of his mouth crept up. "We can't all be naturals."

Rav scoffed but caught herself smiling. As the rest of the night ticked away, Rav pondered fathers and how her life would be different if Ilphas Trisarin hadn't been stolen from her all those years ago. Kymil didn't seem fond of his father, but the sting of her loss had always been dulled for her. Her lone memory of him, her father beaming as he lifted her into his arms, always brought with it an enduring warmth. She watched Annika's chest rise and fall from across their campsite, realizing that despite her attempts to escape her complex history with parental relationships, she had somehow managed to find herself in a surrogate one. Whatever lessons she had missed out on from her father, whatever lifesaving advice he might have had to offer her, the task now fell to a woman who was more similar to her mother than the man she needed to substitute.

At least that means there's no chance she'll leave before she has her way.

Chapter 22

Central Qedrad

The sour taste of the cider stung the sides of his tongue as Tetamii took another draught from the tankard. From his position leaning against the tavern wall, he watched children chase each other around and through the copse of pines that served as the center of Turlaq's Fork. The Qedradan village was as unimpressive as the acidic drink he had been offered upon arrival.

A cluster of thatch roofed homes had sprung up as a way station where the major travel routes running along the western and northern coasts intersected, but despite the traffic the town was sure to see from traveling merchant caravans, it seemed not many wanted to lay down roots here. Tetamii could hardly blame them though. Turlaq's Fork was too far north to benefit from the lumber trade found in the mountainous forests of Achen, but too far south of the Draemoor Sound to have established itself as a coastal port city. Instead, the people of the village eked out an existence in this land that stood out for no other reason than its mediocrity.

He took another swig and winced, the drink no longer warm enough to mask some of the unpleasant flavor. The cider had cooled since the tavern girl had handed it to him, just as the weather had now that he was nearing the northern part of the continent. Wintery winds nipped at his heels over the last few days of his travels, which had been a new experience for an islander, but the change had not been a particularly troublesome one. Cold was not much of an issue for a man who could draw warmth from the World Shroud on a whim.

As much as he would have liked to blame his sour disposition on the drink in his hand or the regional climate, other factors were plaguing his mind. Tetamii looked into his mug and tore miniscule holes in the membrane, allowing heat from the Wellspring into the cider until it began to roil and steam. He refused to choke down this concoction cold. At least that was one problem that was readily solved.

The door to his right swung open, and the young draqesh girl who had greeted him upon his arrival strode out toward him. With draqeshis it was always difficult to discern a young adult from an adolescent; they tended to sprout to their full height by their early teen years. But as Tetamii looked down at the fiery redhead, the top of her braided bun only just reaching his waistline, he could see a confident innocence in her eyes that time and experience hadn't yet beaten out of her. Though now he supposed it never would. *I will be sparing her from that particular torment.*

"Do you want another?" she asked, pointing up at his wooden tankard. "Ma wanted me to make sure you were staying warm out here. She says we may not have enough timber to keep the hearth in your room lit all night."

Tetamii drained the rest of the cider and passed his cup down to her, hiding his disgust as best he could. It wasn't her fault this town's stock of apples were subpar, and for what it was worth, he didn't want to upset the girl. He was never one for wanton cruelty; what he did, he did with purpose.

"That's all right, child. I won't trouble you for more," Tetamii said, adjusting the black leather strap across his shoulder so that his bastard sword rested flat against his back. "Go back inside and play for a while. Children shouldn't be forced to work so hard."

The girl huffed, placing her hands on her hips with a scowl. "I'll have you know this is my thirteenth winter, sir. That's plenty old enough to be done with silly things for children. My ma had this place running on her own when she was naught but two years older than I am now."

"Perhaps you're right," he said with a soft chuckle. "But you shouldn't have to be."

With a quizzical look, the girl shrugged and turned to head back inside. "Let me know if you change your mind. We can open up a fresh cask for you." His stomach turned at that thought, not knowing if a younger cider could be even worse.

The brown leather cuirass he wore creaked as he descended the few steps from the tavern's porch and moved out onto the grassy path. Since making his decision outside Turlaq's Fork, he had taken off his white tailcoat and stored it in his saddlebag. An impression needed to be made, but not at the expense of his anonymity. Tetamii couldn't risk being recognized as an insurgent upon arriving in Alaboq if he expected to be granted an audience with King Berenqar. The city needed to be aware of an approaching elven threat, but they didn't need to know it was him.

He felt a pang of regret as he considered the children playing among the pines in the middle of the town, and the girl not more than a dozen yards behind him who raced toward adulthood, driven by life's pressures to grow up before her time. But this was the last settlement of any notable size on the road to Qedrad's capital; his final opportunity to deliver a message that would reach the king's ears before he arrived.

The tall grasses crunched beneath his boots as he walked toward the town's center, the smoky wisps of the World Shroud dancing at the corners of his vision, eagerly anticipating his touch. He felt no such excitement, only a burning anger in the pit of his stomach. Anger at that incompetent harbormaster and his thuggish lackeys certainly, but they weren't ultimately to blame. Sheep couldn't blame an old and lame guard dog when it failed to protect them from hungry wolves; the fault would lie with the shepherd, who could have found a younger and healthier custodian. As far as Tetamii was concerned, Elikar Thymes was responsible. Not that the Felonian councilman would care, and the fistful of gold libers that now lined Tetamii's pouch said that he shouldn't either.

Pulling the white-and-red elven war mask from its place under his chestpiece, he positioned the wooden oval over his face and reached out to the Wellspring's familiar warmth. The curls and tendrils in the membrane rippled faster at his connection, their agitation palpable. The trio of children in the copse of trees before him peeked around the trunks, staring at the towering, masked figure who stood completely still in the road. They were far too young to recognize the power and history that his mask represented, but their parents would. He tugged at the World Shroud, pulling it taut above the grove of pines while also knotting off a pocket of Wellspring energy within the tavern behind him by folding the membrane around itself. If the children in Turlaq's Fork had to die today, the least he could do was claim them first.

A jagged orange tear ripped open in the air above the treetops seconds before an inverted geyser of flames engulfed everything below. The pleasant pine aroma was replaced by char as the entire copse was consumed by the conflagration, the roar of the air igniting stifling any cries of agony that may have escaped the children's lips. Though with the amount of heat Tetamii had drawn from the Wellspring, he doubted they had felt any pain at all. A few stunned gasps and alarmed shouts sounded around him as the townsfolk stared at the inferno that the center of their village had become. Most rushed off to the wells in what would be a futile attempt to put out the downward spout of flames, but there were a handful of King's Guard who had noticed the strange figure in an elven war mask, one hand held out toward the raining fire and the other held in a closed fist behind. The theatrics weren't necessary, but this was meant to be a demonstration. It might as well be memorable.

He concentrated on the pocket he had formed within the tavern as the guardsmen charged toward him, their breastplates heaving with the effort as they each drew a shortsword from their sides. Tetamii still had a few moments until they were on him, and he allowed the pressure to continue to build within the bubble. Heat energy poured in from the Wellspring, and he knew that everyone in the tavern would notice the rising temperature seeping through the membrane by this point. It wasn't the most inconspicuous method of drawing from the World Shroud, but it was certainly one of the most dramatic. In the last few seconds before a guard's blade could arc down on him, he released his fist, puncturing a slight opening in the bubble as he did.

The tavern ripped apart from the inside, sending splintering chunks of lumber out into the rest of the village as a massive fireball ballooned out behind the debris. A wave of concussive force swept out, flattening the grass forming much of the town's walkways and sending the guards staggering over their feet. In their momentary distraction, Tetamii drew his bastard sword from his back, creating small tears in the membrane along the blade itself. The blade had been forged specifically for him, reinforced for his abilities, and by the time he held it at the ready, the metal had progressed from a deep red to brilliant orange and then to radiant yellow in the blink of an eye.

"One of you will have the honor of carrying a message to King Berenqar," Tetamii said to the ten guards who had gathered around him. "I can respect courage in the face of certain death, so I suggest giving this everything you have, gentlemen."

The guards surged forward as Tetamii unleashed a semicircular spout of flames from the ground behind him, cutting off all but the three soldiers to his front. No matter how superior his training, all it would take was one lucky opening to pierce his side, so controlling their movements was a must.

He swung his glowing blade in a backhanded horizontal arc, catching the first man across his breastplate and sending him staggering into the guard directly behind him. The third brought his shortsword down in an overhanded strike that Tetamii deflected with ease before bringing his own sword back around, gliding it cleanly through his opponent's neck. Head and body fell to the ground independently, the stumps bloodless and cauterized.

The second man struggled to slip out from under the first, who was now wheezing and fumbling with the clasps on his armor. Where Tetamii's blade had struck was a dented portion in the steel, softened by the heat and now constricting his chest. Just as he managed to wriggle free from under his gasping partner's weight, Tetamii was there to plunge his sword into the opening at the armor's neckline. Pulling it free, he held the flat of his blade against the first man's leather straps, fusing the material such that the breastplate's ties would have to be severed for it to come off.

All around them, lances of fire crackled from the sky, puncturing the thatch-roofed homes of Turlaq's Fork and setting them ablaze. Screams and hacking coughs resonated around the grassy field and black smoke began to fill the air. The World Shroud quivered as Tetamii kept it from resuming its typical dancing whirls before ripping a new hole in the membrane. At the base of his skull, a bone-crunching knot began to form, the expected consequence of overextending himself, of siphoning too much power from the Wellspring. During his training, he had been taught to manage his abilities efficiently, to draw only as much as was needed to complete the task at hand. But that same training had taught him his limits. He knew how long he could wield the flames before the effort would kill him, and he intended to use every last second.

Leaving the breathless man where he lay, Tetamii turned to face the next wave of King's Guards who had circled around to the gap in his flaming barrier. Two charged forward, both holding their shortswords in a two-handed grip, while another two waited behind for an opening in the tight space. The pair worked in tandem well, flanking Tetamii when they could and keeping him engaged from every angle. But the length of his bastard sword kept them just out of reach, their swipes missing his body by inches when they weren't battered away.

Rather than waiting to be overwhelmed by the other two guards, Tetamii stretched the World Shroud tight around their armor, drawing heat from the Wellspring into the steel. Panicked cries drew his attackers' attention for a split second, and he took the opportunity to separate their heads from their necks in one wide arc. Before their forms could crumple to the ground, their comrades' cries advanced to screams of anguish as their white-hot breastplates began to meld into their chests, the scent of burning flesh mingling with the smoke and soot that danced on the light breeze. Tetamii watched the two men collapse, first onto their knees and then the ground, their voices silenced by shock. With immediate attention from a witch or herb nurse, they might survive. But if there were any in Turlaq's Fork now, there wouldn't be for long.

The pulsating mass at the top of his neck felt as if it would burst through his skull, but the deed was almost done. Three guards remained, each stepping into the flaming semicircle over their fallen brothers, while most of the village was now little more than a smoldering husk. What few structures still stood Tetamii picked off with more bolts of fire from the sky.

Taking in the wide-eyed shock on his opponents' faces, Tetamii said, "I must commend the three of you. You have to know there is no escape now, barring the one I promised would be allowed to convey my message." The three glanced at one another, their eyes darting around nervously. "Now we see who will be bestowed with that honor."

Without warning, the guard in the back roared and raised his blade high, aiming to strike down his allies. The other two turned, reflexively throwing their arms up to protect themselves from the traitorous attack. But before he could finish the blow, Tetamii's bastard sword spun through the air and lodged itself between the man's eyes. His flesh sizzled as he slumped back to the ground.

Tetamii tutted. "I said courage would be rewarded with continued breath, not treachery." The last two nodded to each other and settled into their offensive stance. Impressed, Tetamii tilted his head in acknowledgment. "Come, then," he said, and they rushed forward.

Tetamii planted the bottom of his boot in the chest of the man who held his blade high for a downward strike, sending him stumbling backward as he caught the wrist of his other foe and twisted the joint around. The man was forced to drop his weapon just before Tetamii slammed a fist into his nose with such force that the skull buckled. Blood fountained across the steel breastplate and onto the charred grass below before a series of follow-up blows caved the man's face inward, forcing it to drain down his throat instead. Tetamii released him as he fell to the ground, choking on his own blood, then turned to stalk toward the final guard.

To his credit, a calm resolve had taken the place of the fear that had played across his face moments earlier. The man leaped into the air, sword arm cocked back so the point of the blade was aimed for a thrust through Tetamii's eye. But he simply sidestepped the blow and caught the man in midair, palming his face and slamming him back onto the ground. Before he could react, Tetamii created more tears in the World Shroud around his hand to wreathe it in flames, cooking the guard's face until he stopped struggling.

He stood with some effort, the world spinning around him. The wrenching pressure that threatened to split his skull apart began to lessen as he released his grip on the World Shroud. The veil fluttered limply around him, as if he had torn it to tatters. Tetamii couldn't remember a time he had siphoned so much power in such a short span that he caused this amount of damage, but the membrane would heal in time. It always did.

He hobbled over to the man who had been gasping for breath, who was still lying on his back and just managing to slip his blade under a leather strap. With a final twist the fused leather tie snapped free and the breastplate loosened, allowing the man to gulp in the air he had been fighting for. Tetamii removed his steaming blade from the cleft skull along the way and came to a stop before his lone remaining victim. He looked down at him, and the man stared back.

"I apologize," Tetamii said. "I got a bit carried away with your comrades and I forgot to spare the most courageous among you. But perhaps not. You could have spent this time crawling away to safety, and maybe I would have been unable to find you. Yet here you remained, a true paragon of bravery."

The man brought himself up onto his elbows, his gaze never breaking from Tetamii's. "If you want me to warn the king that you're coming, you're digging your own grave. Alaboq has enough men-at-arms to slay you before you reach Vinsart Hold. But fine, I'll deliver your funeral announcement. What do you want King Berenqar to know?"

"Just let him know that the embers of old conflicts are burning anew," he replied. "But to ensure you won't forget, allow me to sear it into your memory." Tetamii placed the flat of his glowing red blade against the man's cheek, the metal cooling now that he had released his hold on the World Shroud but enough to cause flesh to bubble. The man's screams followed him as he limped toward the remaining grove of pines north of town and the mount he had hitched there. He would rest for a day in the cover of those woods, allow his messenger a head start. Once word began to spread of a scorcher reigniting the bloody feuds from the War of Arrival, his job, upon entering Alaboq, would be much simpler.

Chapter 23

Central Qedrad

Dulcet tones spilled out of The Royal Stone, Kymil and his lute having found a new home on a makeshift stage of scuffed tables slid against one another. Since they had arrived in Tesigan Crown, a village with a name more regal than it deserved given its absence from regional maps, the bard had assumed the role of master of ceremonies for Aton's Harvest, much to the chagrin of the four men sitting off to the side, their flutes, ouds, and drums all spread dishearteningly across their laps. But the rest of the late autumn festival's celebrants couldn't have been more ecstatic. Rav guessed it had been years since an entertainer with this level of talent had graced their town for more than a bed and a chamber pot.

Candles hung from fishing lines that stretched from awning to awning, their flickering flames dancing in the twilight and forming an illuminated border around the town square. While the rest of the village's paths remained well-trod dirt and grasses, clay tiles had been set in place outside the tavern and the ferryman's boathouse, resulting in a square landing that on most days only saw impatient merchants waiting their turn to ford the Osoburn River. But on this night, the space was filled with dozens of men, women, and children, twirling and stepping in time with Kymil's songs. Their laughter filled the air, only adding to the joy of the melodies.

To her right, Annika sat bundled in her cloak, limbs tucked away from the chill that hardly seemed to affect the rest of the town. Rav had felt the cold creeping into her own bones over the last few days as well, and it was getting harder to remember the time they had spent baking under the Kefyan sun only weeks before. Even Wymund had returned to wearing his thick wool guard's coat, allowing a hint of discomfort to slip past his stoic resolve. From where he stood across the clay square from their bench, Rav thought she saw a slight shiver underneath his crossed arms.

"Is it always colder than a eunuch's trousers up here?" she asked, leaning her huddled body closer to Annika.

The older woman laughed, the air capturing its form as mist as soon as it left her mouth. "I visited the northernmost island of Choii Stier as a child. One of my father's business excursions to try and establish our wines as an exotic import. But climates on the ocean tend to be more temperate than elsewhere, so no, we will be sharing our first taste of the frigid north."

A circle of young woman in brightly colored wool dresses stood nearby, taking turns pointing and giggling at Wymund, who was deliberately avoiding eye contact as he continued to watch the festivities from his post against a lantern pole. From what little she could overhear, the girls were quite taken with his bronze skin, a shade or two darker than they were used to finding here in their Qedradan backwoods, along with his admittedly impressive stature. A smirk crept across her cold-stiffened face as an opportunity for mischief presented itself.

She stood, patting Annika on the knee, and said, "I'll see if I can raise the heat a bit. Nothing like a little embarrassment and jealousy to get the blood pumping."

Rav walked around the periphery of the tiled square, brushing against the shoulders of a few of the women as she went with a toothy grin, before reaching Wymund and grabbing his forearms. "Come with me," she said, starting to drag him out into the middle of the dancing crowd. As expected, he resisted her pull and yanked his arms back into place, glancing around sheepishly.

"What are you doing, Ravael?" he asked.

"I heard someone whispering about a scorcher across the way," she lied, gripping his arms again as she led him out into the center. "If we can get into a position within earshot, we may be able to learn something."

Dragging his feet in protest, Wymund whispered, "We can't just ask them what they know?" But Rav had already taken each of his hands in hers and was leading him in step to the music. His eyes darted around, more flustered than observant. "Who are we trying to eavesdrop on?"

The circle of women had grown tighter, each putting their own spin on a scowl as they stared at Rav. "Oh, no one," she said, winking at them. One of the girls stamped her foot and began whispering to the rest. "I just saw that bunch appraising you and thought I would give them a show. No one wants to buy a horse without first seeing how it runs."

Wymund's face flushed, but his posture improved as he took the lead away from her. "I was trying to ignore their interest, you know. We are on the trail of a dangerous individual and it hardly seems appropriate to play into their fantasies."

She threw her head back and groaned. "Lighten up. The horses need to rest if we don't want to run them into the ground. We shouldn't feel any guilt about what we do while they sleep. If we use the time to blow off a little steam, what's the harm?"

He lifted her hand in the air and spun her around. "I suppose you're right," he said with a small smile, expertly bringing her back into step and leading her into a more advanced sequence of footwork.

Though taken aback, Rav's smile widened. Even the upper crust who attended the never-ending balls in Felona would be impressed by his skill. "I never would've thought you could move like this with that stick so far up your ass." He rolled his eyes and laughed. "You must have the gentle soul of artist somewhere beneath that soldier's exterior."

Clearing his throat, Wymund said, "There's more to me than this coat and a blade. I did have a life before—"

A series of taps on his shoulder caused him to turn, revealing Kymil standing in a half bow, his arm swept out to the side. Rav hadn't noticed the change in musical style while bantering with Wymund, but now noted the tone had become more rustic.

"May I cut in?" His eyes slanted up toward them, impish and dashing all at once. "If dances are being offered by elven roses, only a fool would remain on stage and let the opportunity pass by. Besides, if I held the spotlight for much longer, I fear the local troupe's sour mood would've spoiled the punch."

Before either could respond, the sound of hurried feet rushed up from behind as one of the young women wrapped an arm around Wymund's waist and twisted him away, her chestnut braid nearly smacking Rav in the face from the momentum. His eyes went wide with shock, and Rav only overheard her say something about "sampling the local fruits" before the pair swirled farther away into the mass of dancers.

She took Kymil's hands in hers, and they joined in with the others around them. This new dance was much faster paced, and she was thankful that the bard was now serving as her partner. One quick glance at Wymund gave the impression of a newborn colt, his limbs fumbling about as he tried to keep up with the unfamiliar rhythm. Whereas his mastery of the more formal style was impeccable, he didn't have the natural *feel* for the tempo that Kymil possessed.

While she laughed at her friend's failing attempt, she found her feet lifted off the ground as Kymil spun her in a circle, still determined to be the center of attention though others had taken his place on stage. As she landed, he locked eyes with her and said, "Now that I've successfully swept you off your feet, have I earned the right to know what it is that our mission entails? I haven't heard one word about your dear ill Qedradan cousin since we left Hwen."

Rav blinked, only now remembering their story in the tavern. Kymil had been traveling with them for nearly two weeks at this point, and his ignorance about the scorcher had slipped her mind. However insufferably endearing the man could be, she supposed he did at least have the right to know how much danger he was charging headfirst into. But she wouldn't have him believe it was because he had made her swoon.

She placed her hand behind the small of his back, then suddenly dipped him at the waist. Yet he remained unflustered, releasing one of her hands and cartwheeling over his head before spinning her back close to him. Pushing away slightly, she laughed and said, "Fair enough, bard. Though you may regret your decision to join us after you learn the truth."

"I've never had the patience to suffer regrets in my life," he said. "Anything that would otherwise be one instead becomes a tale to delight my public. I joined you in this endeavor with an eye toward a new story; there will be no disappointment on my part."

She took a breath. "We're on the trail of a scorcher who we believe is attempting to reignite a war between Qedrad and Choii Stier. Or at the very least drag their relations back by centuries." She watched as his eyebrows knitted together and his lips pursed. "I think you deserve to know the risk you are riding toward if you continue with us. I've faced this man personally and only managed to survive through a random and strange act of kindness from another."

Kymil tilted his head, taking a beat until finally, he stuck his bottom lip out in a pout and sighed. "That's all? A glorified game of cat and mouse? I assumed we ventured northward to slay some dreaded beast that was wreaking havoc across the countryside. Something that would really get the imagination flowing." He shrugged, his well-worn smirk returning to its customary spot. "Oh well. I've been known to embellish for the sake of entertainment when called to do so."

Rav's mouth hung open for a moment before she snapped it shut, chuckling as she shook her head. "I don't know if that was bravado or stupidity, but either way the choice is yours."

The pair continued their dance until the song began to shift into a slower beat, at which point she pulled away, the relaxed tempo allowing her to notice an advancing shadow approaching from across the river. The rope that guided the ferry from the other shore creaked at its fixed point as the raft made its way along the lead. Through the mist, she thought she could see two human figures and another larger silhouette huddled together as they neared the bank of Tesigan Crown.

"Ah, leave it to uninvited guests to spoil the romance in the air," Kymil said with a grin that did little to hide the light of curiosity in his eyes. He squinted toward the shadowed shape as Annika joined them, followed shortly by a panting Wymund. "Though travelers eager enough to hire a ferryman at this time of night usually have something interesting to say."

There was a soft thud as the ferry lodged itself onto the bank of the river and a shuffling of feet as the forms made their way off. The candlelight only managed to brighten the mist, sharpening the contrast between it and the silhouettes, but as the shapes moved farther into Tesigan Crown, they were revealed to be an older man with a horseshoe pattern of graying hair and a much younger man in soot-stained clothes, dragging a skittish horse behind him. The older man moved quickly over to a post and began to tie off the raft with a thick cord of rope. Between his practiced motions, he gestured for another man in the crowd of dancers to tie off the other side. Rav figured he was the river town's ferryman, which meant the ash-covered man and his mount were the ones with a story to tell.

A pit formed in her stomach. Their appearance, the direction they had come from, the dazed look to their eyes—she was afraid she already knew what they would have to say.

Taking charge, Wymund strode forward and shouted, "Someone get this man some water and have his animal stabled for the night." Several of the townsfolk did as directed, some scurrying off into The Royal Stone and others taking the horse's reins from the man. Rav and the others followed Wymund, and as they approached, Rav saw dark bags under the man's eyes and a tangle of honey-colored hair that was more windswept than combed. He doubled over and coughed before accepting a flagon of water from a young waitress, drinking most of it in one gulp. After wiping the excess from his mouth on the back of his sleeve, his eyes seemed to focus for the first time on the small crowd that had gathered around him.

"What happened to you, lad?" Wymund asked, holding one hand on the man's shoulder to steady him.

"There was a fire, across the Brighburn," he said, pointing back over the Osoburn River to its twin farther east. "It's . . . it's all just gone." The man tipped the mug up and drained the remaining water.

"What's gone, son?" Annika asked, stepping up beside Wymund.

"Turlaq's Fork," he said, his eyes haunted. Rav recognized the name from their map of the region. It was a town that served as a waystation for Qedradan and Achen merchants.

"My family and I live on the western bank of the Brighburn, but we travel in to Turlaq's Fork often for supplies," he continued. "As soon as I heard the explosions and saw the fire shooting out of the sky, I got in my boat and crossed over to help . . . " A tear rolled down the man's cheek as he stopped to clear his throat. "But by the time I got there it was nothing but embers. Not a single soul was left alive. Whatever it was that caused that . . . well, I didn't want it to happen to another town before I could warn them. So I rode all day and night to get here. Please, you all have to pack up your things and leave before the fire rains down here too!"

A growing murmur spread throughout the crowd, but Kymil held up his hands and turned to face them. He plastered a big smile on his face as he draped an arm across the haggard man's shoulders and said, "Fear not, everyone. Calm yourselves, there is no need for alarm or to leave your homes. If this young man did indeed see gouts of fire spewing from the heavens, then the threat is moving away from Tesigan Crown, not toward it." Annika and Wymund looked first to the bard, then to Rav, each wearing a unique combination of surprise and confusion on their faces.

"How do you know that?" a woman shouted from the back.

"Because my companions and I are on the trail of a dangerous individual," he said, adding a wide-armed gesture to point out Rav and the others. "And in due time, we will have him in our custody. When that happens, Tesigan Crown will be my first stop to dazzle and amaze you all with the tale of his capture." As he carried on, enrapturing the crowd and drawing the fresh arrival into the limelight to wax rhapsodic about his bravery, Rav slid next to Annika and Wymund. Each stared at her expectantly with eyebrows cocked, Annika adding a slight grin.

She shrugged. "If he's going to be joining us in the furnace, I figured he should at least know he may be burned."

Chapter 24

Central Qedrad

The sash that had hidden her ears from a prejudiced populace now covered Rav's nose and mouth. All around her stood the crumbling, blackened husks of what was once the trading outpost known as Turlaq's Fork, now nothing more than an ashen mound of debris and corpses. As the party rode into the devastated area, she peeked through walls that had been burned or blasted away to see huddled, charred forms under tables or in corners, blankets of fine gray ash covering them. Many of the shapes, far too many, were small and forever fused by the heat onto the larger bodies they clung to. Whatever their strategies had been, nothing had saved the people of Turlaq's Fork from the scorcher's onslaught.

A buzzing sound grew louder in her head and her hands trembled on Doe's reins. She dipped her head and squeezed her eyes shut, remembering what Wymund had said in Annika's sitting room those few weeks ago. *"We got that boy out of there, Ravael."* His words calmed her some, enough to quiet the hum and still her hands, but they did nothing for the guilt over the loss of life. All these people had families, friends, jobs, and hobbies. They created goods, maybe even art; formed bonds and laughed in each other's company. But now everything that they had been had gone up in smoke.

"Why?" she asked, and the others pulled themselves from their own thoughts to glance at her. "What was the point of destroying everything here?"

Wymund took a deep breath, his eyes continuing to scan the smoldering remains while he kept his face blank. "We believe he's on his way to Alaboq to deliver news of an elven uprising in the south, Ravael," he said. "Since we stopped his plot in Virdoba, he had to make sure there was a credible threat behind his message."

"So we're responsible . . . " Rav muttered. The wasted years she had spent not chasing down the organization that killed her father suddenly weighed all the heavier.

Annika steered her black mare over, catching her downcast gaze. When she spoke, her voice was gentle but firm. "We don't shoulder the blame for the actions of a murderous scorcher, girl. He's responsible for his own choices, as we are for our own." Rav nodded, but her conscience still needed to catch up.

"Is everyone still lying to me, then?" Kymil shouted. He was kneeling on the ground, hunched over and looking at an impression in the soot. "I keep being told that we aren't after some legendary beast, but my eyes are providing me with evidence to the contrary."

The rest trotted over to the bard and dismounted, joining him around a five-toed reptilian footprint the size of a wagon wheel. At the end of each digit was the imprint of a sharply curved claw that had pierced four inches into the earth below. Rav reached down to place her hand next to it, noting that whatever creature this track belonged to, it would have to be the biggest animal she had ever encountered.

"A dragon?" Wymund asked breathlessly, his stoic mask slipping for the first time since they had arrived in Turlaq's Fork. No one alive had ever seen evidence that the ancient beasts still existed, but their ferocity was well documented in divine texts and artwork, and the knowledge of their cruelty had since been passed down by the High Scholars for millennia. Most believed the Dawn Ones had succeeded in routing the vile creatures before the Departure, but rumors persisted that a few wyrms managed to remain in hiding.

"Children's fairytales meant to puff up the greatness of the Dawn Ones," Kymil responded. Shrugging off their surprised expressions, he continued, "In my trade, I've learned to recognize the fraying threads of a spun yarn. Dragons never existed. They were just a convenient narrative foil to demonstrate the power and glory of the Divine." He inched around the edges of footprint, examining the depths of the impressions left by the claws. "But whatever *thing* left this behind would certainly come close."

"But you must be open to being wrong in the face of all this, Kymil," Rav said. "Evidence of a large, reptilian beast and a village burnt to cinders. That would be quite the coincidence."

"I don't believe in coincidence. In my experience, chance is never random," Kymil replied with a hint of a smile. "Still, it may be that your scorcher wasn't the culprit here. Dragon or no, and I assure you it's the latter, something else was here around the time that the people of Turlaq's Fork breathed their last."

Wymund kept his eyes on a constant scan. "Whatever the case, there is nothing for us here now. We need to press on before the creature that left that track in the dirt decides to come back."

Rav nodded and made to move toward Doe, but something odd caught her eye. Most of the structures in the town had either burned to their foundations or been blown apart from the inside, with charred debris scattered over the trails that ran through the village. But beside one such building, the remains of which appeared large enough to have once been an inn, stood a gray stone well with one side toppled inward. At either side of the crumbled wall, mounds of dirt and rock had been pushed aside and a large burrow disappeared down into the well shaft. Stepping a few paces closer, Rav guessed the burrow was approximately five to six feet in diameter, with walls that were roughly hewn. Small pieces of crumbling stone fell into the darkness below, but she heard no splash. Instead, a deep rumble began to surround her, and she felt rather than heard the vibration.

She whipped around and rushed back toward Doe. "We need to leave. It's still here!"

Her friends turned to her, each still with their feet on the ground as they readied their mounts. But before anyone could reply, an eruption of earth resounded behind her, the scraping of claws on stone sending shivers up her spine like a knife cutting across a plate. She spun in time to see a scaled monstrosity twice the size of the largest horse clambering out of its burrow.

The massive jaws on its spade-shaped head seemed to unhinge, opening wider than seemed possible as it unleashed an ear-splitting, high-pitched roar, its forked tongue lashing about as it cried. Midnight black scales shining with an oily slickness rippled along its thick form as the beast came to a stop on four squat but wide-set powerful legs. A tail that doubled the creature's length whipped menacingly behind it, and along its back sprouted three finlike sails, one emerging straight from the center, with the others offset at angles to either side. Spines ran up the fins, each separated by taut, reddish-pink skin that reminded Rav of an outstretched bat wing. As the beast finished its wail, its eyes fixed on Rav and its tongue flickered in and out of its mouth. A rumbling hiss shook the ground beneath her.

The four horses panicked, their eyes rolling, spittle frothing from their mouths as they reared, tossing Annika and Kymil aside. The bard clung to his saddlebag as he stumbled backward, just managing to pull his indigo-stained cloak free as the animals darted off into the surrounding pines to the north. Wymund unsheathed his longsword from the scabbard at his waist as Rav did the same with her twin daggers. She could feel the arcing waves of energy begin to course through her body; lightning energy she was inadvertently drawing from the Wellspring to fuel her drive for survival. The sensation was familiar by now and not unwelcome in this instance. If she was going to die today, she would rather it be from overexertion than being ripped apart by this reptilian monster.

"Back away from it," Annika said evenly, motioning them toward her with a hand. "Slowly, please. It was in the well, so it's likely just protecting its water source." The other three complied, moving one cautious step back at a time. The low rumble intensified as the beast's mouth opened once again, but this time it showed only a fraction of the wide maw it had presented before. Its claws dug into the earth as it crouched lower, tail whipping more violently now.

Rav felt as if she could see each miniscule twitch in the creature's limbs, each flick of the eyes as it took in the intruders on its territory. She knew this wasn't a warning display. It was a challenge, one that none of them were equipped to meet. She chanced a glance back to Annika, her frail form nearly tripping over the debris covering the area on her way to the tree line. The old woman's gaze met hers, and she seemed to recognize something in Rav's expression. She gave a slight shake of her head and furrowed her brow, but Rav just turned back toward the threat.

"Run for the trees!" Rav shouted to the others as she darted in the opposite direction, drawing the beast's attention with her.

It took her bait as it scrambled after her, legs swinging wide in a low gait that caused its slick underbelly to drag across the ground. Another deafening roar sent dark birds in the surrounding pines scattering into the sky, adding to the din with their own shrieks of terror. Rav gripped tight onto the hilts of her blades and pumped her legs as she ran, feeling the energy siphoned from the World Shroud propelling her forward faster than she would be able to move on her own. But even with the added speed, she wouldn't be able to outpace the monster's longer strides. She could already hear it gaining on her, feel the reverberations of its deep hiss travel up from the dirt and into her chest as it closed the distance.

The force of its forelimbs slamming into the earth behind her almost caused her to stumble, but sheer force of will kept her upright. Her allies hadn't had enough time to make their escape, so her job as a decoy couldn't be over just yet. She angled to the right, leaping for a support beam that had once held an awning aloft but now stood alone among blackened kindling. Planting her foot against the wood, she sprang backward, flipping over as she attempted to land between two of the creature's sails. Her aim was perfect, but her boots found no traction on the oily scales.

The beast reared up and turned its head to snap at her as she slipped forward, instinctually striking out to either side with the daggers, hoping to lodge herself in place. However, her blades simply punctured the thin membrane of skin that stretched across each sail and ripped a line straight through them as she slid down. Bright crimson blood gushed from the two tattered fins as the monster slammed back to the ground, whipping its head around to unleash another screech at the little woman who had harmed it.

Rav landed hard on her shoulder, but tucked into a roll that landed her on her feet. From her crouched position, Rav was readying herself to dive in any direction when the beast lunged. The muscles in her legs felt like loaded springs aching to be released. But heavy footfalls landed behind her, and suddenly Wymund was leaping over her head, sword held cocked in a piercing position. His feet hit the ground inches from the monster's open maw as he thrust his blade up into its soft palate. It jerked its head back and swiped a massive, clawed foot into his side, knocking him several yards through the air into the crumbling stone wall of a small home. Rav could see several deep puncture wounds from the creature's talons in her friend's flank, the dark red that slowly pulsed out of him staining his guard's coat.

"No!" she cried, dashing forward with her daggers, ready to plunge them into the beast's ribs. But it was already on the move to finish Wymund. A tail as thick as a tree trunk slammed into her middle, knocking the wind out of her as she was forced onto her back. Her vision swam for a moment as spots from the impact mingled with the flaring lights that were already present. A sharp pain in her side as she gasped for breath told her that at least one rib had fractured from the blow, but there could be more. It was difficult to distinguish over the thrumming pulses that coursed through her every muscle.

The ruffling of a cloak drew her attention to the left as Kymil ran by, clearly intending to intercept the monster on its path toward Wymund. She watched the bard pull a red silk string from his cloak's inside fold, causing the end to unfurl and reveal a dozen or so stiletto blades attached to the hem of the garment. Leaving a raked trail of ash in his wake, Kymil slid across the creature's path, gripping the right side of his cloak as he went, and slashed the blades forward. Dubious that the small stabbing blades would be effective wielded like this, Rav was shocked to count at least six slashes in the beast's forelimb as it stumbled forward, tripping over its freshly wounded leg, and giving Wymund enough time to regain his footing and scramble out of the way. He bunched up the left side of his wool coat, then held the wadded cloth against his pierced chainmail shirt as he breathed heavily.

But her friend was still standing with his sword held out in front of him. There was fight in him yet.

"I hate to complain," Kymil called, his typical commanding voice now showing a slight tremble. "But I'm not supposed to be the hero in these stories. Might I suggest one of you do something of substance so I can live to spread the word of your mighty accomplishments?"

The monster bounded toward its wounded prey, jaws open wide enough to wrap around Wymund's torso. Rav stood and sprinted toward its left flank, trying to harness the lightning that was flowing through her. If she could move just a little faster, hit just a little harder, her friend might survive. However, Wymund proved to be ready for the assault as he tucked into a forward roll as its teeth clamped shut where he had stood, then lashed out with a backhanded strike as he came into a crouch. The blade caught the creature's left forelimb behind the joint, causing it to buckle as Rav slid underneath to avoid running into its bulk. She plunged both daggers into the underbelly, tearing two gashes into its flesh as she slipped out the other side. Blood and viscera sprayed across her face, stinging her eyes before she could wipe it away and turning her stomach with its odd saline and metallic odor.

Roaring in pain, its life draining from the wounds across its abdomen, the beast thrashed and swung its body wide, slamming into Wymund and knocking him through a crumbling stone wall. Rocks and wooden debris fell on him in a heap, burying him under a tremendous amount of weight.

"We need to get him out of there!" Rav shouted as Kymil appeared by her side.

"The monster might have other plans for us, I'm afraid," he replied.

"I think those wounds I carved into it are fatal," she said. "It seems to be slowing." As if in response, the hiss intensified and the earth shook, causing more rubble to land atop their friend. The creature's gaze bored into them, its hatred for them palpable even as its forelimbs strained to keep it upright. But another piercing roar solidified just how much of a threat remained.

"It seems to have more life left within it than you give it credit for," Kymil said, sweat beading down the side of his face. "Be ready."

"Ready for what?" she asked.

"To rescue me when I do something monumentally stupid."

Whipping his cloak from around his back, Kymil charged forward, his feet carrying him right toward the beast's yawning maw, filled with teeth as long as his hands. Not knowing what he had in mind, Rav trailed behind and hoped she would be able to follow his lead. The beast slammed its feet into the ash and raced toward the bard in response but began skidding to a halt as Kymil flung his cloak out in front of him. The fabric draped over the creature's face, the dangling blades from the hem of his cloak snagging portions of its lower jaw. He tumbled through the air and landed on the monster's neck, grabbing the top of his cloak and yanking it back. A dozen thin blades sunk deeper into its lower jaw as he pulled up, forcing the mouth closed and the head to arc backward.

Those blades don't miss, Rav thought. *Why is he wasting time plucking lutes in taverns?*

Red-faced as he white-knuckled the cloak, Kymil shouted, "I can't hold this for long!"

Rav closed the distance between her and the creature's exposed neck, plunging each of her daggers into the center of its throat. The thick-scaled hide gave only momentary resistance before she was able to slide her blades through and out each side. A wave of crimson blood sprayed over her as she rolled away, barely avoiding the beast's titanic head slamming onto the ground. The rumbling hiss grew weaker, broken up by gurgling gasps until, at last, the shaking ceased.

Breathing heavily, Kymil dislodged his cloak and held it away from him in one hand, crinkling his nose at the gore that covered it. He shook it, forcing fluids to drip onto the ground before he slid off the side of the carcass. "Thanks for that," he said, turning back to look at the slain beast. "But lest your head begin to swell with the title 'Dragonslayer,' I would like to point out the absence of wings and the fact that we weren't engulfed in flames during that encounter. An impressive kill, to be sure, but a dragon it was not."

Rav laughed as she doubled over in exhaustion. She could already feel the Wellspring energy draining away, her body no longer siphoning it from beyond the World Shroud now that she was out of immediate danger. "You are one lucky fool. If you were forced to do that same maneuver ten more times you would fail at each attempt."

His violet-ringed eyes flashed. "Yes, but I only needed it to work once, didn't I?"

The sound of tumbling rocks made Rav's breath catch in her throat. *Wymund!* But as she wheeled around to save her friend that had been forgotten in the glow of victory, she saw Annika already there, scrawny arms shoving aside what pieces of rubble she could.

"Some assistance would be appreciated," Annika grunted, pushing a charred piece of lumber to the ground. "Unless we're planning on leaving Mr. Sylnorin behind. Though I would hate to have wrangled all the horses together for no reason."

Hurrying over, Rav and Kymil joined her in sliding gray stones and blackened wood off the heap, piece by piece. She fought through the fatigue that was settling into her frame, digging her fingers into the rocks until they bled. Making this journey had been her idea. If Wymund had been crushed to death or was bleeding out under this pile of debris, she would be as much to blame as the creature that put him there.

But something stirred beneath the rubble, followed by a hacking cough. Rav lifted one more slab of stone and found herself looking into Wymund's dust- and ash-covered face, dazed but breathing. Working with Kymil, she pulled more of the rubble covering his torso away to find that his longsword had been wedged beside him in the earth. The blade had been bent into an unusable curve beneath the weight of rocks and lumber, but it had likely saved her friend's life by keeping some of the weight off his chest. Gripping his hand, Rav helped Wymund to his feet as Annika held the blood-soaked wool coat to the man's side.

"We're not dead," he said, wide-eyed and seemingly unbothered by the puncture wounds on his flank. As someone with a history of being stabbed fresh on her mind, Rav knew the pain would make itself known once the shock subsided. "That's truly unexpected."

"Maybe next time you'll listen when I tell you to run," she said.

His eyes focused as he turned toward her. "Not a chance."

Rav slapped her friend on the back, causing him to wince. "Come on, soldier. Let's get you into the saddle. We can get you a new blade in Alaboq, but I'm afraid your duckling costume is ruined."

"You may be right," he replied, forcing a smile. "It might be time to try a new animal on for size. Turtles seem well suited to avoiding stab wounds."

They hobbled as a group toward the copse of pines where Annika had tethered their mounts, and Kymil added, "Just make sure that you aren't boiled in a soup."

Chapter 25

Alaboq

Mareq fingered the folded parchment in his pocket, feeling the powder within shift back and forth as he stared at the etching of the Alaboqan coastline on the alley wall. When Ms. Luviire had learned that he intended to return to the alley in the Thistle Hare Warren, she insisted he take the bundle of pulverized herbs with him. "In case you run into anyone who looks like they need a rest," she had said. Coming from an herb nurse like her, he assumed the substance wouldn't be harmful. The person would likely wake up from the most restorative sleep of their life. But the effect would be the same; a dozing Ghost was much less worrisome than one on the prowl.

It had been some time since a Ghost had appeared in the kitchens of Vinsart Hold and days since he had noticed Sylicera Hadac pacing around and micromanaging the staff in anxious anticipation of a new message. Mareq had been worried he missed his window, that whatever secret conversation was being transmitted through Teacher Ias's congregation of spies had already come to end. But that morning, the trade minister made her appearance, more domineering than ever as she fussed over Ptolon's proposed menu for lunch.

Mareq didn't know why there had been a delay in communications, but he couldn't afford to miss this opportunity if the dialogue was slowing. Mareq just hoped he would have the time to test his theory before the Ghost returned. Thankfully, the added time had allowed him days of cautious strolling through the Warren to find an alternate route to the alley. Whether or not another sentry was watching, he had at least avoided the house with the artificial doorjamb.

Remembering the instructions he had inferred from the Shadowmaw script, Mareq took four steps directly away from the etching in the alley wall before turning right and taking another twenty-five paces deeper into the passage. A left turn and another six paces had his nose touching the opposite wall as he shifted refuse aside with his boot. There was nothing special about the wooden paneling here, no board that could be moved to reveal another hidden carving; just weathered wooden slats that could use some care.

Mareq's heart sank. *Only a fool could think himself able to decrypt a secret language without a cypher.* But he had been so sure, and that certainty only made this dead end sting all the more. However, as he shuffled his feet through the garbage that was piled against the alley wall, his boot caught in the groove of a wooden handle. His curiosity roaring back to life, Mareq hefted a canvas sack up and revealed something he had missed before: a weathered oak panel flush with the ground, likely a lid for a kindling storage box buried below. Not being from Alaboq or any other large city, Mareq wasn't sure if it was customary to bury these containers to conserve space in cramped neighborhoods, but it was certainly odd.

He lifted the lid only to discover the box was empty save for another etching of the Alaboqan coastline, nearly identical to the one in the wall behind him. The only difference was the presence of a compass rose in the bottom right corner. He felt his pulse quicken as he reached into the box, feeling for the wooden bird key, but found that unlike its twin in the alley wall, this coastal swallow wouldn't budge. Desperate not to miss out on this chance, Mareq ran his fingers over the etching's only new addition and gasped as the *S* under the compass depressed slightly. Pushing down harder, he heard a mechanism click and watched as the bird turned in place and began to move south along the coastline. The grinding of gears sounded from below until the swallow completed its route, at which point the bottom of the box swung downward. There, in the darkness below, was a set of stairs descending into a stone-lined tunnel.

Without pausing to think about his actions, Mareq gripped the edges of the container and lowered himself into the passageway, taking care to replace the lid and shut the false bottom as he did. He could hear the voices of his older brother and sister chastising him for his restlessness, for his incessant need to find out what was left to uncover under each stone; they never could comprehend his compulsion for discovery. But he tuned them out. As much as he missed his family, they weren't here now. This was his adventure, and he would follow where it led.

Damp, stale air permeated the tunnels as he descended farther, marveling at the craftsmanship of the walls as he went. He surmised they must have been constructed over a thousand years ago, hidden as they were beneath the foundation of the city. *Not to mention the width,* he thought as he shuffled down the steps with his broad shoulders at an angle. The people who fashioned these tunnels had never even heard of a draqeshi, much less met their cousins forging a life in the frozen tundra to the north. So while Mareq had ample head room, his thick frame would cause a tight squeeze as he crept further through the dark, lit only by the alien orange glow of a lichenous plant that appeared to thrive in this musty environment.

Paths branched off from the central tunnel, heading off in all directions as he wound his way through the subterranean labyrinth. It was difficult to keep his bearings without the sun, but orienteering was in his blood. His people had made the most of life in the icy north by forming cavernous networks inside mountains, which were much easier to heat without the wintry winds to battle against. If they could find their way through miles and miles of snaking rock passages, he could at least keep track of which way he turned. Interestingly, Mareq noticed that none of the branches seemed to head in the direction of Vinsart Hold, though he realized that should have been expected. If the Ghosts could pop into the citadel directly, there would have been no need for the trade minister to usher them in though the kitchens. The fortress had been the first building erected in the region, so by the time these tunnels were being dug, the foundation of Vinsart Hold would have already been sealed.

More of the strange Shadowmaw characters were scribbled along the walls of the tunnels, presumably road signs to point travelers in the right direction. He tried to make mental notes of each new symbol he stumbled across, hoping that he could develop a cypher for the secret language if for no other reason than to satisfy his own curiosity, but he didn't have the time to stop and copy them down. It was possible the Ghost was already on their way back from meeting with Sylicera Hadac and was right on his heels, so he kept moving.

The turns and branches that he made weren't arbitrary, despite the illegible directions scrawled onto the stone. Ms. Luviire had described the Ghosts as a communication network of sorts, able to convey messages between members over vast distances; with their apparent fascination with coastline imagery, and the coastal swallow in particular, a theory had taken shape in his mind.

The coastal swallow was notable for its rigid flight path, hugging the shoreline as it traveled to maintain a steady supply of food. This predictability had been harnessed for the improvement of crop yields, with several nations constructing large towers along their shores to house these birds on their migration so that their droppings could be collected and transported to farms inland. One such tower, the Sea Nest Spire, was nestled on the rocky beach of Alaboq's eastern shore. If the coastal swallows could be trusted enough to stop at these points along their route for the purposes of harvesting guano, was it not possible that an organization like the Ghosts could also take advantage of this certainty? Mareq did what he could to continue moving in the direction of the Draemoor Sound and the Spire, hoping that his hunch would finally carry him toward some answers.

Pausing to brush a bit of the glowing orange moss from his chest, he chuckled to himself. This hadn't turned out to be the adventure he had in mind. Sailing rough seas, taming uncharted wilderness, and scaling unconquered peaks were a far cry from the underground maze he found himself in. But despite the looming specter of a Ghost discovering him down in their realm, he was enjoying himself. As a child, he thought he yearned for the thrill of the journey itself, but after a dreadful few months of seasickness aboard Captain Tomau's vessel, he was coming to understand his excitement had always been for discovery, for stepping into the unknown and learning the secrets hidden within. For the first time since settling in Alaboq, Mareq no longer felt stuck. His adventure had resumed without setting one foot on the road.

Though the distance was hard to judge with each gray stone corridor merging seamlessly into the next, Mareq traveled eastward for what felt to him like miles. But as the musty air took on a more fishlike quality, his hopes begin to rise. Although his family's farm in Brey had always focused on dairy production, he recognized that scent all too well, as if it were wafting over from their neighbors' fields even now. Bird droppings were ahead, and from the strength of the odor, he guessed it would be in large quantities. He smiled as his pace began to quicken, shoulders scraping against the stones to either side. These tunnels *did* lead to the Sea Nest Spire, and unless Teacher Ias dictated the use of massive amounts of guano, Mareq suspected he would soon uncover a hub of her communication network.

His eyes had long since adjusted to the dim light, so as Mareq turned one final corner, he saw what at first glance was a dead end. The tunnel widened into what appeared to be a storage room. Piles of wooden crates were stacked high against the far wall and along the walls to either side, meticulously placed such that even the boxes at the top could be easily accessed by stepping on the ones below. Along the lips of each lid were Shadowmaw symbols scrawled in black ink, which he guessed were dates, and as he ran his eyes along them, he saw that whatever this collection held, it likely went back decades.

He reached out to the nearest one and carefully lifted the top to find neat rows of folded parchment, some plain, while others bore the remains of broken wax seals. Messages, then, as he had guessed, and some from sources important enough to emblazon their crests in wax. But as elated as he felt for being right, he knew this hoard was useless to him. It was too vast and organized by a system he didn't understand. He could spend weeks among the letters and never learn anything of substance that would illuminate the trade minister's schemes. Not that it mattered; he didn't have that time at his disposal.

Fearing the sound of a swishing cloak approaching from down the corridor any second, Mareq closed the lid softly and began to turn, freezing as he heard a brief rustle overhead. He shrank down and pressed himself against the stack of crates, cursing under his breath that he had allowed himself to be cornered. But as his eyes darted up to the source of the sound, he exhaled the breath he had been holding. In the roof of the tunnel was another trapdoor, fastened where the opposite wall met the ceiling. This one was lacking the complicated locking mechanism that had been beneath the kindling box's false bottom, and leading up to it were handholds and footholds that had been dug into the stone walls. Several coos accompanied more rustling from above, now recognizable as the flapping of wings.

He hadn't just discovered the Ghosts' repository of missives. This was their entrance into the Spire. *And another exit*, Mareq thought as he placed one foot awkwardly into a notch in the wall.

The holds, like the rest of the tunnel system, hadn't been designed with draqesh proportions in mind, so he had to jam his thick fingers and wide boots into the gaps, nearly needing to launch himself up as he ascended because the next grip was always *just* out of reach. Once at the top, he placed a hand below the wooden door and applied a little pressure, lifting it enough to peer inside. As he pressed his cheek to the wood and looked into the room above, he was immediately hit with a wave of the fishy stench that made his eyes water. Hardened guano littered the floor around the opening, along with bits of straw and mud that had likely fallen from the nests above. Not sensing an immediate threat, Mareq began to swing the door open wide when he heard a voice from within the spire.

"Another one?" the raspy voice said without a hint of alarm. "That's the second one to arrive this morning." Frozen in place, Mareq didn't know whether to rise out of the hole, ready to fight his way out, or shut the door and try to race back the way he had come. He would meet certain opposition within the Sea Nest Spire, but was it worth the risk to retrace his steps only to be pinned between a pursuing Ghost and another returning from Vinsart Hold?

"If Thymes insists on micromanaging his business affairs in Qedrad," the voice continued, more a mutter than a projection across a room, "he would do better to travel to Alaboq himself so that he could pull his own puppets' strings." There was a momentary silence followed by a deep sigh. "Dealing with that woman is almost not worth the coin."

Mareq chanced opening another inch to get a better view inside. Whoever was speaking wasn't addressing him. As he strained to get his face into a position that offered a better view of the room, he could now see the Spire was a circular tower, the walls of which were lined all the way to the top with nest after nest, housing what must be hundreds of birds at full capacity. At one such nest near head height, a tall man with lanky limbs was fussing with something tied to the leg of a coastal swallow. He pulled his hands away and unstoppered a small leather tube, revealing a roll of parchment that had been stuffed within, and broke the wax seal. The man read through the message before folding it neatly and reaching for a nondescript brown cloak that hung from a nearby peg.

"It's not even my turn to meet with her," he moaned as his feet turned toward the trap door. "Where are the freelancers when you need them?"

Sliding the door closed as quietly as he could, Mareq swung himself up onto the top of the closest stack and squeezed his body there below the ceiling. There would be nowhere to hide down below, and not enough time to create distance between them. He held his breath as the door opened wide and the gangly man began to descend, brown cloak nearly swallowing his thin form as he scampered down the wall. At the bottom, the man lifted the lid of a nearby crate and placed the folded message within before disappearing into the maze of tunnels with swift steps.

Mareq shifted back and forth to dislodge his bulky frame without toppling the crates, eventually freeing himself from his hiding spot and dropping to the floor. He listened to the echo of footsteps grow farther and farther away before breathing a sigh of relief. The immediate threat behind him, he returned to his original purpose and fished the new message from the crate. He recognized the wax seal from his time aboard Captain Tomau's merchant ship; it had been pressed onto more than a few shipping manifests even in the handful of months that he spent with the crew. The head of a stallion snapping through its bit, an admittedly heavy-handed crest Kefya had adopted after winning its independence, now represented the seal of the Council in Felona. Inside, written in beautiful flowing script, the message read:

My emissary will arrive in your city shortly. You are to arrange an audience for him with the King under whatever pretense you deem necessary. Haste will be rewarded, as will your usual discretion. — E. T.

Chapter 26

Northern Qedrad

Annika pulled her cloak tighter around her neck, her hand trembling on Olive's reins as the black mare kept pace behind the others. The weather had only grown colder since the party left behind the charred husk that was Turlaq's Fork, and the thick gray clouds overhead told her there would soon be a blanket of snow further complicating their journey northward. She wasn't built for these temperatures, but she wouldn't allow a complaint to slip past her lips. Seeing Rav wince on every uneven patch of road and Wymund gripping the horn of his mount's saddle to stay upright put her discomfort in a different context. Even Kymil had kept his quips in reserve since their narrow escape. A pall had fallen over them, just as it had over the countryside.

Still, whether she protested aloud mattered little. The truth remained that they couldn't spend another night out in the elements, though this final stretch of road wasn't offering much as an alternative. They had passed isolated farms since leaving Turlaq's Fork, but their map showed there would be no more significant settlements along this path until they reached Alaboq itself. A sense of urgency to catch up to the scorcher had prevented them from knocking on doors and asking permission to sleep in barns or stables so far, but as the first snowflake landed on Annika's cheek, she knew certain harsh realities were going to take precedence over their mission. No warning could be delivered if they were dead.

The sky grew dimmer as sleet and snow began to settle onto the road ahead of them over the final hours of the afternoon. Frost-capped pines dotted the path to either side, breaking up the flat monotony of Qedrad's scrublands but obscuring any potential safe havens from the freeze. As time ticked away and the cold sank deeper into her old bones, Annika wondered if it would be safer to turn back. The last home they had passed was three hours or so behind them, at which point a gamble had been made to press on "just a bit further," as Rav had grunted through gritted teeth. Annika regretted not pushing for an early day then, because as she glanced behind her now, she realized it would be much longer than a three-hour trek to make it back. The horses were more fatigued, the path more treacherous. No, their only hope lay ahead of them. With luck, they would reach another farmhouse before nightfall; otherwise, one or more of them would not make it to morning.

Her eyes landed on Kymil, the only one in their group still riding high in his saddle, draped as he was in a fur-lined cloak that had been stashed in his saddlebag. Perhaps fortune could be tipped in their favor.

Annika spurred her horse forward, the animal cautiously placing its steps in the building sheet of snow. She trotted first past Rav and then Wymund, each rider looking drained despite their attempts to appear otherwise. Rav grimaced in her direction as she passed, adjusting her weight in the saddle to favor her uninjured side. Had they been home in Virdoba, Annika could have procured a simple knitting serum that would have healed the woman's fractured rib in short order. The injury was more painful than it was life-threatening, so it wouldn't take a highly skilled witch to infuse a potion with enough power to fuse the bone.

Wymund, on the other hand, was in worse shape. The guard's face had taken on a pallor since their encounter with the scaled beast, and his eyes had lost their once-sharp focus. They had succeeded in staunching his bleeding with his coat, now ruined and caked with dried blood, but that wouldn't mean much if the man wasn't given the chance to replenish his fluids.

Finally, Annika sidled up beside Kymil and spoke low enough that the others behind her couldn't hear. "I worry some of us may lack the strength to survive the night out in this flurry. We'll need to find shelter."

The bard's face bore a stony expression for once, with only the faintest hint of levity left at the corners of his mouth, perhaps out of habit. He kept his eyes trained forward as he answered, "I'm open to suggestions. But as it stands now, the only protection I see are the snowy copses scattered about." He cast a sideways glance at her. "Perhaps we can enjoy the fresh scent of pine as we slowly drift off into our icy tombs."

"With Wymund and his optimism out of commission, we cannot afford another cynical voice in this troupe," she scolded. That made his real smirk return, if only for a moment. "I was hoping that you would be able to grant us a little luck," she added. "Help us spot a cottage or farm where we could stay warm for the night."

Kymil sighed as his shoulders sank. "It doesn't work that way. I could spend the next *week* trying to infuse my eyes, a physical impossibility as far as I'm aware, by the way, and it would still not change our fortune. It doesn't matter how lucky my gaze is if there is nothing out there to find."

Annika huddled lower into her saddle, defeated, as a chilling breeze picked up. She had set out on this journey to prevent another young woman from dying due to her own inexperience, but now she was faced with the reality that she couldn't even protect herself from the weather's whims. What little she had taught Rav about the nature of her abilities wouldn't be enough to keep her alive, particularly with the woman's penchant for meddling where she didn't belong. Annika remembered how she had felt when she learned of her sister's death, the helplessness and regret that had wedged into her heart from that day forward. Rav was on that same path now, running headlong into danger, blinded by the willful ignorance of youth.

It may have been a fool's errand all along. The girl needs real training, not just the half-faded memories of an old woman who's read too many books.

"If you two care to take a break from whispering sweet nothings to each other," Rav shouted from the back, her voice strained, "may I suggest we check out where that plume of smoke is coming from?" She pointed west, to a rising column of smoke that nearly blended with the thick cloud cover.

Her heart skipped a beat. Annika smiled despite her chattering jaw. *Leave it to a thief to have the best eyesight among us.* "I suppose we can, if you are finally willing to admit we should've stopped hours ago, before we had to spend all this time trudging through the snow."

"I'm fine," Rav said, already veering Doe off the main road. "I just worry about your joints freezing in place, old woman. Nobody wants to heft you on and off your horse the rest of the way."

Sparse tree cover grew denser as they ventured farther off the path, though anyone would be hard-pressed to call the area a forest. The landscape was spotted with thin trunks, no two any closer than a few yards, with the ground in between covered in frosted pine needles. However, despite the icy sheen that had formed over everything, Annika believed they were following an existing foot trail through the grove. It wasn't heavily traveled, but there was enough disturbance in the underbrush for her to suspect that someone walked these woods at regular intervals. Someone lived among these trees. She imagined the warmth of a roaring hearth against her face and urged Olive to step quicker.

Snow-dusted thistle hares and glade foxes skittered away as the four horses picked their way through the trees, with a few of the braver ones pausing to peer back at the trespassers before disappearing into the white landscape. The sight of wildlife had almost become foreign to her in these last few days, so she found her attention captured by the creatures as they scampered through the snow. Any animal that had survived the inferno in Turlaq's Fork would likely have been forced away to forage new lands, and she wondered if any of the animals she watched now had moved away from that intense heat to this unbearable cold in just a few short days. But as she watched, a loud, whiplike crack reverberated through the trees ahead, and she turned back to see two small figures running through the trees across their path.

"You didn't set it up right, Qiinan," whined one of the boys, rushing toward a tripped snare on stubby little legs. Annika could hear the rapid patter of paws darting away through the pine needles as the other boy caught up and knelt beside the first. "Da's always gonna get more than us if you don't learn to keep enough tension on the line."

"How do you know it's my fault, Ranar?" Qiinan asked, shoving the other's shoulder. "You probably didn't hide the bait well enough and the fox just snatched it off."

The pair continued to bicker until they heard Annika and her friends approach, turning with wide eyes toward the strangers moving in their direction. They were obviously brothers, the one called Ranar maybe a year or two older than the other, each with the same shade of chestnut brown hair resting in an unkempt mop of waves and curls on top of their heads. She could just make out emerald rings in their eyes, set in square-jawed faces atop wide frames. Each was covered in practical clothing made of wool and leather hides. With eyes like those, their elven heritage was undeniable, but if their ears came to a point, it was so minor as to be nonexistent. Likewise, those jawlines spoke to draqesh parentage as well.

She smiled as she thought of all the geographic barriers separating the majority of the elven population in southwest Anera from the draqeshis to the north. The mountains and rivers, untamed forests and barren wastes, all so easily conquered by love and lust.

"Hello there," Annika called out to them, positioning her mount in front of her injured friends to avoid further frightening the children. "We're looking for a place to escape the cold for the night. Is your mother or father around?"

The boys shared a nervous glance that seemed to contain within it an entire silent conversation before the older one, Ranar, gestured back with his thumb. "Um, yeah. We live back that way. But my da's real strong and my ma's real scary, so if you're bad guys then you're gonna be in trouble."

"Yeah," Qiinan added. "Plus we're fast so you can't snatch us away."

Kymil laughed as he swung down off his horse, creating a dramatic flourish with his cloak that dazzled the boys. "Young sirs," he said as he approached them and gave a deep bow. "Do you like tales of adventure and heroism? About good men and women conquering evil and slaying horrible beasts?" Each word was punctuated with a great leap or a thrust of an imaginary blade, and Annika watched as the boys' wide eyes shifted from concern to awe. Their mouths hung open as they stood transfixed by the bard's performance.

He took a knee in front of them, still more than a head taller than the children as he placed his hands on their shoulders. "Well, these three I travel with are some of the heroes in those stories. And you two can be a part of their tale as the lads who patched them up and sheltered them before they saved Anera from an evil villain. Do you want to be heroes too?" They nodded their heads vigorously. "Good, then lead the way home, champions of righteousness!"

Annika could see their minds at work, daydreaming about being a part of an epic hero's journey as they nearly hopped in excitement back toward their home. Kymil remained out of his saddle, opting to lead his horse by the reins while the others walked along beside him. After what felt like a quarter of a mile trudging through the ever-thickening layer of snow, a small clearing became visible through the trees ahead, just large enough for what appeared to be a short column built of smooth river stones and a wooden door lying flush with the ground. Tendrils of gray smoke danced from the top of the stone column as they rose higher into the sky, filling the area with the scent of stewed potatoes and roasting meat. Her stomach rumbled as she left the saddle, eager to rush inside and enjoy some Qedradan hospitality before the crunching of boots through the snow announced the presence of another person emerging into the clearing from the south.

"This game looks a lot bigger than the ones we set traps for, boys," the man said, his voice a gruff growl that belied the good-natured grin plastered across his face. He wore a fur-lined leather coat over his broad, stout frame and carried the bodies of four thistle hares under one arm. His hair was darker than the boys' own locks but was no less unruly as it draped down to his shoulders, blending into a short-trimmed beard. When he spoke, Annika had to concentrate or risk being lost in the man's heavy draqesh accent, each vowel drawn out in his otherwise rapid speech. Tying the animals on to his belt, the draqeshi crossed his arms and shook his head. "I don't think we have pots big enough to cook them."

The boys raced up to greet their father, Qiinan throwing his arms around the man's leg, Ranar inspecting the spoils of the hunt. "These are heroes, Da!" Qiinan shouted as the man winced playfully from the volume. "They said if we feed them and let them sleep here then we get to be heroes too!"

"Is that so?" the man asked as he patted the boys on their shoulders, gently guiding the younger one off him. He appeared to appraise each of the visitors, that warm smile dropping from his square face for a moment as his eyes passed over Wymund gingerly stepping down from Resin's saddle. But it returned as quickly as it went, producing the effect of a welcoming, squat wall draped in leather and fur. "Well, come on down then. My name is Ormuq, and my wife should be finishing up with the stew about now."

Ormuq lifted the wooden hatch on the ground to reveal a set of steps carved into the earth that descended into a room lit by the warm glow of a fire. He helped Kymil tend to the horses, sheltering them in a nearby copse, then ushered the party down into his home.

Annika found herself in a cavernlike room that was larger than she had expected, extending the length of two or three typical Virdoban dwellings in a narrow line. The walls at first appeared to be made from loose soil, but a slight sheen could be noticed as the flickering flames cast their light around the room, suggesting some form of lacquer had been applied to solidify the structure. At the back of the hollow were two other doorways leading into smaller rooms, through which simple beds and wardrobes could be seen, while the rest of the main chamber was occupied by a dining table in the center and a sitting area toward the far end.

Shelves and cabinets were spaced along the walls, filled with a wide variety of books. Some were traditionally leather-bound while others appeared to be pages held together by loops of twine. There was even a small chest with a mound of scrolls that had missed the binding process altogether. At least one person who lived here was both well read and well traveled to have amassed such a collection.

Frustrated grumbles met them as they reached the bottom of the stairs, coming from a woman who stood with her back to them as she stirred a pot suspended over an open flame. Her long golden-red hair fell like a smooth curtain to the small of her back, its gentle flow only interrupted by a long set of pointed ears reaching out from the sides of her head. She stood at least an inch or two taller than even Wymund's impressive height and wore nothing more than a single layer of cotton clothing despite the plummeting temperatures above.

"I'll never get the hang of this," she said. "The consistency's never right. I don't see why you can't keep cooking the meals."

"Learning new skills is the best way to keep the adventure alive now that you're home with us for good, warmheart," Ormuq said. "Besides, I was out collecting the main course while the boys were out collecting guests."

At that, her head snapped around, her emerald-ringed eyes scanning over each of them with a sharp gaze. Like most of her kind, her features were undeniably delicate and beautiful, but there was an edge to them. Her beauty was not unlike the artistry of an exquisitely crafted blade. And surprisingly, her skin was more akin to her husband's pale tone—not unheard of among elven populations, but certainly a rarity.

"Fantastic," she said without a hint of Ormuq's hospitality. "I hope you all like your soup somehow both watery and chewy." Turning to her children, she added, "Help your father prepare the rabbits. I've had enough *adventure* for the day." She pushed past the small crowd that clustered at the bottom of the stairs, muttering, "I'm going to get more firewood."

Annika watched her disappear out of the hatch and into blowing snow without so much as donning a cloak. Ormuq must have read the surprise on her face because he shrugged and chuckled. "Don't worry yourself over Tiialya. I've watched her trudge around out there like that for hours without catching a sniffle." Waving the rest of them toward the table, he gathered his sons with the other arm and walked toward the bubbling stew. "Put up your feet while we finish cooking. If any of you need fresh bandages or ointments, there should be some in that cabinet near the back wall," he said, his soft gaze lingering on Wymund's side.

Wymund made to move toward the supplies himself before Rav forced him into a chair with a look that would have given anyone pause. As much as the young woman put on a tough exterior, she was all soft inside. Annika helped her collect some clean bandages, along with a paste that she recognized as an analgesic. As long as the plagueman this was purchased from wasn't peddling snake oil, it would at least allow the rest of the journey north to be more tolerable for her injured companions.

The thought of the traveling medics sparked another as they brought the supplies back to the table. They were trapped here for the night. Rav would have no escape from her lessons this time.

Kymil carefully helped Wymund remove his outer layers while Annika did the same for Rav. Much of her side had turned a deep purple in the days since their battle with that reptilian creature, but as ugly as it looked, she was thankful the encounter hadn't gone worse.

"The person who made this cream may have been like you," Annika said as she applied the ointment to Rav's bruised rib, the unsurprising smell of cloves wafting up from the jar. Plaguemen had to rely on natural remedies, after all. Rav winced as Annika rubbed the cream into her skin. "Someone with a passive connection to a Wellspring, I mean. Some of the plaguemen are con artists out to make coin off the desperation of others, but most draw energy from the same source as my sister did when she was infusing her potions."

Tiialya came barreling down the stairs then, long arms wrapped around a bundle of firewood that she carried over to her family. The young boys had managed to skin a rabbit apiece in the time she had been away and were handing them over to Ormuq for cooking.

"Passive witches?" Rav asked, drawing Annika's attention back to the fractured rib. "So they just wake up one day with vials full of healing tonics beside their beds?"

Annika smiled. "No, though I'm sure that would be a dream come true for many of them. Plaguemen draw power from the World Shroud in the same way you do; instinctually, as a protective measure. But in their case, it's not lightning but the essence of life itself." Rav's silence and blank expression told her that she was expected to elaborate. "They cannot get sick, Rav. They heal rapidly from any wound as long as it isn't initially lethal. That's why they're always willing to offer succor to towns overrun with blight. They know it won't affect them."

Rav pulled her shirt back over her bruise with slow, careful movements. "So they aren't really like me, then. If I siphon too much energy, I fall to the ground convulsing with light shooting from my eyes, while they take care of any minor scratch they accrued that day."

"It's not all bad," Tiialya said, carrying over two soup bowls to place in front of them. Her scowl had been replaced with a good-natured smirk. "At least you can get drunk. They could drain every last whiskey barrel dry and only have a full bladder to show for it."

Annika watched her walk away and return with two more bowls, placing them before Kymil and Wymund. The guardsman's color seemed to be returning simply from being out of the cold, and he dove into the soup as soon as it left her hand. Kymil graciously thanked their host for the both of them, that ever-present gleam in his eyes, while she took a seat at the end of the table.

"Do you know much about World Shroud theory?" Annika asked.

Tiialya laughed. "Not in so many words. My mother *is* a scorcher, though, so you could say I've had a lifetime of experience in the matter."

Of course, Annika thought. The woman had walked out into the snowstorm in attire that would be comfortable on the most humid day in Felona. *She's a winterborn.*

Rav's eyes lit up at the mention of another scorcher, and even Wymund looked up from where his face was buried in his bowl. But Annika was determined to finish her point before they could launch into an interrogation. Thankfully, an assist had fallen into her lap.

"Ah, so you do know something about the potential cost of pushing beyond one's limits."

The elven woman looked first at Rav then back at Annika before nodding and relaxing into her chair. "Are we trying to impart a lesson here? If so, it is an important one. You would do well to listen to your mother." Rav scoffed, while Annika chuckled and shook her head.

"It's true those of us with a passive connection to a Wellspring run the risk of pulling more through the World Shroud than we can handle, and for some the cost is greater than others." Tiialya placed a hand on Rav's, locking eyes with her. To Annika's surprise, the woman seemed to have her attention. "While it would be nice if our bodies just worked hard to drive any toxins out, I'm afraid that when girls like us lose control, the outcome is much different. I could stay comfortable out in the ice for hours, maybe days if I had to. But eventually I would shut down, overtaken by a fever that would roast me from the inside out."

Rav's jaw opened as if to say something, but the words seemed to catch in her throat. Before she could find them again, Tiialya added, "And even knowing that, I don't envy what you face with the Illuminated Death. At least I would be unconscious before I went." After a moment, Rav nodded and slumped back in her seat, her brow furrowed.

"Are you making friends, warmheart?" Ormuq said, walking over to stand next to his wife and kissing the side of her head. Though seated, the draqeshi still had to strain his neck some for his lips to reach. Annika could see over his shoulder that he had set two of the rabbits on a spit over the fire while his children continued to work on the others.

Tiialya closed her eyes and smiled as she leaned her head into his, reaching up with one hand to cup her husband's face. When she opened them again, she looked to her guests, a bit of color creeping into her cheeks. "I suppose I do need to apologize for my behavior when you arrived. I've only recently taken up the tasks of running a home, and it would seem I don't have the natural talent for it that I had in my other line of work."

"There's no need for that, madam," Kymil said. "It was my impression that rude introductions are a rite of passage for this lot."

"He's right," Wymund said, finally coming up for air. "We've encountered far worse than hurt feelings in our travels thus far, and no doubt will again." He shot a glance at Annika, his eyes clearly seeking her approval. She nodded. "To that end, perhaps you could tell us more about your mother, the scorcher. We may be crossing paths with one like her, and any advice you could provide would be welcome."

"Certainly," Tiialya said with a shrug. "Though I'm afraid her life is far duller than most expect when they hear she has those talents. She runs a smithy in Draemoor; a quite successful one, at that. It's hard for other smiths to compete with a woman who can heat and shape metals at a fraction of the time and material cost." A look of pride crossed her face as she spoke before she must have sensed the somber tone of her audience.

"But she's never been one for the life of flash and excitement that most associate with people like her. If this 'crossed path' you speak of involves conflict, I don't have any childhood tales of watching my mother fight that you could learn from." Letting her eyes fall on each of them before lingering on Rav, she added, "My only advice would be to finish it quick. Before they have the opportunity to ignite."

"Though it's probably best to stay off that path," Ormuq said. "My wife forgets that not everyone has the same thirst for excitement that she does."

"Unfortunately, we're not just chasing thrills," Annika said. As hesitant as she had been to divulge the details of their quest to Kymil given his inscrutable charm, the information they could gain from the daughter of a scorcher made the risk seem more acceptable. "We believe this man to be fomenting a war between Qedrad and the elves of Choii Stier, likely backed by funding from Felona. However dangerous, we mean to stop him. I've lived through war once before, and I have no intention of seeing it again."

Ormuq placed a hand on Tiialya's back, his boisterous face now crestfallen. "It saddens me that there is such hatred for my wife and her kind in the southlands that they would be willing to stoke the fires of battle. There are still those who consider my people ice-addled savages despite the centuries we have spent living among one another, but at least there is a history of bloodshed to explain such animosity. The Kefyans fought alongside the elves in their war, though." He gave a humorless chuckle. "Perhaps we are not the ones with the addled minds."

While most at the table nodded and murmured their agreement, Tiialya's gaze remained fixed on Annika, her brow furrowed. "Backing from Felona? Does this scorcher's trail happen to lead to Alaboq?"

"It does," she replied.

Nodding to herself, Tiialya said, "It may be nothing, but I took a job in Alaboq some months ago. My last before coming to join my family in this chaos." She gestured to her sons behind her, who had finished with the remaining rabbits and were now racing potatoes across the counter. "I was tasked with delivering a message for a group of Teacher Ias's followers. Normally a group far too secretive for my comfort, but they were shorthanded and willing to pay out the nose for a simple handoff, so I decided to take it. Whatever was in the note, it was sealed with the Kefyan crest and to be delivered to Qedrad's trade minister surreptitiously."

She shook her head and sighed. "It didn't sit right with me, though. Communications between heads of state being passed along back channels is never a sign of innocence."

Annika shared a look with her allies. "Members of the Kefyan Council are the only ones who use those seals." Wymund's jaw clenched as Rav voiced her lack of surprise. Kymil's eyes flashed as he failed to suppress a smile. International intrigue was always a welcome addition in a bard's tale.

"You traveled to the city recently, Tiialya," Annika continued. "I understand that King Berenqar has a reputation for granting audiences quite freely, so I know the man we pursue may not have a difficult time meeting with him. Is there any way that would allow us to have the king's ear as soon as we arrive?"

The woman thought for a moment, picking at the edge of her thumbnail with her forefinger. "I've had a bad feeling about that message for weeks, and now to find out so many lives are at stake . . . " Tiialya knew something. Ormuq rubbed his wife's back, and after sharing a glance and a nod, she sighed. "I do know someone with access to Vinsart Hold, but you won't be walking in the front gates as honored guests. How would you feel about sneaking in the back door?"

Before Annika could answer, Rav leaned forward, her mood apparently having recovered from contemplating her own mortality, her childlike grin reaching from ear to ear. "I would feel right at home. You have your contact get us in the door, I'll take care of the rest."

Chapter 27

Alaboq

The stretch of gold-veined marble in the park was striking in relation to the sandstone that surrounded it, even more so now that the snowmelt had darkened the sandstone's typical lighter shade. It was rare for snow to stick within Alaboq's walls; the city's natural ability to retain heat from the sun often prevented any frozen layer from forming. So as the Hooked Peninsula had been buffeted by snowfall over the last few days, Qedrad's capital city had only gotten cold and damp. Tetamii opened miniscule tears in the World Shroud around his body as he walked beside the marble platform, keeping himself warm and dry. If anyone else in the park had dared to look closely at the man, they might have seen small wisps of steam as the precipitation evaporated off his white tailcoat. But his dour expression seemed enough to avert any wandering eyes.

Statues of Teacher Melan had been placed at regular intervals beside the platform, also constructed from marble but without the strains of gold snaking through the stone. The Kingdom of Qedrad had spared no expense importing the expensive material, but money alone could not duplicate the aesthetic technique created by the Dawn Ones. Still, the artistry was undeniable, and of the two dozen or so statues that lined the expansive platform, Tetamii couldn't find one flaw beyond the sculptor's aversion to depicting her ears. Much like her twin, Teacher Leros, humans and elves alike claimed her as one of their own. It took a rather bold artist to represent either Dawn One without their long hair obscuring the sides of their heads.

Tetamii found a bench nestled between the trunks of two jade canopies, their long, thin branches full of bright green leaves that would keep him dry without the need to draw power from the Wellspring. He sat facing the Dawn Ones' ancient platform, and though it wasn't as visually arresting as the massive Hall of Merchants in Felona, there was always something to admire about a structure that had lasted for millennia.

The platform itself was located between the two Melan neighborhoods, extending about a quarter of those districts' lengths, and surrounded by jade canopies on all sides. At each corner stood a column with carved, fluted spirals running up its three-yard height, and along each side were etched reliefs depicting Teacher Melan on her voyages. One showed the Dawn One perched on the bow of a towering wooden vessel as it crested the waves of an unsettled sea, while another displayed Her meeting with a gathering of four people in long robes, each with brilliant green eyes. The longer edges of the rectangular structure had carvings that demonstrated sequential events rather than single moments from her story. One side showed her and Teacher Leros exploring each region of Anera, and the other showed the Twins traveling lands Tetamii didn't recognize, though he assumed they represented the elven continent of Liiashae.

The people of Alaboq had named this park the Verdant Statuary in reference to their own additions to the area, but as Tetamii took in this ancient tribute to the goddess of exploration, he thought that could only be because they were unable capture the true essence of this place in suitable words.

The sound of hurried footsteps drew him back to the present in time to see a woman slide onto the bench next to him. Her long auburn hair was held in a tight braid that draped down her back, and though she wore common cotton clothes, he noticed they were too pristine to have seen daily use. Likewise, the slight smile she sported didn't reach her eyes, another bit of her disguise that felt forced. From what Tetamii had heard about the harsh woman, the expression was likely as unfamiliar to her as the simple attire she had clearly purchased for this outing. He sighed, wondering how all the lofty contacts he was forced to work alongside could be so inept.

All these years perfecting my craft when it seems I could have failed upward into a position of authority.

"Is tardiness representative of the Qedradan work ethic," Tetamii asked, giving her little more than a sidelong glance to acknowledge her arrival, "or is it more of a personal character flaw?"

Sylicera Hadac bristled at the insult, gripping her hands tighter in her lap as she exhaled sharply. "The duties of a kingdom's trade minister aren't ones that can simply be set aside if appearances are to be maintained." She returned the sideways stare. "Though I wouldn't expect someone unfamiliar with the upper echelons of political life to understand. Some responsibilities cannot be delegated to *hired help*."

"Do not misunderstand your role, Sylicera." Her nose lifted even higher at the pointed omission of her title. "We were both contracted into Elikar's game, but while I was hired on merit, he was only paying for your office. It bothers me little if our employer is forced to pay for the loyalty of your successor." The woman tugged at her collar as sweat began to bead on her face and neck, the air around her head suddenly more akin to a furnace than the wintery weather she had experienced moments before. "Elikar demands allegiance from his employees, but I have always felt that respect for your superiors was more important."

Sylicera swallowed hard but maintained her stoic mask, making no moves to wipe the perspiration from her brow. "I have arranged for a meeting between yourself and King Berenqar two nights from now. The king will be holding a dinner banquet to honor his daughter's sixteenth year, and as is customary, will be granting audiences to a select few visitors during the festivities. I have ensured that you will be one of those few and have primed the king to expect reports of attacks by 'elven brutes' in the south. Your actions in Turlaq's Fork certainly helped to bolster my claims."

For the first time since she had arrived, a small smile crept onto her face. "Staged or not, I am relishing the thought of driving their influence out of my home. The dagger-heads are always seeking to rise above their station."

He had revealed his heritage by drawing heat energy around her, but her pride couldn't accept his slight without offering her own retort. "Bigotry is the hallmark of the small-minded," Tetamii said as he rose from the bench. She opened her mouth to respond but was cut off by a flick of his hand that nearly made her swallow her tongue; a little sweat would be the least of her concerns if he was pushed too far. "But enough small minds can be leveraged to do great things if guided appropriately. Take care that you stay with the herd so that you can be shepherded as needed."

Leaving the woman fuming on the bench, Tetamii marched away toward the market district. He had only two days to prepare for his audience with the king, and needed to procure parchment and ink. Martial prowess wasn't the only skill impressed upon him by his training in the Clipped Gulls. A convincing forged document could be just as effective.

PART III

ALABOQ
CAPITAL OF QEDRAD
VINSART HOLD
LYRI BLOSSOM
MARKET
MELAN NORTH
THISTLE HARE WARREN
SEA NEST SPIRE
VERDANT STATUARY
MELAN SOUTH
THE DOCKS
DRAEMOOR SOUND

CHAPTER 28

ALABOQ

The road leading into Alaboq was well tended, with the grasses and shrubs to either side of the path trimmed short such that no errant strands poked through the blanket of snow covering the ground. And despite the continued snowfall each day since departing Tiialya and Ormuq's home, Rav noted that as far as a mile outside of the city, some team must have been charged with clearing the road. No more than a light dusting of ice impeded their travel over this final stretch.

Likewise, the gate into the city itself was a sight to behold, with two massive and heavily lacquered oak doors stretching at least twenty-five feet into the sky, matching the height of the sandstone walls extending to the left and right. Virdoba had gates through its walls as well, but each entry into Rav's adopted home had been vandalized with score marks and paints, which, along with general weathering, created an air of disrepair upon entering. First impressions counted for something, and Alaboq prioritized welcoming guests with its best.

"It's refreshing to see a major city that reinvests its spoils into general upkeep rather than exclusive galas with imported wines," Rav said, nodding to the line of King's Guard standing to one side of the gate, their breastplates gleaming from the sunlight reflecting off the snow outside. Unlike the guards they had encountered farther south, each of these wore a heavy red wool cloak to match the tunic under their armor.

"Qedrad is a tanistry," Annika replied, her eyes as wide as Rav's felt upon seeing the city's splendor. "When the heir to the throne is not guaranteed by blood but selected from among the noble houses' candidates, each house has a vested interest in demonstrating their worth to the nation so that their own scion can ascend."

Kymil strummed his lute absentmindedly. "Meanwhile, Kefya's Council simply rewards wealth with power, and coincidentally, power with even more wealth. Funny how that works."

Buildings rose seemingly right out of the sandstone below, so much so that a person could be forgiven for believing the city had been carved out of one enormous rock. Rust-colored tile roofs topped the three- and four-story-tall structures lining the main road, each dripping snowmelt onto the street below through a duct system that funneled the water into narrow channels on the sides of the path. Surprisingly, although it was still cold within Alaboq's walls, Rav felt she could loosen her cloak's hold around her neck just a bit. No ice seemed to stick to the ground, as if the city itself trapped heat to deal with weather such as this.

Rows of trees formed a median along the paths of the market district, their cerulean and alabaster petals holding firm against the chill. They rode their mounts with the flow of pedestrians, deftly maneuvering around the men and woman stopping to browse at the various merchant stalls and shop windows dotting the path, keeping their eyes open for an inn near the market's center. Tiialya's friend, a draqeshi named Mareq Iq'Urlset, supposedly had a storeroom located there, and after obtaining room and board, he would be their first stop.

Though finding a healer would also be a top priority. Rav glanced back at Wymund, riding higher in the saddle since they had procured some of the pain-relieving cream, but she knew her friend still needed the attention of a professional. From what she had seen, his wounds had started to close on their own, but she was no stranger to cuts and gashes herself. Just because the flesh healed over didn't mean that it healed correctly. The lasting ache in her side, despite a fading bruise, reminded her of that.

Just ahead, Rav could see a monumental bronze statue of Teacher Leros towering above the buildings at the far end of the market's center, with his hand outstretched for payment. The god of commerce stood watch over all the trade that went on in Alaboq, and a small grin had been shaped into the metal to demonstrate the Dawn One's dictates; business was meant to be amiable and fair, even when fighting for the upper hand.

All around the base of the statue were tables hosting parties of two or more individuals, each in the characteristic bright colors of an Alaboqan, though their silks had been replaced by heavy wool jackets, tunics, and dresses. They wore vibrant yellows and greens, as well as blues and reds so vivid that they seemed to reflect the sunlight breaking though the cloud cover above. Kymil's warnings about their style had not done it justice. The palette was eye-popping compared to her richly attired friends and family in Felona and a far cry from the murky browns and blacks enjoyed by the shady citizens of Virdoba's back alleys. She could almost hear her mother's voice describing the Alaboqan style as gauche and garish, and she hated that she agreed.

She guided Doe out into the circle and saw that the main thoroughfare running through the city had been constructed on a slight incline. To her right, a winding path led down to the docks, at this distance little more than brown lines against the deep blue expanse of the Draemoor Sound, with a fleet of merchant and naval vessels vying for positions in the port. But farther up the hill, past a dense cluster of wooden buildings that looked out of place next to the natural beauty of the sandstone structures around her, was the single largest building Rav had ever seen.

Vinsart Hold was nestled at the highest point of Alaboq's incline, its already-imposing size bolstered by its position overlooking the rest of the city below. Constructed of sandstone in the style of the homes and shops in the market, the citadel looked as if it simply belonged there, as if nature itself had birthed it from the stone. Unlike the architecture she was used to in Kefya, there were no elven-inspired fluted spires cresting the fortress's skyline, nor any of the vaulted dome ceilings for which the most prominent buildings in Felona were known. Vinsart Hold was almost utilitarian in its simplicity, all right angles and smooth surfaces up to its flat, rust-colored tiles, but that understated design only added to its striking impression.

A brief glance around the perimeter of the market center revealed a number of inns, though to Rav's eye, more than a couple were not up for consideration. They were either too full or too empty, and her friends couldn't afford either an excess of prying eyes or a lack of crowd cover during their stay. However, one building drew her attention. It was one of the few she had seen since entering Alaboq that had added its own private row of blue-and-white petaled trees on each side of the door. The sign hanging above the entrance read THE PETALED PATH and depicted a curving cobblestone walkway covered by a scattering of painted petals. She could see through the windows that the tavern was busy but not crowded. A fair price for a meal and pillow could be found within.

Two young stable hands waited outside the inn as they approached, taking coin in one hand and reins in the other before leading their mounts toward public stalls north of the circle. Salted butter and cream could be smelled even before she crossed the threshold, accompanied by an invisible wave of heat from the three lit hearths lining the dining room. Four serving girls darted between tables, carrying cups of what appeared to be a frothy, dark ale from the bar to their customers, who were eating a hearty white chowder from wooden bowls.

While most of the inn's clientele were Qedradan, a bit taller than people from southern Anera and sporting their vibrant wools, Rav could see the thick beards and heavy brows of people who had traveled from the east, possibly as far as Destueqa, as well as the more familiar styles of Kefyan travelers. There were even a handful of Achen trade-masters huddled close to one of the fireplaces, their near burgundy skin visibly goose pimpled anywhere their loose linen clothing didn't touch.

After finding an empty table close to the bar, the party sat as a woman in her middle years approached. She was tall and pretty despite time starting to make its effects known, with lines striking out from the corners of her eyes and mouth and gray strands contrasting with the tight, dark curls hanging around her head. Her smile was pleasant and full of warmth as she stopped next to them, wiping her hands across her apron.

"We had a decent haul of shellfish from the docks this morning," she said. "Can I get all of you a bowl of our chowder? It'll warm you up quicker than the fires alone."

"Yes, that would be much appreciated," Annika answered, pulling a few silver libers from her purse. Qedradan coins were called crests, but silver was still silver. "And a couple of rooms as well. We are rushed at the moment, though, so if you could just prepare the chambers for us we will return later this evening."

"Libers?" the woman asked as she took the coins. "I'll take them, but I don't have the correct change. The currency exchange is in Melan North. We can settle up when you return. Regardless, I'll have your rooms ready for you." When Annika agreed, the woman nodded before turning back to the kitchen.

At the back of the room, a draqesh woman sang about the Divider, the last sole monarch of Destueqa prior to the War of Unification. History hadn't been kind to the man, deservedly so as the moniker referred not just to his desire to hold back the "hordes of icy savages" from entering the rest of Anera, but also his propensity for separating his rivals' heads from their necks. The verses imagined the ruthless ruler having other pieces of his anatomy divided by the people he had wronged, and Rav chuckled. Given the repercussions the world would face if they failed, as well as the injuries they had sustained along the way, laughter felt odd now, but not unwelcome. And by the time the innkeeper returned with bowls of the rich, savory chowder, she couldn't deny that her spirits had been lifted.

"On to Iq'Urlset's home, then?" Wymund asked, scraping the last drops of soup from his bowl. He held his left arm at an awkward angle as he tilted the bowl, his range of motion limited by the incomplete scarring on his side. "Unless we somehow managed to bypass the scorcher, he has already had some time in the city to orchestrate his plans. We cannot afford to squander what time we have left."

Rav shared a glance with Annika, the woman seeming to share her concern. "Maybe finding a healer should be our next stop," she said. "A city this size has to be crawling with real plaguemen. There may even be a witch around who can bring us back to top form." Gesturing toward Kymil, she added, "Take him with you and see who you can find. People seem to offer information up to him for free, so it shouldn't take long. Annika and I will go speak with Tiialya's friend and meet up with the two of you later."

Wymund shook his head, sparing a moment to look sidelong at the bard. The two had grown more amiable over their journey, but that didn't mean her friend liked playing second fiddle to such a charismatic figure. "Tiialya described Mareq as a decent man who comes from humble means. If a criminal and an aristocrat show up at his door, he may balk before we can even begin." Standing from the table, Wymund winced slightly as he stretched before replacing it with a grin. "I mean no offense, but a trustworthy face will likely go a long way in endearing this stranger to our cause."

"Boring is the one personality trait I cannot seem to master," Kymil said as he stood to join him. "It may be useful to have Wymund along in case honor and ethics are the only things capable of selling the importance of our task."

Annika shrugged as she finished her own chowder. "This man has been in Alaboq much longer than we have, Ravael. It may be faster to learn if he knows of a healer than to search for one on our own."

Rav sighed before nodding. "Let's just hope we don't scare him off approaching as a crowd of strangers instead of just two kindly women."

"Oh?" Kymil asked, one corner of his mouth shooting up to match his cocked eyebrow. "Will there be two more ladies joining us?"

Rav shoved the bard's shoulder as she walked back out into the cold.

Chapter 29

Alaboq

Mareq took an instinctive step back from the doorway, keeping a grip on the handle in case he needed to slam it shut. Outside stood four strangers, two with elven blood and another with shoulders even a draqeshi could admire. While the fourth was an older woman, it didn't assuage his fears that Ias's Ghosts had found him after his jaunt through their tunnels. He had already encountered another elderly woman working with them, after all. And while they didn't look outwardly threatening, he took care to note the knives hanging from the younger woman's belt.

"I wasn't expecting company," he said, shifting weight onto his front foot in case he needed to hold the door closed. There might be four of them, but he guessed not even the tall human would be able to budge his bulky frame. "What's this about?"

"We're sorry to trouble you, Mr. Iq'Urlset," the older woman said, bowing her head slightly. "My name is Annika Iatorii. Your friends Tiialya and Ormuq suggested we seek you out once we arrived in Alaboq. She said you might be able to help us."

The tension in his shoulders relaxed as he opened the door wider. He trusted Tiialya's judgment; she wouldn't have sent anyone dangerous his way. Mareq laughed. "Well, I'm not sure how much she promised you. I'm not a man of means, as you can see," he said, gesturing around to his mostly bare living space. "But I'm happy to assist in any way I can. Please, come in out of the cold."

The four visitors filed in, each introducing themselves as they passed before occupying most of the cramped space within. Annika and Kymil took two of the three seats at his small wooden table, the elf's knees nearly reaching the height of his chin with the seat's draqeshi dimensions. Still, he seemed more amused than uncomfortable as he tilted the chair back and crossed one leg over the other. Rav planted herself atop a stack of his storage crates and began to toss a cinder plum from hand to hand while Wymund leaned his back against a wall. Mareq joined Annika and Kymil at the table, eager to learn why Tiialya had wrapped him up with this eclectic bunch.

"I'm afraid we don't have the time to ease you into this," Wymund said with a frown. "What we need to accomplish here is too important to the future of Anera, so brevity will have to take precedence over caution. We understand that you—"

"Irasil be damned, Wymund," Rav interjected, tossing the fruit at his face. "Can brevity take precedence over formality too?" She turned to lock eyes with Mareq, leaning forward with the same mischievous sparkle in her eyes that he recognized from traveling with Tiialya. "We need to break into Vinsart Hold and speak with Berenqar. Tiialya said you could help us with that."

Mareq felt his pulse quicken, his thoughts racing to keep pace with his heart. Tiialya was the one who had told him to be cautious around the citadel, that back-room deals were being made and that she didn't want him caught in the potential crossfire, and now she was sending four people to his doorstep with the impression that he would help them break in? He was stunned. His face must have said as much because Kymil jumped in after only a moment's pause, his voice like silk.

"What my brash colleague means to say is that we have urgent matters to discuss with the king, news that mean the balance of life and death for thousands of people." He flashed a smile with such confidence that Mareq found himself returning it, albeit a smaller one. "We know that King Berenqar meets with us commoners on occasion, but given the gravity of the situation, Tiialya said you may be able to skip us to the front of the line."

Mareq rested his chin in a palm and stared at the table. "Listen, I don't know what she has volunteered me for, but I couldn't help you if

I wanted, which I'm not even sure I would. There's something boiling beneath the surface of Vinsart Hold, some hidden plot that I believe is being kept from the king." His guests shared a look among themselves at that, but he continued.

"The digging I've done has gotten me closer to the truth, but if I become associated with a group of footpads sneaking into Berenqar's chambers, nothing I discover will grant me any favors from the man. I'll be locked up with the rest of you." Mareq shook his head and sighed. "Besides, my only access to the citadel is through the kitchen during deliveries. It's not like I've been granted permission to bring guests. Your best option will be to request an audience through official channels. Within a month or two, you should be able meet with him."

"Months?" Rav scoffed and jumped off the stack. "The man clearly doesn't understand the meaning of the word 'urgent.' Come on," she said as she strode over to the door. "I'll have better luck scouting the place anyway."

Wymund barred her path with an arm, giving her an even look. She crossed her arms and exhaled sharply, but she did stop and took a place beside him on the wall. "You mentioned a secret being kept from King Berenqar," Wymund said. "We are pursuing a man who aims to speak with him, likely under the guise of a trade official given the nature of his ruse. It's a lie of course, one that could lead to ruinous results if not intercepted, and we have reason to believe he has ties to powerful, well-connected individuals." The man's stoic mask slipped for a moment, his eyes pleading for help. "Please, we need to get to the king before he does, and your access is our only advantage."

The message from the Council of Felona rushed to the front of his mind. An emissary would be arriving soon, someone that Sylicera was supposed to assist in meeting the king. He chuckled despite the room's dour mood. "Tiialya always seems to stumble onto the right path. Maybe helping you four *is* the next step in my investigation."

He stood from the table and retrieved the folded parchment from beneath his bedroll, the wax seal still affixed to its back. "Do the initials E. T. mean anything to you?" Mareq asked, sliding the paper across the table toward Annika and Kymil.

Annika's eyes flared. "Elikar Thymes," she breathed. Kymil's eyebrow rose as he glanced at the older woman while Rav and Wymund's faces remained blank.

"Who?" Rav asked. When Annika didn't respond right away, she took several steps forward to stand over her at the table. "Annika, who is Elikar Thymes?"

"The Kefyan port admiral," Annika replied, still not making eye contact with anyone in the room. "He sits on the Council."

"And? We already knew someone else was pulling Swithred's strings and paying this scorcher."

Mareq's chest tightened at hearing that word. They had neglected to mention that little detail. What *had* Tiialya gotten him into? He swallowed hard.

"Why does it matter what title this rich bastard holds?" Rav asked. "We'll deal with him once we've stopped a war."

"It matters a great deal, Ravael," Annika snapped, finally meeting her gaze. "If it had just been some rich merchant looking to maximize profits by maintaining trade flow through Kefya, we could have gathered evidence and presented it to the Council. But now . . . "

"Now at least one member of our government is implicated," Wymund said. The man looked crestfallen, like he was taking the news more personally than the others. "Which means there could be more. Maybe the whole Council." He made to reach for something at his belt, but, finding nothing there, he slammed his fist against the back wall. "All these years . . . ," he muttered.

Some part of Mareq had known all along that the plot he was unraveling led back to the upper echelons of society, and he had already grappled with the danger that posed. But hearing it confirmed made the hair at the back of his neck stand on end. He was getting closer now to finding proof of this treasonous plot, and therefore closer to getting back on the road with a grateful kingdom funding his travels. But knowing concrete details about the force he was hoping to unveil was making him question his involvement. Evading Ghosts was one thing, but was it worth seeing the world if it meant being chased by Kefyan assassins for the rest of his life? On the other hand, how much adventuring could he accomplish in a land ravaged by war?

Mareq sighed. "If you're certain this scorcher intends to foment a war, it doesn't matter if Teacher Irasil himself commanded it. I can't knowingly let the people of this land fall into conflict when there was something I could do to stop it." Wymund's eyes snapped back into focus, and he gave Mareq a slight nod. "It doesn't change the fact that I cannot just walk you into the kitchens, but I'm open to helping in any way I can."

"That's all we can ask," Annika said with a smile. "Your assistance gives us more options than we had prior to our arrival, and the more tools we have available to us, the better."

"Yes," Kymil said, tilting his head back to glance at Wymund. "Because we've all seen how successful this one can be when he appeals to the honor of his fellow guardsmen. Perhaps a more advanced plan than simply asking for admittance is called for?"

"And how many forged documents do you have padding your cloak?" Wymund replied, with less venom than Mareq expected. There was even a slight smirk on the man's face. "Enough to get through the litany of checkpoints inside?"

"Fortune can only be stretched so far until it snaps," the elf replied with a laugh.

"Well, we need to think of something," Rav said. "For all we know, the man could already be speaking with Berenqar now."

"Doubtful," Mareq said, shaking his head. "King Berenqar is open to speaking with his subjects directly, but there is usually an event or celebration that facilitates these meetings. Based on what I've heard from the kitchen staff and an uptick in deliveries over the last few days," he said, pointing toward his stacks of produce, "there's going to be a banquet held tomorrow. My guess is that is when your scorcher will sit down with the king."

"A party?" Kymil said, his chair legs settling down to the floor as he placed his elbows on the table. "I know how I'm getting in, then. Perhaps you as well, *Lady* Iatorii. One night out among the people and I'll acquire an invitation for the sensational traveling bard and the Felonian noble woman on his arm." Turning to give an appraising look at his other two companions, he added, "You two cannot be helped though.

You don't look the part, and I simply don't have the time I would need to transform you into presentable specimens."

Scowling, Rav said, "I don't need to play dress-up like a child to make my way inside. There hasn't been a wall built that I can't find a way over." Looking to Wymund, she said, "But you may need a disguise. If I can get a King's Guard uniform out to you, can you act enough like a guard to work your way into the citadel?"

Wymund laughed. "I don't think that will demand too much of a performance from me."

"Good," Rav said with a nod before walking over and slapping Mareq on the back. "Then all we'll need is a way to get the armor out. Do you happen to reuse your crates?"

Excitement and dread waged a war in the pit of his stomach as Mareq nodded. Preventing the potential for thousands of needless deaths and gaining the gratitude of a king were reasons enough in his mind to aid these strangers, people who Tiialya had entrusted with his name. But he still couldn't help but feel like one of the Destueqan heroes in his bedtime fairytales, running headlong into a dark dungeon where hidden traps punished one wrong step.

CHAPTER 30

ALABOQ

Wymund wouldn't describe the sensation as painful, but as his scar tissue was forced out of the puncture wounds in his side, making room for the new flesh folding together behind, it certainly wasn't pleasant. The fistful of aromatic leaves that the older elven woman had given to both him and Rav tasted bitter in his mouth, and while he maintained his composure out of a sense of gratitude, his friend wasn't faring well at hiding her distaste.

Still, despite her grimace, he could already see Rav's posture had improved in the few minutes since they had started chewing the infused herbs. Her rib fractures would be completely healed shortly, and his side, not long after. The infusion this herb nurse created was more potent than he thought possible, but he chalked that up to his own inexperience. His father never could afford anything more than a tincture here and there from a traveling plagueman, and neither could he on a guard's wages, so the power of healing via the World Shroud was new to him. As he reached to the side to touch his mending skin, he realized it would be difficult to return to his slower natural healing processes.

Mareq stood with Kymil and Annika toward the back of the small room, chatting with the herb nurse he had introduced as Mrs. Luviire. They had traveled north through the city into a cramped district called the Thistle Hare Warren, where the elven woman lived in a little apartment filled with leafy vines and flowering plants that hung from iron hooks in the ceiling. An almost-spicy aroma pervaded the home, but she had explained that the scent changed depending on the purpose of her most recent infusions. Apparently, for a plant to knit flesh and bone together, the cost was a stinging nose and watering eyes.

"A crystalline prism?" Kymil said to Mrs. Luviire, looking off into the air around him with a genuine grin. "I do love it when another infuser has the right words to describe their vision of the Shroud. It adds verisimilitude to my poetic repertoire when I recount the tales of Anera's finest healers. The average audience wouldn't know the difference if I subbed in your experience for my own," he said, just as Rav and Wymund shared a surprised glance. "But that doesn't mean that I shouldn't strive for the essence of truth in my performances."

Mrs. Luviire laughed. "I find it hard to believe you would ever have trouble finding the right words. And if you did, you have fate on your side. The words would find their own way to your tongue."

Wymund watched as Rav's eyes widened for brief moment before color rushed to her cheeks in a flash of recognition followed by what could be either anger or embarrassment. Perhaps both.

"You infused that step, didn't you?" Rav asked, her level voice belying the emotions he knew she was suppressing. "That morning back in Hwen, in Damara's Bounty?"

The bard winked at her. "It would have been unfortunate if the three of you had left before I awoke. I couldn't let that happen, so certain *steps* had to be taken."

Wymund had heard of fatestitchers in his line of work. For many with their talents, it was hard to resist bending the rules to suit their whims, and the only weapon a city guard had against them was to be well informed. Otherwise, their crimes could be written off as happenstance; misplaced items would turn up in their pockets, or they would find themselves inside restricted areas "by accident." If one could prove someone was a fatestitcher with the opportunity to infuse an object ahead of time, an unlikely heist would suddenly become plausible. If not, the fatestitcher lived to cheat and steal another day. All things considered, they were fortunate that Kymil only seemed interested in amusing others rather than his own personal gain.

Rav rolled her eyes and settled back in her chair, letting Kymil's pun slide by unchallenged. Wymund knew the woman had a particular aversion for that flavor of wordplay, so the fact that it warranted no further reaction from her spoke volumes. Her wounded pride had just been healed, her ability to tread silently no longer under question. Wymund filed away the knowledge of how long his friend held on to her grievances, understanding it may be good to keep in mind for his own well-being.

"We should be going," Annika said, reaching up to place a hand on Kymil's shoulder as she smiled at Wymund and Rav. She had a knowing look in her eyes that told him she had already known about the bard's abilities. He didn't like that secrecy came so easily to his traveling companions, but he supposed it wasn't her secret to share. "You have impressions to make if you hope to see us invited to Lady Cailynne's banquet tomorrow evening."

"You are correct, Lady Iatorii," he replied. "We should be off to carouse with the monied folk of Alaboq. There are songs to be sung and people to make swoon." He eyed the two at the table, adding, "Though you both are still a bit worse for wear. I can't have a pair of wounded commoners holding back my swagger."

"He's right," Annika said before either Wymund or Rav could respond. "You two stay here and allow the herbs to finish putting you back together. We can meet back at The Petaled Path tonight."

His side began to itch as the knitting of flesh continued. "Of course," Wymund said. "Perhaps our new friends can point us in the direction of a blacksmith in town. I'll need my sword replaced before tomorrow." If all went well, he wouldn't need his blade during the banquet, but he would prefer a useless blade at his side to being useless himself in a fight.

Mareq looked to the herb nurse, who nodded. "I know just the man," she said. "I can tell Mareq where to take you once you're done here."

Pulling the lute from his back, Kymil moved toward the door. "Come then, Annika. Time is dwindling and I intend to hit each tavern, alehouse, and bordello in Melan North before nightfall." The bard began to strum even before stepping outside into the narrow streets, the throngs of people making way at the sound of his music. Saying her own goodbyes, Annika followed him, leaving the room quiet and still.

Mrs. Luviire came to join them at the table, looking over each of them with a motherly gaze that emanated both concern and disapproval.

"Injuries like those usually stop people from looking for a new weapon," she said with a sad smile. "At least for a time. But Mareq tells me that you intend to keep putting yourselves at risk?"

"Believe me," Rav said, stretching her torso from side to side as she tested her freshly healed fracture, "it's not out of an innate desire to do so. But many thousands of lives could be in danger, and unfortunately for us, we're in the best position to prevent it."

Wymund nodded. "We appreciate your concern and your talents as a healer, but this is a path that we cannot deviate from."

The elven woman thought for a moment, lips pursed and brow furrowed, before glancing toward Mareq, who approached to stand at her side. "Do you still have that packet I gave you?"

The draqeshi nodded and fished a small, folded parchment from his pocket, holding it up between two thick fingers. "You should give that to them. I don't know what they have planned, nor do I want to know, but it may serve a greater purpose than keeping you out of the Ghosts' clutches."

Mareq shrugged, sliding the envelope across the table toward Rav. "Maybe so, though I think these two have other methods of rendering people unconscious when they need to."

Rav picked up the packet and shook it, causing a powdery substance to shift back and forth within.

"Infused hindran root," Mrs. Luviire said. "Chewing on it straight from the ground or steeping it in some tea can help you drift off to sleep at night. But with my little addition, the effects are more dramatic, more immediate." With an impish grin, she added, "Get someone to inhale this, and they'll wake up refreshed and restored. A few days later."

Pocketing the powdered root, Rav shared in the woman's mischievous smile and said, "I can make good use of this. Thank you."

A few minutes passed as Mrs. Luviire described the event that would be taking place at Vinsart Hold the next evening: all the decadent foods and drinks, all the musicians and storytellers aiming to dazzle the crowds, as well as the people in those crowds themselves, comprised of the lords and ladies who lived in the wealthier districts bordering the north and south of the Verdant Statuary. She had worked in the kitchens since before Lady Cailynne had been born and had grown accustomed to the work leading up to the yearly celebration, the event seeming to expand into a larger and larger affair with each passing year. By the time she had reached the previous year's banquet and the staggering number of crustaceans that had been prepared, Wymund's wounds had disappeared.

Moving his hands along his side, it was as if the damage had never been done, and the stinging aches that had been ever-present over the last week of travel were now nothing but a memory. As they departed from her home, the herb nurse directed them toward a small blacksmith shop several blocks away, claiming the man who owned it was the best craftsman in the city. She insisted that Mareq accompany them, as his shop was "tucked away at the end of an alley," and remembering the nonsensical layout of the Thistle Hare Warren's roads, Wymund welcomed the draqeshi's experience.

Squeezing their way through the other denizens of the district proved to be a difficult task, even as he stood a head taller than most around them. Being able to see the best route didn't translate to forcing his broad frame through the masses, so Wymund often found himself falling behind Rav and Mareq as they slipped by stalled carts and haggling customers in ways that weren't possible for him. Still, the journey was relatively short, and after just a quarter hour of being jostled and prodded. the three found themselves striding down a narrow alley toward an open door, above which hung a sign that simply read SMITHY. No catchy name, no eye-grabbing illustration, just a statement of fact. The man's skill must have spoken for itself.

As they neared the door, Wymund began to sweat despite the cool winter air. Heat was billowing out in waves from within the blacksmith's shop, accompanied by the rhythmic clanging of metal on metal. Stepping through the threshold, he could see a barrel-chested balding man, arms as thick as many people's thighs, hammering a shortsword into its proper shape, the blade still glowing a vibrant red. Racks of similar blades lined the wall, along with simple breastplates, shields, and bucklers, none of which possessed any filigree or artistic flair to speak of. The man crafted solid tools, leaving any further decoration up to the buyer, which was too bad. Purchasing a King's Guard breastplate would be much simpler than smuggling one out.

The blacksmith must have noticed the shadows pass across his shop as the three entered, because he paused his work and wiped the sweat from his brow with the back of his sleeve. "Busy," he grunted, sparing them a momentary glance before returning to the task at hand.

"We won't take much of your time," Wymund said, scanning the room for a suitable replacement for his damaged weapon. There were blades of varying lengths on the wooden racks, but none matched the length of his longsword. Most were shortswords and daggers, though there was a smattering of iron hand axes and hammers, which appeared to be more of the workman variety than those crafted for battle. Disappointment creeping in, he said, "Maybe none at all, in fact, unless you keep your longer blades elsewhere. I'm looking to replace a longsword, but it doesn't appear that you have any in stock."

The man sniffed. "No one keeps longswords in Alaboq. Not a market for them." He continued his hammering, sparks and cooling bits of blackened iron scattering off the anvil with each blow. "King's Guard requires shortswords, so that's what we make. You want a longsword, I'll have to make it special. Give me a couple days. You'll have a better-balanced blade than you know how to handle." Wymund couldn't tell if his stilted way of speaking was due to physical exertion or if the man simply didn't care to speak more words than he had to.

"We don't have a couple of days," Rav groaned. "You'll just have to work with what's on offer, Wymund. Pick a shortsword so we can go."

"I've only been in Alaboq for a few months," Mareq said. "But I agree with her. One of these is your best hope to blend in with the King's Guard. In fact, I can't recall seeing a longsword since I left Destueqa."

"It's not that simple," Wymund said, rubbing his hand across his cropped hair. He had been trained with longswords as a member of the Virdoban guard and was accustomed to being able to maintain a certain distance between himself and his foe. With a shorter blade, a skilled opponent would see his defense's openings and pick him apart.

"You're right on that, boy," the blacksmith grumbled, finally setting his hammer down and lifting the completed blade from the anvil to dunk into a barrel of water off to the side. Steam hissed and sputtered as the metal rapidly cooled. "Fights would be all different. Closer than you're used to. But that can be helped."

He pulled the new sword from the barrel and set it aside, then walked over to the wall and picked up a steel buckler from a rack. It was oval in shape, approximately the length of Wymund's forearm, with an adjustable leather strap on the back. "You'll fall back on your instincts. Raise your arm to protect yourself. This will use that to your advantage."

The man grabbed Wymund's arm and twisted it, fastening the strap across it without uttering a word. He took a step back and Wymund tested the weight of the shield, lighter than he expected as he maneuvered his arm around in front of him. "I can see its utility," he said, reaching down for his pouch. "I'll take this one, and a standard issue shortsword for the King's Guard." But before he could retrieve any libers for payment, Rav placed a hand on his to stop him, using her other to tilt the buckler away so that she could examine its back.

"Do you have any with leather stretched across the back?" she asked. The blacksmith sniffed as he eyed her before giving a single nod. Wordlessly, he unfastened the buckler from Wymund's arm and trudged toward a room in the back, leaving the three of them alone. Rav shrugged off his quizzical glance. "I've seen what this scorcher can do to metal. Trust me, you don't want that steel touching you directly when this fight kicks off."

Chapter 31

Alaboq

Kymil was no stranger to pomp and circumstance, but a royal banquet at Vinsart Hold was proving to be an experience all its own. Linked arm in arm with Annika, the pair ascended the sandstone steps leading up to the citadel's main gate, exchanging the restrictive streets of the Thistle Hare Warren for a breathtaking view. With each step they could see more of the Draemoor Sound's sparkling blue waters as it surrounded the Hooked Peninsula, as well as the pops of color that flourished throughout Alaboq. The whites and blues of the Lyri Blossom Market stood in stark contrast to the warm colors of the setting sun, while the thin branches of the jade canopies swayed in a mesmerizing dance on the gentle breeze.

But it wasn't the colors in the world around him that made this experience unique. During his childhood in Liiashae, Kymil had been surrounded by expanses of nature that would be more at home on a canvas than in the real world. Likewise, the coastal beauty of Choii Stier had been known to inspire the minds and hearts of more than a few artists. No, it wasn't the environment but the vibrancy of the people that he found captivating.

The typical vivid Alaboqan dress seemed muted by comparison to the attire of the lords and ladies ascending the steps next to them. The wool cloaks worn by both the men and women to fight off the chill were all dyed with the brightest shades of blues, greens and reds imaginable, but underneath, he caught glimpses of form-fitting silk dresses and doublets, each with their own eye-popping hues. On every exposed inch of skin, the men had painted swirling designs of a color that matched their outfits, while the ladies did the same with strands of ribbon woven into their hair. Kymil's deep violet jacket and pants seemed dull next to their displays, even draped as he was in his fur-lined cloak, while Annika's new navy dress appeared to blend into the evening's setting shadows.

"This won't do," he whispered to her. "I do my best hiding in plain sight. I stand out more when I'm *not* the center of attention." Spotting a young woman who wore a flowing lilac gown that trailed strands of matching ribbon up the stairs behind her, a smile crept onto his lips. He tilted his head closer to Annika's and added, "Though I suppose sometimes I don't even have to try for luck to be on my side."

Hurrying Annika forward, Kymil caught up to the woman and placed a foot on one of the strands. Her dress caught as she stumbled forward, catching herself with an awkward step before she fell onto the sandstone stairs. Without missing a beat, Annika rushed to her side and clasped the younger woman's hands between hers.

"Are you all right, dear?" she asked with a look of motherly concern. "These steps are quite treacherous. The Crown really should do something to repair the cracks before someone hurts themselves."

Kymil laughed quietly as he knelt behind them, impressed with her ability to jump into a ruse without warning. It shouldn't have been a surprise though; complaints flowed from the lungs of the wealthy as easily as air. Flicking out one stiletto blade from underneath the hem of his cloak, he sliced off two of the lilac ribbons. Kymil had reinfused his cloak after their battle with the reptilian beast, but now he hoped his skill alone would suffice without using the luck stored within. Although it would be such a shame for his beautiful cloak to go up in a scorcher's smoke just to save the world.

The woman thanked Annika for her concern and turned to check on her gown as Kymil rose, his disarming smile in full effect. She blushed and flicked her eyes toward her feet before he could speak.

"I do apologize for the state of the grounds, madam," Kymil said. "An effervescent beauty such as yourself should not be required to walk such a harrowing path." Her tan skin was glowing as she smiled up at him, and he brushed a wavy strand of hair out of her eyes. "But do not be troubled, I have dislodged your gown from the stone's embrace. Please, continue your journey to the banquet. I will trace your steps, ready at all times to catch you if you stumble once more."

"I am in your debt, sir," she replied. "Find me inside and I can repay you with a dance?"

Kymil winked at her. "The entirety of the King's Guard couldn't keep me away." With a slight curtsy, the young woman resumed her trip up to Vinsart Hold. Annika found her place beside him once again, linking arms as they resumed their ascent.

"While I can appreciate the game," Annika said with a smirk, nodding politely at other guests as they passed, "next time, I would like to at least be told I'm going to play."

"Oh, you handled yourself just fine," Kymil said, threading the ribbons through his blond waves. Several of the men standing about looked at him strangely while many of the women tittered at the foreigner mixing up their traditions. But he knew what he was doing; all that mattered was that he held their attention. Everything else was detail, and details made for interesting banquet conversations. "People who come from money never truly leave the façade behind. You slipped back into your role with aplomb."

Finally reaching the top, the pair passed through the towering oak doors that led into the citadel's vestibule. A line of five guards stood firmly at attention in front of the main doors, hands clasped behind their backs. Each wore a similar red wool cloak that others in the troop had donned since the temperature dropped, but these were decorated in gold trim, as were the steel breastplates underneath.

Beyond the statuesque lineups were another set of figures, a draqesh woman behind the left door and a barrel-chested human behind the right. They, too, wore the ornamented uniforms, but while their compatriots presented themselves with a practiced stoicism, these two had beaded sweat on their brows as they held a wooden wheel in place with an iron bar. Kymil found himself wondering why the building's architect couldn't have developed a heavy locking mechanism to hold the doors ajar for occasions such as this, but he didn't entertain the thought long. With soldier types, the answer usually had more to do with honor than common sense, and he found that notion far too boring to ponder when he was surround by such splendor.

The walls were covered by expansive tapestries, each one woven to reflect Qedrad's history. One depicted Vinsart Hold sitting alone atop a hill, the rest of Alaboq yet to develop around it, while another showed a fleet of merchant ships departing the city of Draemoor, on their way to begin the Qedradan sea trade supremacy that would last centuries. While its relative dominance had diminished following the War of Arrival and the subsequent losses of ports in Felona and Virdoba, no other Aneran nation yet matched Qedrad's ability to traverse the ocean for monetary gain and military might.

Curiously, tapestries dedicated to both Felona and Virdoba still hung in this entrance hall as well, each represented with Qedradan warships in their harbors, though to Kymil's eye, the boats were defending the cities rather than laying siege. However, he supposed the greatness of those cities was in part due to their historical Qedradan ties, so perhaps it wasn't so strange that they remained in this place of honor. After all, it wasn't the tanistry that had been eager to sever those ties in the first place. Kefya had won their independence, but it was Qedrad that built those cities up.

"People are staring at us," Annika said, continuing to smile and nod at the clusters of people mingling in the walkway. "I believe your hair accessory may have been a step too far. Don't you think commanding the stage for a time would have been enough to make you the star of the night? Or are you starting to doubt your ability to entertain?"

"Never, my lady. The stage and I are two halves of a whole, incomplete when we are apart," he said, taking note of the locked gazes for the first time at her mention of them. "As for the stares, don't let them bother you. They aren't of the indignant variety, but rather ones of awe. You get used to them when you spend much of your time engendering adoration from the public."

Kymil had done just that the night before, performing gripping renditions of Liiashan overtures that flowed seamlessly into traditional Qedradan folk songs at taverns and inns alike. The two of them had spent most of the evening in the neighborhood of Melan North after hearing its southern counterpart was composed of Alaboq's aging aristocrats, who preferred their silent nights over raucous outings. However, he and Annika had discovered a thriving nightlife among the young nobles that lived within Melan North, and by the time he had reached his second song at the third tavern, she had schmoozed her way into the good graces of anyone who was anyone in this city. After one simple conversation with the young administrator of Vinsart Hold's gardens, they had received an official invite to tonight's banquet on the condition that "her music-man" perform for Lady Cailynne. The old woman really did have a unique ability to ingratiate herself with strangers, without the need for the theatrics he employed, and a part of Kymil was jealous of that. While charisma effortlessly oozed from his every pore, he wished he knew if the relationships he formed were genuine or based solely on his own magnetism.

"And when you grow up among these types of people," Annika added as they exited into a larger hall, "you come to suspect that gazing at the entertainer does not differ much from gawking at the fool. Take care that you understand the difference that implies."

"I understand," Kymil replied. "Adoration for a respected guest and amusement at a silly pet may hide beside the same smile. Lucky for us, I'm quite comfortable with either."

The banquet hall opened up before them, nearly choking off Kymil's banter as he realized it was likely the single largest room he had ever seen. Close to three hundred guests milled about, some already seated at the long heartfir tables, the wood a deep crimson that would be difficult to keep pristine, while others stood in groups around the perimeter of the room or in front of the great stage at the far end. Streams of fabric ran from the rafters as acrobats swung back and forth between them, flipping through the air and catching one another with a grace he was sure even Rav would envy.

Attached higher up to the ceiling proper, silk banners in as many colors as there were available dyes draped down, half of them depicting a galleon rising above a roiling sea, which Kymil recognized as the Qedradan crest, while the other half displayed what appeared to be a great fish with a toothy maw and a fin along its back leaping out of the water, the creature too rounded to be any shark. The top half of the animal was always represented as darker than the silk it was embroidered into, while its underside was sewn with white strands. Kymil had heard many tales from fishermen and sailors alike of monstrous sea creatures that stalked the waters of the world. Whatever this one was, he supposed it was native to the Draemoor Sound, and judging by the crest's presence on the throne at center stage, it was representative of Berenqar's House.

A dry, spiced aroma permeated the room as platters of blackened pheasants, thistle hares and salmon were spread upon the tables, along with saucers of an almost pink cream sauce that accompanied each dish. Steamed vegetables of any variety Kymil could imagine filled the places between the savory entrees, and bundles of thin, crispy flatbreads were nestled throughout the feast. Based on the smell alone, this was traditional Ebkarish cuisine, unexpected but not unwelcome as Kymil's stomach rumbled at the memory of the last opportunity he had to indulge in these flavors. If Lady Cailynne had any say on the menu for her banquet, he had to remember to compliment her on her taste.

As if the thought had summoned her, a door at the back of the stage opened to reveal two more King's Guards followed by two figures in relatively subdued colors. One was a man well into his middle years, his short, dark hair graying at the temples and barely covered by a thin band of metal encircling his head. He was of average build and appearance, though some true artistry had gone into the designs painted across his skin for the celebration. Despite the plain attire, even at this distance Kymil could see a softness in the man's eyes that he knew would engender trust in others.

To his left stood a much younger woman, on the edge of adulthood, who shared her father's tanned skin and dark hair. Hers was worn in a long, loose braid that hung to her lower back with an intricate web of silver ribbons woven throughout. She was on her way to becoming a beautiful woman, traits she must have obtained from her mother, given her father's plainness, but she *had* managed to receive his kind eyes. She, too, had a thin circlet around her head, more delicate than her father's but just as unassuming.

The guards flanked them as they crossed the stage and stood before the two thrones positioned there. Without a word on their part, the din in the room softened until he could have heard a feather fall to the floor.

"Thank you all for attending my daughter's celebration this evening," King Berenqar announced to the room. He didn't raise his voice, but somehow, it seemed to carry all the same. "As you know, this year marks Cailynne's sixteenth in these halls, where she has grown from a scampering tot to a gracious young woman, never losing an ounce of mischief along the way." The crowd laughed as Cailynne shot her father a disapproving look that was filled with more love than scorn.

"So please," he continued, "eat and enjoy the entertainment my staff has procured for the evening. I know I will be meeting with a few of you throughout the night in my chambers, but to everyone else I would like to extend my sincerest gratitude for your attendance and invite you to join me in celebrating another year of my darling daughter's life. To Lady Cailynne!"

Berenqar raised a goblet as the rest of the room did the same, repeating his toast and then rejoining their prior conversations. The royals then descended from the stage to the main floor, accompanied by their pair of guards as they made the rounds to greet their guests.

"Do all fathers speak so lovingly about their daughters in these circles?" Kymil asked. "I always pictured the wealthy taking a more hands-off approach to parenting."

"Some do, I suppose," Annika replied. "Though it seems that love for one's child is largely a universal sentiment." With a wry grin, she added, "And as prolific as you claim to be, I'm sure you will feel that bond yourself one day."

Kymil felt a familiar click in his jaw as he smiled down at her, the sound a constant reminder of his relationship with his own father. One of many, anyway, and the memory of what caused it was not even the most traumatic. "Maybe I will someday," he said with some strain. "It would truly be a great evil to deprive the world of my prodigious stock. Though I would not be surprised to happen upon a child with my face on my travels one day, as it is."

Annika rolled her eyes and unlocked their arms, the smile never leaving her face. "That's enough of that for one evening. Make your way onto the stage and keep an eye out for the scorcher Rav described. I'll work my way around the room and see who I can find."

"And if we don't find him?" Kymil asked. "If he's already waiting in the king's chambers?"

"Then it's up to Rav and the rest," she answered with a shrug that belied the moment's tension. "We all have our roles tonight, it's up to us to play them."

Chapter 32

Alaboq

Rav's feet landed with a soft thud on the roof's wooden slats. She had managed not to skid along the thin layer of sleet that had accumulated on the tops of the Thistle Hare Warren's buildings. This time, at least; so far, her journey across the district's rooftops had been a treacherous one. Unlike the sandstone of Alaboq's lower regions, the slush partially stuck to the wooden constructions here, but she didn't blame her difficulties on the weather.

She shifted her feet, the leather wraps fastened around her silk slippers offering more stain protection than traction. Rav cursed under her breath. She had rebuffed Kymil's slight about dressing up like a noblewoman, but Wymund had been right to insist she wear her own disguise while obtaining his inside the citadel. Knotting off her gown at the knees wasn't ideal, but it was less cumbersome than carrying an oilskin bag of formalwear to change into inside. However, that did nothing to lessen her desire to be back in her boots. After leaving her home in Felona, she never imagined she would need to don this type of dress again.

Shut up, she thought, swearing she could hear her mother's laugh.

Ahead of her loomed the exterior wall of Vinsart Hold, its sandstone façade interrupted regularly by rectangular windows. As the sun set farther in the distance and the temperature plummeted, most of the windows had been shuttered for the evening, including the one closest to her location. Looking to her left and right, she found the same was true for each window at rooftop level, almost as if her arrival had been expected. Another side of the citadel was out of the question; she needed to enter the building from this side to be as close as possible to the kitchens. Moving downstairs without being seen would be challenge enough. Creeping down long hallways from a different wing of Vinsart Hold just to meet up with Mareq and pass off the armor would be an added layer of risk. Timing was everything, and anything that delayed her rendezvous with her allies in the banquet hall increased the odds that the scorcher would reach the ruler first.

No, her only options were before her now, and her best chance was the singular open window one story up. From her position, it looked like a fifteen-foot span to the closed window across from her and another twelve feet up to her improvised entrance. The first distance would be difficult but not insurmountable; she had made similar leaps in the past with a running start. But scaling a smooth sandstone wall without equipment would be a real test. No handholds from layers of stone or brick to provide support, just a sheer vertical climb. She caught herself smiling. She was back in her element.

After backing up to the opposite edge of the rooftop, she charged forward and leaped through the air toward the citadel's wall. The window rushed toward her before beginning to rise out of view faster than expected. Her leather-clad slippers hadn't provided the same traction she was used to, but she did manage to grasp the ledge with the tips of her fingers, her legs dangling over the thirty-foot drop to the gardens below. With a stifled grunt, she pulled herself up onto the sill and pressed her body flat against the shutters, listening for any sounds of movement within. The toes of her shoes were pressed hard onto the available area, only a couple inches of lifeline protruding from the wall. After a few agonizing moments of silence, the strained breaths through her nose the only sounds, she suspected that whoever this window belonged to wasn't inside. Breathing a sigh of relief, she allowed herself a few seconds to relax. The easy part was over. Now for the rest.

She tested the shutters to ensure they were locked from within and, finding they were, she returned to the task at hand. Picking an external lock would be a simple fix, but she didn't want to risk the time it would take to manipulate her tools blindly through the seam for an internal one. Directly above the window was another ridge that stuck out from the wall to match the windowsill. It was as shallow as the one she stood upon now, but it was all she had. Reaching above her, she grabbed the edge and hoisted herself up, again pressing against the side as flat as she could manage. With as little purchase as she had, breathing alone caused her body to move farther away from the building than she felt comfortable with, so she tried to take in short and shallow breaths. If she reached her arms straight up, the twelve-foot gap shortened to about four, an impossible distance to cover in her current circumstances. She would need to bend her knees to even hope for that kind of leap, and that move would push her over the edge.

She cursed and tapped her forehead against the wall in front of her. Knowing what she had to do didn't mean she wanted to do it.

Rav carefully crossed one foot behind the other and turned her body so that she faced out at the Thistle Hare Warren, the horizon now seeming to sway. Heights had never bothered her before, but with her weight back on her heels now, she realized how much of a difference it made being on the balls of her feet. She had felt in control before, but now she could only rely on the force of her mass as she shoved her back against the stone wall. If she hadn't worn her leather cuirass under the gown, she was sure the rocky surface would be digging painfully into her skin.

She slid down the wall into a crouch, gathering as much power as she could into her legs and wishing for the first time that she could draw directly from the World Shroud. She wasn't sure if her father's abilities had allowed him to purposefully channel lightning through his body, but right then she would have been happy for that skill to have passed down to her. Waiting a moment for the familiar light show and waves of liquid fire across her flesh to begin, she resolved herself to the fact that her powers weren't coming to the rescue this time.

"Not life-threatening enough for you?" she whispered, addressing the World Shroud itself. "We'll see about that."

Kicking off the lip, she leaped straight up into the air, suspended in flight for what felt like an eternity. But just as it seemed her ascent was beginning to end, her fingers found purchase on the open windowsill above, her bodyweight now held four stories off the ground by the strength of her grip alone. Rav laughed with what was more of a sigh, letting her head rest back against the wall for a moment. However, at any time someone could look up and see a woman in a tied off gown dangling from the side of Vinsart Hold, and she didn't want to be around to deal with what followed. She crossed her right arm across her body to grab the ledge on the other side of her left hand, then let go with her left so that she swung around to face the building once more. Bracing herself with her toes, she clambered up and into the window as silently as she could, hoping this room would be similarly unoccupied.

The room she landed in was dim, the only light seeping in from under a closed door to her left. She removed the sodden leather wraps from around her slippers and began to creep along the plush, plum-colored carpet. An enormous canopy bed took up most of the room to her right, with gilded strands woven into the duvet and draping sheets sparkling despite the low light. This was obviously the bedroom of one of Vinsart Hold's noblewomen, perhaps a member of the advisory council or even one of Lady Cailynne's royal attendants. It was reminiscent of the room she had grown up in, right down to the suffocating, prim décor. If the pattern held, a sitting room would be beyond the closed door, which would have an exit to the citadel's hallways. Not that she had been raised in a castle, but architects of the gentry were always seeking to emulate royal designs.

Her footsteps now softened by the carpeting below, Rav moved silently across the room and placed an ear on the wooden door. Muffled voices sounded from behind it, one with the cadence and volume of authority while the other two seemed to stick with one-word responses. While she couldn't catch every word, she was able to pick out "cinch it tighter" and "will be in attendance" among a smattering of "yes, mistress."

Rav smiled. Someone was hoping to make an impression tonight. She unknotted her gown, allowing the scarlet skirt to flow to her feet and let down her hair. Straight black shoulder-length hair would have been a hazard whipping about in the wind, but at an Alaboqan ball it would be striking. People with love on the brain were prone to jealousy and were easily flustered, just two more weapons she could add to her infiltration arsenal.

"How much longer would you have me wait, Archie?" Rav blurted as she swung the door open, adopting a slightly slurred affect. The three women inside snapped their heads in her direction, surprise plastered across their faces. In the center stood a woman Rav guessed was nearing the end of her fourth decade, but through the pampered life of aristocracy, had maintained the smooth, unblemished skin of one half her age. The only cues were strands of gray interspersed in her walnut-colored hair, which had been fashioned up into a decorative bulb. She was dressed in a lacy, cream-colored gown and was currently being squeezed into a turquoise corset by one of her attendants. The other one, younger than the others by at least a decade, was on her knees and holding the hem of the noblewoman's dress in her hands, along with a needle and spool of thread.

"What is this?" asked the woman being dressed, turning so that the girl at her heels nearly fell over while trying to keep a grip on the dress's tail. "How did you get into my bedroom?"

Rav hiccupped, then giggled. "Sweet Archie told me to meet him here. Are you joining us?" She strode forward with a swagger that usually accompanied one too many whiskies and the dumbest smile she could muster. "It's not what I had in mind for the evening, but I can make an exception for such a beauty. Archie *does* like his playthings, doesn't he?"

The woman's two attendants tightened their lips to keep from snickering, looking anywhere but at Rav and their mistress, who had begun to blush despite a look of indignation. Playing to her vanity had been the right choice. "You have the wrong room, girl. I don't know this Archie and certainly wouldn't invite strangers into my bed on this special day."

Keeping her smile cool and even, Rav lightly slapped her forehead with a laughing sigh. "This isn't the fifth floor. I thought I may have lost track when I had to have a quick sit in the stairwell, but I was just feeling so lightheaded. That is none of your concern, though. Let me just be on my way and you can finish preparing for tonight."

She began to trudge toward the door, dragging her feet in a way that felt antithetical to her typical catlike gait. Even when she really was intoxicated her balance was not *this* altered, but she had to play to the audience she had. Subtlety would be lost on this woman.

"Now wait right there," the woman called after her as she was unable to move from the fitting stool. "I am the Minister of Culture and I can't just have strange women traipsing through my bedro—"

Pretending she hadn't heard, Rav spun back as she reached the door and said, "By the way, whoever you *are* planning to bewitch tonight is a lucky man." The woman's protests died in her throat as her red shade deepened. However, all traces of annoyance were now missing, replaced by the confused look of flattery Rav had been aiming for. "But if he fails to see that and makes a fool of himself, come find Archie and me upstairs. Just make sure that bodice isn't too tight." With a wink that she shuddered to think she had picked up from Kymil, Rav slipped out the door and found herself in a hallway lined with thick red carpeting.

The walls were all sandstone with golden sconces spaced evenly down the length of the corridor, their orange-yellow flames adding to the warm color palette of the palace's interior. A quick mental check to get her bearings told her to head right, which was the opposite direction Mareq had told her the staircase would be from her planned point of entry. According to him, the flights of stairs were located at alternating ends of the hall, floor by floor.

Assuming this floor has the same layout. And why would it? Nothing else has gone right so far.

The corridor wasn't deserted, but it wasn't crowded either, the worst condition Rav could have expected. When the occasional attendant or maid were the only other occupants, a foreign woman in a vibrant gown would stick in people's memories. Rav did her best to walk with a purpose, chin held slightly aloft and only making eye contact with a curt nod as the castle's staff passed her by. As long as she looked like she was supposed to be here, she thought she could make them believe the same.

She reached the first set of stairs without receiving more than a handful of puzzled glances along the way. While she was thankful she hadn't encountered any guards thus far, she would have to find one eventually. Mareq didn't know much of Vinsart Hold's layout and couldn't direct her to the armory, so if she hoped to obtain Wymund's disguise, she would have to nick one in use.

Making quick work of the stairs, she exited into a near identical hallway, though the foot traffic here was a bit heavier. Young men and women darted down the hallwaym carrying messages to living quarters and offices, while more of the cleaning staff seemed to be busy on this floor, taking advantage of the empty rooms while their occupants were celebrating. She set off down the corridor to her left, continuing her exercise in aloofness until she heard a voice call to her from behind.

"Oy," a man shouted. Rav turned to see two guards striding toward her. One was elven, standing a few inches taller than her and sharing her light build, while the man who had called out to her was the prototypical human guard. Each wore a mask of stoicism, the elf's intimidating presence only slightly softened by the sky-blue rings around his irises.

Irasil be damned, she cursed, less at the intrusion and more at their body types. Neither breastplate would fit Wymund's tall, muscular frame.

"What are you doing up in the residences? Visitors are to remain in the banquet hall."

"That may be true for the guests of Lady Cailynne," Rav said, standing with her hands clasped behind her back as she stared down her nose at them. She kept her legs as straight and still as possible, knowing that a guard's eye would be able to pick out the shape of her concealed daggers through a fold in her gown. "But as Kefya's first secretary of culture, my presence here in your city is more than an opportunity to feast and dance. Is this how you are instructed to speak to visiting dignitaries? Harassing them with questions and suspicious gazes?"

"Uh, no ma'am," the man stammered. "It's just we weren't told to be expecting you."

"Yeah, we meant nothing by it," the elf added. "Ambassadors are meant to have a guard detail for their own protection though, and to serve as a guide. You could get lost in this place."

Rav dismissed their concern with a wave of her hand. "I'm just coming from upstairs after a pleasant meeting with your own minister of culture. If you want to explain to her that she was wrong to instruct me on proper protocol, that is certainly your prerogative." Their eyes widened. "Otherwise, I believe I'm capable of navigating a few hallways on my own. Unless you believe a member of the Kefyan Council to be an incompetent fool?"

The first guard cleared his throat. "No, not at all ma'am. Please just hurry on your way to the banquet hall. I would hate to think that we were responsible for you missing any of the festivities."

With a respectful tilt of her head and not a word of thanks, Rav turned back to her path, fighting the urge to increase her pace. Whereas a love-addled brain was susceptible to flattery, men like this responded to authority, orders from higher up on their chain of command. She couldn't risk ruining that illusion now by running away from them. She made it down the length of the hall without arousing further suspicion and descended the next flight to reach the second floor. Just below her would be the kitchens. Now all she needed was a uniform and a place to hide near the opposite stairwell. And hope that their new friend held to his part of the plan.

As soon as she stepped into the corridor, she knew she was in the right place. The din of party goers could be heard through the wall in front of her. Boisterous laughter, scraping chair legs, and shouted conversations all competed for dominance. Thankfully, the enticing lure of the ball seemed to keep everyone on this floor within its grasp, leaving the hallways devoid of inquisitive eyes. Turning to her right, Rav began to move along the maroon carpeting toward the stairwell that led down to the kitchens. She suspected she would pass a stationed guard or two at the entrances into the banquet hall, and she tried to stay focused on how she could get a breastplate off one.

But as she neared the point in their plan that would require her to sit and wait, her mind began to wander, thoughts of the white-coated scorcher bubbling up into her consciousness. It was easy for her to stay on task when actively engaged, but she hated sitting still. How much closer would he get to the king's ear while she squatted in a dark room and waited to deliver the armor to Mareq? As much as she dreaded the idea of facing him again on her own, a part of her yearned to permanently snuff out his flame. It wasn't just that he had toyed with her, beaten her back with barely an effort. He had manipulated her, used her own trauma to goad her into making foolish and reckless decisions. More importantly, he belonged to the organization that had stolen her happy childhood. The Gulls would be further clipped tonight.

The sound of shifting feet caught her attention ahead. She hugged the wall and peeked around a narrow-angled corner to see a lone King's Guard posted near the rear entrance to the celebration. The man was large, more corpulent than muscular, and only a few inches shorter than Wymund, but with the breastplate's adjustable leather straps he could make it work without looking too ridiculous. Across from him was the stairwell leading down to the kitchens and another doorway into a small sitting room. Rav guessed it was typically used to hold early guests who arrived before the banquet hall was prepared, but more importantly, it was currently unoccupied. She touched the folded parchment of infused hindran root that was tucked just under her neckline but thought better of it. The man would need to be out of the hallway before she removed his armor, and she certainly couldn't leave him slumbering in view of any passerby. He would need to be drawn into the open room using his own strength; she would have no hope of dragging his form across the carpet with any hint of discretion.

"Ahh," Rav grunted as she hobbled around the corner, keeping one hand on the wall while she favored her left leg. The King's Guard turned to her, startled that he hadn't heard her approaching from down the hall. "Is there a healer nearby? I think I sprained my ankle trying to make an impression on a dashing young man on the dance floor, and I was told someone back here would be able to help me."

The man hustled over, wrapping a hand around her waist and draping her arm across his shoulders. "Let's get some weight off that foot then, miss," he said. "But as far as healers go, we have a knitter that lives up near the king and Lady Cailynne's chambers on the fifth floor, but no one down this way." He cocked an eyebrow in her direction. "Not sure who would've told you something like that."

Rav placed her free hand on her forehead and sighed. "Oh, my head is just swimming with pain. I'm sure I misheard. It serves me right for being so foolish, trying to impress a man in the presence of all these beautiful women."

He snorted, bringing his fist to his mouth and trying to play it off as a cough. "Well, I don't think you need to sell yourself short in that regard, miss. I, uh, haven't seen another lady here tonight that measures up to you."

Giving her best impression of a bashful smile, Rav said, "That's so kind of you to say. And you are such a testament to your profession, helping an injured woman in need." The man grinned as they finally made it into the sitting room. He carefully guided her down onto a silk-upholstered chair, grabbing a pillow and stuffing it behind her back before kneeling to remove her slipper.

"Please tell your commanding officer that you deserve a more prominent post," Rav continued. "Your comrade inside the banquet was most unhelpful, directing me off to find a healer on my own while he kept watch over people just chewing their food."

The guard froze in his crouch and slowly tilted his head to look up at her, suspicion and confusion comingling in a way that made her heart skip a beat. "There's not a guard in our company who would've sent you out on your own, miss."

Before he could stand, Rav pushed off the chair and slammed her left knee into the man's face, then slid around behind him to wrap her arm around his throat. She was careful not to apply enough pressure to crush his trachea—he did seem to be a decent enough man after all—but she locked her arms together and held fast, hoping to cut off the blood flow to his brain. The man rose to his feet and dragged Rav up with him, then drove her back into the wall behind them. The air was knocked out of her with the impact, but her grip remained strong, and she was able to drive her feet into the backs of his knees, causing him to collapse once again. He wheezed, spittle flying from lips as his skin turned from a reddish hue to a blue one, and eventually his attempts to claw at her arms grew weaker and weaker. As his head lolled forward, she let him fall onto his face, soft snores escaping from where his bleeding nose was pressed against the carpet.

Without a moment's pause, Rav jumped up and shut the door to the hallway, blocking the view of their scuffle's aftermath from the rest of the citadel. She leaned back against the wood and caught her breath.

Of course you couldn't talk yourself out of everything. When has anything ever been that simple?

The rush of adrenaline faded, and she went to work unstrapping the man's breastplate. Wymund and Mareq were supposed to have obtained a basic red tunic to complete the disguise, and she was glad for that.

Rolling this man out of his plate would be draining, and the garment would swallow her friend whole anyway. Once she had pulled the steel shell free, she sat back against the wall, trying to see this opportunity as a calm rest before a potential storm. But if she didn't hear Mareq's footsteps soon, she might just plan a route to the fifth floor, then dart off on her own.

CHAPTER 33

ALABOQ

Mareq was afraid the sandstone floor of the kitchens would crack under the repetitive tapping of his foot, but his attempts to stop the reflex had proven hopeless. There was no reason for him to be anxious, standing in the storeroom with his unloaded crates of produce. He had long been finished with the delivery, but he had spent so much time in this part of the citadel over the last few weeks that he suspected any non-kitchen staff member who saw him would likely think he was part of the team. No, he wasn't in any current danger, trespassing though he might have been. It was the thought of what came next that set his nerves on edge. Creeping upstairs to help steal from a member of the King's Guard and then smuggling a man he hardly knew inside Vinsart Hold. Maybe he had overcorrected from his life on his family's dairy farm, bypassing adventure and landing squarely on criminal enterprise.

"Still on your Ghost hunt, Mareq?" Chaevin called from the sink. Waemish stood to his left, intent on scraping a particularly stubborn bit of burnt fat from the bottom of a pan. "Mrs. Luviire told us you were done with all that, but here you are, still lurking around the pantry like a hungry little mouse looking for a nibble." The two washers snickered.

"It's not like we don't like you or anything, kid," Waemish added. "It's just crowded enough down here as it is. Now that you've come to your senses about Chaevin's fairy tales, maybe you should do something more productive with your day." The younger man elbowed Waemish in his round belly, only eliciting a louder chuckle.

Mrs. Luviire was sitting in her usual chair, outside the storeroom but angled so she could keep an eye on Mareq while she stripped herbs from their stems. He had caught her watching him with that concerned, motherly stare of hers several times already this evening and could only guess what she was thinking. She knew what he and the others had planned, and she had never done anything to betray his trust in the time he had lived in Alaboq, but could he really trust the woman to hide a planned infiltration into Vinsart Hold?

A small but warm smile appeared on her face as she gave him a slight nod, and he felt a bit of tension ease out of his body. He was still wound tighter than he had ever been in his life, but their shared look was the respite he needed from his own spiraling thoughts.

Mareq exhaled, planting his foot firmly on the floor to keep it still. "There's nothing more productive I could do than to keep this place stocked with enough fruits and vegetables. My hope is that you two will never have the chance to step away from that station," he said with a smirk. "I'm just sticking around to see which types give you the most trouble to clean. That way, I know which kinds to increase in my deliveries."

"Plus, I find that Mareq balances the energy out in here," Mrs. Luviire added. "If it weren't for him, I could only rely on Ptolon for stimulating conversation."

The Ebkarish chef chuckled quietly to himself while Chaevin and Waemish playfully grumbled. Mareq was grateful for the camaraderie he had discovered within the kitchens of Vinsart Hold, and their banter provided an escape, albeit a brief one, from the torment in his mind.

Another look from Mrs. Luviire and a slight tilt of her head told him it was time. Mareq had agreed to give Rav half an hour to get in place on the next floor, and those minutes had already drained by like water through one of Ptolon's sieves. He had to move now, or she risked being discovered as she waited for his arrival. Although she was a stranger to him, he didn't want her imprisonment on his conscience, much less a failure that could result in war between Qedrad and Choii Stier.

Hefting an empty crate from his stack, Mareq began to walk toward the stairwell while Mrs. Luviire stood from her seat, carrying several mounds of rosemary and thyme on a wooden tray. As she passed the washing station, she dragged her foot so that it caught Waemish's heel and then sprawled herself out on the floor with a convincing shout. Herbs scattered everywhere as the tray clattered to the ground, and Waemish and Chaevin dropped their sudsy utensils into the basin and turned to help her. Thankful for the distraction, Mareq slipped upstairs as swiftly and silently as he could. The fewer questions there were, the better it was for both him and the staff below. If he was caught, he didn't want any one of them having to answer for his foolhardy decisions.

He made quick work of the stairs despite his shorter legs, his nervous energy compensating for the length of his stride. At the top of the landing, he found himself standing alone in a maroon-carpeted hallway, suddenly feeling more out of place than he expected he would as a trespasser. The gilding on the sconces lining the corridor and even the polish on the gleaming sandstone walls told him he didn't belong here. He thought if the value of everything in his hometown were totaled, it wouldn't measure up to the riches he saw around him now. Coupled with the glimpses of formal attire he caught twirling around inside the banquet hall, not to mention the décor within, he couldn't help but draw himself down behind the crate in his arms. He needed to find Rav and get back down to the kitchens with the armor soon, or else he was positive these nobles would smell the scent of straw and raw milk on him.

"Stop lagging around out here," a voice hissed from his right. He turned to see Rav poking her head out from a sitting room that was adjacent to the stairwell. "If you're going to clod around with those heavy footfalls, you at least need to keep moving."

Her straight black hair was a bit mussed at the front, as if something had been pressed flat against her forehead and shifted around, but she somehow managed to still fit in this place. She possessed a chameleon-like quality, an ability to move back and forth between disparate social strata with ease. Assuming they survived, and averted an international incident, he thought it might be worth tagging along with her and her friends. If nothing else, it wouldn't be dull.

But as he followed her into the room, he began to second-guess that daydream. Lying flat on the floor with his face shoved against the carpet was a bear of a King's Guard, a small, drying patch of blood appearing almost brown against the plush red flooring.

"What happened?" Mareq asked, nearly dropping his crate and struggling to keep his voice low. "I gave you that powdered hindran root, you didn't have to beat the guy into submission!"

"Oh, don't be dramatic," Rav said as she carried the breastplate over and placed it inside. It was clearly heavy for her to move, but it was a lighter load than he was used to hauling. "By the time I got him out of the hall, he was starting to grow suspicious, so I reacted. It's just a bloody nose. I didn't bludgeon him into unconsciousness."

Mareq swallowed, his nose burning in sympathy where the guard's had been crunched. "All right, just be careful please. I know you're after a horrible man, but most of the people in Vinsart Hold are at least decent. They don't deserve to be a casualty of this plan."

He watched her mouth draw into a thin line, biting a retort off at the tongue before the tension in her face relaxed. "You're right, Mareq. He was being a perfect gentleman before I put him to sleep. I'll take more care with where I plant my knees going forward."

Breastplate concealed within his produce crate, Mareq peeked his head out into the hallway, finding it still deserted. Most of the King's Guard would likely be stationed at the entrances or within the banquet hall while the king and his daughter were making their rounds. Based on Rav's assessment of his footfalls, he needed to take advantage of this opportunity while it lasted.

"All right, I'll get this out to Wymund," Mareq said. "Head over to the party and he'll join all of you shortly."

Rav's eyes flicked upward. "Tell him I'll meet up with them later. If they can't secure an audience with the king, I'll make sure that I do." Before he could reply, she darted off down the hallway, combing her hair back into place with her fingers as she went. Unsurprisingly, it fell right into place.

He descended the stairs with the lightest steps he could manage and exited back into the kitchens. In the time he had been upstairs, the two dishwashers had returned to their stations and were now eyeing Mareq, speechless for the first time since he had known them. No one who worked down there belonged upstairs. But he met their wide gazes and kept walking, trying to keep the color out of his face and the stammer from his voice.

"Some preserves were special-ordered for the banquet, and I wanted to hand-deliver them. Better for business if I can make myself known to that crowd up there." Deceit didn't come naturally to him, and though he had concocted this excuse in case he needed it, it still flopped clumsily from his tongue. However, neither Waemish nor Chaevin seemed to notice, as the pair just shrugged and muttered something about never getting to set foot upstairs themselves.

He made his way through the kitchen, passing Mrs. Luviire, who was chatting with Ptolon as she dropped off the stemmed herbs. She touched his shoulder as he walked by, lending her support so that he stood a bit taller on the way out. He had made it. The riskiest part of the plan was done—his role in it, anyway. What the rest of them got up to inside the walls of the citadel was another story, but it wasn't his. All he needed to do now was meet up with Wymund in the Thistle Hare Warren on the outskirts of Vinsart Hold's grounds and pass off the breastplate. Then he could return home and wait—

"Hey, fruit man," a voice called out to him. All the fresh steel in his spine turned to jelly as he turned to see a pair of King's Guards stationed outside the entrance to the kitchens. He recognized them, a human woman and a draqesh man who were often posted at this point of entry. The woman, Karome, was the one who had spoken, and had he not been so preoccupied, he would have realized the shifts had changed and would have tried to find another exit. Karome liked to pick at him, always commenting on how much taller his stack of crates was than the man carrying them, and other than the occasional eyeroll from her partner, Mareq never received any backup from his fellow draqeshi. The comments didn't bother him; he could tell it was the good-natured ribbing of a bored sentry trying to pass the time. But what he did mind now was the added attention.

"Where are the rest of your boxes?" Karome asked. "I can see more of you than just your boots today."

Mareq sighed, hoping to pass his nerves off as exasperation. "Minister Hadac overordered for the banquet, so now there isn't enough shelf space for me to unload. They're shuffling things around inside as they bring more food up to the party, so I'll be back later to collect the rest." He hoped the two guards couldn't see his jaw clench at that unintentional promise. They would be here for the duration of the evening, and now he was expected to return. So much for waiting things out in the safety of his apartment.

You are not suited for a life of criminality, he told himself, marveling at how just minutes ago, he had considered joining Rav's band. He wouldn't make it past the first night with them.

Karome looked across at her partner with a smirk before turning back to him. "Too much coin and not enough sense. Between you and me, fruit man, every one of them who work for the king are just like that. Spending more than they have any need to, and then wondering where all the money went." She laughed and added, "All right, be on your way, then. When you come back, make sure you're carrying something in front of your face so I can recognize you."

He laughed along with her, though it came out at a higher pitch than he was used to. "Will do," he said, his back already to them as he hurried down the sandstone incline. Wymund should be waiting for him a few blocks into the district, already in his red tunic and prepared to head inside. Much to his dismay, Mareq would be following behind him before long, thanks to his own undisciplined mouth. Even though he wouldn't be trailing the rest of them onto their collision course with the scorcher insurgent, he still had the feeling that he was diving back into a boiling pot. He swallowed hard, choosing instead to focus on the reward that was sure to come from stopping this scheme and the promise of the open road to follow. Laying low in the kitchens for the night was all that was required of him. He could manage that.

Chapter 34

Alaboq

Tetamii's hand trembled as he strained to keep himself from crushing the roll of parchment held at his side. He stood in the center of King Berenqar's sitting room, ironically named given that there was only one chair at the far end, and judging by the King's Guard stationed to its right, it wasn't meant for guests. One door off to the left presumably led farther into the king's personal living quarters, while against the right wall was a table holding stacks of parchment scrolls. The simple furnishings told him this room was used for private meetings that didn't require the pomp and circumstance of the throne room, but he wasn't offended. All that mattered was that his employer's message was delivered convincingly. The only bit of décor that was meant to impress was a large semicircular window positioned behind the chair and high up on the wall. Tetamii imagined during daylight hours the effect would be striking, the rays of light cast onto the king as he held court, as if blessed by the Dawn Ones themselves.

He could hear his own galloping pulse in the silence of the room, the thick red carpeting absorbing what little sound there was with only the two men present. But it wasn't Berenqar's tardiness that was fueling his anger; royalty often existed in an alternate reality with their own conceptions of time. It wasn't even the cold stare of the square-jawed guard that drilling into him from across the room. The man's eyes hadn't flitted away from him since he had entered the chamber. No, this was a rage born of incompetence. Sylicera was supposed to be here to aid his manipulation of the king, a trusted advisor to lend credence to his claims.

But the woman was nowhere to be found, and as the minutes dragged by, his fury only grew.

Passing the scroll from one hand to the other, he stretched the fingers that had been threatening to claw into the parchment and shook them out. He had spent all yesterday forging this document, carefully replicating Elikar Thymes's hand, which he had studied prior to his departure from Felona as preparation in the event that such an improvised tactic needed to be employed. It explained to King Berenqar all of Kefya's supposed concerns regarding the "mounting elven threat" within their borders, and how the Council feared the "terrorists" would expand their reach into Qedrad. Tetamii had even learned the signatures of two other members of the Council at Thymes's direction. If the scheme fell apart, Kefya's port admiral wanted plausible deniability. His employer would simply insinuate he was a concerned leader who had unwittingly signed on to the corrupt plan of a colleague.

Double doors swung open behind him, admitting King Berenqar and his retinue of two guardsmen into the sitting room, the soldiers marching across the floor with one hand resting on the pommels of their shortswords. Next to the imposing man and woman in gilded breastplates, the monarch looked less than impressive. From build to appearance, there was nothing special about him, which meant the respect and adoration he had cultivated during his reign was truly a testament to his character.

It's amazing the character flaws one can avoid developing when sheltered from the harshness of everyday life, Tetamii thought, ever thankful for his education with the Clipped Gulls as to the true nature of the world around him. Hiding his annoyance behind a polite smile, he bowed his head as Berenqar took the only seat in the room.

Once he was safely surrounded by his three guards, King Berenqar took a moment to appraise his guest. Tetamii had once more donned his white tailcoat and still wore his sheathed bastard sword across his back. He was surprised no one had asked to take it from him upon entering the citadel, though he supposed he *did* have the backing of one of the king's highest-ranking advisors. Maybe her word granted him more leeway than he had expected. or no one had dared to ask him. Tetamii was a more imposing figure than any one of the King's Guard he had seen since arriving in Qedrad, so he would have respected an attempt to disarm him. They wouldn't have walked away with his blade, but it would have been impressive just the same.

"Was Minister Hadac not also meant to join us in this discussion?" Berenqar asked. "She has of course prepared me for the troubling assertions you plan to present, but her insights would be appreciated."

"I am sure that she is on her way, Your Majesty," Tetamii said, keeping his voice level. "The trade minister is a woman with many responsibilities, but I am willing to begin now in the hope that she arrives soon." He raised the rolled parchment in front of him. "Despite the gravity of this message I carry from the Kefyan Council, I would not want to keep you away from your daughter on this special day."

Berenqar waved away Tetamii's feigned concern, offering a simple smile in return. "Lady Cailynne has insisted that I spend this day each year hearing the troubles of my people and aiding in any way I can. 'Gifts are for the spoiled princesses,' she says. Do not be troubled for helping me do as my daughter wishes."

The king tilted his head forward, and one of his guards stepped forward to retrieve the scroll. The man's jawline could have been chiseled from stone, his face a master class in stoic professionalism, but Tetamii was certain the guard stopped a few inches farther away than he should have and leaned in to take the paper. Unfurling the roll, Berenqar began to read over the forgery in silence, eyes creasing at the edges as his brow furrowed. Once finished, he let the parchment curl back up as he settled deeper into his chair and studied his visitor once more.

"I see that four of your Council's members are not represented here," King Berenqar said. "Are they not of the same opinion regarding this supposed incursion of elves from Choii Stier? I would think that a threat such as the one insinuated in this message would warrant unanimous agreement before bringing it to the attention of another nation's leader."

"The undersigned Council members recognized a pattern of escalation within the elven attacks, particularly within the walls of Virdoba, and felt it prudent to send word to your kingdom before the terrorists reached your borders. I was sent with their concerns before the rest of the Council could be briefed, though I would not be surprised if I had a counterpart following on my heels attesting to their agreement as well."

The king nodded, his eyes still narrowed as he glanced back and forth between the parchment and Tetamii. "I do appreciate the gesture, Mr. Fiadar. It is nice to know that Kefya's leadership cares for the well-being of their neighbors. It is only in the spirit of Teacher Irasil that our two countries have overcome our history of bloodshed to reach this new bond of friendship." The man was taking great care with how he spoke, choosing each word with a deliberate focus. He wouldn't be easily convinced.

"Though I would be remiss to neglect the social conditions of your nation and how that might color this warning. I am aware that many of your countrymen feel . . . *insecure* around their new elven compatriots. Economic hardship has bred competition at all levels of society, and it is tempting to blame the beautiful and talented newcomers for one's own misfortune. I just want to be sure that this perception of danger is not a misconception derived from jealous animosity."

Tetamii smiled politely. He had anticipated this line of inquiry; Kefya's bigoted tendencies were not a well-kept secret. "Yes, of course, Your Majesty. If you would allow me to detail for you all of the trauma that has been inflicted on the good people of Virdoba, and the evidence I have seen in my travels north, I am sure you will come to see that this claim is without bias and meant with only the best intentions for Qedrad."

"Please, illuminate me. Your assessment will be of particular value as a man who finds himself with one foot on either side of this divide."

His smile faltered for a moment. The king seeing through to his elven heritage hadn't been expected. But this was a cultured man, a person who interacted with all manner of individuals and would of course be able to pick out his more subdued elven characteristics. Chastising himself inwardly for the oversight, Tetamii said, "My allegiance lies only with my home, not the people destroying it. It is no matter to me if these dangerous invaders share some of my physical attributes. They certainly share none of my character."

Berenqar shifted in his seat, leaning to the opposite side as he crossed his legs, and never tore his eyes away from Tetamii's gaze. "Invaders is a curious term. It is my understanding that the governments of Choii

Stier and Kefya allow for free passage between their borders. 'Invaders' suggests an unwelcome arrival, which brings us back to the populace's general sentiment rather than any official policy position. If this alarm is being raised out of a distaste for one's neighbors, might I suggest a feast to ease the tensions and generate camaraderie? Breaking bread is often more productive than breaking bones."

"I take your point, but—"

"Furthermore," King Berenqar continued, "solidifying ties and opening new trade routes with another nation is an opportunity that I would not want to pass up for my people. There was a time in our history when Qedradan ports were the envy of the world, and many of us wish to return to that zenith. I will require more evidence than basic hearsay before I walk away from such an economic boon."

Tetamii took a breath, forcing his jaw to relax. He found himself wishing for Sylicera's presence and her knowledge of Qedrad's trade realities, but that only angered him more. Having to rely on a woman he had already concluded was incompetent was a failure on his part, and one he wouldn't make again. If future jobs required that he obtain and study the balance sheets for an entire nation, Tetamii would do it just to avoid this shame. This semantic battle wouldn't be won with numbers, and his appeal using the word of Kefyan authority had fallen on deaf ears. There was only one avenue of rhetoric left for him, then, but fortunately the ruler seemed to be the type to fall sway to it.

Clearing his throat, Tetamii tilted his head downward and closed his eyes. His training had demanded much of him to achieve his physical and martial skills, most of which involved sealing himself away from the emotions that would impair those abilities. Joy and sorrow dulled the blade in equal measure; therefore, neither could be allowed. The Clipped Gulls taught all their initiates to lock feelings away in a mental chest, stored so deep at the base of their minds that it took purpose to retrieve, and only then for manipulative gain. Tetamii had been known to indulge himself over the years, visiting the vault and the memories it contained as a form of penance, but now as he brought the forced tears to his eyes, their true purpose could be realized.

"Please, King Berenqar," Tetamii said past the convincing lump in his throat. "If you had seen the things that I have seen on my journey to meet with you. If you had seen what these *evil* beings had done to your own subjects, just a matter of days from where you sit now, you would know this is far from hearsay." Behind a mask of steepled fingers, the monarch tilted his head to give his guest permission to continue. "I am sure by now you have heard of the tragedy at Turlaq's Fork."

"Indeed I have," Berenqar replied unflinchingly. "A member of my King's Guard returned to us, maimed and raving about a masked scorcher who set the village ablaze like so much tinder. Though we have also heard conflicting reports, with scouts carrying news of a massive reptilian beast being found among the town's remains."

Tetamii nearly lost his hold on his vein of emotions at hearing that, his mind churning at the news. But he dismissed it as rumor; any time there was an unexplained conflagration, some fool was always quick to scream "dragon."

"With the state of my soldier's mind after surviving such a devastating event," Berenqar continued, "I am not quite sure what to believe. I am curious to know what news you may have to add to our understanding."

"I passed through the village on my way north, Your Majesty. I saw no evidence of this creature you speak of, but I can attest to the sheer horror that remains." Tetamii held a fist to his mouth, choking back a sob. "Nothing is left. Buildings have been reduced to charred rubble and mounds of soot. Scorched husks of families . . . women and children are seared to the ground where they huddled together, praying to anyone who would listen for safety."

He met Berenqar's gaze, the ruler still appraising him from above his steepled hands. His vision swam behind a veil of unfamiliar tears, which he blinked away as he reached a hand inside his tailcoat. "As for evidence, I found this on the trail leading north from Turlaq's Fork." Tetamii tossed his wooden war mask onto the ground before him. To the king's credit, the man didn't react more than to redirect his discerning gaze down toward the disguise.

"The elves of Choii Stier are on the move across the lands of Anera, King Berenqar," Tetamii continued. "For reasons unknown to me, they are seeking to stoke the flames of war, and they are not content with terrorizing the Kefyan people. I'm afraid that this is no longer a matter of trade deals and economic consideration. Based on what I witnessed, the ruthless damage that was inflicted on those good people, this is an extermination."

The three guards in the room glanced at each other, sharing a look that told Tetamii he had been convincing enough for them. But Berenqar remained hard to read. After a moment of sustained silence, the ruler finally spoke.

"Speak to me about what your leadership has in mind to stem this assault. I am not wholly convinced, as Choii Stier's High Scholar would have to be a fool to throw away the potential for peace and profit so close to being realized. But I want to be prepared for any eventuality. If a lesson must be learned, I will not hesitate to bloody their delicate noses."

CHAPTER 35

ALABOQ

Wymund tugged down on the gilded breastplate as he stepped into the banquet hall. Its added heft was unfamiliar to one who was used to working with only a chain shirt for protection, but his real issue was that the armor stopped inches above his waistline no matter how much he adjusted the attached leather straps. He felt like he did as a new recruit on the first day of training, one of many standing in ordered rows outside of the Lighthouse before the drills began, self-conscious and out of place. He might have known the ins and outs of a guard's life, but wearing ill-fitted armor in a foreign nation's capital only left him feeling more exposed, as if anyone who glanced at him could tell that he didn't belong. However, he didn't have the luxury of time to worry about his appearance. Mareq had informed him that yet again, Rav had decided to break ranks and go her own way. He was beginning to wonder if the woman understood the meaning of the word "plan."

He scanned the massive room, eyes passing over twirling couples on the dance floor and tables full of people laughing and drinking the evening away. It didn't take long to locate Kymil, who had taken his place on the stage and was commanding the attention of many a young man and woman, all staring up at him raptly as he led the room through an upbeat rendition of a Felonian folk song that told the tale of a sailor's daughter and her three lovers. The song's content didn't fit the occasion, but the bard had a knack for being incorrigible and endearing at the same time, and no one in the crowd, from the stuffiest old man to the primmest lady, seemed to mind the salacious lyrics. Kymil caught his gaze and gave him a wink; he would meet Wymund offstage once the song ended.

Locating Annika proved to be more of a challenge, her navy dress seemingly designed to blend into the shadows of a torchlit room. But he caught sight of her bushel of dark waves toward the eastern side of the hall as she stood facing a pretty young woman and two King's Guard, locked in conversation. Ordinarily he would have chosen to wait the discussion out, avoiding the risk of being unmasked as an intruder, but he needed Annika now. Rav had gone rogue, and a new plan had to be improvised.

Should've left her in the Iron Spiral, he thought, grumbling to himself as he gently pushed his way through the mingling masses.

"You *must* bring a bottle or two with you next time, Ms. Iatorii," the younger woman said, beaming across at Annika. She wore a thin silver circlet over her dark brown hair and carried herself with a grace that belied her age. His sense of foreboding about approaching them only heightened as he realized who the guards were there to protect, but there was no time left for subtlety. "The Iatorii Vineyard was a favorite of my mother's before she passed. Anytime one of our ambassadors was dispatched to Felona, she would always ask that they return with a crate of your finest vintage. My father and I would love to toast in her memory with the drink that brought her so much joy."

"It would be my honor to return with such a meaningful tribute to your mother. My family's business is now run by one of my cousins, but my name still carries some weight. I will inquire as to which vintage was most often gifted to her and send it your way." Annika turned to see Wymund step up beside her, her eyes widening briefly in surprise before she slipped back into her socialite mode. "And I see this young man has also come up empty handed. I asked him to locate King Berenqar so that I might request a formal audience, but it seems his luck has been as poor as mine."

Thankful that the onus of the introductory lie was off his shoulders, Wymund said, "My apologies, Ms. Iatorii. Even at my height it can be difficult with a gathering of this size."

Lady Cailynne frowned. "I'm sorry that you missed him. My father has already excused himself to his chambers to begin meeting with his scheduled guests. I believe he is in with a dignitary from Felona now, a man representing the Kefyan Council." Wymund did his best to keep his face neutral as his heart began to race. "But he will return before the party ends. If you are able to stay, I would be happy to introduce you to him then."

Annika smiled. "That would be lovely, Lady Cailynne." She swung her arm out back toward the center of the celebration. "Please, don't let this old woman dominate so much of your time on this special day. Enjoy yourself, and I look forward to seeing you again later tonight."

The princess chuckled and patted Annika on the shoulder as she passed, promising she would find her once King Berenqar returned. As her retinue followed, one clamped a hand onto Wymund's bicep. "What do you think you're doing?" the man asked through gritted teeth. He felt his stomach jump into his throat, suddenly envisioning himself locked up in Vinsart Hold's dungeons as Rav got herself killed confronting the scorcher in the king's chambers. But before he could respond, the guard added, "You look like a damn halfwit. Next time you pack on a few pounds, make sure you get your armor properly fitted before representing the Crown at an event like this."

"Yes, sir," Wymund choked out, nodding his head, then sighing as soon as the man was out of earshot.

Now that his pulse wasn't quite so loud in his ears, Wymund noticed a shift in the music and could see that Kymil had been replaced on stage by a pair of draqeshi women who were singing a cappella while performing a style of ballet that involved tossing spinning iron rings between one another. The bard strode toward them and arrived with a self-satisfied smile plastered across his face. "I assume my musical stylings set the stage for a successful diplomatic request?"

"I would've preferred to make our case to King Berenqar first," Annika said. "But it appears the scorcher beat us to him. No matter, Lady Cailynne will introduce us later tonight and we will just have to reveal the truth to him then."

"We can't wait," Wymund said. "Rav is on her way to the king's chambers now. If, and more realistically when, she barges in on their meeting, matters will spiral out of our control. We won't get a second chance at this if the king takes her to be an elven insurgent." He watched

Annika's furrowed brow shift from puzzled to some mixture of fear and anger. Even Kymil pouted. "We make our way to speak with him now, or we lose both Rav and our chance to sway the world away from war."

Kymil sighed. "You know, at a certain point this story is going to strain credibility. No protagonist could be *that* reckless. But I suppose we should still save her anyway. I haven't come all this way for nothing."

***

"I didn't realize my dietary requests would fall on deaf ears," Sylicera shouted, commanding the attention of Vinsart Hold's kitchen staff. She stared expectantly at the back of Ptolon's head, but it elicited no reaction from the man, who either out of apathy or spite maintained his focus on the pot of chili sauce before him. The chef raised a wooden spoon to his lips and tasted his creation before nodding and setting the utensil aside.

From Mareq's position against the wall with Mrs. Luviire, he could see Ptolon was unperturbed by the trade minister's dramatic display. But she wasn't one to tolerate flagrant insubordination, so after failing to draw him out into the center of the room for a more public chastisement, Sylicera stalked over and jerked him around by the shoulder to face her.

"When your betters ask for a more traditional sauce to be served alongside their dinner, you would do well to meet their demands, "Sylicera said. "Otherwise, one might expect to experience consequences both professional and personal."

Now that the woman was closer, Mareq could see her bloodshot eyes and detect a slight rasp in her voice. He knew the reaction well, and he felt his stomach tighten sympathetically. Ebkarish chilis made their way north to his home in Brey more frequently than they trekked across the entire length of the continent, so he couldn't blame the woman being unprepared for the spice's heat. However, he suspected the sting of Ptolon's disobedience hit her ego harder than the fiery sauce had burned her gullet. Whatever wrath she was about to unleash, though, he was actually grateful for her presence. If she was down here berating the kitchen staff, then she and her scorcher guest couldn't be meeting with the king yet. The others still had a chance to reach him first.

Ptolon stared down at her with a blank expression, a bored aloofness that would only serve to drive Sylicera's anger to greater heights. "The excess cream I had available was needed to create the glaze for Lady Cailynne's puff pastries. As you might remember, she is quite fond of that dessert and wanted to ensure each of her guests had the opportunity to try one. By the time all of the cakes were coated, I simply did not have the remaining ingredients to make a special sauce for your meal."

"Then someone should've been sent to the market for more," she seethed. "It is a solution even the simplest of chefs could have come up with, but I suppose that would be giving you too much credit."

Mareq saw Ptolon's brow twitch, but before his cool could completely break, Mrs. Luviire hurried over to join them. "My apologies, Minister Hadac," she said, shoving her shoulder defensively between them but wearing a bright smile. "I'm responsible for sending our runners out on errands and managing our supplies. I should've known to stock up on cream once Lady Cailynne requested the dessert course. But we are only halfway into the evening; perhaps we could whip something else up for you while you return to enjoy the festivities."

At the mention of the hour, Sylicera's eyes darted over to the window, seeming startled at how high the moon had risen already. "I no longer have the time. Unlike all of you, those in my position have other appointments to keep." Her voice trembled as she spoke. The woman wasn't just surprised at the time; something had her scared. "I will just have to make do with the trace amount of your meal I was able to choke down, and tomorrow a discussion will be had concerning an acceptable attitude for Vinsart Hold's staff."

Mrs. Luviire just smiled and bowed her head while Ptolon sniffed, returning to his work as Sylicera began to head toward the stairs. The fear in Sylicera's eyes could only mean one thing. The meeting between the scorcher and King Berenqar had already begun, and she was late. There was nothing Mareq could do to warn the others now, and Rav would be essentially walking blind into a furnace.

Mareq acted without a thought, propelling himself off the wall and wrapping his beam-like arms around the trade minister's waist. She struggled in his hold, writhing left and right but finding no weak points. Competing thoughts battled in his mind as he buried his face in her lower back and lifted her feet off the ground.

Congratulations, Mareq, this is the worst idea you've ever had.

"Unhand me, you filthy oaf!" Sylicera shouted as she struck at his arms with her fists. Whether it was the dramatic difference in strength or just pure adrenaline, he felt her blows as little more than pokes and prods.

Waemish and Chaevin stared slack-jawed at Mareq's actions, letting the soapy dishes they held clatter into the sink, and even Ptolon displayed some shock with a raised eyebrow. However, Mrs. Luviire just tightened her mouth and strode over, pointing at the two dishwashers. "You two, get over here and help Mareq secure her. Cover her mouth so she doesn't get any of the King's Guard down here."

The men only spared a moment to share a confused look before following her directions, seemingly responding more to her tone than any genuine understanding of the situation. Mrs. Luviire bent over so that her mouth was next to Mareq's ear and whispered, "Next time, give me a signal before you decide to go off script. I can usually find better ways to stall someone than holding them still."

After stuffing the trade minister's mouth with a wash rag and placing a burlap sack over her head, Chaevin helped Mareq bind her hands and feet before stowing her in the storeroom. Once she was out of earshot, everyone huddled together, waves of anxiety washing over them all.

"Well, that was unexpected," Waemish said. He patted Mrs. Luviire on the shoulder and turned back toward his station, a distant look in his eyes. "When this goes sideways, I'm telling anyone who will listen that you bewitched me with one of your plant powders. I won't be going down for . . . whatever this was." Chaevin mumbled his agreement as he slid his back along the wall into a crouched position.

"I hope this was worth it," the older elf said, looking down at Mareq with that warm smile of hers. For once it didn't seem to help. One way or another, he had just bet his life on the success of people he hardly knew.

But if I hadn't, what would my life even be worth?

"I hope so too," he muttered, collapsing back into his chair.

***

Rav tapped the back of her head against the wall, just soft enough to remain silent but still vent her frustration. Snaking her way up four flights of stairs and down each floor's corridor had been uneventful; a polite nod here and a quickened step there had been all that was required to make her way back up to fifth floor. As much as she hated to admit it, slipping back into her aristocratic roots gave her a sense of power that she had forgotten. The right mixture of confidence and arrogance combined with an eye-popping gown could take her a long way in this world. But as she tilted her head back around the corner, she knew it would take more than an aura of belonging to make it past the two King's Guard posted to either side of the large heartfir doors.

She cycled through the options in her mind and didn't like what she saw. The hindran root wouldn't knock out both, and she didn't believe she could convince both to leave their stations at the same time. *Kymil could,* she thought, but recognized it was too late to wait for her allies' arrival. The very presence of these guards meant the king was already within, his granted audiences already taking place.

A combination approach, getting one to leave and then making the other sleep, seemed more viable, but also opened her up to too many variables, too many moving pieces that could end with her rotting away in a dungeon below the citadel. That left a violent approach, but she could still hear Mareq's plea that these were decent people. A pit formed in her stomach. She could handle these two on her own, but she feared becoming the type of person who fell back on that option too readily. Knotting her dress off at her knees again, she ducked into an unlocked side room and softly shut the door behind her. If the interior entrance was unavailable, she would see what the exterior had to offer.

Rav found herself in a small but beautifully decorated bedroom. A four-poster bed with mounds of thick pillows sat against the wall to the right, ornately carved chests flanking either side. Given the room's size and proximity to the king's chambers, she suspected it belonged to an attendant of some kind, and one who was well taken care of, at that. But the most important feature of the room was the shuttered window, and when she opened it, she found it was overlooking the northern portion of the city wall. The gap between the rear façade of Vinsart Hold and the wall looked to be around fifty feet, far too wide of a leap for her to use the top of the wall as a bridge between windowsills. But as she looked to her left, she saw what she had been hoping for: equally spaced windows, suspended stepping-stones toward her destination.

After kicking her silk slippers off, she planted her bare feet onto the sandstone sill and exited the building. Her skin would offer better traction than delicate footwear, and she was thankful the icy weather had tempered the building's ability to retain heat. As it was, the sandstone was still surprisingly warm beneath her feet. She leaped from ledge to ledge, a task that was much easier to do horizontally than it had been to do vertically earlier in the evening. Rav soon found herself approaching the building's exterior corner, around which she expected to find a large balcony garden or some other indicator that would denote King's Berenqar's window from any other. But as she dug her toes into the ledge offered by a decorative corner block and crept around the side, all she saw was a tan expanse of solid stone where the royal chambers should be.

Clinging to the corner, Rav searched desperately for anything she had missed, eventually glancing up to find a semicircular window near the roof of the citadel, placed so that sunlight would be cast down into the interior below. She began to scale the building, finding handholds on the corner blocks that jutted out just wide enough for the tips of her fingers and toes, and wondered whether another window overlooking a room she hoped to scout was an ill omen or an opportunity to make up for her mistakes in Virdoba. Pain transitioned into numbness as she climbed the twenty feet remaining to the roof, without thought as to what might come next once she reached her goal. It would all depend on what, or who, she saw inside that room.

***

With Wymund as an escort, most of the quizzical glances Kymil had expected were deflected as the three of them walked briskly through corridor after corridor. To the outside observer, he and Annika would appear as guests being guided through the halls of Vinsart Hold by a member of the King's Guard. He had to admit he was concerned that Wymund's straitlaced inflexibility would wind up with him breaking character out of ethical concerns, but the stickler had impressed him thus far. Besides, he was not exactly playing against type.

But there was only so much he could expect from Wymund in the delicate art of conversational misdirection. He trusted the man to be at his side when it came to blades and blood being drawn. His mettle had been on prominent display as he stared down that scaled monstrosity to the south. But as they approached a pair of King's Guard, a man and a woman stationed beside King Berenqar's scarlet-stained heartfir doors, he knew a softer touch would be required. Wymund's last attempt to appeal to a shared guardsmen code had resulted in an embarrassing scene, so Kymil placed a hand on the man's breastplate as he passed him, giving his allies a look that said *hold back*. It was time to dial up the charm, and he couldn't have an old woman or a stone-faced giant lurking behind him to throw off his chances.

"Finally," Kymil said, striding toward the pair. "A couple of people who seem worthy of my time." The guards tensed at his approach, their hands tightening around the hilts of their shortswords as they locked eyes on him. "I was beginning to think the night's festivities were over for me, but fortune has seen fit to pull me toward the two of you."

"What are you on about?" asked one of the guards, his frown creasing an otherwise handsome face. "Be on your way. Guests aren't allowed up here."

"Right you are, the riffraff cannot be allowed to wander about on their own this close to the king's chambers. But my traveling companion and I are no ordinary guests," he said, gesturing back to Annika. "Lady Cailynne extended a special invitation for us to stay in one of the citadel's suites during our visit, something about my good friend's family producing a favorite wine of the late queen." The guards appeared to relax a bit, their shoulders dropping an inch or so as their hands moved to rest on the ends of their pommels.

Kymil leaned in, lowering his voice. "As you can see, though, my friend has most of her years behind her now. She thinks the hour is late and that we should board up for the night. I offered to have another one of you fine guardsmen lead me up on my own later, but you know how people can get in their twilight years. She would be anxious if I was too far away."

The guards nodded their understanding, smiling along with him at Annika's expense. Kymil winked at them, enjoying himself almost too much. People who lived highly structured lives were always the easiest to throw off with a smile and some attention. If nobles were smarter, they would keep a number of bards in their employ to be posted with their protection. Then maybe Kymil would have a challenge. *But probably not.*

"Just when I believed my glamorous night in Vinsart Hold would end with a whimper, I stumble upon two exemplary specimens on the way to my room."

Blushing, the first guard straightened his back and cleared his throat while his partner chuckled. "And how exactly do you think we figure into your night, bard?" she asked.

"Oh, I'm sure the three of us could come up with something," Kymil said. "As you might have heard, we traveling performers have been known to pick up a trick or two everywhere we go."

The pair glanced at each other, though the man had trouble making eye contact with his partner, appearing to be much more interested in his own feet. The other guard tilted her head in thought for a moment, looking Kymil up and down before finally shrugging. "They'll be locked up in there for at least another hour, and the rest of this place is crawling with other guards. I suppose we can find some time to see if the rumors have any truth to them."

"Wh-what?" the man stammered. "Jayli, we can't abandon our—"

"Come off it, Trysul," she interrupted, gripping him on the shoulder. "Nobody's making it up here that shouldn't be. In fact"—she paused, snapping her fingers at Wymund down the hallway, who immediately stood at attention—"you there, once you drop that good woman off in her chambers come back here and maintain our post. We'll be back in, well, you tell me," she said, glancing up at Kymil with a smirk.

The confidence this woman radiated made Kymil wish this wasn't just a ruse, but some things were more important than a tryst. Or so he imagined. He had never thought to put another matter before a romantic rendezvous. There truly *was* a first time for everything.

"We can be brief, or as brief as you like. Either way, what I *know* it won't be is forgettable." Kymil gestured toward the other end of the hall, away from his allies. "Lead the way, you two. I prefer a down mattress if one is available."

"Jayli, are you sure about this?" Trysul asked. His face had only turned a deeper shade of red, yet his smile was reminiscent of a boy who had just discovered an unattended pantry full of treats.

"Stop being such a child before I leave you behind," she said, already marching down the hall and dragging him behind her. The three rounded the corner and found an unoccupied room, which Jayli opened and slinked into, already unfastening her breastplate. Trysul fumbled with his own straps, all thumbs as he battled against his nerves.

Gripping the handle, Kymil said, "You two get yourselves settled, and feel free to start without me. Give me a moment and I'll join you. I like to make an entrance." He shut the door behind him, not granting them the time to react with more than flustered faces. Moving quickly, he plucked a stiletto blade from under his cloak and sank it into the wooden doorframe, passing the knife through the door handle so that if they tried to open it, the door would catch on his impromptu deadbolt. Kymil could still see trailing luminescent tendrils dancing around the infused blade before he turned to meet up with Wymund and Annika. If his luck held, so would the door.

***

Suspended by her ankles from the lip of the roof, Rav stretched her neck to peer through the semicircular window into King Berenqar's chambers. She had torn her gown off at the knees and knotted the length of fabric around one of the sandstone balusters ringing the citadel's roof, which she had come to suspect was a stupid decision, as most of her blood rushed to her head. The silk dug into her ankles and her feet began to throb, a prickling sensation dancing across them that was reminiscent of her connection to the World Shroud but was just her feet screaming for fresh blood. However, she managed to hang far enough over the edge to peer through the glass, her dark hair billowing out and around her from the sea breeze. With one hand, she forced the hair out of her eyes. Then she gasped, her fears realized inside the room.

Standing with their backs to the window were three King's Guard and a man she assumed was Berenqar himself, given the circlet he wore over dark, graying hair. Two of the guardsmen stood to either side of the king at one end of a rectangular table, a map of Anera spread across it, which Berenqar appeared to be studying. The other guard remained closer to a large chair positioned near the back wall of the room. But that was all visual noise, unimportant details next to the tall, muscular elven man standing at the other end of the table, his amber-ringed eyes meeting hers with a flash of recognition. One corner of his mouth turned up in the same smirk he had worn while he toyed with her on the Virdoban docks, and Rav saw red.

She scrambled back up the wall and onto her feet, then untied herself from the crenelation and felt the tingling waves of energy crash over her once again. The man who had batted her aside and left her to drown, who had played on her trauma, was mere feet below her, in the process of manipulating yet another person to his own ends. Only this time, the consequences would be felt across the world.

They were too late; King Berenqar was already being fed lies by this mercenary without anyone present for a rebuttal. Rav certainly wasn't that person. She acted first and answered questions later, but with the surprise of her survival already squandered, her one advantage to catch the scorcher off guard was already off the table.

Unless I do something truly mental.

Her anger at seeing this man again fed into the lightning racing across her skin, the two forces building each other up in a crescendo that demanded action. Spots flared to life at the edges of her vision as she propelled herself off the roof, a fistful of silk fabric in one hand that halted her outward trajectory and yanked her back toward the building. Her bare feet slammed into glass, the window shattering beneath the force as Rav slipped through the opening and landed among the shards, more pieces clinking to the ground behind her. She could feel a slight, warm dampness underfoot, but there was no pain from the lacerations. Only lights, trembling energy, and rage.

King Berenqar and his guards spun to face her, all three swordsmen drawing their blades and entering a crouched stance, with the two closest to the ruler placing protective arms across him. "Guards!" Berenqar shouted toward the set of double doors across the room, a look of panic etched onto his face. Even the scorcher's mouth hung open for a split second before he regained his composure.

The scarlet doors flew open, and another King's Guard stormed inside, shortsword out and buckler raised, followed by two other figures in formal attire. Rav blinked past the flashing sparks and recognized her allies, Annika already working to remove Wymund's stolen breastplate while he maintained a readied position.

One less target to turn into a skillet, Rav thought through the furious hum that was her mind. The armor clattered to the ground as Kymil casually strode to the middle of the room, hands clasped behind him and his typical cocksure grin greeting everyone in turn.

"No other guards I'm afraid, Your Majesty," he said with a slight bow at the waist. "They are rather indisposed at the moment, but you have nothing to fear from us anyway." Glancing toward Rav, he added, "Not even from that raving madwoman over there. She just got lost and found her own way to meet us here. But if you don't mind, we would like to present another side to this web of lies that is being spun for you, and I do hope to be quick about it. I'm expected down the hall and I would hate to keep them waiting."

Chapter 36

Alaboq

"I had hoped to prevent this, Your Majesty," the scorcher said, projecting a calmness even Kymil couldn't emulate. Annika could see through the bard's nonchalance; it was a performance just like any other. But while the scorcher might have been caught off guard by their intrusion, he didn't seem like he had lost any control.

"If only I had arrived sooner, you would have had ample opportunity to create more checkpoints and tighten security. But now at least, the truth lies before you. Two elven assassins," the man said, pointing to Rav and Kymil, "and the people they ensorcelled to get them here. A noblewoman and one of your own men-at-arms."

Two of the King's Guard positioned themselves between the king and Rav while the one remaining faced Kymil; obviously, they had decided the seething woman who was mad enough to slice her own feet open by crashing through a window was more of a threat than the well-dressed, waiflike man grinning like a fool.

Berenqar composed himself admirably despite the situation and spoke to Wymund. "Replace your breastplate, guardsman. I will not hold this mental manipulation against you, but you will not raise Qedradan steel against your king."

"That steel is not meant for you, King Berenqar," Annika said, stepping around Wymund, whose gaze never faltered from its lock on the scorcher. "We hope it is only destined to return to its scabbard this evening, but I can assure you that if we are forced to draw blood, it will not be yours."

Feeling the scorcher's cold eyes land upon her for the first time, Annika thought Rav's description had been lacking. He was a monster of a man, far larger than any other elf she had met in her life, which spoke to a rigid discipline that worried her more than his sheer bulk. Elves didn't tend to build muscle mass as readily as draqeshis or even humans, so the fact that his size rivaled Wymund's was both impressive and horrifying. This man was no mere hired thug; he was a trained mercenary.

"Speak, then," Berenqar said over a guardsman's shoulder. The ruler kept a wary eye on Rav at the back of the room. "If you truly do not intend us any harm, in the spirit of the night, I will hear your story. But know that there will be repercussions for your actions already, regardless of the content of this news. You have all moved about my home with free rein, I'm sure harming untold numbers of my guards just to make it unhindered to my chambers. That cannot stand."

Rav blinked at that; something the man had said struck a nerve. *That foolish girl laid her hands on a guard.* The sooner they explained themselves, the better, then. They had already made a less-than-desirable first impression.

"As my colleague stated," Annika continued, "we fear that your other guest has been feeding you lies, Your Majesty. We believe he is part of a conspiracy that aims to foment discord between your nation and Choii Stier, all in the name of maintaining personal wealth for a handful of noble Kefyans. There are no elven terrorist attacks wreaking havoc across western Anera except those perpetrated by that man and his allies in order to bolster his false claims."

"King Berenqar, you cannot honestly take the word of these invaders over the invited guest of your own trade minister," the scorcher said. The man's pleading voice didn't square with the iciness of his gaze, which remained fixed on Annika. "I have provided you with documentation attesting to—"

The ruler lifted a hand. "No one's word is taken on faith alone, Tetamii Fiadar. But these allegations are troublesome, and I will not forge new ties until all aspects of this tale have been revealed." Annika watched Tetamii's jaw clench, the man unaccustomed to being interrupted and unable to retort. Turning back to her, Berenqar added, "I hope you have evidence to back up these claims. But first, to whom do I have the pleasure of speaking?"

"My name is Annika Iatorii," she replied as King Berenqar's eyes narrowed, studying her face as she continued. "The man who donned the uniform of your King's Guard is named Wymund Sylnorin, a corporal in the Virdoban City Guard, and the pretty one there is the bard Kymil Adii." Kymil's smirk widened into a childlike grin as he winked at the guard facing him. Annika gestured toward Rav and sighed. "And this one is Ravael Trisarin. As a fellow Felonian, I would like to say that she possesses better manners, but she manages to prove me wrong at every opportunity."

"The Iatorii family I know is elven," Berenqar replied, a hint of suspicion remaining in his voice despite the tension leaving the rest of his body. His guards, however, remained vigilant watch dogs, ready to react at the slightest provocation.

"You are correct," Annika said. "They are my adopted family, taking me in after my parents passed when I was a young girl. I was a year or so older than their own daughter, and they always treated me just the same."

The ruler nodded wistfully. "That does sound like the family I heard about in story after story. My wife always spoke of them with honeyed words, how they welcomed her into their home when she visited your country, and as much as she enjoyed the wine, I believe it was that relationship that she cherished the most." He paused before taking a step toward her, pointing a pensive finger in her direction. "In fact, there was one Iatorii in particular she always remembered fondly. A beautiful young woman with cascading blonde curls who played hide and seek with my wife as a child, entertaining her while the families discussed their business. You would be about her age, though I recall her name being Alauvar."

Hearing the name still stung after all these years, but she maintained the polite mask of nobility. "My sister," she said with a small smile. "She loved running around with the little ones while the adults tended to the boring aspects of life. But it is fortunate that you know of her, because it is in her memory that we have traveled all this way to prevent yet another pointless war." Annika took in a deep breath to settle the slight quiver in her voice. "Alauvar was a witch. She died using every bit of power in her to heal her allies against the Council in the Rebellion of the Commons."

Wymund and Rav both spared her a glance. Each of them would have learned the horror stories of that revolution as children, of the violent crackdown the Kefyan military unleashed upon the populace after they dared to elect a "common thug" to the one democratically filled seat on the Council. It didn't matter that Councilman Daleus was a beloved member of the Felonian Woodworker's Guild, a man who had single-handedly made the city's streets safer by organizing a band of volunteers to serve as a neighborhood watch, helping the less fortunate find food and shelter for the evening, and breaking up fights in back alleys. All the rest of the Council saw was a leader of a militia that didn't come from their own social strata, and therefore a threat to their power.

"On the Night of Cinders, Alauvar infused close to thirty knitting serums, healing the charred flesh that the Council inflicted on their own citizens. By the time the last of the flames had been put out around the Hall of Merchants, her body had begun to fail," Annika rasped, clearing her throat before adding, "and there was no one around to take care of her."

"Such a senseless massacre," Berenqar muttered. "You lot start a war to secede from our monarchy in the name of democratic ideals and then lack the decency to uphold the will of the people. But unfortunately, there has been more recent butchery I must contend with. You claim that the extermination of my people in Turlaq's Fork lies at the feet of Mr. Fiadar, yet have offered no evidence. Despite my sympathies for your family, I must have more than sentiment on which to base decisions."

Wymund stepped forward, pulling a folded parchment from within his tunic, the wax seal of the Kefyan Council still affixed to the back. "We regretfully do not have evidence of his involvement in the attack beyond the knowledge that the man is a scorcher, and that the village was reduced to ash. However, I must also admit to the presence of a massive reptilian creature in what remained of the town, which we saw firsthand was capable of unleashing destruction all its own."

Tetamii's stony façade flickered to one of confusion for a second before he recovered.

"My allies and I handled this creature," Wymund continued, "and no one in the surrounding area need fear it for now. But while we may not be able to link this man directly to that attack with more than circumstantial facts, we do have evidence of a conspiracy." Wymund held the folded parchment forward as the guard that had been squaring off against Kymil sidestepped over to retrieve it. "An eyewitness will attest that the contents of that note were delivered through one of Teacher Ias's delivery networks to the ears of your trade minister, Sylicera Hadac."

King Berenqar accepted the note, first examining the wax seal for authenticity. Then, seeming satisfied, he opened the note and read it. Finally, he turned to Tetamii and said, "This E.T. and Councilman Thymes from your document wouldn't happen to be one and the same, would they, Tetamii Fiadar? The choice of the word 'pretense' is troubling, considering a truthful explanation from one of my advisors would have been sufficient to have earned you an audience."

Tetamii exhaled sharply through his nose and offered a soft smirk. "You can't say I did not try to avoid this," he said as he drew his bastard sword from its sheath, tossing the leather scabbard aside. He looked to Rav and Kymil and nodded. "Your daughter will be much more agreeable when I have two elven corpses to point to next to the smoking husk of her father."

Chapter 37

Alaboq

Through the roiling storm in her mind, Rav heard Annika's story of her sister, another young woman recklessly driving toward her own death. Rav instantly felt the distance she had kept from her lessen, but she would have to examine her attachment issues another time, because as soon as Tetamii drew his blade to face off against the King's Guards she knew it was a feint. A familiar pocket of heat was forming before her, the bubble of rippling air enveloping Berenqar where he stood at the side of the room. Another fiery explosion was brewing, but this time, he would not have the chance to finish building the energy.

Glass shards crunched beneath her bare feet as she rushed headlong toward the scorcher, crystalline barbs digging into her flesh with each step. With her left hand she unsheathed one of her twin daggers from its position on her thigh while she fished out the packet of hindran root with the other, flipping open the folded top as she ran. Waves of liquid fire crackled across her skin with each pounding footstep, numbing any pain in her slashed feet and fueling her dash forward. Tetamii settled back into a defensive stance, ready to parry the strike that she was all but announcing with her blade held low and to the side. But as he tilted his blade down to intercept her attack, Rav tossed the packet of powder at his face and dropped into a slide.

A look of shock crossed the scorcher's face before it was obscured first by the cloud of hindran root and then a rush of flames blooming in front of him. The fire consumed most of the infused plant, the scent of singed herbs lingering in the air as Rav kicked the man's legs out from beneath him, sending him crashing down behind her.

Rav came up onto her feet and drew her father's other dagger into her free hand, then turned to see Tetamii propped up on one elbow as he unleashed a hacking cough. Using his sword as leverage, he staggered to his feet as the three King's Guard appeared and flanked him. Tetamii's eyes raged, but he blinked heavily and wiped at them with the back of his gloved hand. It wasn't the full dose, but Mrs. Luviire's concoction was having some effect. Now it would just have to give her enough of an edge to finish the fight on her terms before the energy from the World Shroud consumed her. The aching knot began to tighten at the base of her skull; the countdown had already started.

"Clever," Tetamii said. "But tricks won't be enough to save you, lightblood."

The three guardsmen rushed the scorcher's back, shortswords held high, ready to save their king from the assassin. Tetamii kept his eyes on Rav, but behind him, a jagged orange line appeared, spitting a fiery lance straight into the face of the guard charging up the middle. He screamed and staggered back, falling onto the floor, writhing back and forth as he clutched at his sizzling skin.

Rav realized too late that the heat in the room was continuing to build, now focused near the ceiling, which was suddenly ripped open by a sweltering, concussive blast. Rough slabs of sandstone collapsed into the room, some larger chunks crushing the guard approaching Tetamii's right under a mound of rubble. A dusty haze encompassed the room as the debris settled, the night sky providing more light to the chamber. However, a white-hot flare near the scorcher's position shone the brightest within the cloud, accompanied by another shrill scream. Rav squinted through dust to make out the last guardsman struggling to remove his melting breastplate before a wide, arcing swing of Tetamii's bastard sword silenced him forever.

Wymund and Kymil fell in beside her as the air in the room cleared, the latter's movements trailed by the clinking of loosed stiletto blades from the hem of his cloak. King Berenqar sat slumped against the side wall among hunks of sandstone, dazed, a trickle of blood sliding down his forehead.

"Check on him," Rav said, glancing back at Annika before giving her companions a quick nod. Leaving the scorcher time to draw from the World Shroud would allow him to pick them off one at a time. Fast and overwhelming force was the plan, if one was generous enough to call it that.

Rav leaped through the air to draw his attention while Wymund and Kymil flanked him. Annika skirted the pile of rubble, staying clear of the whirl of blades. Not that the distance would matter if Tetamii focused enough to unleash another lance of fire in her direction, but Rav would do anything she could to prevent that from happening. Her daggers appeared to be little more than silver streaks as strike after strike was bolstered by the lightning her body was drawing from the World Shroud. Any normal opponent would have been gutted in an instant, but Tetamii was far from normal, even with the sedating effects of the infused hindran root slowing his movements. He ducked and sidestepped each slash and stab when he could, parrying those he couldn't, all while knocking back Wymund's thrusts and Kymil's sweeps with well-timed arcs of his blade.

Wymund's discomfort with the shorter sword was obvious, his hesitancy to get in closer to Tetamii preventing his attacks from being as effective. The buckler had already saved his life multiple times, but each heavy blow of the bastard sword was denting the shield. Soon it would be a liability, and Wymund would have to get over his inexperience or he would fall.

Kymil's cloak cracked through the air, the knife tips probing for openings in the scorcher's defenses, but also fanning out in swooping displays to momentarily obscure his vision. As much as it was an unorthodox weapon, the bard masterfully wielded the hem of blades as if it were an extension of his body. Stiletto tips pierced Tetamii's side one after the other as Kymil danced between swings of the heavy blade, not doing enough damage to seriously wound their opponent but succeeding in irritating him and keeping him distracted from Rav and Wymund's more lethal strikes.

Red-orange cracks split the air around Kymil, opening and closing in the blink of an eye, just long enough for small lances of fire to strike out at him. The scorcher was adopting the same strategy of distracting probe-like attacks, but it wasn't having the same effect. Most bursts of flame struck open air a split second after Kymil's cloak fluttered out of the way, while even the direct hits failed to catch the garment on fire. The bard had infused the fabric, but that didn't make the performance any less impressive.

Meanwhile, Wymund took advantage of Kymil's ploy and closed in tighter, keeping his dented buckler up and driving his shortsword forward in strike after strike. Had he been more accustomed to thrusting with a shorter blade, the battle may have ended then, but he simply wasn't fast enough. Despite the openings created by Kymil, the scorcher continued to bat away Wymund's strikes. However, their opponent was on the defensive, ceding ground as he stepped back toward the middle of the room, and each parry of shortsword or dagger was becoming fractionally slower.

Sparing a glance behind her, Rav saw Annika kneeling beside Berenqar, propping the man's head up and binding it with a strip of cloth from her gown. Blood had already soaked through the material and drained down across his face to drench his clothes, but she knew how much scalp wounds bled. Rav wasn't worried about him bleeding out, but a concussive injury to the brain could have its own complications.

Annika caught her gaze. "Focus on the flaming blade, girl," she snapped, and Rav turned to see that Tetamii had turned his blade a blistering orange, waves of heat and smoke swirling around it as it arced back and forth at his attackers.

But the crackling storm of fire lances had stopped. *He can't concentrate on drawing heat in multiple ways in this state,* she thought as she lunged back into the fray. *Thank you, Mrs. Luviire.*

Tetamii roared in frustrated rage as he swatted at Kymil's cloak, taking the barbs so that he could keep his attention trained on Wymund and Rav. The man was tiring, but Rav was feeling more empowered by the second. Each slash and stab was closer than the last, the scorcher's parries becoming more desperate than precise as Rav's reaction time only quickened. Crushing pressure on the nape of her neck reminded her of the cost, but as pulse after pulse of arcing energy surged through her body, she became confident this battle would end before the Illuminated Death could claim her.

Whipping his left arm forward, Kymil released the edge of his cloak toward Tetamii's arm. Three of the stiletto blades sunk into his flesh as the fabric wrapped around the limb, and Kymil pulled the cloak taut, yanking the scorcher's arm out to the side and exposing his middle.

"I can't be any more helpful," Kymil shouted as he turned his body and pulled the cloak across his shoulder with both hands, using every ounce of power he had in his thin legs just to keep the man's arm uncurled.

Already envisioning her daggers burying into his abdomen, Rav plunged her blades forward but only found empty air. She had expected him to wrestle for control of his limb, but instead he had tucked into the grapple, twisting just out of the way before her strike found purchase. A small cautionary yelp from her right gave Rav enough warning to step back and avoid Wymund's equally unsuccessful thrust.

"Enough!" Tetamii barked as he spun, jamming his open palm into the back of Kymil's left shoulder with such force that the bard lost his balance and twirled around on one foot, arms splayed wide to keep himself from tumbling over. "No more games!"

Kymil's eyes widened as time seemed to slow, the consequences of his gambit dawning on him as Tetamii gripped the hilt of his bastard sword with both hands. The scorcher swung the blade in an upward arc that caught Kymil's right arm just above the elbow, severing the limb as cleanly as if it had been made of parchment. Whatever luck the fatestitcher could call upon had finally run out.

The smell of burnt flesh turned Rav's stomach as Kymil screamed, clutching his cauterized stump as Tetamii planted a boot in the bard's chest and sent him staggering back toward the wall. A loud twang and crunch announced the crushing of his lute against the bard's back. Kymil slumped down, folding over his wound with his head bowed. He was out of the fight.

Tetamii turned to face Wymund and Rav, bright light from his searing blade reflecting off his hate-filled eyes. "No one escapes their fate this day. No leaving anyone to die. This only ends with your blood on my blade."

Rav stepped forward in a whirling flurry of steel, closing the gap between them before the scorcher could ready a strike. As many of her attacks were landing as were parried now, the man simply unable to position his heavy blade in time, but her vision was consumed with flaring lights and her aim had been hindered. The hits he took were glancing blows, slices into his sides or arms instead of deep puncture wounds. Her muscles ached with thrumming energy dying to be unleashed, the amount of lightning she was drawing from the World Shroud unable to be used up fast enough no matter how many times she struck out with her blades. All that existed in her mind was the liquid fire that raced across her body and the target before her, until suddenly an orange tear ripped open inches from her face.

Rav managed to dip her neck to the side so that the flames only licked at her cheek instead of consuming her. She smelled her own skin begin to boil but felt no new pain, just shame at failing to notice the bastard sword cool to a deep red, Tetamii having turned his connection to the World Shroud elsewhere.

But that momentary pause was all Tetamii needed. He gripped Rav by the throat and lifted her off the ground before slamming his forehead into her face. She felt the bones around her left eye buckle from the force, and a wave of red cast a tint over half of her vision. Racing footsteps from behind her announced Wymund's charge as she was flung through the air, landing hard on the pile of sandstone rubble in the center of the chamber. Dazed, Rav forced herself up onto her elbows, the ringing of steel on steel echoing throughout the room. Half of what remained of her light-blinded vision was now obscured, the flesh around her left eye already swollen shut, but she could see the silhouette of her friend matching blades with Tetamii's dark outline.

The heavy falling arcs of Tetamii's bastard sword could shatter the forearms of most opponents absorbing the blows with a small steel buckler, but if Wymund's arm was breaking, he was showing no signs of slowing down. He used the shield to disperse the force of each swing, following the trail of the blade down and coming back with a stab or slash of his own. Under normal circumstances, Wymund would have been dispatched within seconds. He was a skilled swordsman, but Tetamii had years of experience on him and could bend a force of nature to his every whim. However, with the mercenary bloodied and drugged, Wymund was holding his own.

Rav staggered to her feet, half sliding down the pile of rubble as she fought against legs that now seemed less like coiled springs and more like fastened locks. Between the open tap from the Wellspring and injuries she had sustained, the strain on her body was too much. It would shut down, and the lightning would claim her. But she stumbled forward while she could, daggers at the ready. Rav was determined not to be the Wellspring's only victim today.

Tetamii returned to a single-handed grip and took a backhanded swipe down toward Wymund, which he deflected easily enough on his buckler. But the scorcher followed up with a right hook across his jaw, and then swung his fist back like a club from the other side, catching Wymund in the temple. Rav watched the shadowed form of her friend collapse to the ground, unmoving and helpless as Tetamii raised his sword directly over him for a killing jab. But as he brought it down, Rav was there to kick the blade aside and slash two deep gouges across Tetamii's forearm. He turned to face her, the sliced arm hanging limply at his side.

"I told you before that I envied you, lightblood," Tetamii said, though Rav found it difficult to focus past the throbbing hammer at the base of her skull. "My death will be at the hand of someone who I have no personal quarrel with, for a matter in which I have no stake. The fate of a mercenary is inescapable. But you are different. You have had the opportunity twice now to die in the service of something you believe in." She could not make out the details of his face, but she could hear him smile through his pain and fatigue. "Thank you for giving me the honor of participating in your martyrdom on both occasions."

Dozens of jagged lines cracked the air around her, forcing her to weave this way and that as she searched for an opening to plant a dagger in his side. Lances of flame licked at her feet, keeping her off balance as Tetamii advanced with each swing of his bastard sword. Rav was in retreat, losing ground as she was forced back toward the pile of rubble and failing to avoid most of the fiery bursts. Even though she couldn't feel the burns, the tissue damage would take its toll all the same. Her movements were slowing, coming in fits and starts as she was buffeted by shots of fire from all directions. The only reason she wasn't dead yet was because Tetamii hadn't decided to end it. His swings were broad, meant more to control her movements than to make any lethal contact. When her heels hit the sandstone debris, she fell onto her back, staring up at where the hole in the ceiling should have been.

Flaring lights were all she saw as her fading mind drifted, taking her back to the starlit nights of her childhood in Felona, lying on the lawn between her parents and picking out constellations for hours. Before any of the fighting, before the struggles with her mother, before her father's life was claimed by the Clipped Gulls for daring to hope his city could be a better place. It was her picture of contentedness, and in that moment she surrendered. The fight was lost; Tetamii had prevailed. Rather than dying in agony as the Wellspring energy consumed her, she chose to exist in this moment for as long as she could. No longer fighting, no longer trying to survive. Tension crept out of her muscles, the burn of the lightning replaced by the actual burns covering her body. But that was all secondary to the peace of the moment as a comforting warmth began to envelop her, allowing her to relax into her last seconds, which she would spend wishing she could tell her mother that she loved her.

But the warmth intensified until suddenly the debris detonated beneath her, sending her somersaulting through the air and landing several yards away. Tetamii's steely voice snapped her out of her reverie.

"Still breathing?" he asked. He sounded exhausted, but tired meant still standing, and that was all the advantage he needed. "You truly are resistant to death's grip. Maybe I'll start by finishing off your friends, and then you might feel a bit more cooperative about taking that final breath."

From where she lay, Rav watched through the new crater in the rubble as Tetamii paced in front of Kymil's slumped form. The scorcher disappeared from view behind another part of the mound, but she could still see her friend, back against the wall and legs splayed out in front of him. He was cradling his severed arm as his silhouette shivered, but when the bard spoke, there was no hint of fear. Just a strange sense of purpose that was at odds with his usual levity.

"It's just as well," Kymil said, looking up at his looming executioner, then turning so that he was looking straight at Rav. He gestured with his amputated arm. "What's the point of going on if I can't mention my disarming personality without eliciting groans or sympathetic looks?"

Rav chuckled despite the pain; puns apparently mixed well with gallows humor. The last time he had made that joke, sitting by the fire with her dagger balanced on his finger, it had pained her soul, but now . . .

Her eyes shot wide as she glanced at the remaining dagger in her hand, the other having slid across the room when she'd landed. Kymil was a fatestitcher. Had he really just been admiring the weapon's craftsmanship that night, or could it have been something more? If he had infused one of her daggers with a bit of his luck, perhaps fortune could still be on their side. Of course, that wouldn't matter if the dagger she held was the wrong one, the one that had remained under her bundled cloak that night on the road.

"Well, allow me to spare you the agony of dying a sad clown," Tetamii said, his form still hidden behind crumbled ceiling.

Rav flipped the weapon so that she held the blade between her fingers. *Show me you can make more than a step creak, music man*, she thought as she flung the dagger at the wall to Tetamii's back with every bit of strength she had left.

The blade spun end over end, passing over the rubble before ricocheting off the sandstone and disappearing from view. There was a wet thud and a metallic clang before the hilt of a bastard sword clattered to the ground in front of Kymil, followed by the shadowy form of Tetamii falling prone. She could see the shape of her dagger's hilt sticking out of the scorcher's lower back at a descending angle, and she allowed her head to rest on the ground once again. The irritating thought that the bard would get to take credit for this victory as well as the reptilian monster swam across her mind before exhaustion took her. The sound of Annika crying out for a healer echoing into a muffled silence.

Chapter 38

Alaboq

Tetamii knelt on the ground, arms chained behind his back at the elbows, his head bowed. Rav had watched King Berenqar's hidden hand administer one of his own infused poisons to the scorcher, a substance he claimed would prevent Tetamii from tapping into the Wellspring as long as he was held under its influence. Still, she kept a wary eye on the man as she found her seat at the long table in the banquet hall. Tetamii was bandaged around his torso, the wound she'd created only partially healed by Mrs. Luviire at the request of the Crown. Her dagger had sunk into the man's liver, resulting in a massive hemorrhage that would have killed him without intervention, but Berenqar believed in criminals "facing what they have done and accepting the consequences." However, the ruler had possessed enough insight to suggest his healer not return the man to his full strength.

The herb nurse's infusions had done wonders for Rav and her companions, though. The first dose had been more of a stabilizing agent, powdered lunok petals inhaled through the nose that worked quickly to staunch bleeding and maintain consciousness. But over the next few days, they were able to convalesce more gently, Mrs. Luviire providing packets of infused herbs to be steeped as a tea that mended slower than knitting serums but was less physically draining.

Rav's feet had been torn to ribbons by the glass shards but were now quite comfortable back in her leather boots. Even her burns had been healed, though she was left with several splotches of skin that were darker than before the injury. Mrs. Luviire explained that sometimes more pigmentation returned during the healing process, and Rav didn't mind. As far as she was concerned, they were beauty marks of victory, and anyone who didn't see them that way could receive some marks of their own.

Both her and Wymund's skull fractures had been repaired as well, and while Mrs. Luviire lamented her helplessness in regrowing limbs, Kymil's smile had been the first to return. The bard sat across from her at the table now, plucking at the neck of a new lute with his left hand and somehow making the instrument sing as well as he had before.

Double doors swung open at the entrance of the hall as two hulking King's Guard marched into the room, each with an arm linked through one of Sylicera Hadac's, the trade minister letting the toes of her shoes drag on the ground behind her. Her eyes were wild and pleading as she glanced back and forth between the men carrying her, straining her shoulders as she pulled against the manacles that bound her hands behind her back.

"This has all been a misunderstanding," she said, tears rolling down her cheeks. "If you would just give me the opportunity to speak with King Berenqar, I could clear this all—"

The pair dropped her unceremoniously on her knees next to Tetamii, who didn't even flinch as the woman appeared beside him. "King Berenqar is on his way now," one of the guardsmen said with a smirk. "Though with everything we found in your chambers, I hope you're better at telling stories than you are at covering your tracks."

The woman straightened her spine and huffed as the guards walked off, chuckling. She flicked frizzy curls out of her face with a shake of her head, her auburn hair now unkempt after a couple days in confinement with no one to keep it braided, and set a cold gaze on Mareq, who had taken the seat next to Kymil. The draqeshi shifted uncomfortably in his chair and looked everywhere but at the woman he had physically restrained.

Rav had learned that Mareq and his friends in the kitchens of Vinsart Hold were responsible for keeping the trade minister away from the king's chambers, an action that was likely the only reason any of them had survived their encounter with Tetamii. If Sylicera had been present, Berenqar might have already been swayed too far to have listened to

Annika's evidence, or she might have been able to summon more King's Guard to stand on their side.

Looking across the table at her new friend, a man at once both timid and bold, she felt a sense of shame at how curtly she had treated him. Rav turned in her seat to shoot a fiery stare back at the woman, overwhelming her icy glare and forcing her to blink and choose instead to focus on the floor in front of her. Mareq's shoulders settled a few inches as he sent a small smile and nod in Rav's direction. That would have to serve as her apology to him. Deeds were better than words, anyway.

Completing the table, Wymund was seated to Rav's left and Annika at the end of the table to her right. With all the resting and healing that needed to be done over the last few days, they hadn't had much of an opportunity to talk, but she was thankful they had both made it out relatively unscathed. Wymund's facial and forearm fractures had been repaired, and the old woman had only sustained a few minor scrapes and bruises that she refused to have helped along, saying something about "not using up resources on the frail when the foolish need them more." However, despite their lack of conversation, Rav could see the woman looked at her differently now. There was less concern in her eyes, and perhaps a bit of peace as well. It was a nice change of pace from the motherly fretting.

The sound of heavy footfalls announced the arrival of King Berenqar and his party: two more King's Guard, Lady Cailynne, and a tall elven man with a shaved head, crimson-ringed eyes, and a hawk-like gaze that shifted around the room, lingering on everyone seated within. One corner of his mouth crept up into a small smile as his eyes settled on Tetamii. This was Vinsart Hold's hidden hand, the master poisoner. True to his connection to the World Shroud, he embodied the opposite of everything Rav had seen in Mrs. Luviire. While they both infused plants and minerals with Wellspring energy, their results couldn't be more different. But it was more fundamental than that. There was no warmth to be found in the man, no joy for life or compassion for others, just cold calculation, which she supposed would be desirable for a man in his position. If King Berenqar had hired a hidden hand who possessed a true passion for his work, she didn't believe he would still have his benevolent reputation.

"Former Minister Hadac," King Berenqar said as he came to a stop before her. "For the crimes of treason and plotting to incite violence, the Crown has deliberated on an appropriate punishment."

"Your Majesty, if you would just give a moment to speak, I could clear all this up," she replied, looking up at him with tears in her eyes that belied her forced smile. "I have always been a loyal advisor to you and to my home—"

Berenqar raised a hand. "Save your breath. This is not a trial, and you should be thanking me for that. If the people of this city knew what you had planned, knew that your schemes could have resulted in the deaths of Qedradan soldiers based on nothing but fiction, I promise you would fare much worse in their hands."

The ruler beckoned to the two guardsmen who had dragged the woman into the hall, and the pair began to march forward. "I have decided that what remains of your life will be spent in service to this nation you call home, starting with the town you helped wipe from the map. You are to be sent to the smoldering ashes of Turlaq's Fork, where you will live under armed confinement and work with the craftsmen rebuilding the village, board by bloody board."

The two guards hefted her back to her feet as she struggled against them, leaning closer to her king. "But these are lies, King Berenqar! There is nothing that ties me to this mercenary's dreadful actions!"

"Enough silver and gold libers were recovered from your chambers to raise anyone's eyebrows," the bald elf said dryly. "I know you organize our nation's trade arrangements, but so much Kefyan currency in your personal possession is certainly curious."

"Not to mention the prewritten documents that altered existing trade deals with our elven neighbors, referencing the 'rise in elven political violence.' If you had truly learned of these attacks with the arrival of Mr. Fiadar to the city, you wouldn't have had the time to craft such comprehensive language on the subject," Berenqar said. "These were prepared over the course of weeks, not days."

Sylicera opened her mouth to protest but was cut off by the hidden hand. "But ultimately it was your ally here that sealed your fate," he said, pointing to the dazed Tetamii, still kneeling beside her. "Before I relieved him of his faculties, he said something about incompetence not deserving loyalty, and hoped that the Crown would find a trade minister who 'understood the importance of completing one Irasil-damned tas k.'" Her jaw clicked closed, and she shot a scornful look at the scorcher before hanging her head.

"On your way with her, gentleman," King Berenqar said with a dismissing gesture. "See that she arrives in Turlaq's Fork in peak physical health. She'll need the strength for the months of labor ahead."

He turned to face Rav and the others as Hadac was hauled away, her shoes scraping along the tiled floor all the way out. "Now to discuss next steps," the ruler said, clasping his hands together and striding toward the table. His daughter had taken a spot behind his chair at the head of the table, resting her hands along the top as King Berenqar took a seat. The hidden hand placed himself beside her, his appraising gaze flicking over all of them once more. Rav wondered if the man was calculating dosages, filing the information away for later, should they be needed.

"As I mentioned to Ms. Iatorii while some of you were recuperating, I believe Kefya should handle their own criminal discipline," Berenqar said. "As much damage as he has enacted on my people, he has doubtless inflicted more in his homeland. With that in mind, I will be returning Mr. Fiadar by ship to Felona so he can face the repercussions for his actions."

Wymund sat forward in his chair to speak but paused as Rav stood, placing her palms on the table and staring at the ruler. "And what happens when he snaps out of this fog? You saw what he did to your King's Guard. What hope would sailors have at keeping him contained?" Wymund planted his forehead into the heel of his hand while Annika inhaled sharply, but Berenqar just chuckled and pointed with his thumb to his hidden hand behind him.

"Ubadrii will be accompanying him," the king said, the bald elf behind him bending slightly at the waist to formalize the introduction. "He will continue administering his infused concoctions to the mercenary to maintain everyone's safety aboard the ship."

"And I will also act as Qedrad's emissary upon delivery of the prisoner into Kefyan custody," Ubadrii said. "An accurate accounting of events will be made known to the Council in Felona so the man's punishment may be doled out appropriately."

Lady Cailynne looked askance at the hidden hand before shifting one of her hands down to Berenqar's shoulder. "Father, would it not be wise to send a diplomat more accustomed to the art of court pleasantries? The relationship between our two nations has always been fraught, and though tensions have cooled, the current situation could lend itself to sparking a new conflict if not handled with a delicate touch."

Unfazed, Ubadrii replied, "I did not arrive at my station in life by being boorish or insensitive, Lady Cailynne."

Berenqar placed a hand over his daughter's and looked back at her with a gentle smile. "While I agree Ubadrii can be aloof at times, I promise he is well versed in discussing matters of state. The task will be in capable hands."

"If I may cut in, Your Majesty," Wymund said after ensuring Rav had settled back into her chair by throwing her a warning glare so sharp she should have winced. "My concern is the motivations of the Council itself. As much as it pains me to say, my country's leadership has been corrupted. We have evidence that Elikar Thymes was involved in this scheme, but we have no way of knowing how many other councilmembers could be wrapped up in this. How do we know we aren't simply returning their man to be unleashed upon the world again?"

The king frowned. "This evidence you provided is circumstantial, but I do agree it warrants some measure of caution. If only your government was filled with loyal civic servants like you, Corporal Sylnorin," Berenqar said. Wymund offered only a sad smile in response. "Maybe it would be wise for another of my advisors to make the journey as well; someone more familiar with the councilmembers. But it's not as if any of them have a friendly relationship with the Council."

"I'll go," Annika said from across the table. Her face was resolute, as if the matter had already been settled in her mind and no further discussion was needed. "I haven't been home in some time, but my roots are deep in Felona. If I don't know a member of the Council personally, then I can assure you I have a connection who does. I won't let this murderer be released into the custody of a group ready to set him loose again."

Berenqar looked unsure, but Kymil picked up his one-handed strumming again and said, "You can trust her, King Berenqar. The entire world's secrets are laid bare before that woman's withering gaze. Not a councilmember will be able to so much as break wind in their own chambers without her knowing."

Everyone at the table laughed at that, pausing for a moment to listen to the upbeat melody. Finally, the king said, "Very well. After all you lot have done for my kingdom and my family, I can trust you to carry this through."

"Good, that's settled then," Kymil said. "Now about 'all that we've done,' Ms. Iatorii may come from money, but I am nothing but a humble storyteller, living life on the road and rolling with whatever punches come my way. Perhaps the Crown could see our peace-rendering services rewarded in some way?" His smile was somehow both puckish and innocent, cutting the tension in the room that he had just created.

"I believe we can make that happen," Berenqar said with a laugh. "Was there anything in particular you had in mind?"

Kymil leaned over and nudged Mareq. "I've heard our new friend here is in search of adventure, and it's been too long since the lads and ladies of the sea have been graced with my presence. A funded ocean voyage to warmer climates seems a fair exchange for stopping a misguided bloodbath."

Rav thought she saw the draqeshi's skin turn a slight shade of green before the man swallowed hard and smiled. Traveling across the water wasn't for everyone, but she knew the restlessness that came with sitting still for too long. Despite Mareq's obvious poor history on the waves, she thought he would jump at the chance to get moving once more.

Chapter 39

Alaboq

"Just set that down right there," Kymil said, sitting on the ship's railing as deckhands scurried about readying the *Lost Horizon* for sail. Rav and Wymund placed the bard's last crate on top of the rest of his pile they had been volunteered to carry aboard. She shot the elf a scornful look as she stood to stretch her back.

"Excellent, I can't thank you two enough for your assistance. I would've helped, but . . . " Kymil shrugged what was left of his right arm and smiled. "I can't risk any strain on my remaining limb. What would become of my art if something were to happen to it?"

"How is it you have more luggage now than when we picked you up in Hwen?" Rav asked, taking a moment to catch her breath against the side of the ship.

"I'm about to embark on a weeks-long voyage at sea, and suddenly all my shirts have far too much fabric dangling from one side. Before I left civilization, I thought it prudent to purchase a tailored wardrobe so that I could always look my best."

"You had us lug four chests' worth of fancy clothes onto this ship full of people who walk around shirtless half the time?" Wymund asked.

Kymil leaped off the railing and clasped his hand on the man's shoulder. "Presentation is everything, Corporal. Remember that." Wymund stood speechless as the bard walked off toward Mareq, who was just boarding the vessel carrying several pouches of tea leaves.

"Did she give us what we asked for?" Kymil asked.

"You mean what *you* asked for?" Mareq answered as he tucked the pouches into a pocket. "Mrs. Luviire infused these leaves to settle my stomach, not produce hallucinations."

Kymil bent down to pat the draqeshi on the back and sighed. "Oh well. I was just hoping to prevent the monotony of weeks at sea, but come. These sailors are sure to have stores of rum stocked below. Let's get a head start, shall we?" Mareq followed, helpless to the pull of the bard's charisma.

Over the side of the ship, Rav could see Annika speaking with Mrs. Luviire on the pier, both women sharing the determined look people have when making decisions that affect others. She recognized it from all the times her mother had arranged playdates and tutoring sessions without first gauging her level of interest. But the memories no longer stung as much as they once did. Maybe it was how close she had come to never seeing her home again, but knowing she was returning to Felona somehow filled her with as much trepidation as it did excitement. After everything she had been through, she could understand now why her mother had been so overprotective of her. But it would have certainly helped their relationship if Rav had just been told the risks of being a lightblood.

Spotting them too, Wymund asked, "That doesn't look like a simple farewell. I wonder what it could be about."

"Knowing the old woman," Rav said, "It's likely about me. Let's go find out."

Rav and Wymund descended the plank and made their way toward the pair. Ubadrii passed them on his way onto the ship and gave a curt nod, leaving Rav wondering if even Kymil's boisterous nature could counteract the hidden hand's dour countenance on this journey. As they reached the bottom the two women clasped hands, Annika nodding in thanks as the other smiled that warm smile of hers.

Not waiting for a greeting, Rav strode up beside them. "Accepting a position as my tutor?" she asked. "I hear it's a tough job, but that may just be because the old woman enjoys hearing herself complain." Her voice was still laced with sarcasm, but it didn't carry the same edge it once did. "I think you'll find I'm a quick study when I don't have an overbearing teacher always harrying me about safety."

Annika laughed. "I've come to realize the only way to ensure your safety would be to keep you locked up under armed guard at all hours of the day. Otherwise, you home in on life-threatening situations like a bloodhound after a scent."

"Speaking from personal experience," Wymund said, "That method of protection is also not effective on her."

"I prefer learning through a collaborative approach, but you'll catch on," Rav said. She glanced around and behind the herb nurse before adding, "Where are your things? We can help you load them on the ship."

"Oh, I'm not going out to sea," Mrs. Luviire said with a laugh. "My life is here. Alaboq would crumble without me around to patch people up."

Rav cocked an eyebrow and turned to Annika, who replied, "And you aren't coming with us either, Ravael." Before Rav could spin on her and launch into an argument, the older woman held up a hand. "As I was saying, I know you always find your way into situations that threaten your life, either through external factors or your own nature as a lightblood. I thought a firm hand was needed to hold you back, to keep you from extending beyond your limits. But after what I saw in Berenqar's chambers . . . "

She paused, her face softening. "Well, you showed a restraint I didn't know you possessed. You pulled back from your connection to the World Shroud just when I thought the Illuminated Death would consume you. Perhaps instead of being prevented from doing some good in the world, you could be trained to use your abilities responsibly. Help others without harming yourself in the process."

"To that end," Mrs. Luviire said, "Annika asked me to learn what I could in Vinsart Hold's libraries about anything that may help you. Some time ago, a man arrived in Alaboq seeking supplies. Mostly lumber and other construction materials according to the records, but it was where he said he was from that caught my eye. The man claimed to be building a place for lightbloods like himself, tucked away in the northern reaches of the Tesigan Peaks. A place free from distractions where they could learn to better understand and use their connection safely and effectively."

Rav looked back and forth between the women. "And you want me to go climb a mountain and learn how to not kill myself when I fight?"

"No," Annika said. "We want you *and* Wymund to go climb a mountain." The woman turned to face him; his mouth turned slightly down in confusion. "I will have word sent back to the Lighthouse to explain your absence, but I think it's important the girl has a friend along to keep her focused."

His frown deepened as he mulled it over, finally tilting his head down to look at Rav. "If that's where you decide to go, I'll join you." One side of his mouth ticked up into a smirk. "You're still in my custody, after all."

Her mind returned to her mother and their home outside Felona, the conversations she was finally ready to have, and, hopefully, the relationship she wanted to mend. But she also knew Annika was right. She was rash, impulsive, and prone to getting in over her head. This makeshift school in the mountains could be her best chance to get a better grasp on what she could do, to reach the full potential of the legacy her father had gifted her. If she went home, it would be a long trek back north to reach this region again. She and her mother had waited all this time to have their talk. What was the harm in waiting a bit longer?

Kymil leaned his torso over the railing of the ship, and Mareq's head appeared next to him. "What's causing the delay?" the bard shouted down. "The sooner you all come aboard, the sooner the crew will let me crack open the rum." Looking back over his shoulder, he added, "They've all been rather rude about the whole thing so far, if I'm honest."

"Will your herbs work even with the spirits this man is sure to force down my throat?" Mareq added as he stared pleadingly at Mrs. Luviire. But whatever excuse he had been searching for, he didn't receive.

"You'll be fine, Mareq." She laughed. "Just as long as you don't drink so much that you can't keep them down. Those will keep the seasickness at bay, but if you poison yourself enough with that swill, you'll have to pay the price." The draqeshi's face turned that slight shade of green again as he slipped back behind the barrier.

Everyone else on the pier turned to look at Rav, who nodded and shouted back. "Wymund and I will meet up with you later. We have something else to do before we head south." She unsheathed the dagger that had stopped Tetamii from killing her friend. "Any chance you want to top off my dagger again before you go?"

Kymil broke into a toothy grin and winked. "Who's to say that was the blade I infused anyway? You may still carry a bit of my luck with you yet."

EPILOGUE

White-gold flames consumed him and the corpse he meant to hide, painless but just as overwhelming as the process had always been. No matter how many centuries one lived, the complete destruction and rebirth of one's body wasn't something that became routine. He felt his form disperse into the conflagration, his consciousness remaining intact due only to his connection to the World Shroud. Normally, bringing another body along with him would prove more taxing, but that was only true for a living companion; he had no need to hold together the corpse's sense of self during the jaunt through a Wellspring.

As far as he knew, the journey from Slaeth to Tellahhr was instantaneous, but without breaths or a heartbeat, time became a loose concept. The fire burned away, and he took a step forward into the dusty, bone-white expanse around him. It had been some time since he had been here; he had forgotten how unpleasant the sunbaked ground and cloudless sky could be, the unrelenting heat amplified by the total lack of a breeze. He glanced around. Everything was flat and still. Bleached, cracked ground as far as he could see. Maintaining the same form had been the right choice. Had he returned to his natural state, the environment would have been much more unforgiving, and the last thing he wanted was another reason for this conversation to be disagreeable.

"Nasargiel," a woman's voice called to him from behind. He turned to see what appeared to be a human woman with short black hair that hung like a parted curtain across her forehead. But her striking emerald eyes, a matched pair to his own, revealed the truth. Not that he would be expecting a human to be out this far. That had been the point of meeting in this location: privacy.

"I see you were successful in retrieving the invader and returning it to its proper place." The woman's eyes narrowed as she frowned, taking a few gliding steps toward him. The movements were practiced, just as his were in this human form, but he understood the desire to maintain the illusion. It didn't feel right to move freely with foreign limbs. "Though judging by its condition, I must believe that at least some on Slaeth made contact with the creature. *You* wouldn't have butchered it so carelessly."

Nasargiel turned to look at the massive reptilian form he had carried with him through the World Shroud. Puncture wounds and gouges marred its flesh, as well as an impressive cleaving of the beast's throat that he surmised had been its downfall. He had been right in his assessment of that elven woman's strength, even if he had been wrong about who she was when he saved her life. Pulling that half-elf from the waters around Virdoba before she could drown could prove to be his most consequential action yet.

"I am not concerned about a handful of adventurers telling tales of victory in taverns across Anera, Yofie. You know as well as I that heroes embellish more than fishermen, and most will assume the group just slayed a monitor lizard; if they believe any of it at all." Yofie's demeanor remained unchanged. She always fretted over everything, but that was no different from most of his people. In truth, *he* was the outlier, the one more prone to curiosity than concern.

Still, there was one factor about the incident that he did believe warranted worry. "What should give you pause is the scorcher that created the conditions for this to occur. The World Shroud has not been sufficiently damaged to allow unrestricted travel like that in millennia. The people of that world are starting to tax the veil again, and the rest of you are content to hide your eyes and pretend everything will be fine."

The woman's frown deepened. "Both are concerns, but you have always been blind to the consequences of your inquisitive nature. The same conditions that motivated our departure from Slaeth are still present, primarily held at bay by the population's ignorance. If you keep interfering, they may discover the knowledge that has been lost to them and return to their old warring ways." Her eyes scanned the remains of the beast before adding, "One side of the conflict has been content to keep their distance and skirmish among themselves all this time, but if Anera and Liiashae build stronger connections to the World Shroud, the Wellsprings may not endure another war of that scale."

Nasargiel shook his head, tired of having this same conversation with his people over and over. "Advancements are being made regardless of my interventions, but you know that already. You have read the same reports. They are learning how the Wellspring is accessed, and one even believes he was able to grant a young girl this talent after birth. *That* is why my presence there is necessary. I have to find her before that knowledge spreads, because you are right. We may not survive a second Rupturing, no matter how far we travel."

Acknowledgments

My writing journey began as early as fourth grade, when I started my first fantasy novel in a black-and-white composition notebook. I found it not long ago, and surprisingly, it's not bad – for a ten-year old's work, that is. After a few chapters, the project was abandoned, as were many others over the rest of my childhood. Not finishing is an issue most writers experience, as overcoming that first hurdle - simply reaching a conclusion, no matter how sloppily – can be daunting. Thankfully, I've had a wealth of support behind me since I resumed writing in earnest several years ago, and getting to the end is no longer an insurmountable task.

First, I have to thank my wife, Morgan, who repeatedly allows me to spend time writing when I really should be doing more of the housework. This book is dedicated to her, and while future novels may have different honorees on the dedication page, I would like to make it known here that without her love and support, none of them would make it to print. Everything I do is dedicated to her, whether it's explicitly stated or not.

Next, my parents always cultivated my love for reading, filling my shelves with stories that captured my imagination. Starting a new book was always encouraged – even when I was grounded, books were never off limits – and any time I mentioned that I wanted to write when I grew up, I was never met with scoffs or reality checks. Now that I'm a father myself and better understand the financial realities of the world, I know that it must have been difficult to not push heavily toward a more stable profession. I ended up in one anyway, but my parents never smothered that dream, and here we are, holding a book I wrote in our hands. I hope

I can foster that same ambition in my son if he chooses to venture down this path.

Chase is the closest thing I have to a brother, and is usually the first beta-reader to get back to me with feedback. I know I don't say it enough, but I truly value everything he has done for me and my family over the years, and I'm sorry for repaying you by bogging you down with so many of my novels to read. I won't stop, but I do feel a little bad about it.

This book would be much more of a mess without my wonderful editors, Diana and Michelle. Punching up the pacing and strengthening emotional beats were Diana's domain, and the onerous task of reining in my tendency toward convoluted sentences was all Michelle. Their insight was invaluable, and if you enjoyed the book, they deserve some of the credit.

Finally, I was fortunate to work with two extremely talented artists, John and Dewi. John took my words and turned them into a beautiful, painterly cover that I couldn't be prouder of, and Dewi translated my software generated maps into the gorgeous images found within these pages. Both were a pleasure to collaborate with, and I hope to again for future novels.

Thank You for Reading

As a debut fantasy author in the self-publishing space, it means the world to me that you've made it this far into the book and haven't wantonly discarded it or buried it at the bottom of your To-Be-Read pile. Without the backing of a major publisher and their marketing team, it makes me happy that you've even found this book among the numerous that are released into the wild every day.

If I could ask a simple favor: it would make a massive impact if you took a minute or two to leave a review online where you purchased your copy. The only way self-published authors can be picked up by the algorithm is by becoming visible with higher review counts, and letting others know that you enjoyed the book might help them discover it as well!

Finally, if you want to keep up with Rav and where her journey goes from here, sign up for my mailing list at blueaxispress.com

I promise not to blow up your inbox, but as the next book nears release in the back half of 2024, you can expect a title and cover reveal, as well as a pre-order announcement.

Thank you again, and I hope to see you in the back matter of the sequel!

About the Author

Ryan Elledge is an epic fantasy, science fiction and horror author who has been crafting stories in his mind since he was a child. He has been actively working toward publishing since graduate school, starting with The Light of Shadows, the first novel in the Balance of Shade and Radiance trilogy. He lives with his wife, son, and their dog, Smaug, who is far less ferocious than her namesake. She spends her days in tireless combat with their robotic vacuum, Bilbo.

www.ingramcontent.com/pod-product-compliance
Lightning Source LLC
Chambersburg PA
CBHW020902200626
46814CB00001BA/142

9798989892617